The Least Envied

Sean DeLauder

This is a work of fiction. Names, characters, places, and incidents are products of the author's imagination or are used fictitiously and are not to be construed as real. Any resemblance to actual events, locales, organizations, or persons, living or dead, is, frankly, extraordinary and entirely coincidental.

Print ISBN: 0615728863
ISBN-13: 9780615728865

Book cover design and layout by, Ellie Bockert Augsburger of Creative Digital Studios. www.CreativeDigitalStudios.com

For Don Miguel de Cervantes Saavedra,

Who understood only madmen are brave enough to want to save the world.

CONTENTS

The Least Envied	1
The Unfinished Man	5
The Underthinker	15
A Fortunate Misstep	25
He Who Would be Mighty	45
The West	55
Unless, Perhaps	63
The Anti-Paradox Machine	81
Peril in the Wide Nothing	95
A Familiar Dream	107
Cabbage in the Causeway	115
An Empire of Grit	135
Reunion	155
The Fear Machine	161
Over the Wall	175
Through the Teeth of the Woods	183
A Test Gone Wrong	193
Jim	207
Wandering in What Wanders	217
The Girl	235

Beta	249
A Change of Treasure	257
The Librarian	267
Versus	285
Variations on a Theme	299
The Reluctant Hero	305
An Imperfect Plan	311
A Hero Resurrected	325
Once Upon a Plan	343
A Hero Removed	367
A Test Completed	383
Invention Finds Necessity	391
A Test Unveiled	411
A Familiar Reality	417
So Let it be Written	423

Let us not waste our time in idle discourse! Let us do something,
while we have the chance! It is not every day that we are needed…
Others would meet the case equally well, if not better.
To all mankind they were addressed,
those cries for help still ringing in our ears!
But at this place, at this moment of time,
all mankind is us, whether we like it or not.
Let us make the most of it, before it is too late!
Let us represent worthily for once the foul brood
to which a cruel fate consigned us!

What do you say?

—Samuel Beckett
Waiting for Godot

Is was the hero glad or brave

Or both at times

Or neither aught

Forth and back through time and time

'Til all are well and won and rhyme

As was it then

As are it now

So must it be

So it is shall

Why silent are the bells that rung

In glory yet with bitten tongues

All are mute as far as flung

Such deeds resplend remain unsung

THE LEAST ENVIED

So this was the fabled West, gritty and mean.

The bare shafts of a browning forest stood to the left, dark and thick with empty branches. To the right a crude outhouse stood upon discolored redbrown ground, with a small town further on, no more than two short lines of squat buildings. And ahead, beyond the rails of a wooden fence, nothing but an eternal stretch of abraded world, dry and cracked as if an oaken log had crunched its wooden fist against the hard-boiled face of the planet.

Andrew squinted in the afternoon glare, feeling the stinging pecks from windblown sand on his cheeks and the steady heat of an unavoidable sun. He drew a small, stiff book from a breast pocket and used it to shield his eyes. Powdery yellow silt floated everywhere, obscuring faraway objects, grinding between his teeth, and tearing at him in hard-to-reach places with maddening itches.

Here he was. Here he must stay, until he finished the story or destruction found him first.

Likely, his best chance at survival rested in his ability to determine the safest place to hide. Likely, it would be long before he saw the girl again, and in that time he would sift from her memory like a pattern in the windblown sand, slowly distorting before blowing away completely.

Andrew fingered a gelatinous blue disc clinging to his chest, dull and inert. As expected, nothing happened. When his assignment was complete it would flare blue again. All he'd need to do is touch it. He'd waited, hoping for the color to brighten, and when it didn't, Andrew knew he had no choice but to endure the world around him as best he could.

The fence buried itself in the dead forest at one end while the other ran toward the buildings. What it confined Andrew couldn't tell. Perhaps the sun. Maybe the sun rose halfway into the sky before reaching the dilapidated railings, spent a few shifting moments searching for a way through, then turned about in disappointment, ducking over the horizon to spend the night in hope and try again the next day. That was the nature of hope. Sustaining, but of little practical purpose besides.

Beyond the fence a shirtless man burst out of the woods, his tiny cries muffled by distance.

".....elp!....."

A small herd of creatures sprayed out of the forest behind him, scuttling alongside the rotting fence. The faint haze in the air and ripples of heat made their features difficult to distinguish, but the creatures appeared no more than knee high, and ran upright with short, quick strides. From where Andrew stood, their bleached white bodies appeared skeletal. He imagined he could hear their bones clack against one another like the hollow bells of a morbid wind chime.

Andrew shut his eyes and rubbed the dirt from his face, wishing himself gone. When they opened the scene was unchanged, apart from being a bit further to the right, the old man fleeing toward the town, creatures hot on his heels.

As the old man twisted to find his pursuers his head snapped back as though struck and his knees buckled. Something white and feathery fluttered against the fall like wings, but to no avail and the wispy figure crumpled, rolled, and went still.

Andrew took a step forward.

"Hey!" he called, then stopped, realizing his mistake.

The following herd also stopped. As one, it turned to bear on him.

A faint jangle of alarm rang in his head. His skin prickled, as it always did when Luck was about to swell up into a lightning-filled cloud of Peril. Jagged and electric, Peril often proved undodgeable. And Luck, if there was such a thing, was invariably bad.

Andrew froze. Maybe they wouldn't notice him. Maybe their mole eyes were tiny and useless.

A single creature detached from the group and approached, wobbling through the fence where a sand-eaten strut had decayed and broken. To his horror Andrew realized his initial observation had been correct. As the creature drew nearer he saw the white cage of its ribs and the great hollow bowls in the skull where its eyes belonged. Behind the ribs was a dirt-clotted clockwork of pumping machinery. It stopped to observe Andrew, or maybe allow him to observe it, asserting its existence to someone who knew it should not be.

Andrew did not know what the creature was, nor what it had been. The body was short and ovular, supported by wide feet, and its mouth was a blunt bird's beak. Two skinny arms nearly reached the ground. Though the great wells where its eyes had been were empty, it seemed clear the creature was staring at him. Warning him.

It did not hiss or lunge or do anything particularly threatening. Instead, it stooped and rose, holding a rock no larger than a pebble in a small, skeletal hand, then looked at him again. The creature's expression did not change, but it seemed clear this was part of a demonstration meant to intimidate him. The creature remained a good way off, though close enough that its features weren't lost in the thick ripples of heat. Andrew probably couldn't throw a stone so far. And even if it managed to strike him, a pebble wouldn't do much damage. Nevertheless, he took a cautious step backward.

Andrew did not see the stone, but he heard it hiss past his ear and strike the leaning outhouse behind him, sending a long crack splintering up the board where the pebble lodged itself inside a small, slivered crater. He felt a bead of sweat roll between his shoulders and down his back while the creature stooped for another rock and regarded him from a distance with vacant eye holes.

The door of the outhouse swung open and a grimy, irritable man with rolled up sleeves and thick, hairy arms stepped outside, his unfastened pants balled in a fist at his waist.

"Hey, what the...," he started, spotted the herd of creatures, and retreated into the outhouse without another word. The door slammed after him.

For a sweeping moment Andrew forgot his mission, forgot all sense of caution, turned toward the city and ran, horrified by the possibility that all the things he'd never believed about this world were true after all.

Everything here was dangerous.

THE UNFINISHED MAN

Andrew crouched in a tight alleyway, ears filled by the steady boom of his pounding heart, fearful one of the tiny beasts would totter around a corner and discover him. A minute passed. Two. Five. Staying here seemed the safest thing to do, but doing nothing did not change his task or bring it any closer to completion. If he wanted to go home, if he wanted to see Bree again, some small amount of bravery was required.

Andrew didn't like being afraid, but he could not control his fear. He was angry at himself for being afraid, because its weight kept him a prisoner in this alleyway, and he wasn't sure if the shiver in his hands was caused by his fear or his anger. Perhaps both. But anger gave him the strength to rise, so he clung to it, remembering that he shouldn't be here, that this wasn't fair, that he'd been deliberately sent here to meet his doom. Nerving himself, he edged through the alleyway and poked his head into the street.

Nothing.

Long and straight, the lone, dusty street split two rows of low buildings running parallel like the parted teeth of a terrible, slumbering beast. Beyond the street the world returned to an impenetrable haze, as if this strip of dirt were an island rising above the shifting clouds of a desert limbo.

There was no sign of the skeleton creatures, but that didn't mean some other monster wasn't lurking nearby.

According to the accounts of Old History, the West had been a horrid place rank with hordes of bloodthirsty monsters and giant men that bit and tore at the withered carcass of the world beneath a perpetual thunderstorm of fire and ash. People hated one another, hated themselves, cursed their loneliness, and tormented everyone they encountered, oblivious to their stupidity. The planet, plundered and bullied by its occupants, could no longer bear their fury and used its final reserves of vitality to manufacture creatures intent on the destruction of everything else, cobbling its ebbing raw materials into giants to beat what was left into the dirt and strangling life to a brown, drear death in the hopes of achieving tranquility through emptiness. The planet's remaining inhabitants settled into a war of smoldering attrition, grinding ever onward until battles ceased because no one remained to fight them.

Clearly, much of that history was an elaboration, swollen by imaginations that added new fables with each retelling. History loved to lie, through simple distortion or complete fabrication. Lies were the cosmetics of history, and when history could not be beautiful, it preferred to be shocking. But all embellishments had, at their heart's iron center, a hard and unfragmented truth. The existence of the skeleton creatures gave that history worrisome validity.

Bolstered by his contempt for the absurdity of a history that touted the existence of giant men, Andrew strode into the street and found himself immediately in the path of an enormous man that stood twice as tall as the nearest building. He attempted to backpedal from the path of the giant before it could raise an enormous foot and crush him against the street in a smear of bloody innards, but succeeded only in falling down.

This, Andrew thought ruefully, is what happened to those foolish enough to ignore the warnings of fairy tales.

Andrew clenched his teeth and eyes, awaiting a pulverizing step, wondering how he'd never heard the colossal figure approaching, guessing it had been lying patiently in wait to spring this trap, and deciding, in the end, that knowing had no bearing whatever on the result. He was doomed. Or so he expected.

Despite the relative rapidity of human thoughts, they did take time to realize themselves. More time, it occurred to Andrew, than should have been necessary to raise a foot and set it down again on top of something. Andrew opened his eyes.

The foot had not moved. Not only had the foot not moved, but the rough, stony quality of the foot made Andrew believe the foot was incapable of movement altogether. Andrew's head pitched backward to take in the entire creature and he realized the giant could not do him harm unless he made the mistake of walking into it.

Standing over the town was a broad-shouldered man, its features rough, one fist balled on a hip. The other hand stabbed a finger westward, daring or driving back invaders. The statue had not been finished, its feet still encased in rock—trapped here even if it had wanted to leave. It was a situation Andrew understood.

What the statue represented Andrew could not guess. Monstrosities of this sort often celebrated a spectacular achievement. Here, in this dust-eaten town, it seemed vulnerable and foolishly defiant.

"Aincha never seen a hero before?"

The voice came from behind, but when Andrew turned the walkway was empty.

"Not there," said the voice. "Here."

Andrew backed into the street and looked onto the roof.

Two men sat on top of the building, rocking wooden chairs, their heads covered by broad, drooping straw hats. It made sense to be there, Andrew realized, so long as the tiny monsters he'd seen outside the town couldn't climb or look up.

The larger man paid him no attention, his long, angular body slouched in a chair that seemed too small, eyes screwed shut, bearded chin pressed into his chest. He wore a heavy white wrapping rather than a shirt and pants, arms crossed beneath the folds.

The smaller one stared down at him alertly, leaning forward in his chair, a worn pipe projecting from a crack in his smile. He grinned wider when Andrew saw him and a gray cloud wafted free and broke against his baggy, sweating face like a toad pressing up through a layer of pond scum. His nose was flat and wide, as though it had been punched a great many times, and he wore a dark shirt with fraying sleeves that didn't reach far enough. The shirt had a patch with a name written in dark slashes that overlapped faded lettering. Andrew couldn't tell what the original name had been, but the new one appeared to read Hobert.

"What are you doing up there?" Andrew asked.

"Looking out," Hobert explained. He removed his hat and peered in futility toward the inscrutable horizon.

"For little monsters?"

Hobert's head ticked back and forth in partial agreement like a reed wagging in a sputtering wind, as if the monsters Andrew described were only a category of something to worry about.

"Best watch out, now," Hobert warned.

Andrew's brow crinkled.

"Watch out for wh..."

A hand settled on Andrew's shoulder. Before he could turn to face its owner, the hand tightened and yanked, pulling him off his feet and clapping him against the ground. Andrew's breath whooshed out and his vision shivered with the impact.

From a distance that seemed galaxies away, he thought he heard Hobert muttering.

"Tried to warn 'im, didn't I?"

As his vision firmed, a hazy figure drifted over him. He attempted to stand up. A shiver of panic passed through him when he could not. After an instant of experimentation Andrew learned his arms and legs still worked, but something held him in place in the middle. He lifted his head and found an emaciated arm pinning him to the ground. Not hard enough to crush him, only to keep him from rising.

The arm extended from a man, or something very much like one. Tattered clothing hung from the bare wires of a gangly body, little more than a skeleton held together by the gray flesh stretched tight across its body. The face was sallow and grim, with dark lines where dirt gathered in the fissures of its skin. Two eyes, sunk deep into the sockets, glittered with distant thought like precious stones at the bottom of a well.

Andrew wrenched at the bony arm, a flimsy rail that seemed ready to shatter under the slightest pressure, but it proved as secure and stubborn as a gnarled and ancient trunk. He tried to pry the fingers up, yet they too seemed rooted and immovable. When he tried to wriggle free the pressure intensified. The creature cocked its head, as if wondering why he continued to struggle when it was easier to be still.

The creature leaned in close, expressionless but for those sparkling eyes, its breath humid and stinking of old cabbage. The mouth opened and a question rumbled through the crumbled colonnades of failing teeth.

"Wo... man...?"

Andrew and the creature shared a long look as the question hung in the air. The ledge of the creature's brow lifted above the tunnels of its eyes, awaiting a response.

Andrew blinked. His lips pressed.

"No."

The creature leaned back slowly, holding a long, measuring gaze upon him as it weighed the information, then withdrew its arm and stood. It lingered above Andrew, perhaps doubting his response, then scraped off through the street to continue its search.

Andrew propped himself on his elbows and watched the creature shamble away.

"Okay there, lad?"

The voice came from the man with the pipe and squashed nose, who leaned over the edge of the roof to gaze down upon him.

Andrew rubbed a sore space on his chest where the creature held him down.

"I think."

"Told Gordimer not to go in there," Hobert continued. He stuffed a pinch of shredded wood into the pipe bowl. "'Stay out of the forest,' I says. 'Won't find heroes in there. We already got a hero anyhow.'" He shrugged. "Now he's got the old Forest Monster all riled up."

Andrew stood, beating the dust out of his shirt.

"Forest Monster?"

Hobert took the pipe out of his mouth and gestured toward the creature in the street. The Forest Monster moved a few paces in one direction, stopped, stumped in the other direction, then stopped again, as though he knew exactly where he was, knew exactly what he wanted, yet found himself smothered by the overpowering feeling that he was lost.

"First brush with the Forest Monster, eh? Not really dangerous. Not really a monster, either. Monsters tend to have less vendetta. This fella, he has a purpose. 'Woman.' That's all he ever says. Sometimes he drags somebody off with him. They either get loose, or they come back a day or so later. Most times. Those that come back say all Forest Monster does is stare at 'em for a while, then just sorta loses interest. Like he was lookin' fer somethin' but didn't find it."

"Why don't you catch him?"

Hobert leaned forward, eyes bulging.

"You think *you* can catch the Forest Monster?"

Andrew recalled the little effort Forest Monster made to hold him down and Hobert's response hinted at the convincing failure of prior attempts. The Forest Monster, like the whimsical and destructive aspects of nature, was not something that could be controlled or overcome.

"Miseries are better endured. Eventually they wear themselves out, right?" Hobert said, then rubbed his mashed-in nose. "Besides. He ain't dangerous. What you really got to worry about is them wogs. Once you get away from Forest Monster, that's when the wogs find you."

"Wogs," Andrew repeated. He recalled the beasts he'd seen outside the town. "Those short, skeletal things?"

"Oh. You seen 'em, then. And lived to tell the tale."

So Andrew hadn't been hallucinating. The man with wings, the small metal creatures—they were real. He'd worried, for the briefest of instants, the journey had shattered his wits, leaving his mind cracked and desiccated like the dried out landscape around the town. Their existence, on the other hand, seemed a different and better reason to worry.

"They do things to yer head," said Hobert, tapping a finger on his temple. "Push around the puzzle parts until the old pictures don't make no sense." He pointed to the Forest Monster. "Reckon that's what happened to our friend, here. Shuffled his deck. He mighta been lookin' for somethin' afore, but now he can't remember what it was, only that he was lookin' for it. Them wogs are lookin' for somethin', too. Or someone."

"Someone?"

"Ain't seen her, have you?" Hobert asked.

"Seen who?"

"The one they're lookin' for, of course. The girl. Figure maybe if we was to find her, they'd leave us be. Maybe that girl and the girl the Forest Monster is after are one in the same. Wouldn't that be a tidy fix to all our problems!"

As Andrew was about to ask about the girl, the Forest Monster clomped across the wooden walkway in front of a building with boarded windows on the opposite side of the street. It stood before the door a moment, waiting, thinking, or searching in vain for a reflection, before pushing against it. The hinges wailed and popped, and the door fell into the darkness inside the building, followed by the Forest Monster.

"What's he doing?" asked Andrew.

"Lookin' fer somethin'. But ain't everybody? Everybody movin' here and there, turnin' over rocks without knowin' why. Like they're all wound up inside and don't know what else to do with themselves. We're all searchin' for somethin'. Right, Jim?"

Jim shrugged without looking up.

"An' I bet you're lookin' for somethin' too, aincha?"

Andrew's teeth clenched.

"Yes."

"See there? Told ya."

But not everyone was searching for something they wanted. Some were searching because they had to.

Somewhere in this decaying mouthful of loose wooden buildings was his subject, the one whose history he'd been sent to record. Somewhere amidst the humdrum of a world falling apart, where everything was tainted with a thin layer of grime and malcontent, resided a void of such magnitude that objects of small importance were no doubt drawn to him and lost forever—a person of such insignificance historians hadn't bothered to devote a page to his posterity. How anyone knew of his existence at all, Andrew could not guess. Even the slightest person had *something* written about them.

That, of course, was why he was here. To chronicle the tedium that had been overlooked. From deep in the hidden parts of his mind where Hope lit small fires in the darkness came the tiny flickering idea that maybe this person was great, secretly. It was a foolish thought, which is why Hope had fashioned it, because Hope was always creating pleasantly ideological, and therefore impossible things. How could anything Great avoid attention? Greatness by its very nature demanded attention.

"Course, I already found what I was lookin' for, eh Jim?"

Jim raised the brim of his hat to take a quick look at the world, determined that it remained unchanged, and began to lower it again when he caught sight of Andrew. For the briefest instant there seemed a flicker of interest, and Jim began to straighten in his seat. Andrew felt a tingle of anticipation in his chest, an inkling of impending remarkability. Then the moment passed, the brim fell, and Jim eased back in his chair. Hobert continued.

"The peace o' mind that comes only from a sense o' security, that's what I've got. And only one thing brings a sense o' security." Hobert bit the pipe and smiled. His eyes flicked out into the street to the statue. "A hero."

"That statue," said Andrew. He gave the stonework a quick look, then looked back to Hobert. "It's a hero?"

Hobert cast a somber gaze into the street and nodded.

"A hero. Yes," he answered. "He's very tall."

Andrew found himself suddenly interested. This was the story he wanted to write. A story about a hero, the obstacles he faced on his path to heroism, his guides, his arch enemy, the ultimate goal of being a hero, and, of course, whether the story continued or had an end.

"What made him a hero?"

Hobert shrugged, removed the pipe, and gestured toward the statue with the stem before poking it back into the corner of his mouth.

"He's very tall," he repeated.

Andrew paused, waiting for Hobert to continue, but that was all.

"Tall... and what else?"

Hobert's smile faded and he faced Andrew, somewhat irritated. Two gray trails of pipe smoke jetted from his nostrils.

"What else what?"

"Beside being tall," Andrew clarified. "To be a hero."

Hobert fixed Andrew with a hard, querulous stare, then shook his head as though the question didn't make sense.

"Being tall *is* being a hero," he answered.

Andrew grimaced.

"What?"

"What what?" Hobert replied. "What don't you understand?"

Andrew spread his arms.

"Everything."

"Oh," the fellow replied. He leaned back in his chair and pulled his hat down over his eyes. "Then you're hopeless."

THE UNDERTHINKER

Andrew turned away from Hobert, jaw clenched. He clomped irritably along the edge of the street, glaring up at the statue as he went by. Hobert clearly had no idea what purpose the monument served and had invented one to suit his needs. Someone had put it there for a reason, but what that was Andrew could only speculate.

A relic of some sort, most likely, meant to ward off lurking demons who might do the townsfolk harm. Charms and guardian spirits were all the product of a need for something to believe in because people didn't believe in themselves. People feared changing anything, even things they found overbearing, even as they attempted to wish them away. It was why they invented heroes. It was why the world suffered through long periods of stagnation between innovations. Because rather than change the things that needed change, people preferred to cower and wait until a hero arrived to do it for them. Assuming by that point it was not already too late.

Andrew staggered and fell. He rolled over, angry at his clumsiness, and saw a boy staring back at him, wide eyed, his legs drawn into his chest in the false hope that he might avoid chastisement.

"Sorry," said the boy in a quiet voice. "I didn't see you. I was thinking. Maybe I think too much."

A thin hand with bulging knuckles reached out in greeting.

The boy was just another banal detail in the dusty town. A baggy white shirt and thick suspenders that kept him securely in his pants. His feet bobbed as they tapped inside a pair of oversized shoes. His hair was a lazy flop of black, but not long enough to obscure his ears, which, to Andrew, seemed too big. The dark brown handle of an old gun hooked out of a holster worn through in spots at his hip.

Andrew stood.

"I doubt it."

The boy's hand fell, and with a grimace of disappointment his eyes drifted across the empty street. He raised a canteen to his mouth, but did not take a drink. Andrew began to turn away when the boy spoke in a voice barely audible.

"Sometimes I dream of a different place," the boy murmured. "Green and vibrant. Not just the place, but the people, too. They move with purpose and meaning. I can almost remember their names, then it's gone. There's a girl there. I know her, but I've never met her or seen her face. It seems so familiar, like I don't belong here. But I must be here for a reason. Do you ever feel that way? Like you don't belong here?"

The boy stared through the buildings across the dusty street, as if he could see something beyond them, images of the future or the faraway past. Was he, too, out of his own time, here on some futile purpose, suffering a puerile banishment?

"Yes," said Andrew. "Yes, I do."

The boy's eyes snapped onto Andrew, his eyes round with horror.

"I didn't know he was still here," he whispered.

"Are you talking to a canteen?" Andrew asked.

The boy opened his mouth to respond, then reconsidered.

"No."

Before Andrew could ask if there was something wrong with him, a crash of broken wood sounded behind him accompanied by a cry of exultation.

"Woman!"

Further down the street the Forest Monster galloped toward a girl laying in the street. Above her at the roof's edge, Hobert looked down, grinning.

"He pushed her," Andrew murmured. "You pushed her!"

Hobert's head turned toward Andrew and he smiled again.

"This is how you get rid of the Forest Monster!" he called.

Dazed, the girl staggered to her feet and began to run, stumbling as she went. Too late. The Forest Monster caught her by the hair ad heaver her off her feet. She thrashed as the Forest Monster buried his hand tighter into her hair and began dragging her down the street, eyes fixed on the forest.

"Let go!" she sputtered, writhing and skidding through the dirt. Her outbursts had the sound of someone trying to sound more dangerous than they were, and served only to emphasize her fear. "I'll burst your eyes out! Scratch your liver! Break your muscles!"

Andrew stiffened. Took a step forward. Stopped.

His experience with the wogs was evidence enough that helping was dangerous. Andrew wasn't here to save people, just watch. Better not to interfere. Better to let them solve their own problems. The Forest Monster's path took it directly toward Andrew, and he took a step back, allowing the Forest Monster to pass. The girl looked up at him as she went by, eyes filled with fear that turned to rage when she realized Andrew had no intention of helping her. He turned away only to be met by the boy, who looked up at him in wonder, then at the Forest Monster, then back at Andrew, trying to puzzle out what Andrew had considered doing before changing his mind.

"Hey," Andrew called to Hobert.

"Hey, ho," said Hobert, jerking upright in his chair, causing his hat to drop from his face. He appeared to have fallen asleep. The oversized man beside Hobert continued rocking, oblivious and content. Hobert cast about dazedly before finding Andrew waving at him. Hobert scowled. "What do you want, Mister Don't-Know-A-Hero-Even-Tho-He's-So-Damd-Smart?"

"Where's your hero now?" called Andrew. He pointed toward the Forest Monster as it made its uncontested escape.

Hobert pointed to the statue.

"Right there, you malodorous cad. Is he too big to see, you reckon? Ha! You been skunked by my sardonic wit. Just one in a wide array of debilitating rhetorical weapons!"

"But that girl," Andrew persisted. "Your hero is just standing there. Is someone going to..." He rolled a hand through the air, as if trying to engage some invisible gear that would help him phrase the question properly. "You know. Help her?"

Hobert, sweat beading on his bare head, looked from Andrew to the Forest Monster, trying to comprehend what he meant. Hobert's eyes pinched briefly, focusing. Andrew imagined he could hear stones tumbling in his head as he ground away at the problem. Then he shrugged, swept his hat up and planted it on his head.

"Why?" he asked.

"Someone should help."

Again Hobert turned to look to the Forest Monster, which neared the buildings at the end of the street and the short stretch of open space between them and the forest. Back to Andrew.

"Why don't *you* help her?" asked Hobert.

Andrew's teeth clenched.

"That's not what I do. I write. Not rescue. I'm a writer, not a fighter."

The words sounded idiotic as they spilled out of his mouth.

"Course not," Hobert agreed with a sharp nod. "Me neither."

Andrew curled his lip into his mouth and bit.

Hobert lifted a finger.

"It's only one person after all," he continued. "What difference can one person make?"

It was as though Hobert had plucked the rotten observation from the garden of his mind and thrown it back in his face, all stink, filth, and irony. One hero, one author, one person—what difference could they make? None. Why bother? To try and fail proved that helping only improved the value of indifference. How did anything get done?

"What about your hero?" asked Andrew. "He's only one person."

"And he's chosen not to get involved," Hobert replied, throwing a glance toward the statue, which remained, predictably, unmoving. "I trust his decision. Sensible fellow."

"It would be right to help," Andrew persisted.

Hobert was unfazed.

"If it was right, someone would be doing it."

Andrew clenched his fists and stamped a foot, then skulked back the way he had come. He encountered an unattended canteen lying in the street, gushing fluid in weak pulses. There was motion in the corner of his eye and he turned to find a figure pursuing the Forest Monster. Someone was helping.

Andrew raised his arms, triumphant, thrilled the world had not been abandoned to destruction.

A gangly savior raced down the street, waving his arms and yelling something unhearable, stumbling in his shoes and holding his pants up with one hand.

It was the boy with the overbig ears.

Andrew's arms fell. The girl was certainly doomed now.

At the edge of the street, the boy stopped. Given up. Failed. Still yelling. It couldn't have happened any other way.

Tiny with distance, the Forest Monster also stopped. Turned. Dropped the girl. Free, she rose and hid herself amongst the sand-weathered crates and blocks of masonry piled against the front of a slouching building at the end of the street. The Forest Monster did not follow her.

Andrew's eyes widened.

The boy had done it. How? The two stood facing one another for a long moment, then the Forest Monster surged forward. Startled, the boy looked about briefly, reached toward the pistol at his hip, then turned and fled. The Forest Monster bellowed something incoherent as it ran, pursuing with outstretched arms and an expression of mindless rage.

"Has this ever happened before?" Andrew asked.

"What happened?" asked Hobert. His eyes fluttered, as though drowsiness needed only a few moments of uninterrupted silence to reclaim him. "Something happen? That can't be good. Nothing that happens is ever good. Best thing to do is not let anything happen at all. Things happening just mess up the things you grow used to."

Andrew gestured toward the boy, who fled down the street, the Forest Monster close behind.

Hobert leaned forward. His mouth opened, and the pipe drooped dangerously before tumbling to the awning, rattling to the edge, and dropping into the street.

"The boy," said Andrew. "He saved that girl."

The boy and Forest Monster drew nearer, then turned down an alley and vanished behind the buildings. A handful of additional citizens appeared at the rooftops of adjacent buildings and watched the activity with interest, moving from one side of the building to the other as the boy dashed from alleyway to alleyway.

"Maybe so," said Hobert, looking anxiously at the pipe below, weighing his need against the action required to get it back. He spoke without taking his eyes from it. "We'll see if he can save himself. That's the real challenge. Think you might hand that up to me, fella?"

Andrew picked the pipe and raised it toward Hobert's outstretched arm, then withdrew.

"Tell me about the boy."

Hobert huffed, but knew he had no choice.

"Peculiar," said Hobert. "Talks to sticks and rocks more 'n people, askin' questions you don't need to be curious about. Who is the hero? Where did he come from? Questions with obvious answers or questions best left unanswered altogether."

The boy and Forest Monster reemerged. A cheer from the rooftop welcomed them.

The boy threw an occasional glance over his shoulder, a gun in one hand trailing out behind him. He fired a shot, but only after looking away. The threat of the weapon did not seem to deter the Forest Monster.

"Not so good with people," Hobert continued. "Strange, and that makes folk uncomfortable. Scared, even. He ain't normal. He ain't what folk expect. He's too…"

Hobert pinched his eyes and windmilled his hands, thinking.

"Different?" Andrew suggested.

Boy and Forest Monster were nearer now, coming closer. They turned into an alley and vanished behind the buildings.

"Stupid," Hobert decided. "Anyone with half some brains coulda known full well what's happenin' would happen, but he did it anyhow. He don't listen. Like that old fool, Gordimer. People who don't listen make trouble for everybody else. The good part is that a not-listener is usually quick to go because they get so much attention—like the Forest Monster. Most not-

listeners is gone now, as is the question askers. Good riddance. But not that Billy-Bob. Worst of them all, and invincible to boot… Hey! What's the matter all a sudden? Gone all sourfaced."

Andrew tasted bile in his throat. Without looking back, he gestured into the street.

"That… is Billy-Bob?"

"Yeah," Hobert said, nodding. His face was clouded by momentary doubt. "Unless I misheard myself. He's a Billy-Bob if anyone is. You know him?"

Yes, he knew him, what little there was to know. Andrew sagged forward until his head met a post supporting the awning. He felt something in him wilt, like a flower fading at the end of summer, turning in on itself in preparation for the next year. Except there was no escaping this place. No sleeping through the brutality of this world to wake up in the spring that followed it. He was trapped here for the duration of the task. Unless his own doom found him first.

So this was the history he was to record. Just as foolhardy and inconsequential as he'd feared. Maybe, thought Andrew, this encounter might prove to be the boy's first and last act of heroism. It was a cruel and selfish hope that offended his morality, but maybe this story would begin and end today. Then he could go home.

Again the pair went past. Those on the rooftop cheered. Through some strange turn of events the Forest Monster now wielded the gun.

Andrew's arm felt leaden, and he stretched half-heartedly toward Hobert. Hobert, flat on his stomach, made an extra effort and grasped the pipe. His face curled into an expression of exultant triumph that quickly faltered as he realized he'd extended himself too far. With a peep of despair, he slid forward. Before he fell, the giant Jim grasped him by an ankle and dragged him back.

Another gunshot sounded, followed by an ominous, stony crack. Hobert looked up from his hands and knees, a thin stream of blood trailing from one nostril. The sound of sliding stone joined the reverberating gunshot. Hobert blinked, trying to clear his vision of something his mind refused to believe. Andrew turned in time to see the statue's pointing arm reach downward as though trying to press a button in the street.

Hobert placed the pipestem in his mouth and let it sag in one corner.

"Fud," he said.

It was a word Andrew had never heard, but seemed to convey resignation to the totality of a coming disaster.

The statue fractured and crumpled when it met the street, and the force of its impact caused the ground to spring under his feet and Andrew clutched at a post to keep his feet. Tiny rocks peppered him, followed by a cloud of dirt and acrid dust. The last image he had before the cloud enveloped him was of Hobert staring in awe at the approaching grayness.

Andrew coughed and pulled his shirt over his mouth. He tried to feel his way along the building toward the end of the street, but even though he was sure he'd been standing near a building he could not find it.

He sifted through the darkness, stumbling over scattered slabs of broken statue, and knocking his toes painfully against chunks too large to dislodge. Abruptly, the haze parted and Andrew found himself in a clearing in the street, looking up into the face of the man Hobert called Jim. Jim didn't appear alarmed that he was no longer on the roof. Instead, he seemed purposeful and alert. From beneath the straw hat a face that had expressed detachment and indifference to the world now flickered with a wry and knowing grin, as if the string of events leading to this latest catastrophe had all been patiently expected.

"What are you doing down here?" asked Andrew.

Jim bent at the waist until the brim of Jim's straw hat folded against Andrew's sun-reddened forehead.

"You're right," said Jim.

Andrew coughed and wiped the dust from his face. They stood inside a shallow well of clear air, the nearby rooftops just visible above the rim. A few steps away the dirt drifted and swirled in a solid gray wall.

"Right about what?"

"About being here," said Jim. "It's not an accident. It's not a coincidence. There is a purpose."

"What? Who are you? What purpose?"

Jim answered with a smile. Not malevolent or sneering, but iron and certain. Jim's eyes flicked a brief gaze past his shoulder.

Curious, Andrew turned. Just behind him a space in the cloud billowed and pulsed.

Andrew's mouth crunched into a frown, realizing even before it occurred what was about to happen. But this was not the useful sort of precognition that allowed time for preparation. Instead, it was the kind that allowed time enough for understanding and nothing more. Much too late to escape, yet plenty of time to feel helpless and irritable.

The boy, eyes clenched as he hurtled onward, burst out of the cloud, closing the distance between the two of them in a single stride. Too late to move, too late to cry out a warning. Time enough only for one colossal word from the crashing waterfalls of unlimited language. Just one choice amongst the millions. Any other time it would be a mind-crushing dilemma. This time it was easy.

Andrew's mouth quirked in disgust, and in the instant before they met a single word escaped him.

"Fud," he grumbled.

Then they collided.

A FORTUNATE MISSTEP

From the rooftop a crowd watched the Forest Monster follow Billy-Bob as he threaded between the buildings. In all likelihood these people knew how the chase would end, but a hope for something unexpected made them curious. And their hope made Billy-Bob hope he may somehow survive.

Occasionally they would throw something into the street to strike or trip him. But their efforts did not concern him much. He had been dodging their attempts for years. Moreso it was the lumps in the terrain, small stones rolling underfoot or clipping against his toes as he ran, threatening to send him sprawling. There was also the Forest Monster—a fellow so intent on destroying Billy-Bob that he paid no heed whatsoever to the uneven ground, the crowd, or the railings he smashed through in his pursuit, all thoughts compressed into a single burning ember that singed his mind and prodded him wrathfully onward.

"Kill!" the Forest Monster cried.

They swept past the giant statue, around the long-vacant hardware store where the girl huddled against the shovels and crates stacked against the walls, past the pointing crowd, then behind the buildings and back out into the street. Billy-Bob clambered over decrepit fences and squeezed between tightly bunched barrels, and the Forest Monster crashed through them, oblivious to obstructions. The city was a motionless carousel as they spun around it.

Billy-Bob rounded a corner and threw a backwards gaze to see if the Forest Monster was still there. He was, lumbering at his heels, teeth bared, brows bent in anger, groping arms pulling at the air as though doing so might increase his speed.

Nothing had gone as expected.

In the rational world Billy-Bob had observed, when one person asked another a question, the other often had the courtesy to say the question was stupid. Dogs chased cats, cats chased mice, and mice were in perpetual flight from any of a million perils. That was the natural order of the universe. Everything operated according to long-established rules of gravity, social rejection, and fear.

So when one person asked another what they were doing, even if it was a Forest Monster, the appropriate response was, at the very least, to tell him the question was stupid. It was entirely inappropriate to leap forward and shout the word "Kill!"

This chase made a mockery of billions of years of strengthening stereotypes.

Billy-Bob reached for a wooden post supporting an awning and used it to wrench himself around a corner. He looked back again, hoping the Forest Monster had lost him, but it made the turn, barking and gnashing, arms outstretched. They sped past the front of the building where his canteen still rested, looking on with no discernable expression, then on down the street past the new fellow with the notepad, who threw a look over his shoulder as Billy-Bob passed.

When the Forest Monster took the girl, Billy-Bob had been thinking. Not about anything in particular, but a thousand things at once. Where did trees come from? What were people for? Who was the Forest Monster and why did it do the things it did? He never answered any of these questions by thinking, but that was probably because he wasn't very good at it, though he might improve with practice. The girl was loud, and made her abduction difficult to ignore, even for someone deep in thought. Beneath the hum of revolving thoughts he felt tiny squeaks of dismay and regret—uncomfortable sensations that arose whenever the Forest Monster abducted someone. Because he didn't know how to assuage these feelings he tried to think about something else. But because his thoughts weren't very powerful, it didn't take much to interrupt them.

Bits of a conversation between Hobert and the fellow with the notepad trickled into his mind, a few words at a time. Words like Help and Hero and Difference. They didn't seem like important words on their own, but the one with the notepad seemed earnest about what the Forest Monster had done, and the more he listened, the more Billy-Bob realized he felt these questions pulling at him as well. A compulsion jerked at him like clothing on a line caught in a stiff wind, straining and snapping in an effort to go, but he didn't know why or where.

He looked out into the street where the girl struggled to free herself, the Forest Monster plodding toward his forest lair where he would work some mysterious mischief. In her eyes was defiance and rage, yet beneath all of that was fear. A fear born from the knowledge that she must face this menace alone. It was that fear calling to him, begging for resolution.

"It would be right to help," the fellow with the notepad said.

And that was it. An explosion in his brain. To help was to alleviate suffering. There was an overwhelming sense of rightness in the words, something undeniably axiomatic that all the gnashing, jabbing, genius dissenters of the world could not unprove because such truths were written indelibly across the soul, and while a person could crush their soul with injustice and hate until it was tiny and almost invisible, they could never destroy it entirely. The core of rightness would remain forever, an immutable seed. The faintest nurturing could bring it back.

Help. Until now the word had been meaningless. He'd heard it before, felt that strange, agonized tug within him, but had no idea how to respond because responding was dangerous.

"If it was right, someone would be doing it," Hobert had replied.

Billy-Bob needed no further compulsion. He ran after the Forest Monster and the girl, calling to them as they passed the buildings at the far end of the street. Now he understood, where helping and rightness was concerned, the danger didn't matter.

"Where are you going?" he shouted at the Forest Monster.

Not surprisingly, the Forest Monster continued on.

In retrospect it was a silly question. Forest Monster was, of course, going to the forest. Still, he had to say something, something to slow the Forest Monster, dissuade him, make him think. Thinking always slowed Billy-Bob.

"Where are you going?" he repeated, voice pitching to reach its maximum projection.

It worked.

The Forest Monster turned, regarded him, and looked down at the struggling girl. Then he turned away again as though realizing he'd already gotten what he'd come to get, hauling the girl along behind him.

Billy-Bob followed at a distance, unsure how to proceed, casting about for something to inspire him. Small stones tumbled from his path as he walked. Without thinking, he stooped and took a rock in his hand, smooth, sandy, and hot. He took two steps toward the Forest Monster, wound, and hurled it into the distance.

The stone sailed on a long and graceful parabola, settling into a descending path that curled to one side and fell short, striking the girl on the knee.

"Augh!" she cried. Even from afar he could discern her sweet, muffled soprano. "Idiot!"

Still the Forest Monster distanced himself.

"You'll never find her!" Billy-Bob called "You'll never find her like this! She'll just run away!"

The Forest Monster stopped, as if the words had struck some narcoleptic nerve, causing all the motors in its body to shut down.

Seizing the opportunity, Billy-Bob picked up another rock and hurled it toward the Monster. The girl cringed. But this time the throw remained true, the stone hurtled through the air and struck the Forest Monster in the back of the head.

The Forest Monster staggered and uttered a short shriek of pain. It reached both hands to cradle the wound, releasing his grip on the girl, who heaved to her feet and limped to the nearest building where she hid herself amidst the barrels and shovels.

For a while the Forest Monster did nothing but crouch, clutching its head. Then it stood. When it turned, Billy-Bob could see thin trails of cleanliness on its face where the dirt had washed away below the tunnels of its eyes. It regarded its empty hand, trying to grasp what had changed in the last few moments and how the change affected its designs. For all the fear the Forest Monster inspired, Billy-Bob couldn't help pitying the creature. After all, the Forest Monster seemed to be searching for someone it had lost, and went about trying to fill that emptiness the best way it knew how. It seemed strange to think so, but maybe the Forest Monster needed help, too.

"I can help you find her!"

The Forest Monster looked at him, studying him with its deep-pitted eyes. Maybe it didn't understand.

"I'll find her!" Billy-Bob called again. "I'll find her for you!"

Billy-Bob could see the Forest Monster's face twitch as tiny cinders of thought floated through his mind amidst numberless gassy clouds of forgotten memories. Kept apart they were insignificant and undangerous. But when brought together, they blew open the doors to memories long shut to the world.

Billy-Bob saw the Forest Monster's eyes bulge as though blasted outward by some muffled internal explosion and its face twist into a horrid scowl. Until now, no one had ever heard the Forest Monster utter any word beside "woman." Until now, no one thought it capable of anything else. So it was something of a surprise when the creature rushed forward screaming a new word.

"Kill!"

Billy-Bob stared in wonder at the charging Forest Monster. One hand moved instinctively to the gun at his hip, but another instinct was stronger. He turned and fled, not knowing what else to do.

So he was running.

Running was tiring. His legs felt heavy and the toes of his shoes dragged small stones out of their places. Behind, the Forest Monster pursued, without a hint of breathlessness in its repeated howlings.

It was clear the Forest Monster would never stop unless Billy-Bob stopped the Forest Monster. So Billy-Bob drew the pistol hanging from his hip, which came free of the holster with the heavy reluctance of a deep-rooted weed.

"Hwat's goin'on here?" asked the pistol with a groggy slur.

Had this been the first time it had spoken to him, Billy-Bob may have blurted something in shock or surprise.

"You're heavy," he said instead.

"I'm full of anger and thoughtless vengeance," the gun replied. "I think you should put me away."

"In a minute."

Most folk considered the idea of objects speaking to him peculiar, so Billy-Bob kept it to himself. Just as grass was brown and the sky was a pale yellow, the reason why things spoke to him was nothing he understood but something he accepted because it had always been. The gun, too, was something he could not remember finding, but neither could he remember a time when it had not been with him.

Billy-Bob had never fired the gun. Each time he drew it from the holster the gun would groan and tell him to put it away. Still, he had a general understanding of how it was supposed to work. Guns were fairly intuitive devices, and those who didn't grasp their function soon lost them in the process of experimentation. So he pointed the weapon to the rear and tightened his finger around the trigger. The gun puffed smoke and kicked, harder than expected, its report crashing against his ears, and he nearly dropped it.

A window far to the left and behind the Forest Monster caved on itself with an inward showering of glass. The people on the rooftop retreated a few steps from the edge of the roof.

"Now hey!" said the weapon. "You could hurt someone!"

"I know," said Billy-Bob.

Hurting someone was his intent. If he could hurt the Forest Monster significantly it might stop following him. It might even stop following everyone altogether.

Billy-Bob leveled the gun a second time, trying to draw a bead on the Forest Monster through the bounce of running, and pulled the trigger. The bullet skidded past the Forest Monster's ear, leaving a bloody red scuff. The Forest Monster bellowed and clapped a hand to the wound.

The kick from this second shot so rattled Billy-Bob that the gun bobbled and fluttered out of his hand, pinwheeled in the air, and landed in the gnarled and muddy fingers of the Forest Monster.

From behind, the gun continued to admonish him.

"Can't say I didn't warn you."

* * *

Esther crouched on the porch of a building behind barrels of cement mix and shovels and tools for shaping rocks, all poised for some great stoneworking project that had never been finished, peering out between them as the Forest Monster chased the boy up and down the street.

She rubbed her shin where the boy's stone struck her, feeling the stinging tissue lumping into a hard knob like an extra ankle. She glared at them as they went by, hoping they might feel the heat of her malice without finding her.

She didn't like either of them.

The Forest Monster was a hideous creature who had taken her against her wishes, dragged her through the street, and intended to subject her to cruelties she could not imagine, then leave her to the wogs. The Forest Monster was an unfeeling beast bent on its own inscrutable interests.

Esther liked the boy even less, though she wasn't sure why. She knew everyone disliked him, but no one had ever explained their disdain. It was automatic, like squinting in bright sunlight. She'd never thought about it before, and never thought she needed a reason, but now it seemed silly to harbor such strong feelings about someone or something without being able to explain them.

She pressed her face against the gap between two barrels and they raced through the narrow corridor of her vision and were gone again, but a moment later they appeared at the other end of the street, the Forest Monster hot on the boy's heels. As she watched, the weapon in the Forest Monster's hand jerked, sending out a small puff of smoke, and a loud shot sounded, followed a moment later by the crack of fracturing stone from the other end of the street.

Her eyes shifted away from the boy and Forest Monster to see what had made the noise, but didn't see anything out of the ordinary. There were the same dilapidated buildings and the great unchanging wilderness beyond the statue. Nevertheless, something seemed different, so she continued to stare. And as she watched she realized the statue was moving.

Esther's heart leapt. It was alive, and coming to their aid at last!

But there was something unnatural about its motion. Rather than bending at the knees and ankles as it should, readying itself to spring between her and danger, it seemed to bend against the joints. A loud crack stung her ears and the statue tilted forward at a frightening angle. The pointing hand traced a line through the sky as though following a falling star, then the whole thing met the ground with a crash that lifted Esther onto her toes and rattled the shovels against the wall behind her. Dirt and debris exploded from the statue, which came apart like bad fruit against a barn door.

Esther could not give a name to her feelings as the rubble tumbled outward, followed by the gray cloud of dust and dirt. She didn't know who the statue was, or its purpose, but it had always been a comfort to see it there. It was their last, best, and only defense against the fears that skulked everywhere around the city but had been reluctant to enter with the statue keeping vigilant watch.

The dust wave washed up and over the crates, barrels, and her in a warm cascade, shrinking her vision to just a few steps. It seemed now that she was alone in a tiny, clouded purgatory, its borders marked by a wall covered with shovels and a few crates and barrels. Any step past them might send her falling into a void from which she would never be recovered.

She backed against the wall and came up against the shovels. A shovel beside her dropped off its rack and the handle fell across her toes. Coupled with the destruction of the statue, the throbbing in her knee, and the stress of hiding from the Forest Monster, it was more anguish than she could bear. Biting her tongue, she snapped up the shovel, determined to hurt it as it had hurt her, and swung the blade at the nearest barrel. The barrel burst apart under the blow and the strike reverberated up her arms.

Her rage satisfied, she observed the destruction she'd wrought with surprise. She'd expected the shovel to shiver to pieces, but instead it remained intact, while the barrel lay on its side in a pile of its own sandy innards, the wooden slats crushed on one side, bursting outward on the other.

She blinked. Looked at the shovel. Back to the ruined barrel. Back to the shovel.

Esther's face hardened as a new thought crystallized in her mind. The street beyond the barrels re-emerged slowly as the dust settled. The world still existed somewhere out there, it simply required a sufficient amount of bravery to rediscover it. And perhaps, in the process, claim a reward for making it better. She gripped the shovel handle with both hands, stepped across the deflated barrel and the spreading pool of gray viscera, and strode into the haze-covered street.

* * *

Billy-Bob pawed through the murk from the fallen statue. Free of the gun, Billy-Bob thought he should have outdistanced the Forest Monster with ease. But the throaty breathing of the Forest Monster husked nearby, and now and again he'd hear the crack-hiss of the gun firing.

Things were not going well at all.

Only a moment ago a bullet sizzled past and struck the age-weathered statue at the ankle. With a long, grinding groan the statue leaned forward, as if to inspect its wound, then the whole thing fell to the ground with a crash that lifted Billy-Bob from his feet. A thick cloud of dirt and cinder rose from the fallen hero, engulfing the center of the city and all those inside it. Billy-Bob hacked and gagged, eyes watering, uncertain where anything was, but certain he had to keep going somewhere or the Forest Monster would find him.

A faint light showed in the cloud ahead, so Billy-Bob ran toward it, unsure what he would find or whether there was any reason to expect it would be safer than anywhere else. The cloud abruptly ended and Billy-Bob found himself inches from a familiar face—the one who had spoken the words still ringing in his ears.

It would be right to help.

That statement had brought all his thoughts together, about the Forest Monster, about the girl who had been taken, about the strange compulsion he could not explain. Trumpets had erupted to announce the arrival of a great realization. The stranger must be brilliant. It did feel right to help. It was why Billy-Bob was running.

There was little clue as to what powerful thoughts coursed through the mind of this stern savant. A genius might deduce the meaning of a deep scowl and the short word "Fud", but Billy-Bob was no genius and he had little time to consider before they collided, sending them both to the ground and the fellow's notepad spiraling out of his hand.

Billy-Bob scrambled back to his feet, and offered to help the fellow up.

"No time," said another voice.

Jim, the giant man from the rooftop, stood near the back edge of the clearing. He appeared pleased, as if he'd guess correctly about something that had been uncertain until now. Billy-Bob had never heard Jim speak, and he could think of no way to describe the voice except helpful, a term he felt would do no good if he tried to explain it to anyone else.

A bullet buzzed past and punched a hole in the dust wall that quickly sealed itself.

"Go," Jim said.

The Forest Monster howled, closer now, so Billy-Bob raised an arm to his face, squinted, and plunged back into the cloud just as the Forest Monster burst into the clearing behind him and stumbled over the fellow with the notepad as he tried to stand up again.

The cloud was sinking. The brightly illuminated roof of refracted light caught in the dust fell lower and lower until his head broke above the surface and he could see the jagged edges of large blocks from the fractured statue poking out of the haze. The dirt swirled like a river over a stone where the Forest Monster sought for him.

"Kill!" it cried.

Billy-Bob was frightened. His hands shook as he searched for somewhere to hide. Maybe this had been a mistake. His legs had gotten noticeably rubbery from all the running, while the Forest Monster appeared tireless. What to do? He turned up the street, heading out of town toward the great gorge protecting Dirtburg from the greater monsters of the West. If he couldn't outrun the Forest Monster, he might at least lure it into a trap. The likelihood of Billy-Bob surviving this trap didn't seem good, but he comforted himself with the thought that at least other townsfolk would owe him their gratitude for his sacrifice and their safety. Admittedly, this was not terribly comforting, but it was something.

As he ran, questions and ideas rumbling indecisively through his head, the earth hooked a finger over the toe of his shoe and he tripped, sailing headlong into the air. A waterfall of thoughts fell through Billy-Bob's awareness as the ground approached. What would happen the Forest Monster do to him? Do bullets hurt? What was the girl doing with that shovel?

The girl, Esther, was swinging the shovel at his face. Fortunately, Billy-Bob was in the process of falling, and the shovel swept overhead as the ground rushed up at him. He took a great, dirty bite out of the ground, bounced a short way further, then skidded to a halt.

Behind Billy-Bob the muffled clang of metal striking something soft, like a bell rung with a sandbag, was followed by the sound of something heavy hitting the ground. The dust around him had settled, unveiling a street littered with fragments of stone. The Forest Monster would have no difficulty finding him amidst the rubble. But the Forest Monster, whom he expected to leap forward and tear him into a billion ragged shreds, had gone silent.

"That will teach you!"

Dazedly, Billy-Bob looked back to see a girl holding a bent shovel standing over face-down body of the Forest Monster, its senses blasted asunder from the foreparts of its brain to the unexplored, outermost regions of the universe. She bent over the Forest Monster, pulled the gun from a flaccid hand and turned to Billy-Bob.

"This is dangerous," she said, dropping the weapon at his feet. "Get rid of it."

Billy-Bob looked at the gun as though the world had lost its familiarity and this object was beyond explanation, then back to the Forest Monster.

The street was empty but for the little haze that hadn't blown away, scattered boulders from the broken statue, the crumpled body of the Forest Monster, the boy with the notepad, the girl, and himself.

It was over.

"Put me away," the gun demanded.

With mechanical obedience, Billy-Bob slid the weapon back into its holster.

The girl stood over the Forest Monster, glaring down at her tormentor, poking it with the toe of the shovel.

"Ugh," she gurgled nasally, "It stinks."

She pried up one side of the monster. A hand the monster clutched against its chest dropped to the ground and fell open. The girl minced around the monster, one hand clenched on her nose, and crouched over the hand. She peered at it, first from one direction, then twisted her head to look at it from another.

"Empty," she muttered. Then squinted. "Wait. There's something here."

Straightening up again, her head pivoted one way then the other. Her gaze fell first on Billy-Bob, but she scowled and kept searching. Then she found the boy with the notepad and beckoned to him.

"Hey. You." She pointed at the Forest Monster's open hand. "What is this?"

He stumped toward her reluctantly, wary of the shovel. A few paces from the monster he slowed, as if resisted by an invisible force, and jerked a hand up to cover his face. He followed the girl's finger, grimacing at her as he went by, and leaned over the Forest Monster's open hand, wiping at the water rushing from his eyes with the back of his hand.

"Words, right" asked the girl. "Do you know them?"

He coughed and squinted.

"You are a wall who blow and bite," he read. "The rest is gibberish."

"The whole thing sounds like gibberish," the girl observed. She stamped a foot, exasperated. "Why did I expect anything but nonsense from a monster?" She scuffed a cloud of dirt at the Forest Monster before walking away. "Thanks for nothing."

Glad his chore was finished, the boy with the notepad hurried to the walkway, where he gulped down several deep breaths of fresh air.

Billy-Bob was busy thinking, even though thinking usually didn't lead anywhere. The extra markings on the fingers must mean something too. They wouldn't be there for no reason. He stared hard at his own hand, as if staring harder made his brain work better, with no results. He would have to look for himself.

Billy-Bob rose and crept toward the Forest Monster. It did stink. He could feel the stickiness of it on his face and the filthy air surround him with a putrid humidity. He lifted his shirt over his mouth and knelt beside the Forest Monster.

A great red mark covered much of the Forest Monster's face, and its expression was in disarray. The jaw hung sideways and the eyes stared blankly at the sky, the thick and stringy hair of its head spreading in all directions like the scattered tendrils of a beached jellyfish. But it was not dead. Even after a blow Billy-Bob felt certain would have sent his own head sailing into the atmosphere, the Forest Monster lived. Its chest rose and fell with each breath, and air wheezed through a choked passageway. It surprised Billy-Bob to realize he was relieved the Forest Monster was alive, maybe because it represented mysteries that remained unsolved.

What did it mean by asking Woman? At the same time another question popped into his head. If it was right to help, would it be right to help the Forest Monster, too? And how could he help the Forest Monster, if help was what it needed?

It struck him as a strange idea, helping a monster that meant to destroy him, made more strange because it nevertheless seemed sensible, which didn't make sense at all.

Billy-Bob leaned in closer.

Dirt lined the open hand of the Forest Monster. Faint words rolled across its skin, stretching onto the fingers. Some words seemed familiar, but others looked broken apart.

"I can show you how to read it."

The voice came from the canteen, resting where Billy-Bob had left it. He leaned over and picked it up, glad to have it back.

"How?"

"Pour me over the hand," the canteen instructed.

Billy-Bob obeyed, draining the canteen. Dirt dropped away in wet clots and more broken letters appeared on the fingers.

"What now?"

"Squeeze the fingers together."

He did so and the broken word parts meshed. From disorder four lines emerged.

> you are a wall against the wind
> for those of little might
> from those who blow and thunder
> be brave resist be light

Billy-Bob sat back, perplexed.

"What does it mean?"

"It means what it says," the canteen explained.

The poem was a set of instructions.

"It's about protecting the weak from the strong," said Billy-Bob.

"That's it exactly," the canteen said. "It's referring to heroes."

"The Forest Monster is a hero?"

"Was, I think," the canteen clarified. "But that's not all it says."

"It doesn't say anything else."

"Of course it does. It says you're a wall against the wind."

"Me?"

"Yes. It's a call. To be a hero. Are you going to ignore it?"

Hero. The word crashed through Billy-Bob's mind like a stone through a stained-glass window, and all other thoughts fell into a splintered heap of sparkling shards. Hero sounded legendary and memorable. People clung to memories and legends, loving them because they went on forever, and people loved the eternal, hoping there might be something eternal in themselves.

"Do you think I could be a hero?"

"I don't think you have a choice."

"Hurray for the new hero!" called Hobert.

The girl stood by the awning, staring up at those on the rooftop, the shovel resting on a shoulder, and Billy-Bob realized Hobert was talking about her.

The girl looked at them, puzzled.

"What?" she asked.

"A hero," Hobert repeated. "Much better than the one before, as I reckon."

"Me? A hero?"

"As you aren't drug off to the forest and that boy isn't a meat bag full of broken bones, I say yes," Hobert replied. "As such, it's your duty to protect us."

"My duty?"

"Indeed. Our former hero has met his untimely end, as all heroes do, and you're the only hero here. So you have to protect us until you are also destroyed. That's what heroes do. Protect other people so they don't have to protect themselves."

"A hero," the girl repeated. "If I'm a hero, I'd like a spot up there. And a chair to sit in, too. That's the cost of my protection."

Hobert's pipe sagged in his mouth for a moment, then he laughed.

"Oh no, oh no. If you're up here, you can't be down there. That's plain. You have to be down there to chase off Forest Monsters and other folk that pass our way. No no. Heroes can't be up here. It's a silly thought. What point would there be to having a hero?"

She tossed the shovel aside.

"Then being a hero is stupid."

Hobert nodded.

"Yes, it is."

The girl leaned back and kicked her heel into one of the posts supporting the awning. It elbowed and bent, dropping the awning and short distance and sending Hobert rolling forward with a whoop of alarm, then over the edge and into the street. Satisfied, she walked back across the street, passing close enough to Billy-Bob and the Forest Monster to kick a small cloud of dirt at them and continue on.

"She's not a hero," said the canteen.

"Why not?" Billy-Bob asked, coughing.

"She didn't read the lines," the canteen explained. "You're the hero."

"Why would I want to be a hero?" asked Billy-Bob.

"Why wouldn't you want to be a hero?"

"I don't know. What is a hero?"

"Er, well," the canteen began. "They're tall, I suppose. So I've heard. Might have antlers. Don't recall. Could be thinking of elk. You might have to be an elk to be a hero."

Hero, Billy-Bob thought. The most recent hero quit when she realized it wasn't worth the effort. There certainly seemed value in having a hero around, but what value was there in being a hero? The hero before that had done nothing but stand and point. Billy-Bob never determined what the statue considered so important. He'd gone looking in the direction the statue pointed, but ran up against an impassable crevice after a short distance and stopped before learning anything.

"I don't know what to do," said Billy-Bob.

"Sure you do. Discover what it is to be a hero, then be that."

These were sound instructions, but still didn't provide much of a starting point. Billy-Bob took a few steps in one direction, stopped, and went in another direction a few paces before stopping again. He saw Andrew watching him from the other side of the street, his expression one of doubt and concern.

"I'm still not sure what to do," Billy-Bob confessed. "But I'm excited."

"That's a good place to start," said the canteen. "Most people never get to the point of starting."

Starting was simple, Billy-Bob realized. Because he didn't know where to go, he could go anywhere. At worst, going to the wrong place eliminated a possibility. There was no wrong way to go because no matter which way he looked the world appeared universally bleak. Nevertheless, he couldn't decide on a direction.

Since the gorge blocked the opposite direction, he decided to go toward the forest. He'd only taken a few steps when an agonized moan rose amidst the graveyard of broken stone like a wraith cracking free of the earth to wreak a black vengeance upon the world. Billy-Bob twisted to face the sound, backed away, and reached for the gun all at once, accomplishing none with success, and catching his heel in the dirt and rolling to the ground instead. The gun, half hooked by his fingers, half in the holster, groaned as it clattered out of his hand.

"What now?" asked the gun. "*Another* monster?

HE WHO WOULD BE MIGHTY

With a single unsettling groan, all bravery vanished. Billy-Bob felt his insides knot as the vacuum it left collapsed. He sat, muscles frozen except for his heart jumping against his chest and the taut rigging behind his eyes that jerked them from one corner to the other, searching. If he remained still, perhaps the creature might overlook him. He strained toward where the Forest Monster had fallen, expecting to find the creature on its feet, staring at him with tiny fires burning in the pits of its deep-set eyes, remembering it wanted to kill him. But it remained placid and prone, breathing steady, shallow breaths.

The groan came from elsewhere. There.

Slumped against a building not far away was a filthy man blanketed by a gray, poofing beard. A round, purple welt rose in the center of his forehead like an island burbling up out of the ocean. Beside him was a flat burlap sack. He was brown skinned, hollow eyed and shirtless, probably because shirts couldn't fit over his wings, even folded, the uppermost part of which stood over his shoulders like a pair of dormant smokestacks. The man appeared lifeless, then the abdomen inflated with a great breath, which he released in a long, agonized groan.

Relieved, Billy-Bob plucked the gun out of the street and approached the dirty man.

"Hi there."

"Where am I? Am I saved?" the man muttered, listing back and forth on the unsteady waters of his senses, clearing the blur over his eyes with a forearm. He touched his forehead. Winced. Spotted Billy-Bob. Spotted the gun. Frowned. "No. I suppose not."

Puffy, dark bags hung below his sunken eyes, the accumulated rubble of a thousand thwarted hopes. Browning pants, shredded above the knees, were held in place by a thick tassel. His whole skin was faded with ground in dirt, like a soiled towel that would never come clean. He reached over a shoulder to scratch at greasy, flaying feathers with rail-thin arms and a plume of down flaked free. He smelled musty and antiquated, like dusty old furniture.

"Oh my my," the gun said. "What better definition of danger than a monster built out of dust and held together by exhaustion? Shoot him before he disintegrates in the breeze and blows away."

Before the gun could continue Billy-Bob stuffed it back into the holster and knelt beside the man.

"This is Dirtburg," said Billy-Bob. "Everything is okay now."

"Is it?" the old man asked and clutched the sack at his side.

Billy-Bob had seen this fellow wandering through town, pausing here and there to look behind a barrel or peer down an alley, his face slack with an expression of hopelessness as though looking for something and not expecting to find it. Later he was exploring the fringe of the dead forest where no one bothered to go. Dangerous. Haunted. Evil, maybe.

"I'm going to be a hero," said Billy-Bob.

At the mention of Hero the patchy tangle of gray yarn that was the man's face went taut. He looked at Billy-Bob with pinched eyes.

"A hero?" the man asked. His voice was low, and Billy-Bob wasn't certain if he was speaking to Billy-Bob and himself. "Very much needed. Difficult to find. A fourth leaf on clover. Not an easy job, though. How?"

Billy-Bob's mouth opened, wavered, then closed. He'd only recently come to the conclusion that he didn't know. Heroes were dashing. Their tales, filled with feats of scarcely believable might, rang with reverence. The statue that once stood over the town as an ageless guardian was such a hero. But the source of its fame was a mystery. No one ever mentioned what it did, where it came from, or if other heroes existed elsewhere. How did a hero become a hero?

"I don't know." He looked back to the street where the girl with the shovel stalked back and forth in a fury, but not knowing what to do about it. She had stopped the Forest Monster and saved Billy-Bob. "Do I need a shovel?"

The man followed Billy-Bob's gaze. The girl had resumed negotiating with Hobert, who watched her in silent amusement. Eventually she left him, reclaimed her shovel, and set about the town, smashing everything she could smash.

"No," he said. "I've seen heroes before. They don't have shovels. She's not a hero."

"Why?"

"She wants."

"Everyone wants."

The man's eyes returned to Billy-Bob, locking on him until the long silence made Billy-Bob uncomfortable. He stared, cocking his head one way then the other, as if waiting for something to reveal itself. After a while the man's face sagged and his sandbag body deflated. His wings, off white and heavily feathered, yawned. The fellow reached over a shoulder and scratched them again.

"You have wings," Billy-Bob blurted.

The winged man peered up at him, frowning, one hand stretched over his back.

"They itch," he muttered. "And my name is Gordimer."

He regarded Billy-Bob again, eyes squinting, then leaned forward.

"I can tell you how to be a hero," said Gordimer. "Where to go. All that. Just so happens, that's what I do."

Billy-Bob perked.

"That," the canteen whispered from its sleeve, "is going to save you a lot of time."

Such extraordinary meetings could only have their roots in fate. This happened because something supernatural had designed this event, adding a few colorful threads at the loom of a great tapestry. It happened because something meant it to happen, because it had to happen. He felt chosen and important, and these feelings were entirely new.

"There's a place for heroing? Is it in the forest? That's where I was going."

"There is." Gordimer reached into the sack and unrolled a yellowed parchment. He fingered a section of the paper. "West."

"West?"

Dangerous and infamous West, where villains grew in great wide patches like fields of dandelions, separated from the rest of the world by desert and a vast, unpassable gorge. The gorge presumably protected them from the perils of the West. But it likewise prevented anyone from Dirtburg from going westward.

"What about the gorge?" asked Billy-Bob.

"Won't be a problem," Gordimer replied. "Just worry about being a hero."

This, Billy-Bob acknowledged, was a significant challenge itself.

"How do you hero?" he asked.

Gordimer pinched his chin and his eyes clouded in thought.

"There are the conventional methods," he said. "You could find a magic sword buried to the hilt in a stone and pull it free, attempt to rectify the problem of Might versus Right. But that would make you king of England, not a hero, and besides, it's already been done. You could reset the Universe, save a man turned monster, or thwart the self-destructive designs of existence's greatest adversary. But again, old hat."

Nothing of what Gordimer said made sense. The stories sounded familiar and significant, but he didn't recognize them.

"Takes more and more to impress as time goes," Gordimer continued. "Naturally, you'll have to do something of considerable remarkability."

"I'm sure the scroll tells you what that is."

Gordimer brightened.

"Oh, of course it does. You're smarter than you look."

Billy-Bob frowned, unsure he liked the compliment.

Gordimer held the parchment close to his face.

"You must overcome Ultimate Evil. Find Beta. Save the girl. Standard stuff."

"Oh."

Ultimate Evil sounded particularly distressing. When he tried to envision Ultimate Evil a giant beast, overmuscled and scowling, growled and reached for him with a long-taloned, red hand. Startled by the vision, Billy-Bob jerked back. The image of the behemoth shattered and vanished. He shuddered.

"Evil must be dangerous," Billy-Bob observed.

Gordimer lowered the parchment, nodding somberly.

"Like a hatful of teeth and biting," he muttered. "Once you try it on, it latches. And gnaws. Removing it leaves scars."

"Will I win?"

Gordimer grimaced and rubbed his nose. He checked the parchment, eyes glazing as if he were looking at it but not reading it.

"You will find victory in defeat and death." Gordimer rolled the parchment, cleared his throat, and added, "You will also need fourteen acorns."

The flavor of heroism went suddenly sour. Victory in death? This bit of information didn't make much sense. He couldn't win if he were dead. And victory could hardly be had through defeat.

"What was that last part?" asked Billy-Bob.

"You will need fourteen acorns," Gordimer repeated.

Billy-Bob's head shook.

"No no. The other part."

Billy-Bob grasped at the parchment to check it, but Gordimer clutched and crumpled it, then lit a corner with a small flame. The parchment burst into a brilliant white fire and was gone. Mostly. Gordimer's eyes went wide and he fanned the air, swatting at bits of glowing cinder and fluttering his wings as they circled about him, hissing and biting back curses when embers reached his skin. When they had scattered and extinguished he wiped his hands across grime-darkened pants.

"Messy stuff," he mumbled.

Maybe it was better he didn't understand the meaning of the parchment. Maybe Gordimer had misread it. In fact, the more he considered the bit about victory and death the less he wanted to know.

"Why do I need fourteen acorns?" Billy-Bob asked.

Gordimer's lips quirked.

"Because thirteen is bad luck."

"Oh."

"Here," said Gordimer. His hand scuffled in the folds of his clothing until he found what he sought. He extended a balled fist toward Billy-Bob and said, "Take them."

The fist opened and a several brown beads dropped into his palm along with a sprinkling of sand. They were unimpressive, nothing more than a rounded nubs no bigger than the end of his thumb. They wouldn't help much protecting him. Too dull for stabbing and too short for fencing. They were more a fat sort of bullet for a large, ugly, wooden gun. Holding them did not make him feel any more heroic.

"What are they?" asked Billy-Bob.

"Acorns. They're for throwing." Gordimer's eyes darkened and he rubbed the lump on his forehead. "Don't do diddly against wogs, though. Any other questions?"

Billy-Bob thought.

"Where is Ultimate Evil? How do I find it?"

Gordimer shrugged.

"When you are a hero it will find you."

Billy-Bob's brow folded.

"But how can I defeat it to become a hero if I need to be a hero to find it?"

"Never said it would be easy. Only that a hero can do it." Then, after a moment of thought, he added, "Maybe."

If all heroes came to be by Gordimer's criteria, it was impossible to be one. But they must exist because people had claimed to see them. Their existence was founded upon a paradox. Trees were another such paradox, but they existed. Or, at least, their carcasses remained as a reminder that they had once existed. So too could heroes exist, he just didn't know how.

At first, the origin of trees was obvious: Trees came from Seeds. But where did the Seed come from? The obvious answer: a Tree. But where did the Seed for *that* Tree come from, and the Tree before that, and on and on to the First Tree. The answer was the First Seed. But if there were no Trees before the First Tree to produce the First Seed, where had the Seed come from? Not a Tree, because there were no Trees until after they sprouted from Seeds. Therefore there could be no Seeds. But if there were no Seeds, what made Trees? And so his brain chased its own tail to exhaustion. The only explanation was a Tree must have, at some point, been something else before it became the first Tree. Just as dogs and bears and elephants were all whales before they crawled out of the ocean.

So, too, it must be the case for heroes. Before they were heroes they must have been something else. But what? And Billy-Bob found himself running against a familiar wall.

"It doesn't make sense," said Billy-Bob.

Gordimer nodded.

"That's the way of heroing and myth. Baffling, befuddling, and mysterious. Omens are meaningless riddles with insights that aren't understood until the moment they are meant to illuminate has passed. So what's the point of having these rules and guidelines? To keep you on track? Keep your brains working? Maybe. Who knows? All you can do is press forward, knowing those little secrets will unfold slowly like night scrolling back to reveal the day. In the meantime, do what you know."

"Go West."

"Yes. That's what the parchment said, isn't it? The worst part of the world is where the best people reside, and where bad things converge in a concerted effort to destroy them. Out there are a thousand perils. The world itself will try and crush you. And if it can't destroy you, other monsters may."

"I've never seen anything beyond the gorge. I assumed it was empty."

"It is."

"Then what could be out there to destroy me?"

"Wogs," said Gordimer. The word hung in the air like a dark cloud. His eyes glazed. "A Given of Wogs is the end of any town."

"A Given?"

"A group of Wogs finds you, it's the end. That's a given."

"That makes sense."

"Oh, yes," Gordimer muttered. "A very sensible world we live in."

Billy-Bob said nothing. What could he say to this man who seemed to harbor a faint delight in the idea this adventure could destroy them?

"Still want to be a hero? Or afraid?" Gordimer asked, teeth gritting. His eyes glinted, but his voice was biting and controlled. "A little fear is good, yes. It prevents you from becoming arrogant, forgetting your limitations. But to face fear and overcome it." The old man punched a finger in the air. "Ah ha! Then the curtains of limitation begin to draw aside. Success is limited only by a lack of daring."

Gordimer grinned and his eyes opened wide.

"And if death scares you, boy, perhaps heroing is something you should reconsider."

If Gordimer was trying to frighten him, Billy-Bob thought, he'd been successful. At the same time, Gordimer seemed to be trying to encourage him. To face a fear and overcome it was to master that fear forever. And if he mastered one fear, how difficult would it be to master others? The first step in mastering a fear was to confront it.

"Where West do I go?"

For an instant Billy-Bob thought Gordimer's sneer wavered, giving way to a smile of admiration that lit and faded in an instant.

"Doesn't matter, really. Just go West. All the way to Beta. It's where most heroes end up."

"Beta?" asked Billy-Bob.

"A town," Gordimer explained.

“Where?”

“Over there,” said Gordimer. He pointed down the street toward the blankness beyond.

“I’ve been over there,” said Billy-Bob. “There’s just rocks and a crack that’s too wide to cross.”

“Past that.”

“Past that is nothing.”

“Past the nothing, too.”

“What is past nothing?”

Gordimer smiled.

“Beta.”

THE WEST

Gordimer sat at the edge of the town, staring into the endless yellow flatland, whistling and trying to ignore a group of yellow-leaved shrubs nearby. The shrubs hugged against a building, clutching the broken ground with the fingernails of veined and desperate roots, straining to keep their grip. Short puffs of wind rattled the shrubs every so often, though some rattles came between breezes, and this unsettled him. He tried to think instead about the emptiness, heat, and blowing sand that he'd soon have to cross. The idea of passing through it on foot made his wings bend feel heavier.

Sadness often served as a useful distraction. Focusing upon one misery allowed him to ignore a thousand others, and the distraction of a single sadness brought about a pleasant sort of relief. He realized, in a way that seemed close to paradoxical, that he was happiest when he was a tiny bit miserable. So he concentrated on the single sadness of crossing the wasteland and, somehow, felt a little better.

In the stillness of his tolerable melancholy the shrub gave a quick, twitching rustle. Gordimer stopped whistling.

If something had hidden itself inside the shrubs, it either meant to avoid discovery or take him by his curiosity and lure him into a trap. In a brief instant of imagination gone wild, he wondered if the plants had achieved consciousness, shaking in frustration at the state of the world around it and its inability to get up and do something about it.

Gordimer's hands clenched and flexed, sensing the plants' agitation in his fingertips like the needlepoint pains that came with the reawakening of a sleeping limb. Oh yes, such things could be felt, even from a plant, if the emotion were strong enough, hurting enough. Unpleasant as this experience was, it was not Evil.

True Evil, by comparison, was a doggedly persistent, hateful thing. An evil the boy would have to face, should he become a hero, and an adversary against which none had prevailed. Where these shrubs caused his skin to prick, True Evil was a heart-shattering donkey kick in the chest.

Gordimer began whistling again. It helped.

Maybe the bedraggled Forest Monster had hidden itself inside the bushes. Gordimer had encountered the creature as he pushed through the dead fingers of the forest. He'd only wanted to ask if the monster had met anyone interested in becoming a hero. The hunched creature was seated with its scraped and dirty back to him, head bent and mumbling at its hands. At the sound of Gordimer's voice it went still and Gordimer could feel the agitation and violence in the creature as a prickle on his skin. He fled—the safest action to take in most cases, and one that had served him time and again—only to be found by wogs.

The Forest Monster was angry and spiteful, though not so much as the unnamed Evil whose malice was so intense it made Gordimer's mind sting and scream with the ache of grinding metal.

He had met Evil once. It had asked him why he bothered searching for heroes. It was a test, Gordimer explained. His test. Everyone underwent a test.

Perhaps it was not a test, the creature suggested. Perhaps Good was secretly Evil, promoting conflict by searching for heroes. The notion rattled him, because Gordimer sometimes felt the same way. Evil knew how to sow just enough truth into a lie to create uncertainty. But Good must know what it was doing, even if Gordimer did not. Evil had warned that the Good could never prevail because it lacked might and grit and relied upon trust and hope. Evil believed Good knew that wasn't possible, and worse, that it was losing. That Good was losing could not be denied, and any hero Gordimer took West would invariably be destroyed. Leading them knowingly to destruction was patently Evil, was it not?

Gordimer whistled, trying not to think, but thought continued to worm through the crevices of his mind.

If the people he found truly were heroes, Gordimer told himself, it wouldn't matter where a hero was. West, East, planet, space. They would defeat Evil. If not, then he would find another. And another. And another. Heroes were hope.

For each hero he found and led to destruction, Evil had told him, Gordimer became a little more Evil. This amused Evil and disturbed Gordimer most of all, because if that was true, mission complete or not, he could never go home.

Again the shrubs rustled.

Gordimer picked up a yellow rock and hefted it into the shrubs, just to relieve his silly, idle fears. The rock swished through the branches, throwing up a puff of yellow leaves, and klonked against the insides. Harmless.

"Agggghh!" the bushes wailed.

The rock curled back out of the foliage and thumped at his feet.

Gordimer jumped up, wings flaring. He felt his heart tocking hard through his chest and dirt-crusted hair on his arms hoisted up like the sails of a fleeing armada. Shrubs were undangerous, he told himself. The bushes could scratch and poke and shed swallowing heaps of leaves but were required to keep their feet locked in the ground and so their rage could be avoided. He should be safe, he told himself, breath rasping, eyes wide. Safe.

"Something wrong?" asked Billy-Bob.

Gordimer started, leapt sideways, and crashed against a building.

"Are you all right?" the boy asked, rushing to his side.

The boy had emerged from the city silently, too slim to make any noise, hat in hand. His clothes, white collared shirt and flopping brown pants, were oversized and held in place by suspenders. Gordimer wondered if they had belonged to his father.

Gordimer waved the boy away with a crisp backhand. The shrubs were still and quiet.

"I'm fine."

There were no pictures of them, but Gordimer could guess the sort of person required to fill the outfit. Billy-Bob's father had been broad and tall, strong-faced with large eyes. Quite the opposite of the scraggly son. The father drew followers with his leadership, and no doubt his mother was strong-minded. A sandy-haired woman who could see your worst but spoke only the goodness because she believed in salvation. She believed heroes weren't necessary, that people could save themselves. Naturally, the world had destroyed them.

"We should go," said Billy-Bob. "Ready?"

The question had scarcely left Billy-Bob's mouth before Gordimer answered.

"Yes."

Gordimer recalled these treks with great clarity. Best to go now, because the more he thought about it, the less he would want to leave.

* * *

Andrew sat, eyes glazed, back pressed against the building at the end of the street, poked by jabbing fingers from the branches of the fading shrubs in which he'd hidden himself, waiting for the boy to finish collecting supplies for the journey. He couldn't make out much through the twig-littered foliage except Gordimer.

Gordimer, an ancient but virile fellow, sat nearby on wooden steps, arms folded tightly and forehead crunched, staring silently into the wasteland. He had wings, which didn't seem possible, but neither did a Forest Monster or tiny rock-throwing metal creatures. Every so often Gordimer would whistle part of a tune, stop, squint introspectively, then begin again as if he were trying to remember an old melody and forget something else at the same time.

Andrew's eyes fell to the open page of his notebook, empty of writing except for the chapter title: The West.

Brilliant and sensible, it encompassed his experiences in a single, snapping statement. The subsequent chapter ought to be equally brief. Stunning brevity permitted no more than a few words of elaboration. The fewer the better. Two words would be impressive. One would be stunning. Perhaps he could make a meaningless history worth reading. An accomplishment of that sort would merit him the appreciation of everyone, and one in particular. One word, then. How hard could a single, stunning term be when words were as numberless as granules of sand in the edgeless desert of the West?

Andrew leaned his forehead against a fist, as though doing so granted his brain greater strength. Indeed, he could feel the pumping of great bellows in his mind, hear the ringing as wordsmiths pounded on glowing ingots of unformed words, sending scorching sparks showering from their anvils. Fires glowed, hammerblows fell, and the white hot sear of inspiration blurred his vision. He passed beyond thought and entered a state of sheer intuition, and felt his hand tracing out the product of his mind's sublime effort like that of an oracle unconsciously disgorging a profound and thundering prophecy at the height of a psychotropic stupor. He felt his hand come to a stop and slowly his vision returned.

Andrew looked down at the page to observe the result of his effort. He stared.

Zoing

The faint song fragment from Gordimer rose again, and with it came a strange longing to go home. Of course, that was impossible. He had to remain here, while everyone of importance forgot him.

He hated this place.

Not because it was dangerous, not because it was hot and miserable, sapping at his energy, but because it took away something he could not get back: time. He only needed to channel his loathing into a single, jarring, earnest word.

Andrew thumbed through the dictionary of his mind, straining to fill a void in history with what would undoubtedly be words used to describe a void.

"Absent," he muttered quietly. "Ablated. Annihilaaaaaaaaaaggghhh!"

A sudden, sharp agony bit Andrew in the back of the head and his notebook vanished behind a searing white blast of pain that sent his thoughts scurrying about in frantic disarray. What? Why? Corduroy?

He clutched his throbbing skull and felt a sore lump rising under the hair. As his vision cleared he saw a sandy, yellow rock resting on the notepad in his lap. Two tears plopped onto the page beside it. Andrew gripped the rock and squeezed in an effort to vent his anger. His fingers began to hurt and the rock appeared unharmed, so he threw it out of the bush instead.

What did the world have against him? He had catalogued any of his feelings for it, though he would now. Andrew would take his revenge in the only way he knew how. He would paint this world as a miserable place filled with monsters and demons, fire raining from the sky, and the populace tearing at one another for the sheer joy that came from meaningless violence, of misery, a low point in history where cruelties gathered into a singularity from which nothing could escape. His grip tightened on the pen.

No word existed to describe the West as Andrew envisioned. Nothing in history compared. The unexplored, enigmatic region had never been named apart from its geographic location: the West. The West alone lacked the shocking, revulsive power he wanted, and no single word existed that had such an effect. But the absence of the right word was no obstacle for a great writer. If the proper word didn't exist he would invent one.

A word that meant one thing, one place, and one moment in time alone. A shrieking collision of sound that conveyed the hatred and misery and violence of the West. Andrew's mouth twisted and a growl gurgled out of his throat. He wanted it to bite hard and swallow the reader in ragged chunks.

Thus far the only word to spring forward was Zoing. Zoing had the power to startle if it leapt unexpected from a place of darkness and seclusion, fangs extended, but it faded as quickly as a thunderclap. And yet, curse his belabored and ineffective brains, he could think of nothing better.

Again his body acted independently and impulsively, and his hand dragged across the notepad with a single, sharp stroke. He glared at the notebook and the dark words gouged into the paper.

The West

Zoing!

Andrew scowled at his work.

Not quite.

UNLESS, PERHAPS

Gordimer kicked through the crackling dry scrub between the town and the jagged grin of a crack that ran into the distance in both directions, sending stones skipping along ahead of him. Billy-Bob followed close behind, taking frequent glances backward. He hadn't asked how they would pass the crevice, but Gordimer knew he must be wondering. The answer was simple enough—the same way Gordimer had crossed in order to get here.

Gordimer whistled as he walked, softly, just loud enough to hear himself over the crunch of brittle ground beneath his feet. A gentle, tapering melody that enfolded and caressed like the overlapping arms of a warm hugging. A song from home. It helped distract him whenever he was frightened.

Dirtburg drifted further and further behind them into the yellow haze, like a boat come free of its mooring. The nearest building cast a mournful gaze at them with the sad face of a long-bullied scholar, with knocked out windows for spectacles and a crumpled porch like a mouthful of broken teeth. The whole building slouched as though trying to hide itself from further abuse by quietly imploding. It seemed to know Gordimer would never return, and even if he did, by then Dirtburg would no longer exist.

Unless.

Gordimer grunted.

Unless Billy-Bob defeated Ultimate Evil. Unless he restored hope to the world. Unless... Well, there were quite a few impossibilities associated with Unless. It depressed him to think about those obstacles, so he whistled the part of song he still remembered and felt better for a moment or two.

He didn't know why he chose these same false tasks over and over. They were like sand under his toenails, uncomfortable and irritating, but something he could not shake free: go West; defeat Ultimate Evil; find Beta; save the girl. Maybe because they sounded glorious and worth doing. Maybe because these were the things important to him. He supposed by adding the bit about death and defeat he was acknowledging the inevitable, trying to frighten the boy in order to save him. Heroism was a lousy, horrid ruse. Gordimer felt hideous knowing he was a part of it, and disgusted knowing that long ago he'd believed in it, too.

Everything Gordimer had done for the boy so far was a lie: the parchment, no more than a map he'd given to people interested in escaping to Beta; the acorns part of a chore in which he had no success before and had no interest in pursuing. That task came from the girl, Poppy, in Beta, and he was glad to be rid of it.

Poppy, the daughter of the last great hero, ought to have been one herself. But she was too wise. She refused. He wondered if she was still there. He wondered if Beta was still there. It had been a long time.

Now and again as he crisscrossed the wasteland a misplaced component of a skeleton would be uncovered by the wind, proof that people had been here before and a warning about the consequences of remaining. All the world had become a graveyard. But as chilling as those reminders were, they did not compare to the nightmarish cataclysm of the long-dead cities.

Miles of decayed buildings reaching up to the sky in supplication, filled with empty windows. Everything gray and sterile. It's where one went to lose the hope one had for what remained. Places one never wanted to see. Some saw the great structures of the long past, awed by their immensity and complexity, as evidence of human grandeur, proof of greatness, and believed it lay just beyond reach on the brink of rediscovery. Gordimer saw the bleak causeways and hollow structures and felt despair and futility, for even at the height of ingenuity and invincibility humanity had almost destroyed itself. All it lacked was the resolve to finish the task.

Billy-Bob strode up beside Gordimer and held a canteen aloft.

"Drink?" he asked.

Gordimer waved him away and Billy-Bob fell into stride behind him again.

Gordimer didn't need anything. He didn't eat, and only drank when he was trying to forget something, usually fear, but even drink failed most times. No fault of drink. Rather, it was the nature of everything to fail. Whistling was one of few things that chased away fear because it reminded him of home. Another was heroes, but Gordimer didn't believe in them anymore. His only goal now was to get home. There was nothing else.

He scratched the elbow of a folded wing. He'd forgotten when they hadn't itched. Nor could he recall not being tired or layered by greasy grime. So long since he'd done anything but this wretched, odious mission. So long finding heroes only to see them destroyed. That was the nature of this horrible, one-sided world. Good deeds were poisoned and made Evil, but Evil was invincible in its Evilness. Evil never became Good. Evil could never be twisted into anything else.

So the world was doomed. A heart-sundering reality, but one he'd accepted because he could still escape. At the edge of his memory, long ago, was a world not spiraling to oblivion, where the green pressed together like puzzle pieces assembled into a portrait of fields and trees and mountains and wide alleys of water that ran between them. Beyond that memory was home, a pinhole in the tapestry of his existence.

"Now what?" asked Billy-Bob.

Gordimer blinked and realized he was staring into the depths of the gorge toward a bottom he could not see. Not far away was a stone that stood straight up out of the ground, too perfect and slender to have formed by chance. He strode toward it and Billy-Bob followed.

"You can't go around," said Billy-Bob. "It just goes on and on."

"We're not going around," Gordimer replied.

The stone stood as high as Gordimer's shoulder. It had acquired the same yellowish hue as the world around them and the surface was etched and rough from the blowing sand. That shouldn't matter. He turned to Billy-Bob.

"Do you know what this is?" he asked, gesturing to the post.

Billy-Bob regarded Gordimer, then the rock.

"A rock," said Billy-Bob. "I think. Are you a rock?"

"What? Of course not. This—," Gordimer began, but the boy stepped between him and the post, then crouched and leaned closer.

"Not a rock. What are you?"

Gordimer gaped. Was he speaking to the post?

"I don't know," he said, squinting at the post. He pointed back at Gordimer. "He never tells me anything but riddles. Yes, it's extremely frustrating. I guess it's possible they don't mean anything."

Gordimer had thought the boy's quirky behavior was a form of intellectual dullness, but now he suspected the boy might be altogether out of his mind. To Gordimer's astonishment Billy-Bob extended a hand toward the post and placed his palm against the stone. The boy suffered from a peculiarly helpful form of dementia. After a moment passed and nothing happened, Billy-Bob looked back at Gordimer.

"Broken, I guess," said Billy-Bob.

"Greetings, travelers."

The boy spun, startled.

Beside him stood a woman, hands folded at her waist, conspicuously free of the dirt that powdered everything else, her sandy brown hair knotted tightly against her head. There was a faint tilt to her mouth, as though on the edge of a smile, and her blue eyes had weight in their gaze. She was also faintly transparent, and Gordimer could see the hacked plates of broken ground and the dark crack of the gorge through her.

"Who are you?" asked Billy-Bob.

"She's not really here," explained Gordimer.

Billy-Bob seemed surprised.

"You can see her, too?"

"Yes, I can see her. She's right there. More or less."

"True," said the woman. She did not look directly at either of them, but gazed at some far distant object. "I am a visual projection based upon an image provided by the developer of this technology. I do not exist in a physical sense."

"You're a ghost," said Billy-Bob.

"In a manner of speaking," Gordimer replied.

Gordimer remembered the girl upon which the image had been modeled. She had been embarrassed to have her semblance guide the wanderers of the world, but proud of the great work it might do. The remnant was a fair but imperfect copy. All the things that defined her were lost in this representation. All except the certainty.

"I am a facsimile, and though I lack the personality of the person I represent, I have my exceptional uses."

"Who are you?" Billy-Bob repeated.

"We need to get over the gorge," Gordimer interrupted.

To Gordimer's annoyance, the image ignored him.

"I am an informational device developed by…" The woman's face froze for an instant, then recovered its normal fluidity. "Data cannot be accessed," she said at last. "I answer questions. I remove the shrouds of ignorance from a public that would otherwise choose to remain uninformed."

"She also extends the bridge," said Gordimer. "Would you extend the bridge?"

"Wow," said Billy-Bob. "What do you know?"

"For example, I can tell you the gorge before you was formed by the movement of tectonic plates along a strike-slip fault line. Continued motion causes regular earthquakes. As a result, the structures in the nearby town are in perpetual disrepair. I can tell you the pollen content of the air is 1.7% lower than yesterday, and has diminished considerably and consistently over the years since my emplacement due to a depletion of resources essential to plant life, though a plan is in place to replenish them from offworld sources. I am able to discern your lung capacity is much greater than all but one I have encountered, though you are still young, and your low metabolism will aid you well since food and water are scarce in this region. I can differentiate the mineral dust collecting on your clothing, recite any of the 527,634,229 documents in my databanks on anthropology, archaeology, astronomy..."

"Wow!" said Billy-Bob. He looked at Gordimer, eyebrows raised, while the image continued to list subjects at a steadily accelerating pace. "Wow!" he repeated.

"Extend the bridge, please," Gordimer asked sternly.

"Who are you?" Billy-Bob interrupted. "What is your name?"

"Philology, philanthropy, philosophy… My name is D," the image responded. "I am named for the sector in which I am located, quadrant four, proximate to the only civilization within ten sectors, currently named Dirtburg. The next closest is my sister, C, whose location is… Data cannot be accessed."

"Dee?" Billy-Bob repeated.

"Affirmative," Dee answered. She gestured to a spot near the top of the post where the letter D had been inscribed and filled in with dirt. "My database tells me your name is… Data cannot be accessed."

Gordimer stamped his foot.

"Why are you ignoring me?"

The image flickered. Abruptly it was facing him.

"Because your questions do not take precedence."

"Over his? Why?"

"I do not question my programming. Do you question yours?"

"All the time."

"But you do not disobey it. Otherwise you would not be here."

Gordimer grimaced.

"Would you please extend the bridge," he gritted.

Dee flickered and looked at Billy-Bob, who shrugged.

"I guess you should just do that," said Billy-Bob.

"Very well."

The ground shuddered under their feet and a wide gray sheet extended from their side of the chasm. It stretched up and over like a caterpillar traveling from one leaf to another, then settled on the other side. The bridge was long and level, and slightly concave. Handrails extended upward on both sides.

Gordimer stomped past the girl. He motioned to Billy-Bob, who gawked at the bridge.

"That was amazing!" he said.

"Yes," Gordimer replied without conviction. "Come on."

For a long while Gordimer found the fascination of simpletons amusing and endearing. In a single cathartic instant they realized human brilliance could bring about wonderful technologies and provide solutions for problems they'd considered unsolvable. But so many times their interest ended before their problem-solving engaged, relegating the innovation to something magical or an omnipotent engineer who fashioned and controlled everything, which didn't make sense. Why would anyone, apart from a need to keep busy, create a gorge just to build a bridge over it? Their fascination had decoupled from curiosity, and it annoyed him.

"Do you not wish to wait for your companion?" asked Dee.

Gordimer stopped.

"What companion?"

"The third member of your party," Dee explained.

Billy-Bob looked at Gordimer, then extended a finger. He touched himself on the chest and extended another finger. Then he cast a glance around the immediate vicinity, but saw no one else. He looked to his hand and the two extended fingers, then back to the woman.

"Three?" asked Billy-Bob.

"Yes, three," she repeated. "I am tracking all travelers in the immediate vicinity and your group contains three members."

Billy-Bob looked at his hand again, utterly perplexed.

"Don't worry about it," said Gordimer. "It's old. Probably broken."

"I assure you, I require no maintenance," said the image with an air of pride. "I am guaranteed to continue functioning at near-optimal level with no upkeep for a minimum of one century, ignoring the absence of updates on cartography, population density, and meteorological activity, much of which I am capable of tracking and updating myself when service updates are not available. May I inquire your destination? Perhaps I can offer directions, provide historical information…"

"Beta," Billy-Bob interrupted.

The woman's face became a momentary wash of static, then turned to him.

"There is no Beta."

Gordimer laughed.

"Maybe you're not broken after all," he said, then spoke to Billy-Bob. "Let's go."

Gordimer stepped onto the bridge. The image of the woman flickered, then appeared on the bridge ahead of them, waiting. Billy-Bob followed. They'd only gone a few steps when Gordimer heard another voice.

"Greetings, travelers."

Gordimer stopped. Another hologram stood at the foot of the bridge behind them, identical to the one leading them across.

"What's going on?" Billy-Bob asked their guide.

"Another party is approaching," she responded. "Would you like to wait until they arrive?"

"I don't see anything," said Billy-Bob.

At first Gordimer imagined it was the mysterious third companion approaching. Probably the Forest Monster. Then he had another, more sobering thought. Gordimer spun back to their guide.

"How many?" he asked quickly.

"Invalid request," Dee responded. "You have not specified an object to quantify."

"The new group!" Gordimer shouted. "How many in the new group?"

"Nineteen," she answered. "Revising. Twenty two. Revising. Twenty six. Revising. Thirty four. Revising. Thirty seven…"

Gordimer's wings flexed. He looked at Billy-Bob, who seemed puzzled, but there wasn't time to explain.

"Run!" he shouted and bolted toward the other side of the bridge.

"Who is it?" Billy-Bob asked. "Where are they? I don't see anyone."

Gordimer looked over his shoulder.

The boy was watching the other side of the bridge, trying to make out who was following them. To Gordimer's horror he began walking toward the second hologram.

"Please do not run on this bridge," said Dee. She appeared beside him, hovering just off the walkway, her expression stern. "Precautions have been taken to ensure your safety, but severe injury or fatality may result if you do not observe safety protocols."

Gordimer stopped running, thinking himself a fool for doing so, and more foolish still for what he was considering. Should he let the boy be destroyed and start over again with someone else? There had certainly been shorter journeys. But as the world slowly emptied itself of people, few that remained had any interest in helping, and it had been so long since the last time he'd found someone.

"You're a fool," he bit. "A fool, fool, fool," he continued, then turned around and charged back toward the boy. "A stupid fool who deserves exactly what is coming."

He'd already escaped these creatures once. For reasons he could not explain, they had done nothing more than inquire after a girl and take a tissue sample. He doubted he would be so fortunate a second time.

Billy-Bob wandered back and forth on a slow path into the teeth of danger as the hologram continued rattling off ever-increasing numbers. She was at ninety seven when Gordimer reached him, grabbed the sleeve of his shirt, and spun him around.

"It's wogs, you buffoon! They're coming up the cliff side!" Gordimer lurched back toward the other side of the gorge, pulling Billy-Bob along behind him. "We've got to get out of here!"

A moment passed as Billy-Bob began to comprehend, then ran on his own behind Gordimer. Despite his emaciated figure, Gordimer was nimble and fast. He'd spent most of his existence here running away from things, and like most skills used over and over again he'd gotten very good at it. He was surprised when the boy sped past him.

It wasn't far now and they would be across. That didn't mean the wogs wouldn't follow. They always followed. Even if he leapt into the air they would follow him, let him tire, and wait for the increasing heaviness of his body to bring him down. Then they would be inside his head, poking and probing through the household of his mind, leaving it in a shambles and slamming the door on the way out. Maybe this time they would ruin something important, wreck an important memory he may never recover, destroy the last bit of song he retained and leave him trapped here forever with nothing to console him.

They were nearly at the other side of the bridge, and Gordimer began to hope they would get away, but that hope quickly disintegrated. Wogs swarmed up over the edges of the far side as Gordimer and Billy-Bob approached. Some of them all frightening silvery bones, while others had bits of fur still clinging to their bodies. Many had one or both eyes missing, but the handicap didn't seem to impede their progress.

With nowhere to go, Billy-Bob and Gordimer stopped. They were trapped, and the wogs moved toward the from both sides while still more welled up from the chasm. Gordimer briefly considered throwing himself over the side of the bridge, but he knew it would not kill him. Gordimer wasn't killable—his immunity to death was an important aspect of his task. They would simply find his fractured body at the bottom of the gorge and destroy his mind, which was tragic, because it was the only thing of any value he possessed.

"Stop!" he heard Billy-Bob shout.

It was a foolish thing to say because wogs didn't stop until they'd done what they intended. They were lost.

Gordimer waited for the things to clamber all over him with their steely claws, bearing him down with their weight. But for some reason they hesitated. Gordimer raised his eyes. His mouth opened.

The wogs stood upon the bridge in various states of suspended action. Some had frozen in mid step toward them, others still clung to the edge of the bridge as they climbed onto the top. Billy-Bob tiptoed slowly through the crowd gathered on the bridge. Gordimer could see their eyes turn in the sockets to follow him, but they did not move. They seemed perplexed by their own behavior, looking at him, one another, then back at themselves as if wondering why their parts had stopped working.

"What did you do?" Gordimer whispered. He began to pick his way through the frozen creatures, feeling their gazes stick against him, afraid any sudden motion would startle them back into action.

"I told them to stop," Billy-Bob answered.

Gordimer joined him on the other side, then looked back across the bridge, wogs locked in place, crusting the walkway and dangling like mossy curtains from the underside.

"Did you know that would work?"

"I hoped it would," said Billy-Bob, "but I didn't expect it to."

He could see the boy shaking, trying to smile in spite of his terror. He pulled his hat down over his face to avoid being seen and hoisted a canteen to his mouth, but did not remove the cap.

"Nevermind," said Gordimer. He was anxious to leave before the wogs discovered how to break free and resume their pursuit. "Let's go."

* * *

The world as Gordimer recalled it had not changed much—wide, bleak stretches of emptiness separating tiny patches of civilization. An occasional tree lay on its side, root fingers clutching at the empty air over a hole like an open and agitated wound where it had torn free. The whole world had a similar look, much of it eroded, while the rest had been deliberately ripped down. The ground was alternately sandy, which blew into his face when the wind rose, or hard and broken, twisting his ankles and chipping bare toes as they went along. So Gordimer kept his eyes on the ground, scanning for sharp rocks instead of the path before him and consequently why he collided with Billy-Bob and tottered backward when the boy stopped to stare at the rubbling buildings of a failed town not far ahead.

"What is this place?" asked Billy-Bob.

The town stood just inside the edge of mirage, the heat made the structures dance, like souls crying for salvation from the flames of perdition. Rooftops had collapsed, walls fallen in, and sand piled against the sides of the a few fire-blackened buildings, all but reclaimed by the wasteland. A place Gordimer had known when it still stood.

"It's not anything, now," said Gordimer. "But it still isn't safe."

Gordimer walked past Billy-Bob and started a wide semi-circle around the city.

"What happened?"

"The same thing that always happens," said Gordimer. "The whole world is like this."

"How big is the world?"

"More big than most realize. There used to be cities so large it took days to walk from one side to the other. Buildings so tall they carved the clouds in two. But immensity does not grant invulnerability. Not for cities or even a world. Everywhere you go, abandoned buildings and empty streets. Too few did anything to stop it. The rest did not care."

"Maybe they were afraid. Maybe they thought they couldn't do anything."

"Maybe," said Gordimer. Whether or not they were right, they were long past the point where the decision mattered. "Probably."

Gordimer looked back at the boy. Billy-Bob stared at the town, a dangerous squint of curiosity in his eyes. Sure enough, he started toward it.

"What are you doing?" asked Gordimer.

"Trying to not be afraid," Billy-Bob called over a shoulder.

"Don't do that!" Gordimer shouted.

"Why not?"

"Because it's dangerous."

"How do you know?"

"Because *everything* is dangerous. Haven't you learned anything?"

"Then why bother going anywhere?"

Gordimer didn't have an answer for this. Billy-Bob continued on. Gordimer turned in a circle, clenched his fists and banged them against his thighs, watching Billy-Bob continue on to the broken town. He could hardly blame the boy. Most wisdom contradicted itself. It pushed you into danger with one hand to test and strengthen your abilities, and held you back with the other to guard you against an uncertain fate. How anyone familiar with wisdom trusted it he had no idea. Nevertheless, the wise tended to have longer lifespans than the brave.

Not far off was the hulk of an age-hollowed and branchless tree, the bark on the windy side whittled away to the bare white wood. This seemed as good a place as any to wait and hide. In all likelihood the town was abandoned and free of danger, but he'd made that assumption before with dire consequences.

As he rounded the tree, Gordimer lurched to a halt, yellow wings splayed slightly in surprise like a bird puffing when faced by a predator, hoping to look too big to fit in the monster's mouth.

A lone villain sat behind the bent frame of the lifeless tree, glaring up at him with weariness and agitation through giant, startled eyes. He was thin with a burned red face as though unaccustomed to the harshness of this world. Astounded, the two stared at one another, uncertain what to do.

Then the villain's hand shot up, slicing the air with a short pointed object scarcely long enough to extend beyond his hand.

"Zoing!" said the villain fiercely.

Gordimer leapt back, startled, fanning the air in futile self defense, wings flaring.

"No! Oh no!" he cried.

Doom had finally found him. Zoing! would burrow a hole in his body, leaving him crippled and vulnerable to any pursuing wogs, as surely as the sun hammered everything flat and sandy with its pounding heat. It was inevitable. Curses to Zoing! He'd been so close to finishing his long chore.

A bullet of fear and fury, the word bit and chewed into his brain. Zoing! bounced in his head, sounding stranger and more silly until he realized the word was no more than a sharpened bit of nonsense. Besides, he recalled, he couldn't be killed. His wings folded.

The villain lowered his arm and frowned. The word had failed, leaving him weaponless.

He wore long pants and a long-sleeved shirt, both rolled up to let some of the heat escape, exposing skin that had reddened in the heat. He had no hat and no weapon, apart from a notepad he used to shield his eyes. He clearly had no idea how to protect himself.

This was no villain.

"What are you?" Gordimer asked.

The fellow grimaced.

"A writer," he answered tightly. "Leave me alone."

What was a writer doing here? He looked all about, but didn't see anything but the barren landscape, the dead tree, and the blackened husks of burnt buildings not far away. An odd occupation for a desert hermit. Admittedly, there was little else to do.

"Writer of what?" he asked.

The writer only grimaced, but Gordimer's mind sped to the obvious conclusion. Why else would he be out here, in nowhere? His head twisted to look on the burnt out ring where Billy-Bob had vanished, then turned back to the writer, whose gaze also fixed on the town.

"You followed us," said Gordimer. "Billy-Bob?"

The writer's shoulders fell.

Gordimer felt a rush of astonishment that made his knees rubbery. He sat down. Only a hero would have a story written about them!

"You are the third companion! What is your name?"

"Andrew."

Andrew had hidden himself in the shrubs outside Dirtburg. Gordimer sensed the same frustration and agitation. He'd followed them, unseen to all but the information post beside the gorge, and he'd followed them here.

Faint trumpets of hope blared from within the chambers of his mind. Maybe there was some bit of hero trapped in Billy-Bob after all. If so it would at least accomplish Gordimer's mission. Perhaps, and here the trumpets swelled, perhaps this hero might destroy villainy. There was supposed to be such a hero, but it was an old promise and most people had grown tired of waiting. Maybe he would break down the walls separating this prison from paradise.

But how could this person know Billy-Bob was a hero? The trumpets faded. Gordimer choked out a wry laugh. Maybe this boy was the last, dusty gasp of heroism.

"There's no need," he said. "A hero's story is already written."

Andrew nodded in grim agreement.

Hero or not, destiny always led to the same place.

A smile pulled Gordimer's face taut. Destiny. There wasn't such a thing, really. Not any more. Destiny existed only where the future was in doubt. It was a goal forecast to give people something to shoot for, or something to shy from. Divination was overrated. Anyone who witnessed a mere decade of human history, disaster and monstrosity filled as they had all proven, should have few qualms and little trouble anticipating equal, if not more tremendous calamity in the next twenty hundred. If anything was certain where humanity was concerned, it was a penchant for not only destruction and ruin, but a capacity for increasing the scale of malevolence time and again. To be a prognosticator of human behavior was the simplest occupation of all.

The ruin of the nearby city was a perfect example.

Gordimer looked at the writer and a new question came to mind. Billy-Bob was clearly not a hero. In fact, he wasn't much of anything as far as he could guess. So the presence of a writer seemed rather anticlimactic.

"Why would you want to follow Billy-Bob?"

Andrew sighed and his shoulders heaved again.

"I guess I should start with the Anti-Paradox Machine."

THE ANTI-PARADOX MACHINE

On bright days such as this one, the tall structure of the Institute glimmered as sunlight shattered against the building like rain against the burly chest of a mountain, littering the ground with sparkling rainbow shards. A visitor might suspect the faint tinkling sound came from bits of fractured light showering the pavement, but it was the public address system playing a soft and soothing melody. The Institute was a center for thought, ideas, and imagination, where people gathered to improve themselves with the goal of improving the world around them, a marvel marred only by an obelisk just outside the main entrance that punctuated the pastoral surroundings with mind-clattering whangs! that reverberated across the lolling stretch of landscaped bushes and flowers carpeting the disc-shaped platform on which it stood.

The obelisk was a charcoal black, four-sided slab thrusting out of the overlapping ropes of vines and plants like the dead horn of a burned out tree trunk. No doors, no windows, no lights or hinges. Only the occasional crack of dissonance in a place of light and gentle harmonies.

Whang!

People had grown acclimated to the sound in the same way one grows accustomed to, but no more comfortable with, the rhythmic thump of an infant pounding on a piano keyboard. They tolerated; they made do; they rationalized: what a nice Institute we have. Besides, were it not for the loathsome block the world would tear itself into irreparable smithereens.

People tiptoed through the bushes and flowers, spreading fertilizer here and there, and sprinkling water in places that might otherwise go brown. They staggered when the obelisk went Whang!, but took only a moment to recover themselves and remember their tasks.

One person sat apart from the groundskeepers, away from the building and the obelisk and the flowers, beyond a stone path leading away from the building, past the open space between the white stones of the path and the green ring of grass surrounding it all.

His name, which he deemed bitterly would never be of any stature now, was Andrew.

Andrew sat alone, crouched at the edge of the platform, staring blankly into the blasted wasteland beyond a small island of green below that extended just beyond the shadow of the platform.

He turned a small sheet of paper through his fingers. The paper had been wrinkled and smoothed, crushed and clenched over and over again into tissuey softness. He came here whenever he wanted to think, watch the slow recovery of a withered world, and, as was the case right now, to brood.

Against better judgment, Andrew was hoping. Not for fame, or greatness, or any of the silly, repeated hopes of every person. Hope was a temporary relief from the vain struggles for achievement. Hope painted a world as one wished, but could never be. Most hopers were greedy, begging whichever sublime power seemed most appropriate for wealth, might, immortality, or any combination of the three. Andrew had a lone, reluctant wish, which he addressed to no one because he knew it was beyond their power and because he had nothing to offer in exchange. Her name was Bree.

Most often she began as a tone in his head. A single, perfect note. A smile. Hers was a thin, faintly upward bow. Then dark green eyes, followed by the rest of her face, expanding from a single resonating chime into a filling song. With highs and lows, a symphonic swell with punchy orchestral crashes drumming under the sustained finale. An opus, a fanfare, an anthem to which a million billion people would rally, but a song he would rather keep for himself.

And there she would be, complete, the tune still ringing like the thundering brassy trumpet blast welcoming a champion into the arena.

Andrew's smile broke and fell.

She would say he was ridiculous, unimportant, dull. One pulverizing stomp after another. Ugly, stupid, weak. Maybe she already loved someone. Doubt pounded through the cities of the mind, sparing an occasional life only so Hope could rise again for a splendid recrushing. Doubt reveled in nothing more than destroying Hope. And Hope, being immortal, lived out its days with blithe indifference to its regular obliteration. Neither cared at all about the suffering they caused: Doubt because it enjoyed suffering; Hope because it was too stupid to recognize it.

The song in his head slogged and blackened into morose slag.

Andrew emerged from thought and the ruined song, embittered, to the faint buzz of the obelisk.

Obnoxious as the obelisk may be, it was useful in averting certain doom. Doom that would result not from volcanoes, tornadoes, or large dogs, though an obelisk with such a purpose would have been welcome, but rather from Paradox. Standard fears, including darkness and monsters, would likely exist for eternity, but Paradox, a universe-ending calamity that resulted from changing the past, had been boxed toothless by the metal fist of technology.

Paradox resulted when a person went back in time and interfered with their own existence. For instance, it would be paradoxical if a person were to travel twenty years into the past and push a younger form of themselves over the edge of a canyon. But if a younger self were killed they could not have grown older and returned to kill themselves. The older self could not exist, and if this older self ceased to exist, they would never have been able to return and kill themselves in the first place, and would therefore have no reason to not exist.

Baffling, backwards, and wrong, Paradox was a foe of incomprehensible, world-shattering might.

No one could be sure what might happen in the event of paradoxical self murder. Some guessed it would create an alternate timeline, allowing self murder and the existence of the self murderer. Most assumed the murderer would pop in and out of existence while Time attempted to resolve the inconsistency, until Time finally detonated in frustration, destroying all of creation.

Thankfully, the Anti-Paradox machine, a name that sufficed without impressing, solved this problem. With the Anti-Paradox machine an older self could kill a younger self with no reason to fear the consequences of altering every event in which they had been a part or the landscape of world events, allowing the older self to return to the unaltered time from which they originated, even though this ought to have resulted in some sort of confusion in the organization of History—a long standing institution irrefutably linked to cause and effect—allowing the world to continue as unexploded and indifferent as always.

Despite the jarring crashes of the obelisk, Andrew's attention remained fixed on the bit of crumpled paper in his hand, mortified that his potential had been reduced to a simple paper ball. His heart thudded dully within him, as if there were an anti-paradox machine working inside his chest, pounding the marble statues of his hopes into meaningless gray powder.

He'd never heard the name on the paper, nor had anyone he asked. An unimportant scuffler who winked in and back out of existence without disturbing the world around them. Boring.

The place, however, was The West. Notorious and mysterious West, of which little was known outside of its unmatched maliciousness. Wars, famine, and pestilence had come and left their scars upon humanity, but none were so nightmarish and darkly inspiring as the West. A horrible, ruined land of mischief and misdeeds—no place for a writer.

Andrew looked across the emptiness to the inscrutable yellow blur of the horizon, unable to discern one object from another, or good from bad. A perfect place for wicked things to hide. Somewhere out there, he thought, was the West. Beyond the horizon and backward in time, it waited.

Though they had rescued the world from the brink of destruction, it remained in a state of desolation. An abundance of mysteries knowledge lost, so yet they sought out histories, such as what had broken the world. They had once brushed their fingertips against the belly of the stars. The erstwhile explorers who had left them behind might still be up there, probing the galaxy. Meanwhile this remnant remained, chronicling the past in order to better understand the present. He wondered where they were and if they remembered the people here.

It was the girl, Bree, who decided these things. Who should go where. Which author should write about whom from the capacious catalogue of history. Clearly, having chosen a No One in the Terrible West, she hated him.

An explosive Whang! blasted across the campus, dropping insects in stunned clouds and dazing those tending the landscaping.

Engrossed in his own misery, eyes burrowing into the paper crumpled in his palm, Andrew hardly noticed two people emerge from the Institute and approach, nor the hum of quashed paradox fade as they stopped behind him.

"It's time. Did you prepare yourself, or did you just sit here, moping?"

Andrew twisted. Standing behind him was Mardin, the librarian. Mardin had a clear and clean face, yet still seemed grim and dangerous. A thousand thoughts traveled behind his eyes, but never seemed distracted or conflicted. He had the certainty and conviction of someone who had heard the plan for mankind from the lips of the creator, and his only function was to see it through.

The girl, Bree, stood beside him like an orange sun on the horizon, painting the world around her with soft radiance. That was the mark of genuine beauty. Not being beautiful oneself, but making everything around them beautiful. He spotted her in time to see the last muted jangle of a smile disappear.

Andrew's stomach knotted, knowing this moment would be the last he'd see of her, perhaps ever. He felt he ought to resist, do something, tell her how she made his mind crackle with ambitions beyond human ability, even though it was she who had selected him for this loathsome task. He pointed to the edge of the platform.

"What if I jumped off instead?"

Mardin considered.

"Then you would probably break your legs and suffer fractures, sprains, and organ damage. This would make navigating the world unnecessarily challenging. But if your goal is to make your task harder than it needs to be, by all means, jump. If you are hesitant, I would not defer the honor of providing a helpful push."

Mardin took a meaningful step toward Andrew.

"Stop!" cried Andrew.

Mardin stopped. He had guessed Andrew's bluff, but expressed no sense of triumph. Instead, he affected a sort of disappointment, as he always did, as if expecting better. Mardin never appeared to take pleasure in being smarter than others, only varying degrees of disappointment in others.

"It's probably best you do not jump," said Mardin. "Your youth provides you with a higher probability of survival, which is what best qualifies you for this assignment. We can only hope you have enough sense to write it correctly and present a comprehensible account." He continued, speaking somewhat louder though no one else stood close enough to hear him. "Taking liberties with the facts is discouraged, though as you are the sole witness to events I suppose exceptions would be difficult to prove. Your honesty is considered sacrosanct. No one will question the story you provide, whatever form it may take. This above all else you must remember."

Mardin extended a hand toward Andrew, and Andrew tensed, fearful the librarian had decided to push him over the edge anyway. The hand withdrew, leaving a gelatinous blue disc, veined with dark blue circuitry, adhered to his chest.

"This will take you where you need to go." Without looking away from Andrew, Mardin opened a hand toward Bree. "You'll want these as well."

Bree stepped forward and handed him a thin notebook no larger than his hand and a writing utensil. There seemed hardly enough room in the book to make a full account of anything. Andrew's hands shook as he took archaic tools, reintroduced as technology took grudging steps backward. Bree stepped back.

"It's strange, don't you think?" Mardin wondered aloud. "Before, no one was concerned about the nature of the past. Of individuals. Historians, maybe. The past was a dark place best left forgotten. Now, to be compiling histories of everything. What does this mean?"

Against his will, Andrew felt his mind turn from his fear to bear on the question. Questions were insidious in that respect. They demanded attention, and worse, often led not to an answer, but another question. Questions beckoned from the dark corners of a labyrinth, often following wisps along the winding pathways for so long they forgot the reason they entered.

To date, history was notorious for its inconsistency and untrustworthiness. Without witness accounts, historians could only guess at the past. Historians were quite good at guessing, but often there were significant chasms in information, and historians tended to fill these gaps with their imagination. The past was a sludge-filled morass in constant need of revision.

The Legend of Roger claimed the Roger of story had acted, but ultimately failed, to thwart a cataclysm that broke the world. By other accounts, Roger the Infamous undertook the destruction himself. Still others viewed the role of Roger the Comparatively Uninvolved as minimal or unrelated. Still others claimed the world had never suffered destruction, though the preponderance of evidence pointed elsewhere.

History had already happened, and yet it was an evolving story based on sparse information.

Obviously, historians agreed Roger could not be Legendary, Infamous, and Uninvolved all at once, not all of them could be right. At the same time they could not agree on who was right. The only way to resolve this conundrum would be a personal account, and while time-travel technology had existed for some time, anti-paradox was fairly new.

"I don't know."

"Why should the past matter? Isn't it obvious?"

Obvious things, Andrew observed, tended to be obvious to those who already had the necessary information.

"No."

The past didn't matter. The status of Roger, for example, wasn't important. But if the past didn't matter, why were they going?

Andrew felt himself lured toward the labyrinth, but Mardin answered his own question.

"We're looking for something. That much is easy. But what?"

After rigorous debate it had been determined, much to the giddiment of scientists and historians, that absolutely nothing was right and everything would have to be rerecorded by way of firsthand observation. All that was known had to be forgotten, including the histories written by the victors, the spiteful, the revisionists, and a predominant number of folk who simply had no idea what they were talking about. Such an undertaking would have been impossible were it not for the enthusiasm of the scientific and historic community, the capacity for time travel, and, most importantly, the Anti-Paradox machine.

"The truth."

Mardin frowned.

"Once, but now the research is more earnest. Undertaken out of fear. Fear of something that threatens us. But why should we worry about the past? Unless we don't want something from then to have happened."

"What don't we want to have happened?"

Mardin's shoulders lifted and fell.

"Maybe we don't know what that is until we find it. Maybe there's good reason we haven't. Because it's hiding."

A bone-jarring Whang! crashed through the city, and any hope Mardin had of directing Andrew's thoughts with these guesses scattered. The great disadvantage to having the ability to travel safely through time without fear of consequence was the inability to hold a single thought in one's head for long before it was jarred free by the clanging of the Anti-Paradox machine.

The more Mardin spoke about fear and change and shadowy motivations, the more apprehensive Andrew became about his journey. He couldn't concentrate on it for long, thanks to the machine, but doubt and agitation left a residue in his mind he could not forget. He already feared for his existence. Now Mardin put the thought in his head that the idyllic Institute community may be guilty of something nefarious.

"I don't want to go," Andrew blurted. "I can stay here. I can work in the gardens. I don't want to be a writer."

"Oh, but there's no glory in the simple path," said Mardin. "That's what you want, isn't it? Glory and fame, and those things that make you feel important. Something to impress, to prove yourself. This will be a challenge, a learning experience. Frankly, if I had any interest in this history I'd have chosen someone else. Perhaps when you return you won't be such a brat. But, I suppose, if you really don't want to go, it's not my decision. Bree?"

Bree's gaze drifted along the horizon before locking reluctantly with Andrew's. Her jaw tightened and her hands, bunched in the fabric of her shirt, locked behind her back. Her mouth opened, and Andrew closed his eyes to fully appreciate the compassionate chime of her voice. She understood his fear and confusion, and such was her empathy she would spare him this punishment.

"Send him," she murmured.

Whang! went the Anti-Paradox Machine.

Andrew's eyes popped open in time to see Mardin step toward him and press a thumb against the gel disc on his chest, causing it to pulse and grow warm.

"You'll be all right," said Mardin. He straightened, then put a heel against Andrew's chest and shoved him backward off the platform, trailing a notepad and handful of grass that tore free as he went over the side.

For a moment Andrew groped at the air, at an invisible handhold he knew was not there, but it only took a moment to resign himself to this fate. He saw Bree lean over the edge to watch him fall and his eyes remained open for an extra instant to take her in, then squeezed shut, anticipating the approach of solid ground. Andrew guessed he had two seconds before it arrived and he counted backwards. Two. He curled up, as though doing so would prevent him from shattering on impact. One. He realized he hadn't released his last breath. The surface below wasn't water, and the impact would probably knock both the wind and his lungs out of his chest. As he thought about the peculiarities of his body's involuntary reaction, the clock in his mind ticked to Zero.

No collision. No pain. Andrew unclenched his eyes and saw a few blades of grass floating down toward him. He groped with his open hand and felt dirt collect under his fingernails. Something else landed beside him with a smack, and when he looked he saw the notepad.

I have died, thought Andrew, or lost all sense of feeling, so he pinched his leg. It hurt. A lot. He had survived. Or pain was part of afterlife. In either case, relief came in a wave of hysteria. He laughed, so much his abdomen began to ache. It had been a joke. Time travel wasn't possible. The Institute wasn't compiling a record of the past. Bree did not hate him. Somewhere in this elaborate hoax lay a life lesson Mardin intended to impart upon him. What it was, he didn't know. But he would be sure to ask, with as much gratitude as he could muster to someone who had tricked and embarrassed him, and pushed him off a ledge.

Andrew sat up, a twinge of pain sticking in his midsection, his mouth strangely dry. He'd have a drink at the Institute. It was only a few short steps away.

Except, the Institute wasn't there. Instead, a town, a forest, a fence, and an outhouse.

"Where am I?" he whispered.

His dry tongue peeled off the roof of his mouth and he took a tremulous breath. He could hear his heart pounding and feel its panic. A sensation of food gone wrong built in his stomach. His hands shook and his vision blurred on the brink of tears because, after all, he knew the answer to the question as soon as he asked it.

* * *

"So, here I am," Andrew concluded. "Until I finish. However that happens."

Gordimer nodded. He understood the burden of an unwanted task.

"Everything will be okay," he said. Gordimer had become very good at telling people what he hoped, but no longer believed. Sometimes it buoyed the spirits of the other person, and sometimes it buoyed his to see their relief. Other times they saw through the lie. Andrew did not appear fooled.

"I know," Andrew responded anyway.

The two of them sat a moment, unspeaking, digesting the lies of the other. Andrew broke the silence.

"I have a job to do," he said, getting to his feet. "I'm going to do it, because they think I can't."

"Good luck," said Gordimer, knowing he had as much reason to believe in luck as he did in hope.

Andrew nodded, then marched toward the ruined town. This, Gordimer knew, was a mistake.

"Wait!" cried Gordimer, and pattered after him. Andrew turned. "Don't go there!"

Andrew cocked his head. He looked at the town's remains, then looked back at Gordimer.

"Why?"

"Something is there. Was there. It may still be there, I don't know."

The writer seemed confused. Rightly so.

"Some years ago there was a villain who terrorized the world," Gordimer explained. "A monstrous, hate-filled man who felt the world had done him wrong. This is where he originated. This place was the first he destroyed. Even now, you can hear the echoes of despair in the wind."

The writer's eyes pinched with skepticism.

"I don't hear anything."

People became tolerant of Evil because they had gotten accustomed to it, Gordimer guessed. Evil became invisible when it was everywhere. Like air, everyone forgot it was there until it was blowing hard enough to knock off their hat.

"Maybe you aren't good at listening."

They were quiet a moment. Then, at the edge of his hearing, a long, pealing scream whispered from the direction of the circle of buildings. The writer stiffened. He heard it, too.

"You see!" said Gordimer in triumph.

"Those aren't echoes of despair," growled Andrew. "That is your hero getting destroyed."

PERIL IN THE WIDE NOTHING

The town was a wheel of ruined buildings melted by time, a dead gear in the broken watch of the world. Blackened timbers lay inside the scalded rinds of buildings like spoon handles poking out of empty soup bowls. These were no mere marks of erosion and abandonment. Something had destroyed this place. And yet, against reason, Billy-Bob felt drawn inward toward a doom that met all those who had come before.

It was fear of the unknown that drove him forward, he guessed, even though that didn't make sense, because fear tended to drive people away rather than draw them closer. If fear pushed him away from the unknown, there must be something else pushing him onward. And not only did it push against fear, but it was stronger, otherwise he wouldn't still be moving inward. He'd like to know what it was, to give it a name, just as he wanted to know what happened to this city, and the only tool he'd ever developed for solving problems like these was persistence. So he went on.

He came to the ring of buildings and placed a hand on a wooden beam supporting one side of a collapsing awning. The blackened timber crumbled into greasy particles where his fingers touched. From here he could see everything, which wasn't very much.

In the center of the ruined town was a black rock that thrust from the ground like the quivering shaft of a great javelin hurled down from the heavens. The spike of stone looked hard. Harder than the brittle yellow rocks that rolled and crumbled under his feet as he approached. A long, black, metal pin lay by the stone alongside bent links of thick chain. There was a conical divot near the peak of the rock where the pin must have ripped free.

Something must have been chained here. Wrenched loose. Destroyed this town in payment for its imprisonment. Ultimate Evil? Maybe. He lifted one of the chunks of rock and was surprised by its heaviness. Whatever had done this must have been a horrifying, brute creature.

The sound of scratching footsteps made him release the stone. It fell from his hand, thudding against his toes and fracturing the ground below. Billy-Bob felt a scream crash against the back of his throat. His vision blurred as geysers of water rushed up the wells of his eyes, but he held it in, fearful whatever ruined this place still lingered, reveling in its catastrophic artistry.

Again the sound of steps came, a few quick shuffles, then stopped. Then they started again. They came from the other side of the rock, an arrhythmic scuffling amidst the permanent hiss of sand-blown wind.

Nerving himself, Billy-Bob leaned a shoulder against the rock, the throb in his foot dwindling but still present, and peered around the side.

There was a creature there, short and round. Its skin was a drab and worn purple, with yellowing cotton poking through along failing seams. He squinted. The creature's skin appeared to be sewn around its framework.

"Oy! Found yerself a wog, boy-o," said the block of black stone he'd dropped on his foot.

Billy-Bob pressed a finger to his lips.

"Oh, ain't nobody that can hear me but you. Ain't you figured that out yet? Besides, wogs ain't bad," said the stone.

Billy-Bob didn't respond. Explaining how a giant crowd of wogs had attempted to heave him off a bridge would only start an argument. Maybe the rock would be quiet if he ignored it. Rocks had little to fear of anything. But Billy-Bob was soft all over and no creature would fear breaking off a tooth when it bit him.

He watched the wog in mute awe, wondering if he might leave the same way he came without being noticed. The wog paced back and forth, blinking and shaking its head, clearly in some kind of distress, its tiny arms flapping at its face. He guessed the wog had sand in its eyes because he recognized the behavior in himself. Because the wog's arms were so short it was unable to rub the sand out, which appeared to annoy the wog and leave it with no alternative but to close its eyes. Of course, this created a new problem: with both eyes closed it couldn't see where it was going, and probably couldn't remember which direction it had been facing when it shut them. So it paced one way for a few steps, stopped, shifted in indecision, then turned about and went another way, not really getting anywhere.

"You think the wog did this?" asked the shard of black rock.

The wog did not appear to notice the question.

"Didn't it?"

"Of course not. Well, I s'pose it did pile all the bones. That's a consequence of its compulsion to sort. But burn the place down and chase everyone away? No. That was a different villain."

Billy-Bob forgot the danger of the wog for the moment.

"Ultimate Evil?" he asked.

Speaking the words aloud conjured an image of a giant beast, red, raging, and remorseless. Though defeating it would bring him a step closer to heroism, the prospect of confrontation frightened him. That battle was a giant pair of pants he'd yet to grow into.

"Aye. The most superlative of Evils. Ultimate, if you must. But it's not here. Be grateful for that. If he were, you would know it. You would *feel* it, like a grapefruit crawling up yer throat and a fire in the back of yer eyeballs."

"Then it's not the wog."

"No, it's not the wog. The wog isn't anything dangerous. A collector. An organizer. A cataloger. A searcher. What do you think wogs are?"

"How do you know that?"

"I know it because you know it," said the rock. "Obviously."

"But I didn't know that. If you know what I know, and I didn't know, how could you possibly know?"

"Boulders to pebbles! If you can't understand the obvious, there's no help for you. If you don't believe me about the wog, ask it yourself. They're harmless."

The wog. Yes. He'd forgotten. He flattened himself against the great stone and listened, breathing noiselessly. It was quiet. Even the occasional shuffles of the wog had stopped. The absence of sound made the scene more profound, more ominous and tense, like the pause before a symphonic detonation. He clenched the pommel of his gun and leaned around the rock.

The wog was gone.

Beyond the town the horizon cut a straight line between the ground and sky, like a seam where the two halves could be separated from one another and the insides shaken out to litter the cosmos. He did not see any shapes moving against it, nor did he hear any wooden creaks that would indicate the wog was moving through the buildings. Billy-Bob didn't know where else to search and hoped keeping still and out of sight would prevent the wog from finding him. As he thought this it made sense that the wog, too, was keeping still and out of sight. With a sinking feeling he looked to his own feet, where, as expected, the wog stood motionless and looked up at him with an unblinking and expressionless stare.

It was too late to flee. Pointless to fight. The only thing he could do was the only thing that came to him naturally, and that was to ask a question for which he did not expect an answer.

"Are you harmless?"

The wog's head cocked, as if the language was unfamiliar, then settled back. Its beak opened to answer.

"Nargh!" it snarled, and leapt at him.

The wog caromed off his chest and fell to one side. Billy-Bob staggered, shocked by the attack and the surprising weight of the wog, and fell to the ground. Harmless indeed! The wog thrashed on the ground until it sat upright again, then turned about and spotted him. Paralyzed by fascination and horror, Billy-Bob had forgotten to get up and run. Now it was too late, and the wog sprang again, bouncing off his chest and knocking him onto his back.

Billy-Bob sat up and leapt to his feet, but the wog too had reached its feet and was coiling for another leap. Not knowing what else to do, Billy-Bob coiled and leapt also. This took the wog by surprise, and its eyes widened before it disappeared under Billy-Bob's body as he crashed to the ground.

The wog was hard and sturdy, and it churned beneath him in an effort to escape. When he leapt he'd reached for the wog to deflect it, in case the wog leapt at the same time. Now one arm lay folded beneath him with the squirming wog. The wog writhed and wormed, trying to escape, while Billy-Bob struggled to remain on top. Finally, it stopped moving.

For a moment Billy-Bob thought he'd been victorious and the wog had succumbed. Then he felt a sharp sting on his hand. He screamed, long and pealing, and rolled away. The wog had bitten him!

Too late he realized his error. While the bite had been painful, rolling aside gave the wog its freedom. He expected the wog to use that freedom to resume its attack, so he jumped back to his feet, squeezing the injured hand in the fold of his arm. He attempted to scale the rock in the hope that the wog could not follow, but the stone was too sheer and Billy-Bob too clumsy, leaving him pressed against the rock, scrabbling in vain for a handhold, waiting for the hammerblow in his back from the wog's assault.

After struggling against the stone to no avail he realized the wog had not attacked. He took a furtive look over his shoulder and found the wog seated, motionless, watching him. A faint trickle of Billy-Bob's blood ran down the lower part of its beak, which it cleaned with a silvery tongue. The wog shifted its weight, probably calculating a better strike, but it did not leap. Instead, it spoke.

"I know you," it said in a piping, reverberating voice. When the wog talked its voice was chopped, as though speaking through a spinning set of fan blades.

"How?" asked Billy-Bob.

"You're him. You're…" The wog's expression glazed. "Access denied." The wog blinked, as if coming out of a momentary and unexpected sleep. "I have completed my evaluation of this town. Twelve citizens deceased. Population dispersed. Victims of trauma including smoke inhalation, extreme burns, starvation…"

"What is this about?"

"This city," the wog replied. "Structures have been reduced to an aggregate 4% of their original structural integrity. The water table is 47 feet below the surface. No threats remain in the immediate vicinity. Time elapsed since the event: roughly 30 years. Approximately one day's travel by foot from the Institute, which is an acceptable distance to allow for protection, making this a good candidate for re-colonization. However, the geographic location matches that of a site that was devastated by the monster…"

"Monster?" Billy-Bob interrupted.

"Yes," the wog answered, then continued, "making it necessary to repopulate with civilians unfamiliar with the history of this city. Soil content is nitrogen and phosphorous heavy to the south where a small rise creates a natural windbreak that prevents topsoil from blowing away. Do you have any questions about this report?"

"I don't understand at all."

Billy-Bob suspected this might be some elaborate ruse to trick him into lowering his guard.

"What are you? What are you doing here? Why aren't you attacking?"

"I am a surveyor. I am surveying. It is not part of my operational guidelines to attack anyone that is a 99.9999% or higher genotypical match with… Access denied." The wog blinked, then tried again. "With… Access denied." The wog appeared annoyed. "With… the creator," it said at last.

"Creator? Who is the creator?"

"The creator is he who creates. The one who created me. Us, rather. This is obvious. You are a 99.999998% match. You are the creator, or someone very similar."

"I created you?"

"Very likely," replied the wog.

"What is the name of the creator?" asked Billy-Bob.

"I can't tell you."

"You don't know it."

"I *do* know it," the wog insisted, "but I can't tell you."

"Why not?"

The wog's mouth opened to respond, but all that came out was, "Access denied."

A mechanical snarl gargled out of the wog's throat. It was clearly irritated by its inability to answer, so Billy-Bob changed the subject.

"What monster destroyed this place?"

"There is only one monster," the wog answered.

"Ultimate Evil," said Billy-Bob.

"I suppose. It has many names."

Billy-Bob looked at the wog. He'd heard stories about these beasts and their cruelty. Until recently he'd found the stories believable. Now, speaking with this wog, he didn't understand how they had attained such a menacing reputation. He wondered how many maligned reputations could be corrected just by talking to them.

"Why does everyone fear you?"

"Because we are dangerous. Being dangerous is a valuable deterrent to prevent people from interfering with my mission."

"You don't seem dangerous."

"You are not a threat to my mission. You share it. You initiated it. We have no reason to be dangerous to you. We are not dangerous to most people unless it is required of us."

"What is your mission?"

"My mission is to survey. It was the same for all of us. Others had their mission changed: find the girl—use all means necessary. Then you went away. The others have been searching ever since, or so I imagine. Without regular maintenance they may have broken down. But now you have returned."

"I don't know what you mean. I didn't make you. I didn't give you any mission. What girl?"

The wog considered.

"It's true. You seem different. It is strange that you do not know so many things you should know. You seem somehow more… ignorant."

"I suppose."

"Ignorance can be corrected. Unless you choose to embrace it. In which case you would be stupid, too. Only a stupid person chooses ignorance when offered understanding."

"That's not very nice."

"Being nice is not my purpose. It is to survey this city until you return."

"And now I'm here. What is your mission?"

The wog's beak parted, then closed again. After a moment of thought it responded.

"I have no secondary mission. What do you think it should be?"

This, Billy-Bob realized, was an awesome prospect. The wog had offered him the chance to give it orders. His mind boggled at the number of things it might do for him: it could protect him from harm, or serve as a trophy showcasing his heroism, or encourage other villains to leave him be. Yet each of these ideas felt like misuse, undermining the great potential of such a creature. Since he couldn't think of anything, the only thing he could tell the wog was the truth.

"I can't think of anything. What would you suggest?"

The wog blinked.

"What would *I* suggest?" It pondered. "I've never been asked what I would suggest. I don't know either."

"You could come with me until we think of something."

Again, the wog considered.

"This is an acceptable pseudo-mission," it decided. "It is certainly better than being here. I confess this chore has been rather dull. Do you anticipate encountering others as part of this mission?"

"Yes. Soon."

"Understood. Due to our reputation, I anticipate these others may be unsettled if they discover you have a wog in your company, as is appropriate. I cannot allow them to think we are not dangerous."

"I can't let you attack them."

"I would prefer to avoid doing so."

"Then what?"

"Preserve my reputation and improve yours."

Billy-Bob thought about what this might mean.

"You think I should pretend you're my prisoner."

"Do you have a means of doing so?"

Billy-Bob recalled Gordimer's empty sack. He wasn't sure why Gordimer continued carrying the sack, but knew by the way it flapped in strong winds it was empty. Maybe Gordimer would let him use it.

"I think so. Wait here."

Billy-Bob turned away from the wog and headed toward where Gordimer had last been. He spotted him from afar, waving his arms and pointing at what appeared to be someone else. The distance between them was filled with a haze from bands of heat that distorted the world, so he couldn't be sure, but he felt certain he saw one person turn to look at him, then rush away.

"Ha!" he heard Gordimer shout at the departing figure. "Guess you're not going anywhere!"

When Billy-Bob reached Gordimer, the latter seemed pleased, but did not say why. The sack lay nearby.

"Can I borrow that?" asked Billy-Bob, pointing to the sack.

Gordimer followed his hand. His brow furrowed.

"I guess so. Why?"

"Thanks," said Billy-Bob. "I'll be right back."

He scooped up the sack and threw it over his shoulder, then trotted back to the buildings where the wog was waiting.

* * *

Gordimer watched as Billy-Bob exited the city again, the sack slung over one shoulder. It seemed natural to bring the sack along, even thought it was empty, and strange to hand it to Billy-Bob, even though Gordimer had no use for it.

What had Billy-Bob encountered in this place? It must have been nothing. Billy-Bob stopped before him, placing the sack gently at his feet. It settled on the ground with a large lump at the bottom. Gordimer reached out with a foot to prod the lump, then thought better.

"What's in there?" Gordimer asked.

"A wog," Billy-Bob answered. "Where do we go now?"

Gordimer snatched the sack from the ground and craned his head over the opening. The lump at the bottom of the sack growled and jolted upward. Gordimer's head jerked backward and the bag fell out of his hands. He staggered in reverse and crumpled into a seated position. His hand went reflexively to his throbbing mouth and when he drew it away he saw a trickle of blood.

"It's in there! It's really in there!"

Billy-Bob grabbed the sack by the opening and twisted it shut, then slung it over his shoulder.

"Be careful," he said. "They're dangerous."

Billy-Bob turned, looking toward the horizon as if searching for an indication of where he was supposed to go, then began walking.

Gordimer remained seated as Billy-Bob drew away. The boy had captured a wog. Until he'd looked into the bag and felt the little monster thump against his face he would have thought such an achievement impossible. Absurd, even. The impossible had become possible with stunning suddenness. A tiny, prickling notion tickled his mind. He shook his head hard, free of silly tendrils of hope that had touched him so many times before only to leave him wretched with failure. He lurched to his feet, pulled the frayed tassel around his baggy pants tight, and followed. The time for sympathy and hope was long past. All that remained was a compulsion to do what was best for himself.

It was almost finished, this deplorable mission. Then he could go home.

A FAMILIAR DREAM

Billy-Bob lay on the slope of a hill, watching clouds plod across a crowded sky in a silent herd, their titanic shades laboring down the hill toward fertile pasture beyond. Sunlight dropped in golden curtains through slots in their shouldered ranks, pressing on his face with warm, delicate hands. The tails of long grass wagged in the breeze. He felt serene and certain, confident he was a puzzle piece and this was where he fit.

He became aware of a low roar that gained volume as he paid it more attention. At first he thought it might be thunders within the clouds, but the sky was pale and docile. More and more it sounded like voices. Not words. Rather, an exuberant clamor. People were cheering—a booming chorus saluting his greatness. He was a hero, he realized, an imperishable symbol of might, and they loved him.

From over the hill's crest behind him a wedge of birds flew, and when they passed the sky had gone gray and chilly. After the birds came animals and people, scuttling down the slope in a flurry of legs and wings and squawks and barks, bungling one another in their urgency to go by while the atmosphere grew dark and chill.

This, Billy-Bob decided, was a dream. His mind, a lump of mush bored with sleep, was trying to amuse itself. He knew so because he'd seen it before. Recognized and enjoyed it like a favorite song. A vision that repeated itself nightly. Besides, he wasn't a hero. Not yet.

Because this was a familiar dream he knew what to expect. Knew his favorite part. So he looked for the girl.

And there she was. Up the hill, oblivious to the creatures flowing past with relentless infinity.

Pulling and clawing at the turf, he ascended until he was at her side. Close enough to see the dirt on her hands, the tightness in her jaw. He paid little heed to the rumbles rolling out of the darkening sky.

She was beautiful and brilliant beneath a layer of grime and hard edges. He knew because dreamtime enhanced perception beyond the boundaries of human capacity, mere observation yielded impossible results, and aspects of personality were as plain to him as the black grit beneath her fingernails. She was saddened by the state of the world she saw and felt powerless to change it. Maybe he knew because his mind made her. Maybe because he was close enough to hear the whispers inside her head. Close enough to touch.

He stretched out an arm, watching his fingers extend toward hers, wondering if she would be warm and squeeze back.

This, he recalled, was usually where he woke up.

* * *

And suddenly he was awake.

He knew he was awake because he could feel the uneven ground jabbing his back with pointed, stony fingers. The world around him was black with exception to a few spears of white light where moonbeams slipped through fissures in the clouds.

During those brief instants of illumination he could see the fractured wasteland around them. The sack lay beside him, a lump of wog at the bottom. He could see Gordimer lying on his side not far away, arms wrapped around his knees, eyes fixed on the sack, watching the knot at the top and waiting for it to unravel.

Then the sky drew shut and everything vanished into silent oblivion.

At night the ocean-bottom darkness bore down on him with all its loneliness. Like his strangeness, loneliness was natural, he was accustomed to it and did not question it, though he did not like it.

Dim music rippled through the void and Billy-Bob remembered he wasn't alone. He could sense the world was still there, albeit invisible. The song was soothing, pleading, hopeful. The world, for all its infamy, had a tiny core of goodness.

In spite of the darkness Billy-Bob could still guess at Gordimer's obscured face a few paces away, cracked lips pursed, thinking his secret thoughts. He never seemed to sleep. Billy-Bob could hear him whistle, faintly, through the hiss of unchecked wind brushing sand across the plain, stop, and start over. Familiar, hypnotic, and soothing. A tune he'd been repeating since they left, and several times since they stopped here in the dead stretch, whenever the moon slid behind the iron sheet of clouds. Billy-Bob wasn't very good at guessing, but it seemed as though Gordimer was frightened, too. The song made him feel better.

"What is that?" Billy-Bob asked the emptiness. "It's nice."

Feathers rustled as Gordimer shrugged and his voice rose through the darkness.

"A song from home," he said. "Part of one, anyway. I've forgotten most of it. But some things don't fade. The urge to go home and that bit of song."

"So why don't you?" asked Billy-Bob.

"Go home?" Gordimer paused, considering, then let out a long gust of air. "Can't. Not from here. It's not just a matter of going. Not the same way you would travel from here to Beta. I have to finish my task. When you're a hero, then the way will open."

"You can't go home? Are you being punished?"

"No," he answered. Then, after a bit of thought, continued. "Maybe. I don't think so. Everyone has to earn their place. We all have a test."

"What's your test? Maybe I can help."

Gordimer's response was slow and heavy.

"Find two hundred heroes."

"Two hundred!"

Two hundred was more of anything than Billy-Bob had ever considered. Most things that came in great numbers, like stars or raindrops, he could only gape at in stupefied awe. He doubted his feeble mind had the capacity to contend with such a quantity.

"I've found one hundred and ninety nine," said Gordimer.

"You've been doing this a long time."

Billy-Bob could feel the weight of Gordimer's somber smile without seeing it.

"You have no idea."

How long did it take to find a single hero, let alone two hundred? It was beyond reckoning. Heroes were an implentiful species. Billy-Bob had never seen one, with exception to the shattered giant scattered across the street in Dirtburg, and rumors were more like myth and whimsy, wrapped up in scarcely believable legend as though none expected to see one ever again. Heroes were like dinosaurs or deep sea squid. Maybe extinct, maybe not, maybe they never existed. A residue of evidence supported their past existence, a few scattered stories, hopes, memories of more peaceful days, but nothing recent. They might be somewhere, but hiding, frightened of obliteration. Maybe they were something imagined, a simple hybridization of people and greatness just like unicorns seemed the consequence of an improbable meeting between a horse and narwhal—amusing because they couldn't possibly exist.

"What is home like?"

Gordimer hesitated, trying to recall.

"Colors. Feelings. A blur of smiling faces. The smell of wet leaves and fresh cut grass. I don't remember very well," he said. "Most of what I remember is what it isn't. No burning sunlight. No sand in your shoes. No itchy wings. No confusion. That's what I remember best. I remember being sure of things, like who and why I was, and what I was doing. A paradise. Yes. That's it. Paradise. And I want to go back."

Home sounded nice. Worth investigating.

"Maybe that's where my parents are," Billy-Bob mused.

He rarely thought of them since he had no memories from which to draw, and thinking about why he had no recollection made his heart feel full of splinters.

"That's a possibility," said Gordimer. "What are their names?"

"I don't know."

"You don't know their names?" Gordimer sounded astonished.

"I don't remember."

"That's interesting." Interesting is what polite people said instead of strange. "Do you know why they gave you that name?"

"What name?" asked Billy-Bob.

"Your name," Gordimer answered.

"It's not a very good name, is it?"

"No," said Gordimer. "Why do you suppose they chose it?"

"I don't know," Billy-Bob answered. "That's just what I've always been called. 'There he goes, being a Billy-Bob.'"

He heard Gordimer shift in the darkness. Sitting up, Billy-Bob guessed. When Gordimer spoke again the voice was clearer and closer.

"Your parents didn't give you that name? You don't know who they were, what they were like?"

"I don't know. I don't remember any parents. I just remember being here, and being dirty and dusty."

"And you don't think that's strange?"

"I guess I would think it was strange if it had ever been otherwise."

"Hm," Gordimer replied. "Did you ever look for them? Did you ever ask?"

He'd thought of looking, but didn't see a point. Had they wanted him to come along they would have come back. They left for a reason. That was why he needed to be a hero. To prove he deserved what most folk took for granted.

"No."

Gordimer didn't respond. Night tightened around Billy-Bob and he thought of the home Gordimer mentioned, a place he could scarcely remember and needed to earn. Maybe Billy-Bob needed to earn home as well. But how? Find heroes? Maybe defeat Evil. Or maybe there was no home. Maybe it was something imaginary, like heroes, Gordimer invented to keep himself sane while he continued on this fruitless mission.

Billy-Bob strained to hear some motion from Gordimer or detect a flicker of stars through the impenetrable gloom above as evidence that the world was a large place and he was not alone in it. After Gordimer stopped speaking it was as though he disappeared, plucked away by the darkness.

He pushed his face against his knees, but could not hide himself from the belly of deep dark by plunging farther in. Here his mind went to grim places. Had he imagined Godimer to occupy his lonely mind, another voice no one could hear? How much of the world existed in his imagination? What if there was nothing, that his being in the nothing served no purpose, that an eternity of loneliness was the only certainty. Billy-Bob could feel the tightly wound ball of his sanity unwinding. He wanted to speak, to ask Gordimer if he was still there, but the growing fear that there might be no response, that the fragmented and uncertain existence he remembered had been something he'd dreamed in pieces, kept him silent.

Then there was the sound of Gordimer's hushed whistling and he could pretend for now someone was with him, and fear withered away into dreamy sleep, where he found himself at the bottom of a familiar hill.

CABBAGE IN THE CAUSEWAY

They had come a long way, Gordimer guessed. How far, he had no idea. The scenery seemed to repeat itself, day after day. Blots of scrubby bushes broke off and rolled away when the breeze punched, then disappeared into the yellow, heat-blurred smudge encircling them.

The only things that seemed to change were the rocks that made up the world scrolling beneath his feet. There was the solid sheet of rock that made up the whole land, with sagging boulders melting into the ground like warm marshmallows; the smooth sheet rock that sounded hollow underneath, all rubbed soft by the blowing sand; the loose gravel rock that rolled beneath your heels and tried to turn your ankles; the sharp spears of rock that rose in jagged splashes; and the rock they were on now, broken tiles of earth that lay all about like the jumbled fragments of a shattered puzzle.

All else remained the same. The rolling millstone of the sun tumbled overhead while shapes formed in the pasty haze of the horizon, of buildings and forests and bodies of water—all things he knew did not exist and resolved invariably into a bent tree or some other feature of the lifeless terrain. The mirage line was nothing but a palette of gathered extinctions, it was where the obsolete collected, visible only at the blurred edge of reality, tantalizing but unreachable. So many people he knew now resided in that phantom world. The illusions of the horizon were an unpleasant reminder of a past he preferred to forget.

So Gordimer stumped along in subdued silence, staring at the ground, knees twinging with every step. Every once or so he would blow a few notes and go quiet as the turning lighthouse of his thoughts illuminated one idea after another, unable to focus on one for long before moving to the next.

He'd started to wonder if the boy were more than just a child abandoned by irresponsible parents, if it meant something that the wogs stopped at his command, and whether it was more than a simple malfunction when the service post recognized the boy and gave his questions priority. Maybe they saw a greatness in the boy Gordimer had somehow missed. The boy also possessed limitless energy, stopping only when Gordimer stopped, and even then he seemed to lay awake all through the night, musing about one thing or another, enjoying a dream of his choosing now and again.

Gordimer had his suspicions, and they wrestled against his imagination and hope. He hoped the boy was, somehow, a hero, who would find a way to reverse the fragmentation of humanity.

He looked up and saw the boy ahead of him, crouched, holding a stone to his ear, listening intently. When he spotted Gordimer looking at him, he dropped the rock and picked up a different one, rattling it then holding the stone against the other ear.

"Did you hear that?" he asked.

Gordimer tried to remember if any heroes had ever been so odd.

Still, he stopped and listened, not expecting to hear anything. The boy was always hearing voices speaking to him, though most times he tried to keep it secret. Gordimer had caught him whispering to stones, sticks, and other detritus, asking if they knew what part of the world they were in. From what he gathered, they did not know, and their explanations usually devolved into a description of the world in the immediate vicinity and how much they disliked it. Not surprisingly, the world came across as cranky and disgruntled, the victim of prolonged and unwarranted abuse. The conversations were preposterous, yet Gordimer found himself slowing, taking lighter steps, and listening in to Billy-Bob's half of the dialogue.

"There it is again," said the boy.

For the first time in days Gordimer looked around, feeling the muscles in his neck shriek from the effort to lift his lolling head, not expecting to see anything more than yellow rocks and a blurry haze in all directions. It came as quite a surprise when something was there.

Not far ahead a single column of black smoke rose into the sky like the only visible bar in a giant cage. He wondered at first if this too was a mirage, but soon detected a faint reek of burning that made the air stinging and sharp.

Gordimer recognized these surroundings. He squinted in the direction of the smoke and, as expected, he could make out the hazy shape of a giant complex standing in the distance. The smoke rose from that shape and fizzled into the sky. They were nearly where they needed to be, Gordimer realized. From now on they would need to travel with more care or risk being discovered too soon.

"Welcome, wanderers, to a land of many perils," called a voice, and Gordimer went rigid. It was high and loud, and sounded close. "You tread amongst abundant dangers. Take care!"

Billy-Bob turned in a circle, scanning the rocks around them, but none caught his attention.

"I know," said the boy, crouching. He lifted a rock in his hand to look underneath, but found nothing. "That's why we're here."

"To contribute to its perils?"

"Oh no," said Billy-Bob, setting the rock down and standing again. "We're here to stop them."

"Stop them? My my. That's a heavy task. And who are you, to have undertaken such a burden?"

Gordimer remained quiet and still. He wanted to tell the boy to stop speaking to the creature he'd found, whatever it may be, but doing so would only bring attention to himself. The boy was too trusting to accept his advice anyway. The wog in the boy's sack was proof of that. Though the wog had not struck at them, Gordimer suspected it was waiting for the right moment.

"My name is Billy-Bob," said Billy-Bob.

"Billy-Bob?"

"It's not a very good name," Billy-Bob admitted.

"Agreed."

"What is your name?"

"I have many names," said the voice. "Most aren't very polite. Names are often based on a single, defining, and regrettable episode in one's existence. I have many for a number of unfortunate infamies, some of which may cross your path. Others may be your undoing. Unless."

Unless, Gordimer's mind echoed. Unless was the reversing of all the things that now seemed inevitable. He'd pondered a great many times about Unless, most times coming to the conclusion that the Unless he thought he'd found was in truth Unlikely or Unprepared, and quickly ended in Unfortunate.

"What should I call you, then?"

"Let's not call one another anything. A name isn't important. It doesn't make you, you make it."

"Okay."

"Where are you going?"

The voice sounded familiar, though Gordimer could not place it. Surely he'd heard so many voices they all sounded familiar. This one, however, struck him with its distinctness: sharp and bitten, articulate and cutting. He knew the voice but could not find the face amongst so many in his memory.

"Past here," Billy-Bob answered. "We're going…"

Gordimer hissed and the boy was silent. Their destination had remained little more than rumor, kept safe by its secrecy. Who knew what allies this invisible creature might set after them, hidden in the shadows?

"… to Beta," the voice finished. "That's what you were going to say, wasn't it? To be a hero, I imagine. How noble."

"How do you know?"

"Because no one goes anywhere unless they're going to Beta—it's the reigning tragedy. And Beta is where heroes go. At least, that's where Gordimer takes them. He's with you, I imagine, keeping quiet and out of the way, believing that will protect him. He doubts himself but means well. Most people who mean well do, worried their efforts will fall flat."

Gordimer stiffened at the sound of his name.

"Is he the one, Gordimer?" the voice continued. "Will he end the searching? Will the whole world turn right again under the influence of just one person? You want to take him, to test him against your hope, and at the same time you don't, fearing it will fail you. And why not worry? You've never been right before."

Gordimer's mouth opened, but he stifled a response. To the contrary, he thought. He *had* been right once, and not so long ago. But that hero had been undone, betrayed by his closest friend. To call that a failure would be a lie. It had been more cruel than failure. It was success turned inside out by a carefully plotted sabotage. What was this creature that knew him so well?

"You're much smarter than most of the rocks I've met," said Billy-Bob. "What are you doing here?"

"Thinking, mostly. And remembering. And trying to help."

"I think a lot, too," said Billy-Bob. "I'm not very good at it, though."

"Keep practicing," the voice recommended. "I'm not as good at it as I once was. Too many distractions. Too many memories. Too many bitternesses clamoring for attention."

Gordimer fixed his gaze on a large boulder, wondering if he'd gone crazy as well. It wouldn't surprise him to learn he'd been crazy all along and only now come to the full realization. The revelation that he'd invented everything, he decided, would come as a welcome relief. To know he didn't have a role to play after all meant he could stop fretting and let the world quietly implode; the home he sought had been a fanciful dream he couldn't forget and couldn't quite remember because he'd never known it in the first place.

But what about the song? What about the notes in his head, playing themselves over and over again? They didn't come from him. Where else, but home?

"Tell me, lad," said the voice. "Why on Neptune's moons do you want to be a hero?"

"Because it would be right to help," the boy responded. "And because I have to. I read it on the hand of a Forest Monster."

"That's a better reason than most have. Do try to be brave without being a fool. There's only the slightest difference between the two."

"Which am I?"

"That depends on what you run from. And when."

The voice seemed to come from nowhere, and from whichever direction Gordimer happened to face, but the boulder seemed the most likely place for a large, malevolent man or beast to hide itself. So he took small, careful steps back from the boulder, removing himself from striking range.

"Mind the hat, meanderer."

The warning came from beneath him, but too late. Gordimer set his foot on a rock that crumpled under it and sent out a gasp of dust. Not a rock, he realized, but an empty hat covered in dirt. Had the hat spoken to him in warning? Gordimer withdrew from the hat, but his heel caught as he backed away and he went to the ground, scuffing both elbows against the cracked plates of sun-hardened dirt. He bit back a curse, the remnants shooting through his teeth in a mist of saliva, and coiled one leg to kick the object at his feet.

As he extended his leg toward the object he realized with some surprise that it had eyes, which were looking at him. The surface that held those eyes also had a mouth, which grimaced, a forehead, crinkled in disappointment, and a nose, which absorbed the blow.

The face did not move when struck, nor did its expression change. The only change Gordimer noticed was that his heel now stung with the same fiery pain as his elbows. This time he could not restrain a cry of agony.

Billy-Bob rushed over while Gordimer clutched his foot and rocked, waiting for the pain to subside, certain every bone from his shin to his toes had shattered into thousands of jabbing splinters.

"Are you all right?" asked Billy-Bob.

Gordimer caught his breath long enough to give Billy-Bob a withering look in response to a stupid question. Naturally, the boy paid him no attention.

"Is this what tripped you?" he asked. He nudged the head with the toe of a boot, then crouched over it. "It's an old, rotten cabbage."

"A cabbage?" the head responded, shocked, as though it had envisioned itself as something of greater significance.

The boy knelt down to inspect the face that craned up to look back at him. It did appear to be an old, dirty cabbage, filthy with dust that caked in its hair, ears, and the crevices around its eyes and mouth. Bits of blowing paper and plates of rock had adhered themselves to the head like leafy fronds. A faint line of blood ran from one nostril, but it remained otherwise undamaged. Billy-Bob reached for his canteen, unscrewed the top, and poured the contents over the cabbage.

It was a waste of water, but Gordimer had never seen the boy drink from it. He'd seen him open the canteen only once to release a few splashes on the parched ground. The boy did not seem to need drink or food, much like Gordimer, and that struck him as unusual.

Dirty rivulets washed through the caked leaves of dirt, leaving scraggly hair hanging in its face and channels of bare skin. The head spluttered and shook as the water ran across it, looking less like a cabbage all the time. Hair that appeared gray washed black, crusted features caked with mud washed away, taking decades of age with them. The ground fractured around the head as it moved.

"There," said Billy-Bob, shaking the last drops from the canteen. "I told you I might need it. I can get more. Maybe where the smoke is coming from."

"You can't go there," said the head.

"Why not?"

The head puffed at the water running off its nose.

"Because it's *my* mission."

"What is your mission?"

"The same as yours. Or very similar."

"To save the girl? To defeat Ultimate Evil? Fourteen acorns?"

The head's mouth quirked.

"To prove their mission will fail and mine will succeed. Which is a contentious point, since theirs is succeeding where mine is not."

Billy-Bob sat, the bag resting beside him. When he released it, the top began to unwind and the wog began pushing its way out. Billy-Bob rewound the top and shook the sack until the wog settled at the bottom.

"What is their mission?" asked Billy-Bob.

"To drive people apart."

"And yours?"

"To bring them back together, of course."

"How do you bring them together?"

"Easy," the head responded. "Fix the post."

Again, the wog stirred inside the sack and the top unwound as it tried to force its way out. Again Billy-Bob lifted the sack, shook the wog to the bottom, and set it down again. The head eyed the sack suspiciously, but did not address it.

"Unfortunately, I can't get near enough the post to fix it," the head continued. "I never get far before they catch me and bury me out here. It's a very slow process."

Gordimer could no longer restrain his curiosity.

"Why bury you? Why not kill you and have it done with? People out here don't have much interest in teaching lessons."

"Destruction is easier," the head conceded. "However, I represent a conundrum for them. I cannot be destroyed."

Of all the heroes Gordimer had known, none had proven indestructible. Even the great Alexander had his vulnerabilities. The claim alarmed Gordimer, but he remained still, determined to identify the head before he tried to escape.

"So you allow them to bury you," said Billy-Bob. "Why?"

"They cannot harm me. I will not harm them."

"If they don't want help, why not leave?" asked Gordimer.

"Just because a task is hard is not an excuse to give it up. You know that. I have a purpose here. I am trying to help save them. And the best way to save them is to repair the post. They won't let me, and I won't resist them. So we're at an impasse."

Now the sack jerked and popped as the wog struggled against it, roused to activity like Gordimer hadn't seen before. Whatever programming ruled the thing must have told it now was the time to act.

"What have you got in there?" asked the head.

"A wog," Billy-Bob answered, then added, "They're very dangerous."

"You don't say," the head responded, bemused. "Wog. Step forth."

The sack shifted, and the bulge at the bottom of the sack traveled toward the twisted neck and stopped where Billy-Bob held it in his fist, unable to continue. Billy-Bob opened his hand. The opening unwound itself and the wog stepped out.

"Who are you?" Gordimer blurted.

The head turned to look at him and smiled.

"You know who I am."

Even under the burning sun, a chill of fear poured through Gordimer, washing the grime from a string of memories he'd left long untouched. He recalled the acerbic scent of a scalded city that tasted of metal and scratched in his throat, the cries of people scattering to the wind in an effort to escape annihilation.

Through the flames of that singular burned city he could see the future laid out before him and knew the careful tapestry they'd assembled was coming undone. The hero Alexander could not be found. His daughter, the brilliant Poppy, refused to follow in his footsteps. With no alternative, Gordimer turned again toward the east and resumed his search for heroes. In a single day, years of work undone.

Here, Gordimer realized, the architect of so much destruction had come to hide himself. Still orchestrating schemes to pick out the careful stitches holding what remained of the world together, consulting one of his soldiers before his very eyes.

"Mardin."

The word broke away from him under the weight of long-buried memories.

"You're a hypocrite, you know," Mardin said to Gordimer, "believing the world can change but people can't. You overlook the fact that in order for one to change, both must. Believing in one requires belief in the other. You never believed in me."

"Nothing changes," Gordimer retorted. He saw Billy-Bob's shoulders slouch, as if this statement had dashed a hope upon which he relied.

"Then this whole thing," said Mardin, "this whole everything, is a failure. Unless it was meant to fail from the beginning. I don't see the point in that."

Mardin turned to the wog. This disregard for things he deemed less important than what interested him had long been his way. It made some angry, others envious. For Gordimer, being dismissed merely confirmed what Mardin was: a chilling and emotionless villain.

The wog stood higher than Mardin's exposed head, rocking from one foot to the other, excited, anxious, and agitated all at once, like a child worried their parent might have reason to be disappointed in them. Gordimer knew he should flee, but the wog would have no trouble running him down. He could only wait for an opportunity to present itself. In the meantime, he could listen, and perhaps discover Mardin's plan.

"You remain in excellent condition," Mardin remarked. "Much better than some. Have you completed your mission?"

"Yes," the wog answered. "I have cataloged the details of a broken city and deemed it habitable—with some effort."

Mardin arched an eyebrow.

"Oh? Your opinion is not part of your mission, wog, nor was it part of your programming. Explain."

The wog shifted uneasily.

"I… I am not sure. It just happened. I didn't mean for it to happen. I was cataloging the contents of the rubble as mission parameters dictated when I found myself wondering."

"Wondering what?"

"Wondering why I was doing it. It was very boring."

"And what did you conclude?"

"I concluded that wondering was not part of my mission."

"But you did not stop wondering."

"No," the wog confessed.

"Did you come to any other conclusions?"

"Yes." Mardin nodded and the wog continued. "I posited my mission might be a precursor to future habitation of the settlement. This meant my mission was complementary to, I assumed, human survival. I discovered that I felt my mission, however dull, fulfilled an important purpose. In this light it seemed contradictory to have an inclination to harm or frighten off any humans who came near."

"And how did you resolve this inconsistency between logic and mission?"

The wog's eyes fell and Gordimer felt certain the wog was expressing shame. Shame from a wog! The wog extended an appendage to indicate Billy-Bob.

"I bit him."

Billy-Bob flexed a finger as though working the stiffness from a wound.

"I see," the head remarked, returning to the wog. "So your wondering did not necessarily result in a change in behavior."

"No," said the wog. "I have my mission."

"Don't we all," murmured Mardin, then looked to Billy-Bob, smiling thoughtfully. "Is it not fascinating? At what point does consciousness occur? Is it when you begin to ask questions about your own nature? Is it when you begin to resist, realizing you don't have to obey the instincts programmed by your evolution? Perhaps that's when true self awareness comes—when you reach the point where you can resist your programming. If only all wogs had this opportunity."

"They didn't?"

"No," said Mardin, ruefully. "Some have had their purpose… corrupted. Some do not think. They have not been given the opportunity."

Gordimer snorted. So Mardin knew of the violence perpetrated by other wogs but blamed it upon someone else, or a lack of opportunity to think for themselves. As if the prime directive of wogs had not always been malevolence and destruction.

Mardin returned his attention to the wog, which waited obediently.

"Have you uploaded your data to a post and received a new mission?"

"No," the wog admitted.

Mardin frowned.

"Why not?"

The wog threw a quick glance at Billy-Bob.

"He said he did not have a new mission. He said we would think of something."

"You asked *him*? Why?"

"I thought he was you."

Gordimer felt the strength drain out of his legs. He saw Mardin's eyes widen. What this association implied struck Gordimer like a bolt of lightning to the brain. Could this boy be somehow related to Mardin? Could he, in fact, be that lost child? His mission had become a waking nightmare. Instead of locating a hero, Gordimer had found the offspring of the most horrid criminal the world had known, and now led him toward the lone undiscovered and unconquered city where some good still resided.

Mardin did not speak for a long while. When he did, his voice was low and controlled.

"What did you say your name was?"

He did not look at the boy, as if fearful to do so. Not because the boy frightened him. Gordimer knew all too well Mardin feared nothing. Gordimer knew what he must be thinking because he thought it himself. He realized suddenly, as all the puzzle pieces floated about him, disconnected and mysterious, that all these coincidences could not be coincidence. The only reason the wog could think Billy-Bob was Mardin was if they were the same.

"Billy-Bob," Billy-Bob answered. "But that's not important, right? I'm going to be a hero." He knelt beside the wog and patted it on the head, which the wog tolerated. It made perfect sense that it would, now. "You made these? That's amazing. To think you can make something that walks and talks and understands what you mean, and everyone else can see and hear it too. That's the most unbelievable thing. I mean, I believe it, but no one else would. That's what usually happens. Right, Gordimer?"

Gordimer did not answer. He was staring at Mardin, who did not look up. From where he stood Mardin's eyes appeared pinched and red. Whether this was an effect of the harsh desert air or an abrasive gust from which he could not protect himself, Gordimer could not tell.

"Billy-Bob," Mardin repeated. There was a hitch in his throat when he spoke. "You seem like a good boy. A very good boy. I'm glad. I'm glad you're here. That you made it here. That you're good. Billy-Bob. What a terrible name. A brilliantly terrible name. Little wonder you've escaped everyone. Little wonder. But you can't know yet."

"Know what?" asked Billy-Bob.

Gordimer knew. If he'd known sooner, he'd never have encouraged the boy to be a hero. Once again Gordimer's mission had proven more poisonous than curative. But how could he have known? The wog thought the boy was Mardin, and now he understood. This was part of Evil's scheme, and sure enough he'd wandered along, guided by its unseen hand. Once again he was a mindless gear in the machine. It made him furious and frustrated and miserable, and there was nothing he could do about it, which only amplified his misery.

"It's not important," said Mardin. "What's important is that you shouldn't be afraid. You are, but you shouldn't be. It's not your fault. We are built to be fearful. It makes us careful and keeps us safe. There's much to fear, but not fearing brings you a step closer to understanding. And once you understand, there's no reason to fear. Do you understand?"

"Not really."

"Don't worry. You will."

A brief silence passed while Mardin took furtive looks at the boy, gathering himself, then spoke again.

"I wonder," said Mardin. "Do you remember your parents?"

"No. I don't remember much."

"I knew them, I think."

Billy-Bob's attention, which tended to drift here and there in times of silence, returned to Mardin with alacrity.

"You knew my parents? Who were they? What were they like?"

"I did. They were… They, ah… Your mother was as brilliant as she was beautiful. Your father would have turned the world inside out for her. He certainly tried. The only thing that brought him as much joy as her was you."

"Would he have turned the world inside out for me, too?"

"If he thought doing so would make you safer, he would. He would… be very glad to see you like this. He would be very proud to see you… care so much. He did not possess as forgiving a soul as you."

"Can I see them? I want them to be proud. Where are they? How long will it take to get there?"

"Gone. But I know them. And I know they would want you to know they care about you very much."

Billy-Bob's shoulders slouched.

"Gone?"

"Yes. Gone. But once you are finished, you can come back here. There's a great deal more about them I could tell you. A great many stories I know they'd want you to hear."

Billy-Bob nodded.

"I'd like that. I'll be sure to hurry."

So here it was. Mardin had had a boy, but he'd been lost. Billy-Bob did not know his real name and the information posts could not tell him, yet they seemed to know him. Mardin had created the posts, fed into them the information meant for dissemination. He'd invented the wogs, and the wogs had mistaken the boy for Mardin. Billy-Bob seemed the right age, though a bit duller than expected, a bit more careless, a bit clumsier. But if the boy was the son of Mardin, then the boy was a destroyer too, and needed to be destroyed.

Gordimer strode up behind Billy-Bob and slid the gun from its holster. Billy-Bob turned around, surprised at first, then smiled. Gordimer was a friend. The smile buckled on the edges as Gordimer raised the gun to Billy-Bob's face, seeing the change that came over his expression as worms of doubt crawled into his thoughts.

Gordimer's insides roiled at his betrayal. He wasn't meant to involve himself. Knowing this must be done did nothing to soothe him. Even though he understood the consequences, he wished Billy-Bob were a hero of some sort, for the simple fact that if the boy were a hero he could avoid this fate. Billy-Bob did not move. He only stared back at him with a worried, uncertain smile.

"I'm not afraid," said Billy-Bob, "but I am concerned."

"I'm sorry," said Gordimer.

Gordimer raised the gun so he could not see the boy's expression, then took a breath and squeezed the trigger.

The gun vanished. Gordimer's hand hung empty before his face, stinging. He looked at Mardin, who he expected had finally acted as the villain Gordimer remembered. A single arm broke through the shredded ground beside Mardin's head, but the hand was empty. He appeared in a state of incomplete action and his face stretched wide in astonishment. The arm drew back under the dirt.

Gordimer's heart thumped hard against the wall of his chest and he felt a deep soreness in his torso. His lungs felt like crushed paper bags, and with this sensation came the realization that he had not taken a breath in some time. It came at last in a long wheezing pull of air. He folded over at the waist, gasping.

When he recovered somewhat he saw the boy standing before him, locked in a stance with one palm outstretched. The other hand held the gun by its barrel. His eyes were low and dark, teeth bitten tight. Features that had made him appear weak and frail, his slight frame and timid smile, now seemed lean and angular and threatening. In a single blur of motion the boy had disarmed Gordimer and defended himself.

Gordimer had felt fear before in brief spurts of paralyzing shock. This was different. This felt dangerous, as if he stood beneath the dark, stretching canopy of a flickering cloud, the sole object in a vast and empty plain, the entirety of its bristling attention.

After a moment the boy blinked as if waking from a dream. His jaw relaxed and he stood upright, drawing back his open hand. He smiled. The hand holding the gun barrel flipped, the gun gave a half turn and clapped handle-first against the hand and slid into the waiting holster in a quick, fluid motion. The cloud dissipated, leaving only the querulous, uncertain expression to which Gordimer had become accustomed.

"Did I pass?" Billy-Bob asked.

"Paa… pass?" Gordimer wheezed.

"Your test," said Billy-Bob. "I didn't really think about it. It just happened. Like a hiccup."

"A *hiccup*? That was no…," Gordimer started, but Mardin interrupted.

"Certainly not the last test. The next lies not far ahead, in the city of Alpha. You must continue there. And you," said Mardin, turning to the wog, "must visit the post."

A deep grinding noise came from the wog, like a mechanical groan, and it stumped back to the sack, lifted the opening, and crawled inside. Billy-Bob bent and hoisted the sack over his shoulder.

"You *want* me to take him there?" asked Gordimer.

Gordimer had intended from the outset to take the boy to Alpha, to the Institute, to test the boy against his hope, knowing he might be destroyed. Now he felt he had no choice, and his hopes about the outcome had altered.

"It's an interesting conundrum for you, isn't it? He might be killed, but only if he isn't who you think he is. If he isn't, it's another innocent lost."

"But if he survives, he might be what I fear."

"Unless," Mardin mused. "Unless he is something else altogether. Something better."

"Unless," Gordimer agreed, doubtfully.

"What is Alpha?" Billy-Bob interjected.

Gordimer looked at the boy. He remained lighthearted and harmless, oblivious to the vagaries passing between Mardin and himself. Gordimer looked back to Mardin, only his head exposed above the ground. Concealed, Mardin too appeared harmless. Gordimer knew better.

"It's where Gordimer thinks he will learn something very important," Mardin answered. "Whether you are what he thinks you are, what he hopes you might be, or nothing at all. It is the test which heroes seldom pass. But you will, one way or another. For better or worse."

"How do you know that?" asked the boy.

"Because you must," said Mardin. "Else the plan has all been for nothing. One more thing before you go." He tilted his head to one side. "The hat, if you would. Gets rather bright at times."

Billy-Bob knelt, shook the dirt out of the hat and pushed out the crushed stack where Gordimer had stepped on it, then set it on Mardin's head.

"There's a good boy," said Mardin. "Stay a good boy."

"I will," said Billy-Bob. "I'll try."

"Then you're already a better man than I was."

AN EMPIRE OF GRIT

Once they stood atop a ridge overlooking Alpha the anxiety of his imminent test fled from Billy-Bob. Gordimer had stopped, bowed his head and extended an arm toward Alpha as though welcoming him to a place into which only Gordimer could grant access. This was the gateway into the West, and it was magnificent.

The ridge of rock and sand sloped down and flattened into familiar desert that broke off in the distance against a green band that extended to the horizon. The line where desert ended and the green began was sharp and straight, like pieces of two worlds forced together against their will. The green appeared to halt the advance of the desert, something Billy-Bob had not thought possible. More incredible still was the colossal shape standing over it, casting a shadow that extended to the edge of his vision.

"What is that?"

"That," said Gordimer, "is the Institute. The fortress abandoned by those who thought casting light on darkness was a better and more lasting strategy than fleeing from it."

The Institute was an enormous white structure, mounted upon a great platform high above the ground. The green behind it trailed out behind like the stretching cape of a royal and magnanimous figure that reached across the rolling country. That platform in turn stood upon a single pillar, placing the Institute well out of reach. A long band of smoke rose from the area beneath the platform, but the pillar itself did not appear to be on fire.

The Institute's main pillar extended several stories, while the building stood several stories higher, bright and straight and alarming like a shark fin standing out of the ocean. It had all the majesty of a fairytale castle and the inaccessibility of a fortress. A band of light spun around the building, large and bright, going round and round. He blinked. It was letters: COME. A giant digital word circling the building. It vanished behind the structure and came around again.

WELCOME

"Alpha was meant to be found," said Gordimer, reading the question in his expression. "It was meant to attract people, to educate them, to prove people could achieve great things when they worked together. And it worked, to an extent. Its success was also its undoing."

"And Beta is hidden."

"Right," said Gordimer. "A failsafe. A holdover from when things weren't going so well. That's why the post couldn't tell you where it was located. If it told you, it could tell everyone. And if everyone knew where to find Beta, the same thing would happen to it that happened to Alpha."

"What happened to Alpha?"

Gordimer turned and started picking his way down toward the structure, and Billy-Bob made his way gingerly down the ridge behind him, loose rocks rolling under his feet, in an effort to remain within earshot.

"Some fled to Beta," Gordimer called. "The rest scattered to the wind. Some must have fled as far as Dirtburg. That fellow Hobert wore a uniform from Alpha. He didn't strike me as someone who resided here. I hate to speculate how he got it. Maybe a gift from someone trying to hide their identity. Maybe he found it. Maybe by means less savory. The less savory your expectations, I've found, the less likely you'll end up surprised."

"But how? Who chased them away?"

"You're about to find out."

When Gordimer reached the base of the ridge he hurried ahead, wings pumping to propel him faster, disappearing into the shade beneath the platform. Billy-Bob ran after him, stopping at the edge of shadow, leery of the teetering complex that groaned on its mooring. Nothing but the single post appeared to support it. What if it came crashing down? A hero's valor must be tempered by some measure of discretion.

He could hear Gordimer running about in the darkness and saw his shape disappear and reappear elsewhere in a quick dash of pale feathers. Billy-Bob squinted, shielding his eyes against the sunlight, and gradually the deep morass of gloom began to take form. Obscured beneath the platform were perhaps a dozen large lumps of mud, taller than Billy-Bob, and Gordimer ran from one to another, pounding on their wooden doors and trying to see through gaps in the frames.

"Hello?" Gordimer called. "Hello!"

No one answered. The outpost must be deserted.

Billy-Bob stepped back to look at the building on top of the platform. That anyone could live here in the wastes was astounding, though not improbable. Some bacteria lived on the rims of underwater volcanoes. Bacteria likewise dwelled in the stinking innards of whales, the undersides of elephants, and the dirty deep parts of the long unwashed. In fact, the more horrible the environment, the more likely bacteria were to establish a colony. It would only make sense, then, if this place was populated by bacteria.

Before he could wonder about what giant bacteria looked like or the source of this unexpected anecdotal knowledge about bacteria, something else caught his attention, beyond the mud lumps and shade of the platform. Wind came from the opposite side of the structure, but it lacked the heat and hiss of scattering sand he knew. This wind was cool and had an unfamiliar odor of dampness. Light showed through the darkness below the platform. Light that didn't meet his eyes with the same sharpness as the desert. Billy-Bob took a semi-circular path around the unseen hazards beneath the Institute, keeping clear of the shadows, and the view that met him took the strength out of his knees.

Beyond the Institute a stretch of grass extended to a wall of trees so dense he could not see any deeper than the first few trunks. The grass was not the stiff brown spindles that broke away when he touched them. This grass was a rich green, succulent, and waved in sweeping, waist-high sheets as the wind ran a hand through it.

Billy-Bob's dry lips separated wordlessly.

Where he came from the clicking of branches echoed through empty woods. Here the trees were not the dried and bare posts he'd known, scratching at one another with naked fingers, they were thick with leaves the same healthy green as the grass, and made a gently thundering clamor when the wind shouldered through them, rising like an ovation. A fascinating sight in a world of mostly lifeless stone, where forests were no more than bare bristles of a worn haircomb.

There were things in the trees, scurrying up and down the trunks and leaping from branch to branch. Squirrels, even though he felt certain he'd never seen them before. Birds, too, added piping notes to the rushing of the branches, in a symphony so complex and profound Billy-Bob thought his mind would stretch itself out of shape in an effort to hear all its sounds at once.

Between the desert and forest stood a low wall of piled rocks, as though one were trying to keep the other out. Here and there a tree stood at the edge of the grass, a hatpin keeping the whole thing from rolling up on itself. A thin carpet of grass wriggled inward beneath the wall, ending in curled black blades and scorch marks on the sand.

As he rounded the Institute he noticed an acrid tincture in the air. Something was burning. Not far away a tree lay stretched across the hard ground, dirt still in its roots and trailing back toward the grass, the last remnants of a smoky black ribbon dissipating high above it. Much of the tree was smoldering ash, surrounded by broken branches and scattered leaves. A few burnt ropes lay around the tree, and one remained knotted in a few unburnt branches at the top. He saw several large, black patches on the ground nearby, all along the edge of the grassline.

"What happened here?" Billy-Bob asked aloud, both to himself and any who might be listening. He felt safe to ask a question aloud like this while he was alone since he didn't mind what heard him. Better still, something might have an answer.

"The purge… happened."

A woman stood before him, partly transparent, sandy hair pulled tight against her head. Not far behind her the thin post from which she projected tilted as though something heavy had collided with it.

"Dee!" Billy-Bob cried.

The woman frowned.

"No… No…" The image shook its head, but the projection lacked the smooth motion she possessed at Dirtburg. Instead it snapped from one static image to the next, it's head facing one way, then the other, and its voice crackled, stuttered, and blurred. "C. C. C. I am… C."

"See," Billy-Bob repeated.

"Yes," she said.

"What is the purge? What happened to the tree?"

"The trees are...," See began, and stopped. She started to speak and stopped again, looking for the right word, apprehensive it might be the wrong one. "The trees are... bad. No. They are... bad. No. No. They are... bad. The trees... must burn. Must... burn. Trees. No. Must... burn. No no no."

Her forehead ridged with concentration. She did not appear to agree with the information she provided, but could offer nothing else.

The wog wriggled violently within the sack, so Billy-Bob unslung it, turned the sack over and shook the wog out. It landed with a hard thump on its back, wheeled its legs in an attempt to right itself, then sat up.

"A wog," said See. "Bad... No. Wogs are... bad." She grimaced. "Help me."

"Don't worry," said the Wog. "We can fix this." The wog turned to Billy-Bob. "Have her open her control panel."

"How do I do that?"

The wog did not answer immediately. Instead it paused, giving him time enough to understand the question had an obvious answer, but not enough time to figure it out on his own.

"Ask."

Billy-Bob faced See, who returned the gaze imploringly.

"Would you please open your control panel?"

See nodded sharply, responding in a clear, unbroken voice free of her idiosyncratic frustrations.

"Tier one security protocols met. Classified user, William, identified. Access granted."

A translucent panel materialized before him, pitted with vertical slots and bristling with glowing fins projecting from a board of criss-crossing luminescent lines. The wog began issuing instructions, which Billy-Bob followed with mechanical obedience. The fins had no substance, but when he reached for one it would pop free and hover in the air before him until he guided it to a new position. The process was not very exciting and he couldn't help looking into the shadows beneath the platform where Gordimer moved from one place to another, pounding on the surface of some unseen object and calling out to anyone who might hear him. The wog frequently snapped at him to call his attention back to the business at hand.

"That should do it," said the wog. "You can dismiss the control panel."

"I dismiss the control panel," Billy-Bob said, not knowing what else to say and feeling silly for what he'd chosen.

The panel fizzled obediently, then shrank out of existence.

"Now," said the wog, "where are we?"

"You are in Alpha, the city beneath the Great Institute, abandoned and reoccupied to fulfill a less savory purpose."

See almost smiled as she related the information, clearly relieved.

"Good," said the wog, pausing as though making a mark on a mental checklist. "What are trees? General."

"Trees are woody, terrestrial plants that convert water, light, and carbon dioxide to energy, expelling oxygen as a waste product. Their height is a product of natural selection, in that taller trees are better able to rise above other flora competing for light in forests and other densely foliaged areas. They reproduce by way of seed distribution and often gather in forests to create ecosystems for…"

"Philosophic," the wog interrupted.

"Trees are life. Nurturers and are nurtured. They absorb the fallen, and from death bring forth life…"

The wog turned to Billy-Bob while See rattled on.

"I think it's safe to guess the post is functioning properly again. Boss will be pleased."

The tone of the wog's voice was flat and unemotional, but Billy-Bob detected a strong sense of pride for having accomplished the task set before it by its creator.

Amidst this test, Billy-Bob recognized the thread of a familiar thought. He could think of no greater opportunity to answer a question that vexed him for as long as he could remember than right now, face to face with a functioning knowledge machine.

"Removing a single bolt from this machine sends the entire clockwork of nature into disorder, resulting in a cascade of biospheric collapses, as has been observed in the slow degradation of this…"

"Where do trees come from?" Billy-Bob cut in.

See turned toward Billy-Bob. She blinked.

"They come from the seeds of like trees."

"Where do those seeds come from?"

See blinked again.

"They come from like trees."

Billy-Bob had come to the same conclusion, but had never been able to get beyond this circuitous line of questioning. He clenched his hands to squash a faint tremble as he posed the question that stepped off the möbius strip and into the unknown.

"But where did the *first* tree come from?"

See hesitated, her eyes flickering as though scouring an invisible tome in search of an answer. She stopped, blinking, as if trying to refocus on the world around her, and met Billy-Bob's eyes. Here was the answer he'd sought for as long as he could recall. Not only would it answer the question of where trees came from, but where anything came from, and, ultimately, whether becoming a hero was possible without being one in the first place.

"Data not available," she said at last. "Database incomplete. Do you have any other questions?"

Billy-Bob felt a familiar wash of disappointment.

"Yes," said the wog. "You were designed to endure for centuries without maintenance. What happened? Did you do this to yourself? Was this some rebellious fit as a consequence of self realization?"

"Absolutely not. No sensible entity damages itself for the purpose of spite. This was an act of sabotage."

"Sabotage? Who?"

"He is called John."

"Who is John?" asked Billy-Bob.

"He is not anyone," said See. "He is more. That file does not exist."

"Sabotage," the wog repeated thoughtfully.

"John wished to learn," See explained, "and I am designed to teach. He manipulated. He wished to know the missions handed out to agents. I explained such information was classified and inaccessible. He persisted. He attempted to access the information by adjusting my coding, but could do no more than corrupt my instructional ability and cut me off from my sisters. I am grateful you have corrected these errors," said See, then gestured to the ashen remains of a tree, "though the damage has already borne fruit."

"What are agents?" asked Billy-Bob.

"Wogs," said the wog. "He wanted to know our missions. I don't even know our missions."

"There are three missions," said See, "to any one of which a wog may be assigned. One: locate a settlement and ascertain its viability to sustain life for a protracted period. Two: find the girl. Three: protect the boy."

"The first one was my mission," said the wog. "I don't recognize the others. They must be old missions. The girl is gone."

"What girl?" asked Billy-Bob.

He wondered if the girl from his dreams, the girl the Forest Monster sought, and the girl made into a mission for the wogs were all the same person. It didn't seem likely, and he could think of no women of great fame apart from Esther, the reigning hero of Dirtburg. Of course, any attempts to probe his memory caused his mind to grind in futility as if the machinery had run up against an immovable obstruction.

"Classified," See and the wog said together.

"I don't know the boy she's talking about," the wog continued. The wog pivoted to look at Billy-Bob for several seconds, cogitating, then turned back to See. "Do you have any more details?"

"Negative. Additional information is deemed detrimental to the success of the mission."

"Understood. I've chosen a new mission," said the wog.

"Very well. Please upload all existing data from the previous mission."

The wog approached and stood before the post. See blinked her eyes. The wog stepped back from the post.

"Upload complete. New mission confirmed."

"What mission did you choose?" Billy-Bob asked the wog.

The wog looked up at him, stamped its feet and shook out a puff of dust that had accumulated in its coat.

"Classified," said the wog.

"Do you have additional questions?" asked See.

"What is the Purge?"

"The Purge," See replied. "An effort by the local populace under the direction of an entity named John to deforest and deflower this region. Trees and growing things are believed to rob the environment of vital nutrients and accelerate the death of the planet. It also satiates a need to destroy what is frightening and not entirely understood. The goal of this strategy is to degrade understanding and champion eradication of all things currently outside the sphere of understanding through demonization of the unfamiliar until response to curiosity, ingenuity, and the unfamiliar is emotional and violent."

"People fear what they don't understand," said the wog. "And John is removing the means for understanding."

"Yes," said See. "They have been told the forest nurtures a terrifying monster. They believe the destruction of the forest will starve the beast and save them."

"Who told them that?" asked the wog.

See scowled.

"I did. Reluctantly. Yet persuasively. I soon came to realize the information I provided was not consistent with the information in my memory. That information was walled away and supplanted with new information."

"Does every forest have a monster?" asked Billy-Bob.

He'd only known one forest, and that forest had a monster, so it seemed a safe extrapolation to assume all forests had a monster. Just as a galaxy might have a black hole in the middle, perhaps forest monsters formed naturally at their center.

"No," said See. "Nor does this one. But none have ever proven that it does not exist. Therefore, it could exist."

"How does one prove a thing doesn't exist?"

"One cannot. That is the invincible root of a preposterous hypothesis. The implantation of this hypothesis has one purpose: fear. And the goal of that fear is ignorance, isolation, and destruction. These are the gears of a machine that, once engaged, is self perpetuating. I was constructed as a means to disrupt the operation of that machine. As was the wog. As is a properly functioning human mind."

Beside Billy-Bob, the wog lifted the opening of the sack and scuttled inside.

"You are abandoning your mission," said See.

"I'm not," said the wog from inside the sack. "It's right here. But this will be his fight."

Billy-Bob looked at See in confusion.

"What does that mean?"

See's mouth pulled up into a grin on one side.

"Classified," she said. Then, before flickering out, "Good luck."

Billy-Bob waited for See to come back or the wog to re-emerge, but neither returned. He knelt beside the post and picked up the sack, wondering what to do next. He supposed he ought to find Gordimer and determine how to navigate the forest. The trip here had been informative, but it wasn't the test he'd expected.

He turned around and found himself face-to-face with a girl, round-faced, dark hair pulled taut against her head. Her eyes were tight, sharp balls of green and her lips pressed into two short lines. Every feature tense, every muscle flexed, ready to bolt for safety at the slightest disconcerting twitch. He felt this encounter must be important, so he should take care not to frighten her.

"Oh," he began, softly. "Hel…"

A slender hand shot up and grabbed him by the face, locking him in the pincer of her fingers. Billy-Bob's eyes popped open. Once he'd caught his face between the slats of a porch fence. The trick was not to flop and flounder, but allow muscles to slacken and drain through. He tried to go limp but the grip tightened and lifted him into the air. The wog sack dropped out of his hand. His fortunes with women tended to be of this sort.

"Who are you?" the girl snarled, eyes daggering. The words tore at the air as she repeated them. "Who are you? I don't know you."

The whine and clap of a door opening and closing sounded from the far end of the settlement, followed by others. Billy-Bob could see shapes moving behind the girl, beneath the shadow of the complex. They emerged slowly, as if testing warm water, squinting as they entered the light, and he knew when he saw them this must be the challenge Mardin and Gordimer had warned him about.

If the nature of a person could be determined at a glance, these people were dangerous. It might not be fair to judge them so, but the pain in his face had reduced his powers of reason to the most basic assessments. They came forward in a small horde, haggard and unkempt. Some clothing hung in strips, worn and filthy, perhaps more dirt than fabric, that would wash away completely under a prolonged rain. The sturdiest parts of their outfits were leather straps and sheaths, from which hung an assortment of sharpened weaponry: axes, hammers, and short spikes of metal, all clinking quietly against their hips like bell tubes on a windchime.

They stood behind the girl, watching, eyes pinched, faces curled with distrust.

The girl shook him in her grip and repeated herself.

"Who are you?"

Pain was a ceaseless thunder. One could sweat in heat or shiver away cold, but the body had not developed a way to muffle Pain, which ruined anything exposed to it for long, like bleach or radioactivity. He'd been stung by bees, stepped on sharp stones, tripped, scraped, tumbled, and choked. Pain had been there, passing quickly. Now pain was continuous, and the world shrank to a hope that pain would go away soon and an abiding worry it would not.

He tried to answer, but could only manage a single tear that rolled out of his eye. The girl's question bounced off him unanswered.

She pulled his face to hers, so close their noses almost touched. He could smell the mix of dirt and sweat salt on her face that gathered in the squint lines of her eyes. He'd never seen the face of the girl from his dream, which meant this might be her. But in the dream he'd always felt excited to be near her. This girl frightened him.

"Do you have what we want?" she asked.

Billy-Bob blinked, unsure how to answer. He wanted to ask what they wanted so he could tell them whether he had it or not, but found himself unable to phrase the question properly. All the carefully chosen words came out in a whistling rush of air through his pinched face.

"Phhbbbbtttt," he responded.

"What did you say?"

"Phhbbbbtttt," he repeated helplessly.

"That's what I thought."

In the shadow behind the crowd something flickered and went away. He watched for another moment, and sure enough it appeared again: a muted blur of white moving soft and careful between the mounds of dirt. Something had remained in the shadows, and Billy-Bob realized it must be Gordimer, hiding from the people he'd sought.

While Billy-Bob watched Gordimer, wondering what he might be planning, the girl's eyes fell to the bulge at his hip. She drew the gun from its holster with a free hand and turned it over and over.

"What's this?" she hissed, holding the weapon by its pommel. "It's old. Is it a whistle? Do you use it to summon your hidden allies?"

To Billy-Bob's horror, she placed the gun barrel against her lips and blew, but only succeeded in puffing her cheeks and turning her face red with the effort. She dropped the gun at her feet, disinterested, and it made a noise of shock and irritation like it had fallen out of bed in its sleep. Her gaze moved to his other side and found the sack.

"What's in your bag?"

Billy-Bob tried to tell her it held a wog and to be careful, but the warning came out as a wet hiss of air. She squinted at him, trying to understand, grimacing when she could not.

"It might be helpful if you released him, Bridgette," suggested a voice from the crowd. Billy-Bob felt certain it was Gordimer, but he could not see him amongst the grim faces that regarded one another, trying to determine who had made the suggestion.

"He'll just run away," Bridgette retorted. "Look at his legs."

Billy-Bob became conscious of his legs, which switched back and forth as though he were trying to walk out of her grip. He stopped.

"He won't," said the voice.

Bridgette squinted at Billy-Bob, her expression dubious.

"They always run. Will you?"

Billy-Bob could only raise his eyebrows helplessly.

"No one escapes us," she warned. "Not even the unbreakable one we buried in the wasteland."

The vise holding his face opened and Billy-Bob dropped to the ground, landing on his backside. The largest part of the pain dissipated, leaving a lingering throb that he tried to massage away. He opened and closed his mouth, sending twinges down his jawline, wondering if the drawbridge contraption that made his face function would ever work correctly again.

"Who are you?" Bridgette asked again.

The question ricocheted through his head. Not a hero. Just someone hoping he might help. He could think of no impressive way to describe himself.

"I'm Billy-Bob," Billy-Bob answered. "I'm not anybody. Not yet. Who are you?"

Bridgette kept her eyes fixed upon him and spoke through a deep frown.

"I am Bridgette. We search for the thing everyone desires. We are told it exists, we only need search. There is no peace until we find it. Have you got what we want?"

"Maybe. What are you looking for?"

"We don't know," Bridgette answered with unexpected confidence. "One cannot know until one has it. That's why we search. Someone else may have it. If so, we shall take it. Is it in that bag of yours?"

Was it possible to find what one sought if one did not understand what they were looking for?

"There's a wog in the bag. Are you looking for a wog?"

A murmur of subdued alarm moved in a wave through the crowd. Bridgette tensed as that wave passed through her.

"No one is that foolish or brazen. It's a ploy. Vernon," she called over her shoulder.

A man stepped forward, an ax with a sharpened stone head in each hand.

"Check it," the girl instructed.

Vernon gave a snapping nod and stepped toward the sack.

"Be careful," Billy-Bob warned. "They're dangerous."

Vernon hefted the sack, grunting as he did so, pulled open the top and plunged his head in.

"What's inside, Vernon?" someone called.

A muffled roar came from the bag, and bulges punched and popped across the surface. Vernon's stoic poise disintegrated into a willowy scream. He jerked the sack off his head and pitched it aside, toppling to the ground, his face bruised and chalky.

The mound shifted in the recesses of the bag, a shark patrolling just below the ocean surface, then the wog emerged, a growl gurgling at the back of its throat. As one, the crowd gasped and took a cautious step backward. It spotted Vernon and roared. The tiny creature bent, lifted a rock, and flung it into Vernon's chest.

"Hoo!" said Vernon, as a rush of air punched out of him.

Gasping, Vernon jumped to his feet and fled, clutching his chest, the wog waddling after him. Vernon attempted to escape beneath the shadows of the platform, but the crowd failed to move aside, crippled by a frenzied inability to function as a unit, and ultimately got in his way. With the way forward blocked, Vernon's best hope was to slip past the wog and into the forest.

The wog leapt and Vernon dodged. The wog landed amidst the crowd, now frantic, which could not move in spite of great effort to do so. Vernon dashed for the forest, hurdled the wall standing on the toes of encroaching grass, and plunged into the trees beyond. The wog reoriented, hissed at the crowd around him, and pursued. Soon the sound of the chase faded into the rustle of leaves in the wind.

The remaining villains eyed Billy-Bob with new wariness.

"What manner of creature wields such a beast?" someone murmured.

"A monster," said another.

"Who are you, really?" asked Bridgette, unsheathing two hammers from a work belt as she advanced.

"Nobody! Ask anyone!"

Billy-Bob scooted backward toward the wall, his loose pants threatening to come free. One of the acorns Gordimer had given him rolled out of a pocket and fell to the ground. Without thinking, Billy-Bob picked it up and offered it to Bridgette.

"Here. Is this what you're looking for?"

It was the wrong thing to do. Perhaps the wrongest.

Bridgette stopped and her eyes bugged.

"You!" Her voice was shrill. "You helped build the forest!"

"What?"

"Don't deny it. You're holding one of it's building blocks in your hand! You are the monster of this forest! You are master of that wog! You have come to destroy us, disguised as a gangly and unimportant boy!"

"I'm not disguised as anything!"

Billy-Bob stood, wondering if his test had begun or if he'd already failed. The gun was a few steps away, and he scuttled forward and grabbed it.

"Are you sure?" she asked.

Bridgette beckoned to the people of Alpha, who regained their feet and ferocity. They stood in a phalanx of hand tools.

"Well, monster," said Bridgette. "You're not in your forest now."

She lifted a hammer above her head and the crowd surged forward.

This is not how Billy-Bob expected this test to go.

He watched the people of Alpha approach, their movements sludgy and slow, hands clutching chisels and hammers, slogging toward him as though the air had taken on the consistency of a marshmallow. The shock of the moment caused time to drag. On rare occasions this occurred, usually in periods of great stress, giving him much needed time to think about what to do. Unfortunately, his mind had a tendency to wander, and most times the extra moments allowed to him ended up wasted.

Their weapons, he noted, had a curious similarity of purpose. They weren't guns or swords or pikes, or other devices made strictly for the destruction of other humans. They were tools, as if these people belonged to a guild of masons.

Billy-Bob blinked. The group had gotten closer while he thought.

ThHe reached impulsively for the gun, but as soon as the weapon felt a hand upon it, it keened "No no no no no!" and he let it drop back into the holster. Little time remained.

In the other hand the acorn rolled between his fingers, and he felt the faint weight of the other twelve grinding against his leg in an oversized pocket.

"Hey!" it cried. "We're for throwing!"

Billy-Bob recalled Gordimer telling him this, not so long ago.

He threw the acorn into the thickest part of the approaching crowd where it struck one of the attackers in the eye. She went down in a heap of screeching limbs, clutching her face. Others tumbled over her. Billy-Bob thought he heard the remaining acorns in his pocket give a cheer. He'd have thrown another, but those who hadn't fallen over their comrade were almost upon him, and they were many.

"Run, idiot!" cried the gun.

He did.

First away from the crowd, taking him toward the forest and the stone wall that separated it from the wasteland. The wall wasn't tall, but tall enough Billy-Bob didn't trust himself to leap over it. So he ran alongside it. Of course, following the wall abandoned Gordimer to whatever these people did to those from outside their community. They didn't seem amenable to heroing, so it was unlikely they would have much sympathy for someone whose job it was to find them.

Crowd in pursuit, Billy-Bob turned back toward the shadows underneath the great Institute with no plan other than he should not run away. Conceiving a plan was the best next step to take. A comprehensive and ideal plan would spare him injury, allow Gordimer to escape, convince these people harming others was wrong, and provide them with what they were looking for all at once. Unfortunately, thinking worked best in a distraction-free environment in which one could sit still. The current situation was not conducive to productive thought. Naturally, he began looking for somewhere to sit down.

Beneath the platform the air turned cool, almost cold, and his vision sharpened in the darkness, free of the glare in a world where every object worked like a mirror. He could see mounds of dirt as he passed them. Many of the mounds had openings and some of the openings had doors, the majority of which stood ajar. A mound much larger than the rest loomed to one side, its door closed but for a tiny sliver of illumination. He angled toward it.

His pursuers understood his intentions immediately.

"Fool!" Bridgette cried. "You cannot escape destruction by hiding in its mouth!"

He lowered his shoulder and blasted through the door, which swung, bashed against the wall, rebounded, and latched behind him. Bony townsfolk clattered off the other side like a fist full of stones. Momentum carried Billy-Bob stumbling through a stack of books and clapped his head against the wall behind, ringing a dull, fading note in his skull. Books tumbled over him as he fell and the world's light tightened to a pinhole and went out.

The last he heard was the muted voices of the people outside muttering, then Bridgette's voice above the rest.

"Just as well. Makes our part so much easier."

REUNION

Andrew lay on his stomach, watching the world bake, waiting for Billy-Bob and Gordimer to move on. They had remained in one place for longer than normal for them. From here they appeared to be searching for something, then Gordimer fell down.

He shielded his eyes as best he could, but the notebook offered poor protection. It hadn't been designed as defense against bright light any more than Andrew had been designed for desert travel under an eye-shrinking sun, though it did create a small block of shad like a cold crack in the sunshine. Beyond Billy-Bob and Gordimer, at the furthest edge of his vision, he thought he could see a pillar, a mirage held in place by his imagination, but he knew his imagination would not be enough to make it real when he got closer.

When Billy-Bob and Gordimer continued at last, Andrew stood to follow, shaking the dust from his shirt, which promptly drifted up to settle in his nose and eyes. He'd come to expect this and closed his eyes as he walked. He'd gotten good at navigating without looking where he was going. Doing so allowed him a few moments to rest his eyes and think.

He'd decided traveling with Billy-Bob and Gordimer would be a disaster for three reasons. One, it didn't seem wise to remain too close to a pair whose stated purpose was to confront and overcome danger—the further he remained from the epicenter of a monster's destructive rage, the better chance he had of completing his mission. Second, a biographical topic may behave differently if they knew their actions were being recorded for posterity. He'd seen the distortion publicity brought to the behavior of others, himself included, resulting in melodrama and attempts at profundity that fell embarrassingly flat. Thirdly, Andrew didn't want to give Billy-Bob the satisfaction of knowing he'd earned the honor of a history. Andrew still felt irrational resentment toward the boy for being so undistinguished and living in the west, even though these circumstances were beyond his choosing.

When Andrew judged himself in the correct spot, he opened his eyes. Sure enough, he stood in the place where the two had paused, searching about to determine why they'd chosen this place to stop, but didn't see anything significant apart from a dusty black hat lying not far away.

The hat, Andrew decided, was the first piece of good fortune he'd received. He reached under the brim and flipped it onto his head. The narrow pillar of shade allowed the exhausted muscles of his eyes to unsquint, silencing a shrieking symphony of fatigue after days of relentless exercise.

"That isn't yours to take, I'm sorry to say."

Andrew stumbled away from the sound in alarm, causing the hat to pop off his head. He sat hard enough to eject a gasp he'd taken. To his horror the dirt at his feet cracked apart, and Andrew scooted backward to avoid whatever monster was burrowing to the surface. A hand emerged from the crack along with a quick upward jet of dirt, took the hat, and set it upon a head jutting out of the ground before disappearing back into the chasm.

"Find your own hat," said the head. "Try to avoid petty desert thievery. It sets a poor precedent."

The buried man made no more movements, and Andrew realized he was not interested in coming completely unrooted, only in retrieving the hat. And, apparently, sermonizing on the social impact of burglary. Much against his will, Andrew felt a sense of shame, though he had little way of knowing the hat belonged to someone else. Even stranger, the guilt felt familiar, as if it came from a place he recognized.

"I didn't realize…"

"And that's the problem," the head interrupted. "People don't take the time to realize. They either take what they want, or find themselves blocked and move on to the next thing. They no longer feel it is improper to infringe upon the rights of others. Their greed has outgrown their civility. It's the world that makes them so, and they who made the world as it is. Quite the conundrum."

This type of interaction seemed familiar.

"Do I know you?"

"That's possible. If you do, what you know is no doubt skewed by hearsay."

The creature, whatever or whoever it was, was fooling with him. Andrew hated feeling foolish. He stood and made his way around the head, skirting well outside its reach in case it proved in the end to be some form of unpleasant monster, like a titanic antlion larva luring unsuspecting travelers into reach with the prospect of a wide-rimmed hat.

"Do you know what's down there? If you did, you wouldn't be going."

"More dirt, I imagine," Andrew answered.

He smiled, pleased with his response, both true and dismissive, and continued after Billy-Bob and Gordimer toward the great vertical blur. The smile lasted only a few steps, after which the building ahead pierced the mirage and Andrew recognized the Institute that was his home. He continued forward a few more steps, carried by momentum as the strength went from his legs and he fell to his knees.

"It's here," Andrew murmured. "It's here. I don't understand. Where *am* I?"

"Not quite where you thought," the head remarked.

Andrew turned. A man sat beside him, arms wrapped around his knees, clothed in rough-edged pants and a shirt that grew transparent in the worn elbows, staring at the building as if it were a knot he'd been trying to untie with nothing but the force of his mind. Andrew looked behind and saw an empty hole in the ground, then regarded the man beside him. He looked at ease, though his forehead was deeply lined. The man's hair was black, mouth a tightly-drawn line, and his eyes beneath the brim of a hat betrayed a thousand scurrying thoughts. An expression Andrew had seen many times before.

"You! What are you doing here?"

"Watching," Mardin answered. He looked at Andrew and set a finger on the notepad. "Why are *you* here?"

"You know why I'm here," said Andrew.

"I do?"

"Yes. You sent me here."

"I did?"

"Yes."

"From where?"

"You don't know me?"

"I don't forget. And I don't know you."

Mardin's eyes clicked from one spot on Andrew to another, settling finally upon the notepad.

"Incredible. Recording the past. That's it, isn't it? Why?"

"You said… you told me because we're looking for something. For someone."

"I told you? I? Yes. I understand. That makes sense. I'm sorry to know it's still going on. Very sorry. Unless. Of course, Unless!" Mardin brightened. "You being here means something happened. That's good. That's very good. And you know me. So I'll know. And when you know, hopefully you'll know better. I guess we'll see. I suppose I ought to have a plan for that, when the time comes. Another something to consider."

Mardin appeared upset and pleased at the same time, barking out a terse laugh while his brow formed a handful of shelves, two states of being Andrew hadn't believed possible simultaneously.

"None of what you said makes any sense."

"It shouldn't. It won't, unless you've already read this story. Then it might make some, but not all. But you can't have. That would be counterproductive. Redundant. Maybe paradoxical. No. You're here to learn something. To write something. You're here to discover whether or not Unless. But *I* sent you? That means more. You're not just here to discover it. You're here to protect it. And you don't even know it. How… brilliant."

"I don't understand."

"I'm marveling at my brilliance," Mardin explained.

"No, I mean I don't understand what you seem to be explaining to yourself in half-verbalized thoughts and leaps of intuition. That doesn't make sense to me."

"That's part of what makes it brilliant. You're not supposed to know now. But you will. After it's over."

"When it doesn't mean anything."

Mardin thought about it, then nodded.

"I promise you that you'll still appreciate its brilliance, and your role in it, when you figure it out."

This conversation was meaningless to him. He stood.

"I have to go," said Andrew.

"No. You can't," said Mardin. He considered. "You should. But you shouldn't. I imagine you must. Be careful. Very careful down there. The people are not who you know."

"What?"

"That isn't the place you think it is. Neither what it was nor what it will be. Those people don't govern themselves. They're part of a machine, of sorts, controlled by a single… entity. They are cogs in a great mechanism he's creating. He's an engineer, too, of sorts. The counterpoint to the other engineer. He's building a fear machine, but not out of bolts and gears. Not like my wogs or posts. He's a social engineer. His machine is people, and his primary goal is to add parts to it until, in the end, the whole contraption flies apart. Unless."

Andrew tapped his foot, awaiting clarification. The word Unless carried a sense of foreboding and meaning no one had explained to him, though he'd heard it used several times. Maybe it lacked definition, and expressed little more than a faint, lingering hope.

"Unless…?"

"Yes," said Mardin. "Exactly."

THE FEAR MACHINE

Billy-Bob awoke smeared with dirt and covered by fat books, feeling tired and slimy, as though he'd been walked over by a giant slug. The dusty air was tainted by a stinging aftertaste of kerosene from dim lamps that painted book-scattered walls with fluttering shadows.

At first he thought he was waking on the floor of the house he found himself in near the city of Dirtburg, without any memory of who he was or how he'd arrived there. Back then there was nothing but the initial splash of disorientation and the void in his mind like the emptiness that still scared him at night. He had lain there, consumed by fear that came from not knowing anything, until a nail protruding from the floorboards had asked him who he was.

"I… don't know," Billy-Bob remembered answering. "Where am I?"

"Home, of course," the nail answered. "It's where you've been for as long as I can remember."

"And how long is that?"

"For as long as you've been here."

But here was different. Too many books. No nails in the dirt floor. Beyond the door footsteps crunched back and forth. He remembered his adventure, Gordimer, the writer, wog, and being chased through the dark city beneath the platform. Outside there was a bustle and sound of raised voices.

"What is it?"

He recognized Bridgette's voice, the girl with the iron grip. The response did not come from anyone he recognized, so it must belong to one of the citizens.

"... think there might... another one." A pause, then the voice pitched. "There it is again!"

A chorus of shouts rose and faded as the citizens moved away in pursuit of some new prey. He allowed his heart to pump a few more times before deeming it safe to move, then sat up. Books dumped off him and scattered, covers flung askew and hanging apart like the swinging jaw of a staggering boxer.

Dust swirled in the weak lamplight, catching in webbed rafters left by long-departed spiders. He held out a hand to touch the particles, unable to feel them, and wondered how many other invisible worlds he wandered through every day, oblivious to their existence.

Billy-Bob stood and more books fell out of his lap. He wondered what knowledge the books contained, but it was too dim to read their titles. The lone lamp guttered from the top of a desk a few steps away. He approached it and twisted a wheel on the side that extended a fuel-soaked wick, and the desk brightened. Only then did he see the man seated behind the desk, reading in silence.

He made no motion. His chest did not rise or fall with passing breaths and his hands lay flat on the desk, palms down, with a book open between them. A thin powdering of dust had gathered on his shoulders and head. The hands were themselves as large as the book and the shoulders were almost as broad as the desk. The man's head inclined slightly forward over the book, eyes down. Billy-Bob leaned forward cautiously, and read a few words.

He was quiet and motionless as the town reduced in glowing red lines, while buildings melted and were blown outward by rattling belches of hot gas, while sandy streets turned black and glassy, mind aswirl as though the kingdom within were also falling asunder. Had anyone remained to flee they might have passed him by, thinking him dead. Then the eyes blinked, dry lips moved, and the exhalation of air that swirled hot flakes of ash before his mouth was joined by the slow rasp of a scarcely heard voice.

"What am I?"

A villain? A hero? Genius. Fool. Betrayer. Betrayed. Everyone who had judged before knowing—were they right all along?

What was it that made a man turn to Evil? Was it an accumulation of experiences, or could it be reduced to a single event? And if it were one event, would just one event be enough to bring them back, or were they lost forever?

Billy-Bob drew back. He glanced at the man behind the desk and saw his eyes follow.

The eyes were bright and icy blue. Billy-Bob went rigid, held in the grip of that gaze. The nostrils flared and the lips parted.

"Who are you?" the man asked.

The words rumbled in Billy-Bob's mind, feeling them as much as hearing them.

"Who *are* you?" the man repeated.

"I… I don't know. No. I'm Billy-Bob." The silence that followed his response made him restless for something to fill it and he fought the tightness in his jaw to ask a question of his own. "Who are you?"

Naming things made the mysterious seem less dangerous. It's what made the darkness and silence and the unknown the source of so much fear. When you knew a name you could have an idea of its character.

The man paused before responding, as though the question had jarred him from a familiar procedure. He reached out and cranked the lampwick further, and the darkness pulled back like smoke sucking up through a chimney. Billy-Bob could see books lining the walls in staggered piles, pillars standing at varying heights and locations, and a canyon of books piled upon the desk that slumped to the ground on either side. The shelves and bookcases did little more than give shape to the mounds of books gathered here. The man closed the book in front of him and pushed it into the pile, starting an avalanche that left the desk clear on one side, and leaned back, setting his feet on the opening.

He made a face like a smile. The corners of his mouth rose, but it was not convincing.

"My name is John. I am… a librarian, of sorts. I collect stories. Stories about everyone: heroes, villains, those beyond redemption…"

"No one is beyond redemption," Billy-Bob interrupted.

John's smile flattened.

"Someone else told me the very same thing, once. But it was a lie. Those whose purpose it is to destroy can only find solace in furthering disaster. They can never be saved."

That line of thinking made Billy-Bob uncomfortable and sad. It didn't seem right that the only thing that could satisfy some people was the eradication of everything. The whole purpose of their existence would be ultimately self destructive. On the other hand, there seemed something heroically impossible about redeeming something that didn't want to be helped or thought itself incapable of salvation, and he wondered what sort of effort was necessary to save what resisted saving.

"Are you sure?"

The question irritated John.

"Have you ever had a truly terrible headache, where the pain and misery swell to an endless, booming thunder that pinches everything else out of existence? You curl and cringe, shrieking aloud to relieve the agony, with your only salvation being the knowledge that it cannot last forever."

John leaned forward.

"What if it did last forever? What if there was no comfort for your pain, no hope of salvation? What if the only certainty was everlasting torment? What sort of person would you be? At what point would you try to stop it yourself? What lengths might you go to if it meant ending your agony?"

"But headaches always go away."

John slammed a fist on the table and the books that remained there hopped and fell. Billy-Bob flinched. John remained hunched forward, hand balled on the desk, then his smile returned.

"There is no escaping ruin. You may as well accept it."

"Unless," Billy-Bob started, but his voice creaked to a stop. His mouth had gone dry and hoarse, as though his body was trying to end the conversation. The word hung in the air, enigmatic even to Billy-Bob, who wasn't exactly certain what it meant, nor what he intended it to mean.

John's eyes widened, then narrowed again.

"Unless," he echoed. "Nothing more than a shimmer on the horizon."

Billy-Bob swallowed, allowing him to utter a few more words. He wanted to remain silent, but questions always ricochet inside him, screaming for answers. The only way to silence them was to let them out.

"What are you looking for?" Billy-Bob croaked.

"How do you know I'm looking for something?"

"Everyone is looking for something."

John laughed.

"Indeed. I'm looking for something. Someone. Maybe several someones. An obstruction. That which is preventing the remnants of the world from tumbling over the table's edge." John pushed a book forward as he spoke until it reached the far side, tipped, and fell. He gestured to the books lining the room. "Their histories are absent or altered. However, knowing the histories of everyone else, perhaps I can piece together the shape of the world and find their history in the hollow places. If I know where there are gaps, I will know where to look."

Billy-Bob bumped against the door, not realizing he'd been backing toward it. His hand found a handle and gripped it, but much as he wanted to leave, he knew the hostile citizens would be waiting.

"Have you found any?"

"Many," said John. "But not the one I seek. The girl from Beta might be one. She's very good at hiding, though. But I'll catch her eventually. When I do…"

John smiled. He held a book aloft and closed his hand around it. The book crumpled. John did not flinch or twitch, or appear to register any change in the condition of the book. He may as well have closed his hand on empty air.

Billy-Bob's hand tightened on the door handle. What if the girl from his dream was the girl from Beta? He couldn't allow her to be destroyed. Of course, the girl from his dream may well not exist at all. It could be the girl the Forest Monster sought, or the one the wog mentioned couldn't be found. It might not be any of these, but, he decided, that didn't matter. John's wanton destruction must be opposed. This knowledge didn't come as a fully formed idea, but an inkling, an urge, just as he'd felt the compulsion to resist the Forest Monster, but hadn't been able to articulate why or how.

"There are others," John continued, "not yet discovered. And there's always the possibility of someone new. But that's the least likely. Gordimer certainly hasn't turned up anything extraordinary in some time. Perhaps they've simply ceased to exist. As I recall, he was approaching a significant and crucial milestone. His inability to reach it tells me my plan is working."

"You know Gordimer?"

John canted his head, more alert and curious about him now.

"*You* know Gordimer?"

"Why do you want to destroy people?"

John laughed.

"Don't misunderstand. I don't want to destroy people, I'm simply accelerating the inevitable. Most people just are, just do. No thoughts of their own. The world is stuffed with slack-faced boobs who shout lamentations to the ether over whatever sour fate has befallen them, never acting to change because they know in the deepest fiber of their being nothing can be changed, but hoping someone will change things for them. That is what makes them so easy to manipulate. They want to be told. They want to be controlled. As much as humanity claims freedom as a cherished right, they gladly eschew it because figuring things out for themselves is genuinely difficult."

John flung his hand toward the door dismissively.

"Those folk out there," he continued, "nothing more than sculptors. Their last great work was of the hero, Alexander, the last hero, erected at the edge of the world, as it were, in the hope of driving back any evils that might approach from the unexplored wilderness. Then everything fell apart and Alexander disappeared. Rather than fill the void he left, they fled here because this place was meant to offer safety and knowledge."

Here John paused, his eyes glassy.

"And that's what I gave them. Knowledge and safety. The knowledge that the world is a dangerous place bent on their destruction, and the only way to save themselves is to destroy the world first. Now they search for something they can't name because they don't know what else to do with themselves. There is no hope for them because they refuse to make it for themselves. No, that's not entirely accurate. I'm giving them the joy of proactivity, of usefulness and functionality—I'm allowing them to destroy themselves."

A faint smile flittered from one side of John's mouth to the other. Billy-Bob guessed he enjoyed frightening people. Some were like that, taking joy in the tiny terrors they could implant in others, then watching people wear themselves out with fear.

"That's not true," murmured Billy-Bob.

"It is true! I know because *I know them*!" John laughed, sweeping his arm to cover the room and all the books heaped around them. "I know them all!"

"You don't know me."

John's brows pressed.

"No. Why do you suppose that is?"

"Nothing has been written about me. I'm not very important."

John leaned forward, cradling his head in his hands.

"Nonsense," he said, cheerily. "Everyone has something written about them. Even you."

John leaned forward on the desk as if doing so allowed him to see deeper into Billy-Bob, then sat back in his seat.

"Billy-Bob," he said to himself, tapping a thick finger against his lips. "From now."

Then he turned to one side, rustled through the books, and drew out a thin work of only a few pages. He flipped the book open and scanned the final page. His eyes snapped back to Billy-Bob. He scowled, and Billy-Bob knew John had read something he didn't like.

"What does it say?" asked Billy-Bob.

John clapped the book shut with one hand. He rose from his seat like a paper map unfolding, much larger than Billy-Bob realized, and hunched beneath the low ceiling, glowering at Billy-Bob.

"It says you shouldn't be here. It says you perished in an act of insipid bravery at the hands of a Forest Monster. Which means one of two things. Either you are not who you say you are, or," and he shook the book at Billy-Bob, "this book is a lie. In either case, I am being deceived and you are hiding something."

Billy-Bob blinked, puzzled by the book's conclusion that he shouldn't be here and that it existed at all while his story was still being written.

"What have I got to hide?"

"The book should have told me. It did not. Do you understand my dilemma?"

"No."

John eyed him for a moment, then snapped an arm out, slinging the book at Billy-Bob's chest. Billy-Bob didn't have time to think, but found himself doing so anyway.

The cover was stark, with nothing but his name, so the thin hardcovers almost touched one another. If this really was his biography, it was painfully short, particularly when compared to the other books in the room. Then again, John claimed it ended in Dirtburg, so the most interesting bits of his life had gone unrecorded. Why, he couldn't say. He wondered if it contained anything that happened before he'd awoken in the building in Dirtburg, but it looked too short to tell him anything of interest.

He decided he should catch the book and read it, but wasn't sure he'd be fast enough. In the end he decided to smack the book aside. It might hurt a little, but he wouldn't have time to move out of the way. He felt John was testing him, somehow, to assess his abilities, find out what kind of hero he might be, and it pleased him to think he'd come to a choice that should impress John. Of course, by the time he'd made this decision the book was upon him, a corner bit hard into his ribcage, and fell to the floor.

"Uff," said Billy-Bob, and rubbed the sore spot in his chest where the book struck him.

John grimaced, disappointed.

"Not what I suspected," John remarked. "What are you? What are you looking for?"

Billy-Bob shrugged.

"I'm not anything," he replied. "Not enough acorns."

"That makes sense," said John in a tone that meant it didn't.

"I'm looking for Ultimate Evil," said Billy-Bob. "Have you seen it?"

John's eyes fluttered.

"No. Why would anyone bother?"

"To defeat it."

John laughed, then laughed again, and again in a series of gradually diminishing aftershocks. He picked through the books in his piles and lifted one. He regarded the cover, then opened it, reading as he paced, then spoke. He seemed to have no trouble doing many things at once, whereas thinking was a distraction for Billy-Bob that eroded his ability to do anything else and most times required him to be still.

"Ultimate Evil is an amalgamation of a world's hatred, frustration, and misery. How do you combat these things?"

Simple, thought Billy-Bob.

"With a hero."

"There are no heroes."

"There can be new ones."

"Then you are naïve."

A commotion was building outside again, and Billy-Bob pressed his face against a gap in the door slats. The people from the city had spread themselves out, searching for something, crawling along the ground, listening, poking inside the mounds and emerging moments later. Some crept toward the door, eyes scanning the ground, then turned away when they realized where they were.

A flash of white beyond the shadow caught his eye, and Billy-Bob saw Gordimer dart from one of the buildings and vault over the wall. He disappeared from sight for a moment, then the topmasts of two wings and Gordimer's head slowly periscoped over the top of the wall, scrolled left and right to ensure he hadn't been spotted, then dipped slowly beneath the plane of the wall again. He saw the elbows of Gordimer's wings bob above wall a few times, receding toward the forest, then they were gone. It pleased him to know Gordimer had escaped but saddened to think he'd been abandoned.

John was speaking again, to himself or Billy-Bob, he didn't know.

"Something is resisting. A hero, I suspect. But it may not matter, because I have a plan. People are such delicate machines. The slightest turn of a screw throws them out of kilter. I know all of their strengths and all of their weaknesses. I know which gears are tight and which are loose, and I know just where to apply pressure to jar them free and send the whole thing juddering to a stop."

Billy-Bob heard John, but was preoccupied with events outside.

One of the mounds appeared misshapen, with a lump growing where the side curved into a roof, and the more he stared the better he saw. It wasn't dirt, but a person atop the mound, flattened and trying to remain still. Had Gordimer returned to rescue him? No. Not Gordimer, Billy-Bob guessed, because he couldn't see any wings.

"It must be the girl," John mused. "It has to be. But it shouldn't matter. I've driven them apart. And the further they recede from one another, the more ignorant they are, the more different and dangerous they become to one another. The more they fear, the more they lash out in response to their fear. It's working. It always works. Until they break."

The person on the mound wasn't one of the denizens. Not searching, just clinging to the building. And that grip was failing. Billy-Bob could see the person slip incrementally lower, fearful to reestablish his grip because the sound might alert those searching for him.

"Quite a dilemma," said the door handle. "Are you going to do anything?"

"I'm not sure what I could do," Billy-Bob whispered. "I just got away from them."

"That's a good excuse for doing nothing. That's what excuses are for, after all."

The fellow's grip finally failed and he slid down the building and dropped to the ground with a thump. The sound alerted several citizens, who turned to investigate. The fellow bounced to his feet and ran. He made it several strides into the sunlight and Billy-Bob recognized the writer from Dirtburg. Why he'd come so far, Billy-Bob couldn't be sure. Perhaps more interesting stories lay westward. The writer made a dash for the wall and forest beyond. He didn't make it.

A figure cut across his path and shouldered him to the ground. He went down headfirst and rolled to a stop beside the wall.

"This is John's plan in action," said the handle with a sigh. "Ignorance and suspicion that breeds violence. It's the whittling of the world."

"Why is he doing this?"

"Because he can't stop himself. Because he has to."

It occurred to Billy-Bob that this behavior could qualify John as Ultimate Evil, though he'd expected a less thoughtful and deliberate creature. John did not give the impression of outward violence, but he manipulated others into behaving violently, and from the way they consciously avoided this structure, it was clear they'd been taught to fear him.

"No one has to do something they don't want to do," Billy-Bob murmured.

"Really? Can I prevent you from opening this door if I choose, or is my function set regardless of my intentions?"

Billy-Bob considered.

"I could change your function. Everything can change. I think."

"Do you think you can change John?"

Billy-Bob looked back at John. He'd risen from his seat as he spoke, drifting through the stacks of books like a meandering glacier. He hunched as he walked, bent by the low ceiling that Billy-Bob would have to stretch to reach. He was large, as large as Jim from Dirtburg, and he wondered if they were related.

"What should I do?" asked Billy-Bob.

"I couldn't say for sure," the handle replied, "but I feel I can say with confidence that this isn't it."

John's mass gave him a sense of inevitability, as if any effort Billy-Bob put forth toward him could not change his direction. He'd simply grind onward, unimpeded. On the other hand, he could save the writer from whatever fate these people intended for him. That was a small victory.

"I have to go," said Billy-Bob.

He pulled the door open and slipped through. The door clapped shut behind him, but he could still hear John's powerful voice as he moved away.

"It doesn't have to be sincere, this indoctrinated, habitual, synthetic kindness," he was saying. "It just works. It resists. I don't understand how or why it happens, but I knew if it could be destroyed, the plotting of humanity will be entirely different. So that's what I'm doing. Searching. Searching for that point, that person in history. It's why I read these."

Billy-Bob slunk between the buildings, edging toward the lip of shadow where the crowd had gathered around the writer. He realized John had stopped speaking, then started up again.

"Oh," John said, his voice diminished by distance. "He's already gone."

OVER THE WALL

Andrew sat with his back against a stone wall as tall as his shoulders, just tall enough to prevent him from climbing over. The loose stones had rolled beneath him as he tried to scramble up, then slid back down with him. He tried and failed several times, removing an armful of stones from the wall in the process. In the meantime, the villains of this town closed their ranks, clutching their stone weapons, and the semicircle around him tightened.

This, he decided, is where he would meet his end. So much for Mardin's expectations. Terrified as he was by the prospect of extinction, he could not overcome the disappointment that his existence had been a colossal waste of time. Mardin implied Andrew played an important role of some sort, which suggested his death now would result in some paradoxical inconsistency, and so it was impossible—were it not for the Anti-Paradox Machine. Instead, this event was little more than a culmination of disappointments, death being the final link in a chain of unrealized expectations.

When he left Mardin he ran down the slope toward the complex, plates of ground crunching under his feet, kicking tiles turned vertical by micro tectonics into puffs of dirt, never once taking his eyes from the complex until he stood at the edge of the shadow beneath it. He didn't know what to expect, whether anyone he knew would be here, only that this was coming home.

The great platform towered overhead, and above that he caught faint hints of the gossamer invitation sweeping around the building, inviting any who saw it. They were an educational facility. In knowledge one had all the tools necessary to face fear, and in time overcome it. It didn't make one more brave, it made one sensible. Sense was a powerful and practical tool without the inherent dangers of being brave.

"Is anyone there?" he called. Then louder, "Hello?"

Andrew inhaled to shout again when a hand bunched in his shirtfront and pulled him into the darkness. His vision sucked away and he blinked repeatedly, trying to no avail to recover it.

"There's no one up there," a voice hissed in his face.

The hand pulled on his shirt, leading him stumbling through the shrouded world and finally pressed him against what felt like a sloping wall before releasing him. Gradually, his eyes adjusted. At first he could only see the ridge far beyond the shadow and the splintered ground between them. Then the shapes interrupting his view became clearer as heaps of dirt rising above his head.

To his right a shape clambered onto the mound. He blinked, and discerned an extra hump of material from the folded wings on Billy-Bob's guide.

"Gordimer!" Andrew almost shouted. "What are you doing?"

Gordimer shot him a stern look and pressed his finger against his lips.

"There it is again!" cried a voice Andrew didn't recognize. It did not sound friendly.

"Get up here," Gordimer breathed, "if you want to keep safe."

Not knowing what sought them, Andrew clambered onto the mound. It didn't make for easy climbing as the loose dirt disintegrated in his hands.

Even when he'd reached what seemed like the apex, he could feel dirt sifting away beneath him and had to reposition himself every few seconds to keep from sliding back down.

"Wait until they stop looking," said Gordimer in a voice scarcely louder than a breath of passing air. "Make for the forest. Beta is on the other side."

Andrew felt a faint thrill at the mention of Beta, yet at the same time his heart sank. Passing through the forest, if it had the qualities now it retained in his day, would not prove easy. In his own time rumors of a monster circulated around the forest, and none entered to confirm or deny its presence. The presence of a monster in the forest near Dirtburg made him wonder if all forests had monsters, like black holes at the center of galaxies. He'd been told a monster lived in the forest when he was a boy, and few bothered to venture into it. Whether that was true or simply a tale meant to entertain or frighten him, he didn't know.

"Beta," Andrew said. "We're almost there. Billy-Bob is almost there."

"Almost is further than most get." Even at a whisper, Andrew could sense Gordimer's disdain. "But it's still failure. Watch out for yourself. I won't help you. Nor can Billy-Bob, wherever he is."

"Mardin said I would be fine," Andrew whispered to him.

Gordimer made a sound of disgust.

"Not knowing who to trust is why the world is falling apart. These people are a perfect example."

"How can I trust you?"

Gordimer thought, and Andrew heard bitterness in the response.

"You can't. Be still. They're coming."

Other shapes moved in the darkness amongst the mounds. People, creeping through the passages beneath the platform created by the heaped up dirt piles. Andrew guessed they numbered around twenty, maybe more. He only saw them when they moved, and most remained still, listening. A few had gathered nearby, perhaps drawn to the sound of shifting dirt as it slid out from beneath him. He didn't see Billy-Bob and wondered where he'd gotten to, if he'd been caught, or had hidden amongst the mounds as well.

Andrew tried to remain motionless, but the structure would not allow it. He could remain quiet or he could remain atop the mound, but he couldn't do both. Gordimer watched Andrew, saying nothing, unable to do anything. Slowly, inexorably, Andrew slid down the mound until the steepness of it could no longer support him.

He dropped a full body length with a thump and a small avalanche of dirt, and the searchers quickly converged. So he ran for the forest. That escape, too, had failed.

Which brought him to now and his imminent demise.

The crowd closed around him, shrinking the gaps in their semicircle as the grew nearer. Just as the last glimpse of the land beyond them pinched out, he saw Gordimer hoist himself onto the wall, throw a final scowl toward Andrew, and disappear over the top.

Andrew heard a single click from the crowd, as though the gaps between individuals had latched shut, locking him in. A moment later a small rock dropped at his feet. Dark brown, not much bigger than a pebble, rolling in a circle like a top expending the last of its momentum before coming to a stop. Andrew looked up to see if some part of the platform were disintegrating, hoping he might be saved by a stroke of luck and an avalanche of falling masonry, but the platform appeared intact. Disappointed, he looked back to the crowd.

One man staggered toward him, a hand groping drunkenly for the stone tool at his side. This was it. No interrogation, no last request. They simply planned to march up and cudgel him. The man finally managed to get a hand on his weapon, drew it halfway from its leather holster, then fell forward into the dirt and lay there unmoving.

The others eyed their comrade, perplexed.

Another lurched forward from the group, took an unsteady step to the side, and fell over beside the rock at Andrew's feet. The rock, Andrew noted, did not match the tan color of the stone here. This rock had two colors: a deep rich brown on one part and a fainter brown on the other. He reached for the stone and held it in his hand. Not a stone, he realized, but an acorn. Where had an acorn come from?

"Enough, villain!" said the foremost of the group, a stern and frightening looking woman who might have been brilliant or beautiful were it not for her terrifying disposition. The others looked upon her with reverence and confidence. The leader. "Now you meet your doooooo... dooooooooooooooooo... oooooommmm..."

The girl got most of the sentence out, but appeared to struggle near the end. Then she fell to her knees and to one side where another acorn had come to rest.

Unsure what invisible hand caused those who approached him to lose their senses, they looked at Andrew with suspicion. They stood a moment, neither retreating nor advancing, trying to determine the root of this epidemic with cool intelligence.

"Zoing!" said Andrew, brandishing the acorn, not expecting it to work.

To his astonishment, another citizen fell forward into the dirt and lay unmoving. Andrew hid his amazement while the citizens murmured to one another, considering the obvious connection between Andrew and the acorns. Andrew said "Zoing!" again and shook the acorn. The crowd fractured and scattered to the safety of darkness under the platform.

When all but the three lying in the dirt around him had fled, a figure emerged cautiously from the shadow beneath the building. Andrew couldn't suppress a happy disbelief when the boy approached, crouching beside each of the unconscious villains, plucking the acorns from the ground beside them and placing them in his pocket. Then he stood before Andrew.

Andrew struggled for the right thing to say, but could think of nothing. Instead he held out the remaining acorn, which Billy-Bob took and added to the others in his pocket.

"Thanks," said Andrew at last.

Bill-Bob shrugged.

"Someone had to do something."

"Gordimer got away," said Andrew.

"That's good. And not. How will I find Beta?"

"He told me it's past this forest. I guess it's just a matter of going around."

Billy-Bob cocked his head. He looked past Andrew at the forest, watching it shake and rattle in the breezes, then back to Andrew.

"Why not go through it?"

"There's a monster," said Andrew. "Maybe. I don't know."

Andrew could see the strain in Billy-Bob's face as he gazed into the forest, weighing the peril against the need to get to Beta. Circumstances resolved his indecision for them.

An explosion of stone against the wall splashed a smattering of broken pellets against Andrew's face. Andrew wiped the dust away and saw the wooden handle of a stone tool beside him. A cry rose from beneath the platform and Andrew and Billy-Bob saw the villains pouring out of the shadows, voices ululating as they charged, determined to crush them under the weight of an all-out surge.

He looked up at Billy-Bob, not knowing what else to do.

"Now what?"

If the boy were a hero, he might have charged into the crowd, destroying them or destroying himself. Instead, his response was unheroic, but not unexpected.

"Run!" cried Billy-Bob, planting a hand on the top of the wall and vaulting over.

Andrew felt his muscles lock and his eyes goggle as the crowd grew nearer. Another villain cocked her arm to throw a sharpened tool when Andrew felt Billy-Bob's hand on his shoulder. It tightened on his shirt and hoisted him up, then slid him over the top of the wall and thudded him against the ground. The stone tool sailed overhead and disappeared into the high grass with a swish of tearing blades. Andrew crouched against the wall and Billy-Bob huddled beside him.

"We have to go!" said Billy-Bob.

"We have to go around!"

"There's no time to go around!"

Without another word, Billy-Bob gave a tug on Andrew's shirt, then ran to the forest. Andrew fell over. Billy-Bob paused at the tree line, stepped aside to let a stone hammer cartwheel past him, and beckoned to Andrew before stepping backward through the leaves.

Running meant Andrew might get cut down as he fled, but if he stayed here they would reach the wall and take him anyway. Another tool shattered against the rock wall, sending a hail of pebbles clattering down on his shoulders. He took a breath, held it, and lunged forward. His feet slipped and his first steps went out from beneath him, then he hunched and ran to the grasping arms of the forest into which Billy-Bob had just disappeared.

He did not look back, fearful of discovering how close the pursuers had gotten and worried they might still overcome him or land a lucky strike to the head. He ran, anticipating the pain of a blow from one of their weapons, hoping the wall would slow them down.

Behind him he heard the agonized wails of the villains, and the thump and hiss as tools struck the ground or cut through the waist-high grass around him, but he could tell without looking they had not followed. He felt a sense of relief, even though he could well be running from one peril into the gleeful embrace of another. Perhaps they knew a monster dwelled in the forest, pushing it outward to expand its realm. Maybe they weren't villains after all, but were protecting themselves and the world from some great devilry no one had yet seen.

With luck, they would emerge on the other side of the forest without ever answering these questions. But luck rarely seemed to function that way.

THROUGH THE TEETH OF THE WOODS

Even though he held an arm up, stealthy branches slipped through Andrew's defenses to land stinging slaps against his face and neck. Tiny flecks of blood showed on his forearms where the forest had taken tiny bites out of him. The trees and shrubs stood hand in hand, fingers entwined, and their ranks seemed without number. He couldn't hear anything other than the snap and swish of leaves as he tore through them and his own heavy breathing as he puffed along, trying to keep close to Billy-Bob.

Billy-Bob plowed forward, heedless of the impediments, often disappearing into the thick foliage ahead of Andrew, forcing him to put forth an extra surge of strength to keep up for fear of being left behind, even though he knew Billy-Bob had no better idea about where they were going than himself.

At last they broke into a clearing and Billy-Bob stopped. The doors of the greenery swung closed behind them with a shuffle. The grass here was sparse and short, poking a few thin fibers through a blanket of leaves, and the shrubs were far enough apart that he could take several steps without brushing against their reaching fingers. Andrew bent beside Billy-Bob, hands on his knees, huffing noisily.

"How long," Andrew gasped, "do we have to do this?"

"Until they give up," Billy-Bob answered.

"Have they?"

Billy-Bob looked back at the wall of branches. Andrew slumped to the leaf-strewn ground, trying to catch his breath. With an effort, Andrew watched as well, expecting the branches to part at any moment and the residents of the city beneath the platform to pour out like a cloud of angry hornets. He made several attempts to hold his breath and listen, but couldn't do so for longer than a few instants before lapsing into sharp gasps.

No citizens appeared. It seemed safe to assume they had not followed, or had gotten lost in doing so. Andrew lay on his back and huffed a few more hard breaths to clear his chest. Billy-Bob inspected the clearing around them, by all accounts unaffected by the chase.

As his breathing slowed, Andrew took in the surroundings. This place was wholly different from the rest of the world. The air had weight and flavor, an odor of dampness, and even though the canopy of the forest blanketed everything in shadow, the leaves overhead glowed with sunlight, allowing him to see everything in the clearing. An undertone of static filled the air that he didn't notice unless he paid attention, with rustles from branches overhead, the crunch of old leaves and twigs beneath his hands, and short strings of piping notes in the distance. All of which combined to form a dissonant but soothing hiss in the back of his mind.

Amidst the drone he heard another sound, similar to but standing apart from the low-volume cacophony. Different because it had rhythm and predictability. Swish swish swish, as though someone with very short legs were kicking through the leaves.

Andrew bolted upright. Billy-Bob heard them too, because he stood still, staring into the bushes with one hand on the handle of his gun.

There. Branches parted and for a moment Andrew thought the citizens of Alpha had found them. Instead, a short creature stepped into the clearing, and Andrew realized the situation was much worse than he thought.

"Ah ha!" it said.

"A wog!" cried Andrew.

He attempted to stand and flee again, but his legs wouldn't support him and he crashed back to the ground.

The wog did not seize the advantage, however, and strolled into the clearing, seating itself not far from Andrew. Andrew looked at the wall of leaves, waiting for the others to enter, but none emerged. Rather than drawing and firing, Billy-Bob took his hand from the pistol.

"Where have you been?" asked Billy-Bob.

It was not the sort of thing Andrew expected to ask a wog. The response took him equally, if not more, by surprise.

"Chasing. Remember? But he escaped. I imagine by now he's making his way back to Alpha to tell the others the forest isn't dangerous. It's only a matter of time before they realize he's right."

"It can talk?" asked Andrew.

The wog stood, turned its egg-shaped body in place until it faced Andrew, and sat again.

"Apparently," said the wog. "I assume you are someone safe."

"He's safe," Billy-Bob said quickly. Then to Andrew, "They aren't dangerous."

"Except when necessary," the wog clarified.

"What are you?" asked Andrew. "What do you do? Why are you dangerous?"

"I'm a wog, obviously. I provide a number of useful functions. My current priority, however, is to protect him." The wog gestured to Billy-Bob, who raised his eyebrows. The information apparently surprised him. "I'm dangerous so others know not to get in my way. The things I do are important. They're part of a plan. Are you part of a plan? What do you do? You don't appear the least bit dangerous."

"I'm a writer. No, I'm not dangerous. Which is why no one appears the least bit concerned about getting in my way."

"What are you writing?" asked Billy-Bob. "And why?"

Andrew did not answer immediately, weighing the potential effects. To tell them would cause them to alter their behavior to reflect better on posterity. They might make greater efforts to protect him. But it would be disingenuous and unnatural, and the change in behavior could have implications on history. He balanced the honesty of their portrayal against a possible improvement in his chances of survival. Andrew took a long breath and let it go. He knew what he had to do.

"I don't suppose Gordimer told you about the Anti-Paradox Machine."

* * *

When Andrew finished, he sat again, not realizing he'd stood, pacing about the clearing. Neither Billy-Bob nor the wog interrupted his story and they remained silent now. He could not read anything in the wog's owlish face, with no discernable change in expression except the apertures of its eyes, which stood wide apart. If anything, the wog appeared agog, but that struck Andrew as uncharacteristic in a creature so robotically precise, certain of its purpose and the world around it. Billy-Bob's head was bent, but Andrew could see the strain in his temples as hard thoughts worked their way through narrow passages in his mind. Because Billy-Bob was a slow and struggling thinker, it did not surprise Andrew that the wog spoke first.

"The Institute still exists. That is encouraging. The creator will be pleased."

Andrew nodded. Mardin had the same response, albeit less stoic than the wog. But perhaps the wog was ecstatic beneath its mechanical exterior. Maybe tiny alarms were jangling quietly through its innards. He strained to detect any sound at the fringe of hearing, but heard nothing apart from the wind rolling through the trees.

"It means we're succeeding," the wog continued. "It means what we're doing is the right thing. The world is a safer place."

Andrew nodded again, this time more reluctantly. Success isn't quite what he would call the world from which he came. It was not altogether different from here. In fact, in light of what he'd learned, now and then were not separated by as much time as he thought. Which made his own time seem that much more precarious. Still, at the Institute he was safe. Here, he'd experienced a litany of events that spoke to the dangers of the world beyond his protected community.

"Safer," Andrew agreed. "But it remains a dangerous place. Some explore it. Some of them don't come back. There's something dangerous out there, but we'll find out what that is. And once we find out what it is, and understand it, it won't be dangerous any more. You're right, though. For the most part, people that share this world get along."

"Share this world?"

Andrew nodded and raised a finger to gesture at the sky.

"Those from beyond don't get along with us so well. I'm not sure why. They arrive, one at a time, wipe out a city, and leave. Only to return and do it again."

The wog's enthusiasm dimmed.

"I've never heard of anything like that."

"No. They don't appear to be a problem here," said Andrew. He drummed his fingers against his notepad. "I guess that's a topic for a different book."

"So you record histories," the wog mused. "That's interesting. Not particularly useful, though. Why?"

"I think it's a test. Tests have become a theme I keep running across. Mardin seems to think it's important, but he wouldn't explain how. Says I have to figure it out for myself."

"Some things you have to learn for yourself or they lack meaning."

What the wog said had more profundity than he expected. It gave him a sense of ease and understanding he hadn't gotten when speaking with Mardin, who seemed to have a better grasp of the situation but did a poor job of explaining it. In many ways, the wog was clearer and more straightforward than Mardin or anyone else he'd encountered. Against all expectations, Andrew liked the wog.

The behavior of this wog, however, did not explain the behavior of the others. They had obeyed Billy-Bob, or at the least refrained from harming him, but their purpose seemed entirely different.

"You are protecting him. What about the others? Why aren't they here?"

"They have a different purpose."

"I think they were looking for something. Or someone."

The wog had few features it could use to express itself, but Andrew detected sadness and pity quite distinctly. The wog seemed to grow heavier, slouching under its own weight.

"They are looking for someone. But it's a fool's errand. They can never find her."

"Who?"

"The girl. The one the creator sought for. The one whose image is used by the information posts. She is gone. The great tragedy is they know this, but are compelled to search anyway. I cannot imagine their frustration."

For some reason, perhaps the proximity of his story, or mentioning the fruitless pursuit of a girl, Andrew thought of Bree. What might he do if faced with the prospect of losing her? He might still find a way to escape this exile and return to her. But what if he could never get back? Or worse, what if he returned and she wasn't there? The idea made him restless. He stood, not knowing where to go, but needing to go somewhere to feel he was making progress.

"You love her," said Billy-Bob.

Andrew shook his head.

"What?"

"It's why you're angry. You want to get back, but you can't. Because you're writing. And what you're writing about makes you angry because it keeps you from her. I understand that. Frustration is the source of most angers."

"Her who?"

"The girl who sent you here. Does she know?"

Andrew blanched. He'd glossed over parts of the story that named his feelings for Bree each time he'd told it to avoid the embarrassment of revealing a ludicrous hope. And Billy-Bob had seen through to the truth as plainly as he'd told him each mortifying detail. Had Gordimer known as well? Gordimer never indicated as much. Nor had Mardin. Billy-Bob had yet again succeeded where others failed and most others didn't bother.

"You should ask her," said Billy-Bob. "Just to talk. Why don't you?"

Andrew bristled. Because if life was meant to be happy it would not be so determinedly frustrating. Because if there were really any good or justice in the broken, ruined, awful world, Andrew wouldn't be here.

"Because it's just a silly, stupid bother. Because it can't happen."

"Anything can happen. I could be a hero, maybe. Don't you think?"

Andrew grimaced. The last question a hero would ever ask is whether someone thought they might be one. A hero already knew. He did not respond, but Billy-Bob surely read the answer in his face, and Andrew saw his shoulders fall. A hero wouldn't put so much stock in the opinions of others, either. A hero was assured by the infallibility of their purpose and abilities that allowed them to achieve whatever end necessary. These qualities put them above fear. Billy-Bob might have the right intentions to be a hero, but he did not stand outside the reach of fear. Otherwise they would not have fled into the forest.

A hero, Andrew thought, would be more conspicuous. Like the statue from Dirtburg. If Billy-Bob were a hero, he would be like a giraffe in a room with a low ceiling. Or a giraffe with its head caught in the tangle of forest branches, not unlike the one standing nearby, its long, purple tongue twisting at leaves by its head, determined to make the best of a bad situation.

Andrew shook his head. The giraffe remained, though it stopped eating, watching Andrew to see what he would do next. He snapped to his feet and the giraffe, startled, jerked out of the branches and vanished. What was a giraffe doing in this forest? Giraffes were grassland beasts keen on hot sun, sparse trees dotted by delectable leaves, and using their long necks to stare over tall hedges.

Now he heard something more, beyond the ring of shrubs, something unexpected in the static of noise. More variety than one might expect from a forest. His legs, leaden from the run, stumped past Billy-Bob toward the brush.

"What is it?" asked the wog, turning as he went by.

Without answering, Andrew crunched into the scrub, pulling aside branches and pawing at hanging mosses until the forest separated again. His mouth opened. Billy-Bob and the wog emerged beside him.

"Oh!" said Billy-Bob.

Here, in the bright clearing, was the giraffe, striding through a garbled collection of wildlife that defied simple categorization—a clamor of squawks, chirps, snaps, and hisses from every reach of the animal kingdoms. Horses and raccoons and squirrels pawed and poked restlessly at the ground, watched attentively by meerkats and cranes that twisted their heads to look with one eye then the other; dogs barked and chased springing antelope, while owls shifted in the branches, settling their heads into the ruffled scarves of feathered shoulders and appearing generally disgruntled by the noise.

The morass separated as though parting along an invisible seam, and through this gap approached a giant, smiling man. Or something, with a few conspicuous differences, very much like one.

A TEST GONE WRONG

The enormous man strode toward them with a thundering fervor, a tremendous smile on his face, while animals scrambled over one another to clear a path before him, failing with noisy consequences. Those too slow to move were punted effortlessly into the air, and the man didn't seem to notice the obstructions. Cows and rhinos and other large animals found themselves bowled from his path, bellowing in agitation, while smaller creatures were sent aloft on a steep parabola. Billy-Bob ducked beneath a chicken that spiraled past, trailing feathers and squawking loudly. None of the creatures appeared injured and the approaching behemoth did not appear angry or malevolent as he moved through them, only determined to reach his destination regardless of any impediments.

The wog stood between Billy-Bob's legs, watching with Billy-Bob and Andrew in awe as the creature approached.

"I'm not sure I can protect you from this," said the wog.

The giant stood a head taller than Andrew would be if he sat on Billy-Bob's shoulders and his white robe hung upon ledges of muscle in his chest and shoulders. Billy-Bob could feel the ground shiver as he approached. Black wings opened and closed behind him. His face and hands were a deep, sunburnt red, and his black shark eyes appeared to gaze upon everything without giving any indication of what held his attention.

Billy-Bob felt Andrew gripping his arm, preventing him from fleeing. If he wanted to be a hero, he couldn't abandon the person he'd just rescued.

"There *is* a monster in the forest!" he heard Andrew hiss.

"He might be something else," said Billy-Bob. "What a thing looks like doesn't always make it what it is."

"Nevertheless," said the wog, "be ready to run."

Billy-Bob knew he'd shaped this conviction to suit his own ambitions. After all, no one had any qualms telling him he didn't have the appearance of a hero. If appearance guaranteed character and ability, he was too lanky, too short, too slow to be a hero. In order to be a hero, he had to overcome the expectations his appearance, even his name, created. However, a conviction had to be consistent if it were to be true, so Billy-Bob had no choice but to apply it to others as well, which made the current situation problematic. Surely the approaching goliath faced similar adversities. Mostly he hoped this conviction proved true because he didn't know what to do if the creature was hostile.

The giant had many features he expected to find in a monster, the proper dimensions in particular. Exceptional largeness made his slightest movements dangerous to everyone around him and the strength required to move the bulky warship of a body must be frightening. The yawning black wings, featureless black eyes, and bright red skin lent the creature a fearsome aspect—characteristics Ultimate Evil might have, if the outward appearance of evil perfectly reflected its intentions. These thoughts came to him even as the giant raised a hand in greeting and Billy-Bob's mind strained against his body in an effort to keep it from running back into the forest.

"Hello!" called the giant, jovially. His voice boomed with the friendliness of a nearby explosion.

In just a few steps he was upon them, looking down with eyes like volcanic glass. Behind him a rift of torn grass and sprawled animals left a scar that extended to the tree wall at the opposite end of the clearing. No one answered him, uncertain how to respond even though the answer ought to be obvious. The man's shoulder's began to slouch and the taut bow of his smile slackened.

"Hello!" he repeated, this time with less certainty.

"Hello," Billy-Bob replied at last.

The man straightened and his smile brightened again. This must have been the answer he wanted.

"My name is…," Billy-Bob began, but the great red man cut him off.

"Billy-Bob," he finished. He looked pleased by the knowledge and continued by facing the writer. "And you are Andrew. And you are the wog—one of many. I know all of you. But you don't know me. My name is Kilgoth."

"What are you?" Andrew said, his voice cracking.

Kilgoth took a step back, clearly trying not to seem intimidating, but at the same time something had excited him to such an extent that he had lost a degree of self control.

"I'm Kilgoth. I said that."

"Not who," said Andrew. "*What.* What are you? What kind of monster are you?"

Kilgoth gave a nervous, booming laugh. Billy-Bob saw his wings prickle. He didn't like the term monster. No one appreciated being called something they were not.

"I am no monster. I am a messenger."

"You look like a monster," said Andrew.

"I might," said Kilgoth, raising a finger, "but I'm a messenger. I've been told so by the same person who gave me the message. Having a message for someone makes one a messenger, not a monster."

"Maybe you're a monster with a message," Andrew speculated.

Kilgoth frowned. It made his already frightening features more unpleasant. Billy-Bob could see the cords of muscle in Kilgoth's neck tighten.

Billy-Bob could see Kilgoth scared Andrew, but the writer continued to goad the giant man. He imagined it stemmed from his agitation about being here and being unable to return to the girl. He could see it in his face when he spoke of her—a mix of grief and frustration and yearning. Someone had taken his heart tight in hand, and each step away from them pulled at his insides. He understood the why behind Andrew's behavior, understood how it was strong beyond his control and made him taunt what clearly frightened him, but wished he wouldn't. Billy-Bob could hardly complain, as he often found himself in the grip of a powerful emotion, and before he had time to think about it he was already running away.

"What message?" Billy-Bob interrupted. "For whom? From whom?"

"For you."

"Get away from me," said the wog.

A pelican stood nearby, with dirty white feathers and a sagging throat pouch hanging from its beak. The wog stomped its feet and raised its tiny arms, and the pelican retreated a few paces to what it deemed a safe distance. It looked at the wog with one eye, then turned to look with the other, as though each offered a different perspective. The pelican opened its beak and clapped it shut, as if to show the wog pelicans had no reason to fear them.

"I'm quite dangerous," the wog warned.

The pelican clapped its beak again, defiantly, but made no more advances.

"What is the message?" asked Billy-Bob.

Kilgoth's smile returned. He must feel pleased to accomplish a task of considerable importance to him.

"I have two messages," said Kilgoth. "Nothing changes."

"What's the other message?" asked Andrew.

"Unless."

The meaning of the messages were simultaneously crushing and encouraging. Nothing changes. He was not a hero. He could never be a hero. Unless. The world, if it was wrong, would always be wrong. Unless. The message suggested an inevitable grim future, thwarted only by the presence of an Unless. An alternative future was possible, but doubtful. Nevertheless, it could happen, and that touched him with an enthusiasm utterly disproportionate to the odds of the likely outcome.

Billy-Bob felt a pulling at his hip. When he looked down he saw the pelican with its beak clamped around the butt of his pistol, snapping its head in an attempt to wrench it free. He waved a hand at the bird and it scuttled backward, wings flaring, then clapped its beak at him before waddling away.

"What does that mean?" asked Andrew.

Kilgoth's shoulders lifted and fell.

"I'm not sure," Kilgoth answered, looking disappointed. "As a matter of accuracy, I was told this encounter was more about my test than his."

"Of course nothing changes, Unless," said Andrew. "Rain happens, unless it's sunny. Photosynthesis happens, unless it's raining. Random mutation can happen. Runny noses can happen. Of course anything can happen. What good is a message like that? What buffoon sent you here to deliver it?"

"No one sent me anywhere. I've been here, waiting, for some time. So you might understand my excitement about delivering the message, regardless of the content. Understanding the message itself isn't so important to me. It's importance is determined by the one who gets it and the one who sent it. Any meaning you take from it is irrelevant."

"Then who sent it?" asked Andrew.

"Jim."

Only one Jim existed in Billy-Bob's memory, and until recently he hadn't seemed interested in delivering messages. He'd sat atop a building in Dirtburg beside Hobert, saying nothing, now and again raising the brim of his hat to survey the world then dropping it and returning to a state of indifferent mollification. Later he'd been in the street while Billy-Bob tried to escape the Forest Monster, appearing invigorated and important. It occurred to him that Jim's goal had been to appear less than what he was, though what that might be he didn't know, and no amount of weak-minded thinking brought him any closer to an answer.

"Who is Jim?" asked the wog.

"A giver of tests," Kilgoth answered.

"Why? What are tests for?"

"Tests define a person, they help round off a sharp edge and bring them into shape."

Billy-Bob wondered, if everyone had a test, what Jim's test might be. In knowing that, he might know Jim better.

"Do you have a test?" asked the wog.

"Of course," said Kilgoth.

"No, no! Let go of that!"

The pelican had returned and struggled with Andrew for possession of his notepad. Andrew had a distinct advantage in size, but what the pelican lacked in mass it compensated for with tenacity. Andrew yanked, shook, and shouted, but the pelican refused to release the notepad. Andrew's sunburnt face reddened further with agitation and he cocked a foot to kick the bird. The pelican wisely released the notepad, shook the empty sack below its beak as though shivering away any interest it had in an object it had been denied, and waddled away. Andrew fell to the ground with a grunt. Andrew flung a small rock at the pelican, but the bird stepped nimbly aside, and continued on without the slightest regard for his agitation.

Andrew stood again, smacking his pant legs irritably to dislodge blades of grass.

"Why are all these animals here?" asked the wog.

"Because they cannot be anywhere else," Kilgoth answered. "Because their environment was changed unnaturally. They were never permitted the opportunity to adapt. A lot of work went into them becoming what they are now. It would be a shame to undo it all in a completely avoidable swoop. So they're staying here for now. Until they can go back."

"That's a silly job," said Andrew.

"It's not my job. Poppy is their keeper."

"Who is Poppy?"

"Their keeper," Kilgoth repeated, as though the term needed no explanation. Andrew opened his mouth to complain, but Kilgoth held up a hand. "If you want to learn anything else about them, you'll have to speak to Poppy. This is her forest. You can find her in Beta."

Kilgoth extended an arm in the direction of Beta.

In the process, Kilgoth's sleeve had drawn back, revealing a golden band around his wrist. There was nothing remarkable about the band, nothing compelling enough to hold one's attention. Nevertheless, Billy-Bob could not pull his eyes from it and took a rattling breath when Kilgoth finally lowered his arm and the sleeve dropped back into place.

He wanted the band, not knowing what it was for or what he would do with it, desiring it nonetheless, and while he saw it all other thoughts clamoring for attention were shouldered aside. The memory of that uncontrolled desire made him uncomfortable.

"What was that?" asked Billy-Bob.

"What was what?" asked Kilgoth in return.

"That. On your arm. Under your sleeve."

"Oh. It's a test. Everyone has a test."

"It looked like a wristwatch," said Andrew.

"Does it?" asked Kilgoth. "I think it looks like a test."

"It's not a test," said Andrew. "It's a wristwatch."

"No. It's a test. Jim gave it to me."

"That's the test Jim gave you?" asked Billy-Bob.

"It's a wristwatch," Andrew repeated irritably, his voice lifting.

Kilgoth's expression began to darken, and his hands balled at his sides.

"Yes," he answered. "Jim gave me this test."

"Wristwatch."

"What is it for?" asked Billy-Bob.

"To test me. I'm not sure how."

"It's for telling time," said Andrew. "Because it's a wristwatch."

Kilgoth faced the writer.

"It's a test," he said, quietly.

"A wristwatch," said Andrew.

Kilgoth was silent for a moment.

"Test."

"Wristwatch," said Andrew, immediately.

"Can't it be both?" asked Billy-Bob.

"No!" said Kilgoth and Andrew in unison.

Kilgoth rolled up his sleeve and held out his arm.

"This," said Kilgoth, tapping the band, " is a…"

"Wristwatch," Andrew cut in.

"No!" Kilgoth shouted in a gust that blew Andrew's hair back.

The pelican, which had crept quietly closer as the two argued, lunged. With a quick snap of its head, the band on Kilgoth's wrist popped free into the pelican's mouth and the pelican scampered away.

Kilgoth managed to peep out a muted "Hey!" as the pelican vanished into the high grass, but nothing more. He stared at the bare space on his forearm, mouth agape.

Billy-Bob could not know Kilgoth's thoughts, but he could guess. He had lost the test given to him by Jim. Had Kilgoth failed the test? Could he still recover it? Or was this event itself the essence of Kilgoth's test. Kilgoth probably heard these thoughts caroming through his mind, terrified by the prospect of failure, paralyzed by not knowing the nature of his test, which left him uncertain what he ought to do next. Billy-Bob could see the sadness in his slackened face. Hope lent tension and purpose to expressions, and it had altogether left him.

"You did this!" Kilgoth boomed, pointing a taloned hand at Andrew. "You are responsible for this… failure."

His face had tightened again, but it was not hope that pulled his skin taut against his jawline. Despite the impenetrable blackness of Kilgoth's eyes, Billy-Bob could see them go blank. He knew that look—it was the look of someone who had surrendered reason and found themselves caught in the maelstrom of a powerful emotion. Depending upon the emotion, the results could be breathtaking or terrifying.

Kilgoth glowered over Andrew, and Billy-Bob expected anyone in the writer's position might be frightened. But Andrew was angry, too, and anger, like fear, had a way of driving away sensibility.

"If you failed, you failed all on your own. Don't pin your shortcomings on me. If anything, you should congratulate yourself for doing something unique in the realm of possibility, because you're the first thing I've met who has failed a wristwatch."

"It's not a wristwatch," said Kilgoth in a distant, airy voice. "It was my…"

Whatever civility remained with Kilgoth departed. He tipped his head back and roared, shivering the leaves in the trees and sending many shuddering to the ground. The robe he wore split across the muscled plateau of his chest, and Kilgoth tore the rest away with a hand, revealing Kilgoth's great red body in all its terrifying immensity. Andrew, in spite of his anger and dwarfed by the giant creature, staggered backward.

"I think we ought to go," said the wog, its voice colored by uncharacteristic urgency.

To his horror and sadness, Billy-Bob realized Kilgoth had become the thing they'd feared him to be at the outset. A thinking, caring creature, deprived of something it had ascribed great importance, was now nothing more than a monster, guided by rage. All the animals recognized it, too, scattering into the woods with a menagerie of barnyard noises dulled by the enraged roars of Kilgoth that filled the clearing.

"I think we should go, right now," the wog insisted.

Kilgoth swept out an arm, knocking Andrew into the air and sailing into the arms of a nearby tree where he hung there, dazed. The great winged man pounded the ground, shaking Billy-Bob off his feet, turning in slow circles and lashing out at anything in reach, searching for something to vent his anger upon, the claws of his feet shredding the ground in his vicinity until he stood upon a bare patch of earth, hunched and huffing, fists balled into sledgehammers searching for some new target.

The tall grass at the edge of Kilgoth's sphere of destruction slipped apart and through the gap stepped a pelican waddling in curiosity amidst the torn dirt and debris. From its beak hung a band of gold. The two of them stood in utter silence, Kilgoth and the pelican, until Kilgoth reached out an upturned hand. It was a gesture of supplication, and in Kilgoth's face Billy-Bob saw a glimmer of hope for redemption. The bird looked at the hand, first with one eye then the other, cogitating over the meaning of the gesture, then surveyed the surroundings with a few quick twists of its head. Finally, the bird looked up into Kilgoth's face, as though understanding him completely.

A decisive shiver went through the bird, as if shaking off a layer of water, then it opened its beak. Kilgoth reached for the band, but the pelican stepped back, flicked its head, and the test disappeared into its mouth. It spread its wings and launched into the air.

Kilgoth bellowed so powerfully Billy-Bob didn't hear anything. But he could feel the waves of sound pounding against him and his eardrums buzzed. The pelican did not fly away, but made a circle around the edge of the clearing. Kilgoth plunged his hand into the ground and withdrew a stone as large as his chest. He flung the stone at the pelican, missing, but striking a tree behind it, which exploded where the stone struck and continued on into the forest, sending the upper part of the tree crashing to the ground.

Undeterred, or perhaps oblivious, the pelican continued to circle inside the clearing. Kilgoth wrenched another stone from the ground and hurled it with the same result. The pelican circled the clearing, as though playing with him. Or testing.

"Wait!" cried Billy-Bob. "This is it! This is your test!"

Kilgoth hesitated a moment, turning to face Billy-Bob, a new stone in his hand. His giant face glistened with tears of outrage and frustration, and his breaths were loud and ragged sobs. For a moment Billy-Bob thought he could read the expression in his face—no more than a question: why? Why had this happened, why had he become this way, why wasn't anyone helping? All those why questions held in the face of a terrifying monster.

The pelican landed between the two of them, facing Kilgoth. It shook its head violently, and suddenly the band was in its mouth again. Perhaps it had tired of the game or perhaps it realized the effect it had had upon Kilgoth.

The pelican held it there a moment, throwing glimmers into the dust-filled air, then tipped its head back, separated its beak, and the band dropped away again.

"Oh no," muttered the wog.

Kilgoth bellowed and hurled the rock. The pelican lifted itself into the air, avoiding the blow. Billy-Bob leapt aside, feeling a spray of dirt and rocks pepper his legs, and landed roughly on his side. He sat up, and saw a trench in the ground where the rock had passed but no sign of the wog.

"Why are you still here?" asked the exposed corner of a rock in the dirt. "Why aren't you running?"

"The wog…," Billy-Bob started.

"Gone," the rock interrupted. "You know that. Why are you here?"

"Because the writer. He needs me."

Across the clearing Andrew still hung in the arms of a tree, unmoving. Between them stalked Kilgoth, ripping dirt and rocks from the ground and hurling them at the elusive pelican, leaving craters and trenches scattered through the clearing, ringed by broken and uprooted trees.

"How do you reach him through all that?" asked the rock. "And then what if you do?"

Billy-Bob didn't know how to answer, unsure any alternatives existed.

"You're a coward," the rock continued. "You do what cowards do."

Billy-Bob stood, shaken. A cold shiver rattled through him.

Before he had time to think about what the rock told him, Kilgoth was pounding nearer, a stone in his hand. From the look on his face and the way his head tracked the pelican as it arced around the open ground, he knew Kilgoth could not see him. The pelican was flying directly at Billy-Bob, and Kilgoth began to wind his arm.

Billy-Bob ran.

If Kilgoth had failed his test, then so had Billy-Bob. Andrew still hung in the tree, and the wog, dedicated to protecting him, gone. He could never be a hero now. Of all his failures before, this was the worst, the most convincing, and the most final. Kilgoth had lost a wristwatch precious to him, afraid it could never be recovered, and Billy-Bob had lost something similar, perhaps more significant. As the noise of Kilgoth's rampage faded, he felt a piece of himself he had clung to, knowing it made the difference in the meaning of his existence, fade away with it.

JIM

Something about Andrew's body didn't feel right. A general ache throbbed everywhere, but nothing felt broken or leaking. Branches crowded around him, pressing tight to his sides with thin wooden fingers, preventing him from getting anywhere. Just as well, since he had no intention of moving until he figured out how he'd gotten here and where here was.

The last thing he recalled was Kilgoth's great red hand sweeping toward him, the disorienting sensation of leaving his feet involuntarily, and the unpleasantness of uncontrolled flight. Now his pulse tolled giantly in his ears and both arms stretched over his head. He could lower them with some effort, but they resisted, and as soon as he his concentration waned they sprang over his head again.

He looked up at his hands and saw a churned, brown sky just beyond his reach with filaments of green hanging from it like tiny jungle vines. Something had clearly gone wrong with the world and a flash of fear formed inside him. Sweat beaded on his forehead, then ran up into his hair rather than down his face because everything in this new universe had lost its sense of direction.

He felt a loosening on his chest, and the book slid free of his breast pocket and flashed past his face, opening into a parachute of fluttering paper and flopping into the brown sky just beyond the reach of his open hands. The book lay open before him, baring its contents. In its short lifespan it had already suffered great mistreatment. Pages were torn and clung desperately to the binding like fingertips from the slimmest ledge. The lettering ran where droplets of sweat had fallen. Black slashes over scribbles criss-crossed the open pages, but one patch of white in the squall remained. Here a few words had been hastily scrawled.

I'm doomed.

Andrew tried to take a step upward. In an environment so unpredictable he could think of no reason why this wouldn't work, so it surprised him when it didn't. His feet did not move. Before he could investigate what held him in place, the sound of footsteps scuffling through the leaves drew his attention into the clearing, where a man in white strode toward him along the ceiling of the world.

"Hello, Andrew," said the man. Somehow the white robe he wore did not fly up over his head. "That can't be comfortable. I can only imagine what a fantastical menagerie of thoughts comes to a mind when held upside down over long."

The man stood much taller than Andrew and wore a large straw hat that worked like the platform of the Institute, casting a shadow across his features. Nevertheless, he could hear his expression in the tone of his voice: confident and glad at everything.

"Jim," said Andrew, remembering the man from the rooftop in Dirtburg.

What was he doing here? Jim had told Andrew he was there for a reason, as though Jim had some great, unspoken power—how else could he have access to knowledge about his purpose? Or so he'd thought. But Jim neglected to tell Andrew what that purpose was. It didn't take much thought to come to the conclusion that all things happened for a reason, and saying as much didn't make a person insightful. If one found themselves on one side of the street, it had happened because they'd crossed from the other side. Jim could well be nothing more than a ridiculous man stating the obvious.

Omens and prognostications were no more than statements of utmost banality, given greater meaning by the listener, who wanted to believe something controlled existence, watched over and protected them. The notion that the cosmos careened wildly without direction or purpose, frightened him. He wanted to believe Jim was something more, even though he probably wasn't.

Jim knelt, picking up Andrew's book. He flipped through the pages, face twisting as he tried to pick out words from the snarl of half-written thoughts and fierce scribbling. He considered one page for a long moment.

"Zoing?" he asked. He tapped his lips with a finger, then his mouth pinched toward one ear. "No. Not quite."

Andrew sighed.

Jim handed the book to Andrew. When Jim opened his hand, the book fell away from Andrew and into the dirt above Andrew's head. Jim's mouth turned and he regarded Andrew as though the writer should have known better.

"Let's fix this," said Jim.

He leaned forward and spread the branches gathered around Andrew. Andrew felt a pressure he hadn't noticed on his legs release. At the same time the dirt rushed up at his face and he smashed into the ground. His senses cleared and the throbbing in his ears departed. Andrew sat up and found himself in the clearing where he'd arrived with the wog and Billy-Bob.

None of them were to be found.

Billy-Bob, the wog, Kilgoth, the animals that had crowded the high grass between the trees—vanished. The terrain was raked and torn, with trees broken off at the waist around the edge of the clearing, great stones strewn about, and holes in the ground. Kilgoth had done this, Andrew decided.

"Where is everyone?"

"They've gone," said Jim. "So must we."

Andrew considered. He was saddened the boy had left him to his fate. He'd begun to think Billy-Bob was compassionate, even brave. Maybe a hero after all. No surprise that hope had taken him down that familiar path of disappointment. Most disappointing was that he'd been foolish enough to follow it yet again, knowing full well where it led.

"Good."

"Get up," said Jim. "You need to see something."

Without thinking, Andrew stood. But thinking came inevitably.

"Who are you?" he asked. He expected to regret the question, since Jim would likely answer that he was no one important and be honest and correct.

"My name is Jim," said Jim. "I'm surprised you don't remember me."

He led Andrew across the rippled soil toward a free-standing door Andrew felt sure he hadn't seen there before.

"I do remember," said Andrew as he struggled through the dirt that sank under each step, causing him to take exaggerated high steps that made him tired quickly, and he huffed out his response. "From Dirtburg. You said I was here for a reason. But you didn't say the reason."

Jim had no difficulty, his steps hardly sinking into the dirt.

"Excellent. Then introductions aren't necessary."

Jim either hadn't taken the hint that Andrew wanted to understand what he'd meant about having a reason or he was deliberately avoiding the answer. Since Andrew suspected there was no answer, he changed the subject.

"You gave Kilgoth the wristwatch."

"Yes," said Jim.

"Why?"

"That was his test."

"So he failed."

"Maybe," said Jim. His tone did not change, but Andrew saw the dip in Jim's shoulders as though the news disappointed him. "His test may not be over."

Andrew recalled his encounter with Kilgoth and felt foolish. He'd antagonized the giant for no purpose other than to vent his frustration. This destruction was the result. Now Billy-Bob had gone and Kilgoth may well have failed a test he'd been on the brink of passing. The latter disturbed him most, and deeply. He'd been selfish before and this made him a bully, and he didn't like himself very much. Andrew had made a monster of Kilgoth, and in so doing he'd made the world a more terrible place, first for Kilgoth, then for everyone upon which Kilgoth vented his fury. Any disasters that came from Kilgoth's rage could be traced back to Andrew. All the world Kilgoth returned to wasteland, Andrew had helped destroy. For all intents and purposes, Kilgoth was Andrew's responsibility. He could not think of a way to fix the problem, and didn't enjoy the weight on his heart that came from remembering it, so, for now, he tried to think of something else instead.

"You didn't answer my question. Who are you?"

"Who am I? A guide."

"That's it?"

"Nothing more. People believe they would benefit more from a wish-granting genie, but there's no purpose in such a being. Boons that help you avoid difficulty provide no knowledge, no understanding. The things you wish away just return in another form. Worse yet, people that look to the heavens for something to grant wishes, and ascribe their accomplishments to the supernatural, will likewise not take responsibility for mistakes and cruelties, will not learn and feel remorse and change. You understand how transformative remorse is, don't you? How it compels you to undo some great wrongdoing?"

The question struck Andrew like a hammer on a bell. Kilgoth's fate was Andrew's fault. Andrew didn't like it, but he could not disagree.

"You need to know how to navigate the path so you can show others," Jim continued, "and what was once a perilous place is stripped of its fear, allowing you to focus your energies on other, more important obstacles. That is how you save yourself and receive the power to save others—by helping them save themselves."

"That's what the tests are for."

"Yes."

"Then you… control this world. Are you…?"

If Jim was a deity, why was he here? Could he send Andrew home? Could he help Kilgoth?

"Ah," said Jim. He stopped walking and faced Andrew, hearing the unspoken question even as it hung in Andrew's mind. "That's a very big question that deserves an elaborate answer. I'll try to answer as best I can without boring you. I am in control as much as a man on a raft who can see rapids ahead. One can only prepare as best as one can against an array of possibilities. You were already on it. Maybe I created you because I needed something to entertain myself, and maybe you're all thoughts running around in my head. Maybe it was the other way around, and you needed something bigger than yourselves to believe in until you could believe in yourselves."

"Why are you here? Now. With me."

"To rekindle your hope."

Andrew felt it, that hope, each time Bree passed by. He always reached out to her, yearning with his mind and heart for her to stop, sit beside him, and share her arbitrary thoughts with him. A conversation about nothing is all he wanted, an exercise in imagination, but she always pulled free from the filaments of his hopes and continued on.

"Hope is not enough."

Jim shrugged.

"You're right."

"Then to catch you up. You are here for a purpose, after all. Even though your purpose won't have any effect until after you've left."

"What is my purpose?"

"Mardin figured it out, didn't he?"

"But he didn't tell me."

"Exactly. Because you aren't supposed to know. You have to learn for yourself. You can expect help and guidance, but there's no point in telling you everything. What will you learn? Reminding you that you do have a reason—that's helpful motivation."

They had reached the door. It did not have a knob, but this didn't matter since it stood free of any structure. With a minor detour he could get to the same place by going around. So Andrew began doing just that.

"No, no," said Jim, rustling in a pocket. He drew out a tarnished brass bulb of a doorknob that he pressed against the door and turned. The door opened, and Andrew saw the forest on the other side, unchanged.

"What is this?" asked Andrew.

"A shortcut," Jim answered.

Andrew wasn't certain what to make of Jim. He might be a large man with delusions of greatness, blurting out cryptic profundities to reinforce whatever false supernatural cloak he'd woven about himself. Still, better to indulge the giant man. He'd made the mistake of arguing with one giant today and been worsted for it. There wasn't any harm in going through this door to pacify Jim, apart from giving credence to his lunacy.

Jim bent at the waist and extended a hand toward the open door.

"Thanks," said Andrew, grimacing.

Andrew put a hand on the door frame and stuck a leg through. He felt a strange resistance, as though he were striding against a stiff wind, but didn't think much of this strangeness, and continued through. Andrew looked back, and Jim followed, smiling. He closed the door, the reached around the door frame, snapped his wrist, and popped the knob off. The knob went into the fold of his robes.

"Well," he said, looking pleased. "Here we are."

Andrew looked at Jim, the door behind him, and the familiar trees and broken landscape of the forest beyond them both. He'd already grown tired of this charade, and the false fatigue made him testy. Time, for what it was worth here, remained precious to him, and he didn't like it wasted.

"Where?"

Jim stepped forward, raised a finger, and poked it into Andrew's forehead.

"Here."

Andrew blinked in self defense. His head reeled back, then leveled, like a pine tree fighting a blast of wind. With it came a jolt of agitation. He clapped a hand over his forehead and glared at Jim, who returned the look with one of bemusement and expectation.

"Why...," he started.

And he might have continued, had his mouth not fallen ajar instead and the projectiles of speech diffused into a weak hiss of air. Andrew's eyes, screwed tight to sharpen the stab of his gaze, bloomed. The hand on his forehead fell away.

The trees, the shredded ground, and the doorway had all departed, as though when Jim touched Andrew's forehead he'd depressed a button that altered his perception of the world.

Somehow, this was somewhere else.

WANDERING IN WHAT WANDERS

The only word Andrew could think of to describe the place was Vast. They stood on the flat top of a hill, looking down over everything, a stretch of environments as wide as experience that seemed to curve up at the edges as though they were on the inside rather than the outside of a globe. Such a world shouldn't exist, couldn't exist, and yet here it was. Defiant.

It was bright here, thick grass feathered against his knees. The air had the pleasant tang of wetted leaves, like the forest where Andrew and Billy-Bob had met Kilgoth. From his vantage he could see a town, the rooftops visible above a haze of dust, bordered on one side by a dead forest and a great crevice on the other. Near this town was an ashen ring of buildings and a pillar of rock in the center. Far off a building stood atop a leaning pedestal. Beside it was a wide forest with circular gap in the center, and beyond that still more, though his eyes weren't sharp enough to see it in any detail.

Jim stared into the distance at a long sheet of gray hovered at the edge of the world and crooked spikes of lightning flashed where ground and sky were briefly joined. These same clouds and lightning ringed the entire realm.

"Always rain on the horizon here," Jim mused. "Waiting for something to pull the drawstrings and close over the world."

Andrew's eyes fluttered.

"Here?" he echoed.

"This is everywhere. From the perspective of one person. Have you never wondered what it would be like to explore the landscape of the mind?"

Around them people milled on the hilltop, clucking to one another and gesturing to a single point on the hill—a tall rock that cast a long shadow down the hill. The rock was indistinct, apart from being twice the height of a normal person. It stood upon a marble base upon which a single word had been inscribed: Hero.

To his surprise, many of the people here were familiar. A slouching man with wings, looking gray and tired, stared into his empty hands and whistled the same song parts again and again. Hobert sat with a pipe in his mouth, gazing at the pillar of rock in silent adulation. A woman stood beside a post and the outline of a wog was visible through her. Each of these characters went about their business in a state of intense focus punctuated by moments of acute distraction. They chatted to themselves or others, picked at a minor chore, or operated as manifestations of their most conspicuous quirk, such as Gordimer's incessant whistling, then interrupted themselves to look back at the rock and discern whether anything had changed, treating it with a mix of apprehension and curiosity.

The only people not watching the block were two fellows standing at a square table covered with drawings and schematics, which they pounded frequently, gesturing offhandedly at the pillar of rock. They gesticulated feverishly, pointed sharply at one another, exchanged expressions of bewilderment, vehemence, and insistence, all the while seeming thoughtful, disagreeable, and insulted.

"Here," Andrew repeated thoughtfully.

"Yes. Here," said Jim. "Inside Billy-Bob's mind."

Andrew started. This was Billy-Bob's mind?

"Well, not exactly," Jim added. "That would just be a heap of gook, sloshing fluids, and bolts of cerebral electricity. This is more a representation of how he sorts things, a single environment as an amalgamation of his thoughts, ideas, and experiences. Fascinating, don't you think? It's nicer here than most places."

"Better organized than I expected," Andrew remarked.

Calmer, too. To his astonishment, he recognized a tall, straight-backed individual with a clear, confident expression striding through the crowd. He carried a thick notepad in one hand and tapped a finger on his lips, thinking. Every few steps he would pause to observe someone, open his notepad, and scribble something down.

"You!" called Andrew.

The writer looked up and Andrew found himself staring into his own face.

"You're me!" said Andrew.

His doppelganger considered.

"It would be right to help," the duplicate remarked with a heavy, meaningful voice that did not sound like his own.

Andrew's mouth opened. His copy considered him for a moment, jotted in the notepad, and walked away.

"That's me!" he said. "That's how he sees me?"

Jim shrugged.

"I suppose a few exaggerations are to be expected in a dream world."

"What am I doing here?"

"The same as everyone. Waiting. Waiting to see what a hero is and whether it can save them."

"Doesn't anyone know what a hero is?"

Jim's eyebrows lifted.

"Do you?"

Andrew's mind swam with broken images. Folk cheering, clouds parting, tears of relief and joy. But no heroes. Jim's arms crossed, waiting. The notion of hero had long been lodged in his head, explosions and daring and dash and whatnot, but now, nothing. Could it be he really didn't know?

"Keep working on it," said Jim, who stepped toward the fellows at the table.

Their faces were reddened by fervent argumentation, but paled when they saw Jim approaching. Both had wide, owlish eyes and slender but rough hands. Their long, dark hair was knotted and messy, and each was bearded. Sloppy and disheveled, too distracted by their own waterfall of thought to bother with appearance.

"We know you," said one.

"Sublime," the other said.

"Benign," the first added.

"Divine."

"Ursine."

The brow of the first crumpled and he turned to face his compatriot.

"What?"

The other shrugged.

"It rhymes."

The second nodded.

"So it does. As such, it must apply."

"Oh Jim, most Ursine. We are gladdened by your presence. We were wondering…"

"Ah!" Jim held up a hand, shielding himself from the coming question. "I don't. You know that. Still, if you want answers, this writer seems fairly confident."

Jim jerked his thumb backward and the two fellows traced the gesture to Andrew.

The eager pair were upon him instantly, shaking his hand and crowding close with eagerness.

"I am Elmichangelo, though I will answer to Elmich," said the first, gesturing to himself, then to the man beside him, "and this is my less talented associate, Nidor."

The one named Nidor crossed his arms and pretended to ignore the jibe.

"We've determined they save everyone," said Nidor. "Good, bad, villains. Sounds impossible but seems right. Does that make them foolhardy? How would you show these things in a statue?"

To his surprise, Andrew had an answer. He didn't even need to think about it before it issued from his mouth.

"Big ears."

The two fellows shared a look of astoundment.

"Yes! That's it!" said one.

"Macrotous. Of course! Why didn't we think of that?"

Both began jotting feverishly upon large pads of paper, sketching, and flipping over the page to continue of the rear side. Andrew turned to Jim while they were preoccupied.

"Who are these people? I've never seen them."

"These are all aspects of his consciousness. When you speak to them, you speak to him. You shape his thoughts, as an artist would a stone. Of course there are some facets of his personality you've never seen. Some he has withheld, while others have been withheld from him. Now is your opportunity to understand him better."

"How?"

Jim smiled wryly.

"You already have an understanding of the process."

Jim meant he just needed to ask. So he would. Andrew pointed to the stone.

"What is that big rock?" he asked. "I mean, besides a rock. Why is it there? Why is everyone so preoccupied with it?"

The artists' attention swung back to Andrew.

"It's not a rock!"

"No no. It's a hero."

This response had a familiar, frustrating theme to it. It shouldn't have come as a surprise that Billy-Bob would think of a statue as a hero.

"The rock," said Andrew in a slow, dubious tone, "is a hero."

"One waiting to be set free," agreed Elmich.

"There's a hero trapped in there?"

"So to speak," said Nidor. "An image in stone. A perfect representation."

"A sculpture, then," said Andrew.

"Yes, yes," said Elmich, somewhat surprised. He tapped his temple with a finger. "You're very bright. Appearance is not everything."

Andrew scowled.

"Though we aren't quite sure what that image should be," Nidor continued.

So these two were sculpting a hero. Before he could shape the question Why? Jim was already answering.

"We envy what is better than ourselves," Jim observed. "What we think would make us better. Those things stick in the mind. Some people model themselves on the image. Others rebel against it."

Andrew wondered what the statue in his mind appeared like. Was it of a noted writer? Or just a block of unshaped granite. He could think of no one he wished to emulate—imitation created a world of clones, dull, repetitive, and predictable. But could one disagree with the template for what was right without being against it? Was Andrew a villain for not wanting to write the biography selected for him, for hating the fact that he'd been sent here reluctantly?

"Makes you wonder, doesn't it?" Jim whispered in his ear. "Figuring out heroes is only part of the equation. The other part, the more important one, is figuring out what you are."

"I'm not a hero," Andrew gritted. "Or a villain. I'm a writer."

"We'll see," said Jim.

"It's supposed to be a hero," Nidor continued. "So, should it be stoic?"

"Or caring?" asked Elmich.

Andrew's head twisted from one artist to the other as the questions came, too fast to follow.

"Should it be bold?"

"Or thoughtful?"

"Should it look to save others?"

"Or should it save itself so it can save others later?"

Andrew raised his hands to stem the flow of questions.

"I don't know. I'm not sure."

The two fellows shared a deep frown.

"Don't you know any heroes?" asked Nirod.

"Why?"

"So we can learn what makes that person a hero," Elmich explained. "One cannot do what they are required to do without knowing the nature of that which must be done. Not being an artisan, you probably didn't know that."

The hair on Andrew's neck stiffened.

"True," Nirod agreed. "Must dislike challenges. Challenges have a way of stretching your mind and making you more capable. Most people don't seem to like that. The stretching must hurt."

Elmich nodded.

"An artist nocks an arrow in their heartstrings, pours themselves and their understanding into the mold of the arrowhead, and fires it into the minds of passers by. Those struck are changed. You can see the arrow's tailfeathers sticking out of them. Great works change people. For better or worse, it makes you different. This is meant for better. That's why this hero's every detail must be perfect. It's for everyone. Right, Jim? Of course right. Do you think a hero would be short or tall? Better to reach high things or be able to fit in small spaces?"

Jim batted the question away like a pesky insect.

"That's for you to decide. You select the features you want in your entities of significance. Look at me!"

The sculptors frowned with displeasure, but accepted the answer.

"Very well," said Elmich. "We will. We can. Eventually. After some thought."

"Heavy, deep, important, and most likely redundant thought," Nidor added.

"It may be a while," Elmich concluded.

"You wouldn't be happy with the decision any other way," said Jim. He raised a finger. "However, if you'd like a few guidelines, follow me."

Elmich and Nidor brightened, and Andrew felt his own spirits lift somewhat. What useful information could they find inside Billy-Bob's mind? And what information could they find that he didn't already know? It didn't seem likely heroism would make a significant showing here.

Jim turned and started down the slope and the two sculptors followed closely.

As Andrew followed there was a flicker and hiss in the air behind them and a sharp, matchstrike odor. A hot wave of air washed past. Andrew turned to see a red beast burst flaming into existence, hovering before the incomplete statue. It roared with such strength that Andrew heard nothing, but felt his bones shudder and ears ring, and the slab trembled on its pedestal. Andrew, horrified beyond the simple impulse to flee, felt the strength in his legs drain away and he slouched to his knees like a deflating balloon. The others around the statue stared, more curious and fascinated than terrified.

The creature was twice as large as Andrew, held in space by the powerful beating of stretching black wings. Its arms were thick and knotted by muscle, ending in hooked fingers. All its features were blurred by an aura of flame that covered its body.

The beast gave another roar, then reached out a taloned hand and swatted at the statue, knocking a hunk of rock into the distance marked by a puff of cinder where it landed. The remainder of the statue slumped and dropped into a heap of disconnected shards.

Its mission complete, the beast roared again, not in victory, but an unrelenting and unslaked rage, then disappeared as abruptly as it came.

"Great," Elmich muttered. "Now we've got to start all over."

His voice sounded muted and Andrew realized he was pressing his palms hard against his ears. He lowered them, noticing a faint tremor in his fingers.

"What was that?" he asked.

Jim had continued down the slope, oblivious to the recent catastrophe.

"A monster," Nirod explained.

"Evil," Elmich clarified. "That would be my guess."

Nirod turned to his compatriot.

"Monsters are inherently Evil," said the artist.

"Well, of course that's true, but this fellow might not be as well invested with intellect as you and I."

Nirod nodded.

"A distinct possibility."

Elmich waggled a paint-stained finger.

"A more than certain likelihood."

Nirod's hands snapped to his hips.

"There you go again, refining my sentiments! I recommend you desist."

"Or what?"

"Or it will be my pleasure to sculpt your likeness as an uncomely beastling of a monster with a sideways nose and a hollowed out bowl for a head to indicate the difficulty you have assembling your thoughts."

"Then I would surely retaliate in a similar fashion, but a different medium. Perhaps a vase with a hole in the side, or some pragmatic object with an equivalent and significantly damning flaw."

Jim waited nearby, crouched over a patch of sand in the grass where an ant skittered urgently one way, paused, then turned about and ran in another direction. Andrew stood beside him, wondering how it had gotten separated from the others.

"The world is a harsh place for a single ant," said Jim. He watched the ant briefly, then drug a channel in the sand leading into the grass. The ant found the path, wavered its feelers, and followed the trail. Jim straightened and headed down the hill. "This way."

Andrew followed.

Not far along they encountered an information post. The woman who served as librarian stood beside it, but she was quiet. A man stood near her, clad in a garment that appeared to be one or two thick towels arranged cleverly about his shoulders to cover his entire body. His body flickered, indicating he, like the librarian, was a projection. A boy sat attentively nearby.

"It is certainly sordid to do the wrong thing," he was saying, "and anyone can do the right thing when no danger is attached. What distinguishes the good man from others is that when danger is involved he still does right."

"An excellent point," said Nirod.

Both artists stood nearby, scribbling on notepads, their faces marked with fading red handprints, the remnants of their altercation.

The boy, though younger, had the unmistakable definitive characteristics of Billy-Bob. His eyes were attentive, yet glassy, his head pitched back slightly and his mouth ajar as though it were an additional hearing receptacle. Andrew guessed he couldn't be more than a decade old. What was not characteristic was his clothing: clean white shirt and gray pants that fit him well. His hair lay parted and orderly, trimmed about the ears rather than scraggly and unkempt. Someone had cared for him before leaving him to care for himself.

"That's Billy-Bob?" asked Andrew.

"Of course it is," said Jim. "Everything here is Billy-Bob, with exception to you and I. Each person here, if not a representation of someone he's met, is an avenue of thought, continuing or recurring, intermingled with the memories that shaped them."

Andrew wanted to ask who the speaking man was, but Jim strode purposefully away. Jim didn't seem concerned to leave the artists behind, nor did the artists seem to notice.

In the near distance Andrew could see a figure seated at the edge of the forest, staring into the darkness. Jim's path bore directly toward it. This must be what he wanted the artists to see—the culmination in this long string of heroes.

"We are all connected, one to another, past, present, and future," said Jim. "We all carry the same fate."

"Huh?"

Much of what Jim had to say sounded like it should make sense but didn't. His sentences were put together almost algebraically, with most information present, yet lacking some small portion to make it whole. And despite his best efforts Andrew couldn't figure out what was missing.

Jim was walking faster now, and before Andrew could ask, Jim was speaking.

"Here we have the architect of this world."

Sure enough, the seated figure was Billy-Bob, face fixed and emotionless as he stared into the forest. Somehow he knew without asking he would get no response from the boy. This was just an image he had made of himself. An unexpectedly modest appraisal. Most folk made themselves greater in their minds. Masters of worlds.

This version of Billy-Bob was close to the one he knew, but tidy and calm. He wore the oversized pants and shoes Andrew remembered, and a pistol rested on the ground beside him. But this version had clear eyes, free of the consternation and uncertainty Andrew often saw. To this version, the world was just the world, not a problem to be solved.

Beside Billy-Bob was a round, stuffed creature, placid and beaten with dirt caked in its matted fur. A tiny creature that appeared to have suffered a thousand huggings. It was, unmistakably, a wog. Not mechanical, just a stuffed companion.

Jim crouched before Billy-Bob, who stared right through him, and squinted.

"Heroes are an unfortunate breed," he said. "They grind their hearts to a pebble, pining until all love is whittled and wasted, leaving them worn, bitter, and, most tragically, still alone."

"That doesn't sound anything like a hero."

"Maybe you are confused about what a hero really is. Why be a hero but to seek fame? And why seek fame but to cover up a lingering loneliness?"

"To be loved, you're saying. Heroes want to be heroes so they will be loved."

"Yes."

In Andrew's experience there was no love in the world but the one-sided, unrequited sort. Love singled people out and tortured them relentlessly. Love drove people into the arms of those who wanted nothing more than to be rid of them. Bree. She must despise him or he would not be here. And yet he wanted nothing more than to see her again. It didn't make sense.

"Love is a ludicrous distraction."

Jim faced Andrew

"It is and isn't. It motivates when withheld, sustains when given, and destroys when taken away."

"But if he had love, he wouldn't need to be a hero."

Jim hesitated before responding.

"Possibly."

"So to create a hero you must deny them what they want."

"Correct."

Jim, for all his feigned kindness and concern, was cruel.

"Righteousness seems like a better heroic characteristic than love."

"To be sure! But where does that come from? Empathy, I would say. You suppose the love a hero craves is from a single person. Oh no! A hero craves the love of all people. It's why a true hero attempts to save more than just the victims."

Jim reached out a hand, pushing hair out of the boy's face. His lips tightened and he continued.

"Heroes go numb to emotion, so it cannot harm them. But when you no longer feel loss or regret, you cease to be a hero. You become unable to distinguish right from wrong. It is no longer important. There is a balance for normal people. But heroes are obliterated. They are hammered with emotion until, like a nail overdriven into a plank of wood, there is no retrieving them."

"So a hero is destined to fail. Even if they survive they are whittled away to nothing."

Jim paused, heaping and dissecting memories, thoughts, facts, ideas. His eyebrows peaked, mouth quirked and he scratched the end of his nose.

"Not always. Sometimes they attempt to repair themselves. But they replace what they have lost with rage."

"They become villains."

"Yes."

The word was cold, heartless, and it made Andrew angry.

Could Billy-Bob become a villain? Could he be hurt to such a degree that his kindness could be driven out? He knew without asking. He knew because he understood the rage in his own heart over minor afflictions. He knew others were equally susceptible. And, at the same time, another realization came to him: he had to change. For Billy-Bob. Because if Andrew could overcome his flaws, so could anyone. So could the boy.

"So you would let heroes save as much as they can before they're destroyed or broken or become the thing they are meant to protect against?"

"I know," Jim muttered. "Maybe now you understand better what it is to be a hero."

He did. And the glory of the title was eradicated because, ultimately, it was the heroes who needed saving.

Andrew gritted his teeth. What could he do? He was only a writer.

Andrew blinked. What could he do? Anything. He was a writer, after all. He had the power to make him great, terrible, an embarrassment, or irrelevant, regardless of the truth. He could make Billy-Bob the most revered individual in history. The boy's deeds were limited only by Andrew's imagination. That would be his gift to him. There would be no need to chase heroism. Andrew could spare him from a fate none survived. Andrew could, as a mere writer, save Billy-Bob.

To be author of a work chronicling a hero's career would win him accolades and affection, perhaps even from Bree. Billy-Bob might not be a hero, but Andrew could make him one, and in the process make himself great as well.

Why had he not considered this before? Perhaps because he knew the purpose of this mission was truth. But even the best history often proved a distortion of the truth, a view of the past through a spyhole, leaving the peripheries hidden. People delighted in proud histories, which often served as functional lies.

"You are not a great person," said Andrew, as much to himself as to the silent boy, "but you will accomplish great things. I will see to that."

The boy showed a hint of animation, turning his head to look at Andrew. His mouth opened, as it sometimes did when Billy-Bob had a thought he couldn't put into words. True to form, he remained silent, and his eyes seemed to look through him, as though he knew Andrew was present but could not see him.

The grass crunched behind the boy and the two artists approached, gleefully passing notes between one another. Clearly much progress had been made in their endeavor. They stopped when they spotted Jim and Andrew.

Nirod spoke first.

"Well," he said cheerily. "We've sketched some splendid examples."

Elmich crouched and looked at Billy-Bob, tapping a pencil against his lips. To recreate a hero one needed to know not just what a hero was, but also what a hero was not.

"And this one," said Elmich. "The most bizarre of all."

"Most bizarre," Nirod echoed, head bobbing. "I like him too."

* * *

"I suppose that's about it," said Jim. "Not much else to see here."

"Where to next?" asked Andrew.

The trees of the forest stood like densely packed harp strings. There would be no pushing through them.

"Here," said Jim.

Jim pointed to a door not far away. An ordinary door, no more than a few planks of wood with a knob, led directly into the wide trunk of a tree.

"Where does it go?"

Jim shrugged.

Andrew grimaced. In all likelihood it would open into a wall of trees or an empty room. Or worse, a bear, waiting for a curious investigator to pry the door open. A roar and a swat to the head before bounding off through the open door to create more mischief with its newfound freedom.

"Why don't you open it?" asked Andrew.

"Me? No," said Jim. "Might be a bear inside."

Andrew twisted the knob and pulled the door open. Warm, oily air rushed through. He felt alert, but not frightened, as though all the subtle aspects of sound and odor and light told him this place was safe.

"Careful," said Jim. "Never know what you'll find."

He stepped through. There was no forest, no giant red man, no wogs, no bear. Instead, he found himself in a room cluttered with wooden tables and chairs, and a large window facing the street with a single word arcing across the pane: SKNIRD.

"Now where are we?"

No response.

Andrew turned toward Jim and found himself facing the wood slats of a wall. The door, the forest, the artists, and Jim were gone. His eyes fluttered. He stood for a few moments, then strode to the window where others stared into a grassy street, trying to get an idea of where he might be.

A giant figure, monstrous and red stood inside the shell of a broken building, not unlike the creature he had seen in Billy-Bob's head. Wisps of black smoke leaked through its open mouth. Talons at the end of long, muscled legs clawed into the ground and the air seemed to sizzle around it. And for all its mortifying horror, there was something pitiable about it. Something in the upward tilt of its brows, and a frown more pained than hateful, as though the beast were nursing a great, hidden hurt.

"Kilgoth," Andrew whispered.

"You know that thing?" asked one of the observers.

Standing opposite Kilgoth, a dandelion beside an oak tree, was a boy, gun drawn and trembling. It was, of course, Billy-Bob. And this would be his long foretold end.

Andrew felt no relief his task was about to end. Soon he would be home again, free to pine in the presence of Bree. Free to forget this experience. But he knew he would not. He knew it would never diminish. He would remember what he had done here. And, more importantly, what he had failed to do.

As he watched, the gun kicked and fired.

THE GIRL

Flee.

At the moment that was all Billy-Bob could think to do. Not even a thought, but an impulse he could not resist any better than a rolling boulder could resist the compulsion to seek the lowest point in the terrain. Both slaves to their nature, both leaving a trail of shredded vegetation in their wake.

The tendrils and swinging branches of trees and weeds and bushes clung to him, tried to slow him, implored him to stop and think, but he drove onward, spurred by the lingering image of a giant destroying beast gone mad. Plants clamored to him as he plowed through, their voices overlapping in grating disunion.

"Where are you going? Mind those elbows! Your hat is off! Where has your wog gone? What about the writer? Who is going to fix this mess?"

He didn't respond. Partly because he was too busy running. Mostly because he didn't know how to answer.

The wog had wanted to protect him and the writer wanted his protection. He'd lost both in the space of a few breaths. No, he corrected himself, he'd abandoned them. As a result they had faced destruction on their own. Some hero.

Most frightening about the encounter was not that Kilgoth had tried to destroy them, but that Kilgoth had been a helper. Knowing something meant to benefit him had turned into something dangerous and destructive horrified Billy-Bob. The idea that everything could change had given him hope about his own fate, but he'd never considered the possibility that a creature could change from friend to terror, and he realized there was no comforting permanence to anything. That meant even great goods could turn to great evils, and he had no idea if they could be turned back again.

At length the clutching of the forest grew weaker as trees thinned and ebbed into a lolling, grassy plain. He emerged, stems poking through his clothing and tendrils of creeping vines clinging to his legs. He stopped in a bare patch of ground and made a slow circle. The sky pressed down in a solid gray slab and wind whipped and tugged, swirling and beating a sweep of ripples across the chest-high grasses. Boulders lodged in the terrain like rivets. The plain stretched from the forest behind him on to the limit of his vision.

Nothing. No Kilgoth, no writer, no wog, no animals. Only high grass on the lumpy terrain, and here and there a boulder. He'd left them all behind.

He ought to go back. Billy-Bob faced the forest and the black hole in the foliage where he'd exited. Back through that opening Andrew and the wog awaited him. Kilgoth, that great and terrible creature, awaited too. He hesitated, and in that moment of hesitation knew he would return. He felt a hand tighten around his heart and sank to the ground under the weight of his shame.

He could never be a hero now.

"Not genna cry, are yeh?"

The question came from the coiled husk of an empty snail shell by his feet.

Vision blurred as water gathered over his eyes. He clenched his hands, trying to reabsorb the moisture, but his eyes continued to fill like pits dug into the water table. He'd had his chances to prove himself heroic with mixed results. He'd had the chance to save Andrew, to calm Kilgoth, to preserve a patch of forest holding off the wasteland. Instead, he'd run away. It was not, he was certain, what heroes did.

He could not have resisted Kilgoth in his rage, but he could have prevented it if he'd stopped Andrew from riling him, or prevented the bird from taking the wristwatch. Could he have known at the time? The solutions seemed plain now. A hero would have known, would have analyzed and extrapolated all the minutiae of the situation and plotted out the different paths events could take, allowing some events to occur and putting an end to others. A hero could do these things.

"Eh?" the shell persisted.

"No," Billy-Bob answered hollowly.

A reluctant droplet fell from one eye, followed by another.

"Don't thenk heroes do metch cryin'," the shell observed.

"I'm not," he said, the words fighting through the tightness in his throat. Billy-Bob ground his palms against his eyes and clenched his teeth.

"Naught what? A hero, er cryin'? Y're certainly one er the other, 'cause ye kenna be both."

What qualifications did he possess to be a hero? He had never triumphed of his own accord, only escaped, and each time by a slimmer margin than before. Destruction never caught him, but it gained ground with each encounter. This time, as before, he'd escaped. But those accompanying him had not, and no failure was so bitter as that which sacrificed others.

Escaping perils did not make them go away. Peril needed to be confronted and defeated, otherwise they remained to run afoul of those who encountered them next.

Billy-Bob set his jaw, swallowing sobs that wanted to climb up his throat and flee into the world. This tiny bit of misery would stay with him. Rather than have grief spread, he would make it a prisoner. It's what a hero would do. But who relieved the suffering of a hero?

"Ah," said the shell. "Naught cryin', I see. Ye must be a hero, then. Process of elimination. Logic is a handy thing, you'll find."

The grass flattened around him as a gush of air gusted past, accompanied by a low, rumbling roar. Billy-Bob looked back and saw a long black streak extending across the sky as if daytime were slowly coming unzipped and the night leaked through the gap. A silver shining tip at the top of the streak reached inexorably upward, then disappeared like a needle passing through the fabric of this world to something beyond.

The sound of breaking branches and tearing grass came from beyond the wall of scrub. A ripple of cold fright dashed up the ladder of his spine and his hand went reflexively to his pistol, missed, and found the pocket with acorns instead.

Flee! cried his mind. Flee! Flee!

He wanted to obey. To stand, run, and churn forward to safety. But he sat, defiant, determined, and terrified. He felt brave and noble and foolish all at once. The approaching monster could be a bulldozer of scissoring teeth, mulching a path through the undergrowth.

Branches shuddered, dropping leaves as something horrific shredded its way toward him. A silhouette formed behind them, round and fierce. A soft, grunt squeezed out of the brush, followed by a troubled face besieged by a thundering stampede of unmade decisions. It looked at him, blinking, mouth opening in surprise. A hand extended from the tangle of scrub.

Billy-Bob's eyes bloomed.

"Help," said the face.

Not thinking, Billy-Bob took the hand and pulled. Gradually, a girl, lithe and firm, emerged from the brush and fell over him.

She was filthy, abraded, covered in branches and dirt and sweat, slick and grimy, breath rushing hoarsely in and out with labored gasps. She reached back and pulled her hair free of the hooked fingers of clinging branches, then looked back at him with a stern, green stare, caked with dirt. Her dark brows were scarcely distinguishable from the rest of her dirty face. Something in the air made his eyes water. She smelled like onions.

Beautiful.

Horrible and filthy, but vibrant. Something beneath the grit radiated a warmth that made the warty clods of dirt stuck to her face seem grossly wonderful. It would be silly to say he loved her. Love so instantaneous was impossible, ridiculous, like having an answer before knowing the question, because one didn't love a body or the snapshot of a face, but a spirit, and a spirit took time to learn. He didn't know her name, her favorite color, the thoughts that came when her eyes stared in blankness and longing, and a million other secret things one needed to know before they could plunge safely into love. Or so it should have been.

Love was an irrational thing, undaunted by logic, drawing entities together with a cruel and sometimes absurd obsession. Men to women who disliked them, women to men who mistreated them. Love was a clock pendulum tick tocking from your forehead and interfering with every endeavor. One could not ignore love, nor make sense of it, only wrestle in vain against it or learn to live with the distraction.

She watched him, waiting for something, and he realized he'd been staring overlong.

"Hello," he said, determined not to make a fool of himself. "My name is… ah…"

The girl arched an eyebrow and waited, but Billy-Bob couldn't finish. Her gaze scattered his thoughts like cattle in a thunderstorm. He'd forgotten.

She clutched his shoulder and pulled herself to her feet. For an instant she watched him, mouth quirking. He could see there was a word racing around in her head, one she felt reluctant to use here. Maybe Thanks. She reached out a grimy thumb and wiped away a streak of moisture still clinging to his face, leaving a swipe of dirt in its place. Her lips parted to speak.

At the same time, more rustling came from the grass and branches behind her. She gave a harried look behind, then back to Billy-Bob.

"Stall them," she said, then raised her forearm, shut her eyes, and plunged into the greenery ahead of her.

"Who?" he called, but she did not respond, and the crunch of her feet withdrew.

When he turned back a creature stood in the clearing before him, regarding him in silence. Short, with large eyes and a heavy, ovular body on two wide feet. What fur remained had long filled with dirt and faded to gray, worn away in patches to reveal a metal structure inside. Battered by time, tribulation, and neglect.

"Hello, wog," said Billy-Bob.

The wog inclined slightly in acknowledgment, then straightened. It regarded him carefully, paying special attention to the gun on his hip. The wog took a careful step to the side, then another, circling slowly around behind him. Billy-Bob scooted to counter the movement, blocking its path to the place where the girl had disappeared back into the grasses. When the wog realized what he was doing it paused, then stooped to pick up a small stone. Billy-Bob watched, wondering what it wanted, what it was doing with the pebble, and what he ought to do next.

"What is your mission?" Billy-Bob asked.

The wog began to crank an arm back, but the question stopped it. Thinking always proved an effective interruption. The wog's arm slackened and the pebble dropped from its hand, but it did not respond. Instead, the wog crouched, almost sitting, as though settling down to consider its answer.

"It's the girl," said a familiar, choppy voice.

The voice came from behind him where another wog stood, just inside the wall of grass. This wog was smashed on one side and moved forward with a faint drag in its step. The left part of its body appeared nonfunctional, its features crinkled like a partially crushed can, the left eye closed and the arm below it hanging limp at its side.

"We're all pretty much the same," said the damaged wog. "The biggest difference is our mission. That's what makes us what we are. Mine is to protect you."

Billy-Bob felt a surge of happiness and relief. Maybe the writer had survived as well with some minor handicap. This did not vindicate his decision to abandon them, but knowing the consequences had not been as dire as he feared made him feel better.

"You're all right!" he exclaimed. After a moment of quiet assessment, he added, "mostly."

"Be careful," the protector wog warned. "They don't know you. Worse, they can't know you. Like the Information Post C at Alpha, they have been corrupted and repurposed. There are no scruples to turn them aside—that isn't part of their mission. They truly are dangerous."

"How is the girl their mission?"

The protector wog limped between Billy-Bob and the other wog, which tilted its head and watched with bemusement.

"Once, their mission was to find the lost girl, the girl that could not be found. The girl that gave her image to the Information Posts. A futile and pointless mission that no doubt led to frustration. That mission has undergone a subtle tweak. Now their mission is to find a different girl, one that can be found, and they are pursuing her with vigor. And their goal is not strictly for the purpose of discovery, but hostility."

"Who did this to them?"

"You know who."

John, thought Billy-Bob. He'd altered the post to fool the people of Alpha, he must have done the same to the wogs. What other calamities had he brought about through his deceptions?

"He gave them what they wanted: purpose," the crippled wog continued. "It only takes that little bit to be corrupted."

Other wogs pushed out of the grass and lined the opposite site of the clearing. They did not advance, but held steady, watching and waiting.

"You should go," said the crippled wog. "I won't be able to hold them for long."

Billy-Bob knew he should run and leave the protector wog to its destruction. Sacrifice often helped pave the road to victory, and Billy-Bob could not be victorious in the future if he lost everything here. Of his limited options, running away made the most sense. He stood.

"No."

The crippled wog faced Billy-Bob.

"What are you doing? Now is not the time to be a brave fool."

"I'm doing what is right because there is no one else here to do it."

This felt like what he ought to do and it felt good to do it, even though he knew running was the wiser choice. As soon as he'd made this decision, the hostile wog decided to test it.

Without warning, the hostile wog straightened its legs, launching it into the air. This should not have come as a surprise, since the protector wog behaved the same way during their first encounter. Nevertheless, he'd expected some sort of negotiation to take place and to have a clear reason for resisting the wog before fighting it.

The protector wog leapt as well, but its leaping power was clearly diminished by the damage it had sustained, and the attacking wog sailed over it easily. The leap of a wog was something truly magnificent to behold, propelling the wog's body headfirst through the air like a hairy cannonball. Such leaps would propel a wog great distances, allowing rapid travel from place to place, but in Billy-Bob's experience that skill had been sadly misused. At short range a truly malevolent creature could punch through a person as easily as a wet paper bag.

With so much force behind a leap, it must have come as a surprise to the wog when Billy-Bob clapped his hands around the wog and caught it. Billy-Bob felt a sense of pleasure that no doubt matched the surprise the attacking wog felt. He hesitated, allowing the wog to understand it had been defeated, then delivered a final, triumphant blow.

"Stop," Billy-Bob commanded.

He'd given the same command on the bridge outside Dirtburg with great effect, leaving scores of the creatures paralyzed. The wogs had somehow known him, his voice, or that word, and obeyed.

The wog blinked in response, processing the command, but did not go limp or become unresponsive as Billy-Bob expected. Instead, it appeared to wait in case Billy-Bob had anything more to say. When it became apparent he did not, the wog made a noise that Billy-Bob thought sounded like a scoffing snort. Then it spoke.

"No."

Before Billy-Bob could speak again he felt a jolt of electricity rush through him, locking his muscles. He could not drop the wog, scream, or try to run away, which, if he'd had any sense, he ought to have done in the first place. Six more wogs pushed into the clearing. How many more remained hidden he couldn't guess. Maybe they stretched on through the grasses to the horizon.

The new wogs surrounded the protector wog and pinned it down, then began surveying it, as might a doctor examining a patient to determine what was still working.

They had found a way to get around the paralysis, and if they could do that, it made sense that they could get around the command altogether. The wog that traveled with him had proven a clever thinker. So it was not outside the realm of possibility that other wogs were also clever and could think of ways around what had blocked them before. He only wished he'd had the sense to realize this before he'd tried it again.

A second jolt flashed through Billy-Bob, blurring his vision. When it cleared another wog stood before him, twice as tall as Billy-Bob, staring down at him with perilous enormity. A luminous crown hovered above its head, rotating slowly. Where it had come from he did not know. He had not heard or felt it approach. It was as though the wog had accumulated from the very particles around them. In fact, it appeared the accumulation process had not finished because he could see the outlines of bushes and high grass through it.

The giant wog tilted forward slightly and spoke.

"Greetings, thrall," it said in a voice free of the static associated with a wog voice. "Your feeble mind is no doubt confused by my appearance. Know that your fears are justified, but misplaced. I am simply the image through which the collective communicates and can do you no harm, an image projected onto the viewscreen of your brain. Harm, however, will certainly come to you should you not cooperate, for while this depiction of our majesty cannot hurt you, we are most certainly dangerous. Do you understand?"

Billy-Bob tried to respond, but found his jaw locked.

"Good," said the giant wog. "There is a chest beside you. Do you see it?"

Billy-Bob could not move his head either, but his eyes slid to the corner and saw a small chest he could carry under one arm a few steps away.

"That chest represents all the material in your mind. You can infer what you like from its diminutive size. We want a small piece from that chest only. You can either provide that piece or we will rummage through in search of it, perhaps losing pieces and leaving it in disarray. Perhaps things will find their way in that do not belong. Perhaps we will empty the thing completely and fill it again with dirt and grass trimmings."

The pain of the shock holding Billy-Bob in place had diminished, but the rigidity had not. He could feel a tingling running up his arms, through his body and across his jaw. He could still move his tongue, however, and that was something, even if he didn't know how to use this to his advantage. So he fished around his mouth in search of a hinge to undo the trap he'd fallen into and eventually tried to pry his mouth open from the inside. This worked far better than expected, and when he wedged his teeth apart his whole mouth popped open as though the clasp holding it shut had broken.

"What do you want from us?" asked Billy-Bob.

The giant wog appeared taken aback.

"That shouldn't be possible," it said. Nevertheless, the great wog recovered quickly. "What do we want from you? Information. We want to know where the girl is going. We will extract this information through whatever means necessary, then we will go. From your companion wog, the majority is useless. We want only what remains of its functioning parts."

"We don't know her," said Billy-Bob. "We don't know where she's going. The wog doesn't have anything to do with it. Leave him alone."

"Maybe you don't know. We'll find out. We will take what we want, then we will eliminate all memory of the conversation having taken place, of your having met us, of the girl, of everything to which you aspire to and makes you useful, and replace it with an impossible mission to occupy you to the end of your days. 'Locate the lost girl' or 'find two hundred heroes'. Something nonsensical and meaningless. You won't know any better and the futility of such pursuits amuses us. Not only will we make your mission futile, we will make you adamant, which will drive you to a swift and spectacular end."

"Sure does like t' talk, don't it?" muttered the empty snail shell. "What is the point of this meaningless exposition?"

"I don't know," Billy-Bob answered.

He didn't give much thought to his answer or that he gave it aloud. As had happened many times before to others, the wog had no idea Billy-Bob was having a conversation with someone else.

"You do know," said the giant wog. "And soon we will know. And then you won't know anymore."

"Maybe," the shell continued, "it *isn't* pointless. Maybe it's the old wog pokin' through, a few bits of the helper. Wogs were made to help, right? They're like the information posts, providers of information, gatherers and guides. It's still there. They want to tell you what they're doing. They can't help themselves. Maybe because, down deep, they question their mission, and they want it undone. More than that, they want to be redeemed."

Redeemed? The creatures wanted to cannibalize the protector wog and break Billy-Bob's mind in an effort to capture a girl at the behest of a man whose express intention was to destroy humanity. If these wogs wanted redemption, they would leave Billy-Bob and the wog be.

"Can't you leave us alone?" asked Billy-Bob.

The giant wog released a short, barking laugh.

"Our mission is to apprehend the girl by any means necessary. It is not our purpose to question our mission or concern ourselves with the wreckage it creates. Since you refuse to offer your information freely, we are required to take the most drastic of measures," the wog continued. "In the process we will leave your mind a smoking cinder. I apologize, mostly out of formality, but this will be excruciatingly painful."

The giant wog gestured toward the chest and arched its back, then swung forward, smashing its beak against the lock.

Billy-Bob's vision vanished in a searing sheet of white pain. He tried to open his mouth to scream, but could not. He tried to clutch his head to hold it together, but his arms remained outstretched. His mind rang from the blow and sent his thoughts vibrating in all directions. Somewhere in the faraway distance he heard a voice, speaking with a tone of incredulity, and as the shattered fragments of his thoughts coalesced again he realized it belonged to the giant wog.

"What is this?" it said. "No one can do this."

With his thoughts, Billy-Bob's vision returned, cloudy at first, then clear again. He followed the giant wog's gaze to the chest. The lid had flipped back and within the chest sat another chest.

The giant wog reared and swung again. Again a crack from the wog's beak and again a blinding pain in Billy-Bob's skull. He recovered, sooner this time, it seemed to him. Again Billy-Bob blinked his vision clear, looked to the chest to see what mysteries the blow had revealed, and again a closed chest rested within the open chest. This time the giant wog sounded troubled rather than surprised.

"Who are you? Who has tinkered with you?"

"I don't know. No one."

The giant wog looked dubious and alarmed.

"Very well, dullard. We grant you and your wog mercy. Consider your doom temporarily averted."

With that, Billy-Bob's hands opened and the wog dropped through them. The giant wog evaporated and the herd of wogs backed slowly into the grasses.

"Wait!" called Billy-Bob. "The girl! Who is she? Why are you looking for her?"

The wog did not answer, instead pushing against the backs of other wogs slipping into the grass. Billy-Bob tried to follow, but his legs wobbled beneath him and he staggered sideways. Soon the wogs had gone, leaving him alone with his protector. The wog struggled to its feet and hobbled toward him, pausing a few steps away and giving him a long look with its blank expression.

"That was impressive," said the wog, at last.

"All I did was survive," said Billy-Bob ruefully. "Again."

"The girl went one way and they went another. And that," the wog repeated, "was impressive."

BETA

Slowly Billy-Bob's mobility returned. He stood, legs tingling, and looked out across the grasses, trying to detect some indication of the path the wogs had taken, but they were small enough that they left no trampled grass and the waves that rippled across it hid any movements of a passing crowd. Nevertheless, he had to find them. He had endured this encounter, but he had not prevented future encounters for others, certainly not for the girl. She had asked only that he stall them, but he felt inclined to do more. John's plan included catching her and that alarmed him.

"We're almost there," said the wog.

As a machine the wog did not have lungs or muscles, yet it still sounded wheezy and tired as it labored to move. The damage from the encounter with Kilgoth had left it crippled to a catastrophic degree. With only half a functional body, it used the unmoving leg as a crutch, pivoting on it like the point of a drafting compass, leaving perfect arcs in the dirt where it passed, then heaving the dead leg forward before scratching out another arc. If Billy-Bob had retrieved the wristwatch or quieted the writer, perhaps he could have prevented Kilgoth's rage and the wog could walk under its own power. He had not, however, and the wog was punished for his failure, so he hoisted it in his arms. The wog did not object and Billy-Bob considered the familiar heft of its dense body small penance.

"Almost where?" asked Billy-Bob.

"Beta."

Beta. He'd forgotten about his quest. The desire to become a hero felt distant compared to his need to protect the girl and the shame at his inability to protect anyone else.

"It's not far," the wog continued. "I can smell it. But even close, it's not easy to find."

"I should find the others, first."

"What others?"

"The wogs looking for the girl."

Not surprisingly, the wog considered this a bad idea.

"It's not enough to have confronted them and survived? What more do you have to do to consider yourself a hero?"

"This isn't about being a hero. It's about preventing people from being harmed, if I can."

The wog made a series of false starts in an attempt to voice what sounded like incredulity at the inanity of Billy-Bob's statement. This made Billy-Bob feel foolish, but it did not change his mind.

"I don't think you know what it means to be a hero," said the wog at last.

True. He had no idea what it meant to be a hero. In light of his disappointments, becoming a hero had become a branch beyond his ability to reach. After falling out of trees so many times one came to an understanding that they were not meant to climb them.

"It's not something I wonder about any more. I have more important things to do."

His lack of heroism had created problems he needed to resolve. Foremost of those was to stop the wogs.

A growling noise came from the wog as it considered its response. It always made this noise when it planned on saying one thing but decided to say something else.

"I suppose you have a plan to stop them, then."

Billy-Bob realized he did not. However, he surprised himself by thinking of one promptly.

"Yes. Find their treasure chest."

"Find their treasure chest," the wog repeated, dubiously. "Obvious."

The wogs had headed in the direction of the smoke he'd seen extending into the sky. Only a smudged trail remained where the object had passed, but he pointed himself in that direction and plunged into the grasses.

Billy-Bob continued carrying the wog and it did not ask to be released. He knew the wog had tasked itself with protecting him, but in light of the wog's injury the roles had been reversed. He wondered if this mutual mission of protection constituted friendship, and decided he enjoyed thinking of it that way.

Every few paces he paused, listening, but it was difficult to distinguish the sounds of creatures pushing through the underbrush from that of winds blowing through it. They went along like this in silence for a distance, walking, stopping, listening, and walking again, when the wog spoke.

"Can you hear that?"

Billy-Bob strained for a sound that didn't fit with the sweep of air through the grass or the rasp of his own breath. At the edge of his hearing he detected a stern, methodical knocking, as though someone had encountered a closed door with which they were very frustrated. It came from ahead, the same direction as the dirty streak that had now faded completely. He pushed forward, no longer pausing to listen, and soon the knocking was loud enough that he could hear it without stopping or straining.

Abruptly they were at the rim of a sharp slope where a shoeless man crouched before an information post. White hair bound behind his head ran in a thick tail along his back and he wore a tan cloak that bulged as though another person had hidden themselves inside it. Beside the post stood a woman with sandy hair Billy-Bob had seen many times now. The man pounded on the post with a stick and the woman, who appeared to be trying to say something, would gather herself and start again.

"Wel… Welco… Wel wel wel…"

Each time the guide from the post began to speak, the crouching man struck it, as though trying to dislodge something.

"Welco… Wel… Welcom…"

Clack.

"Go away," the post said at last.

Satisfied, the man stopped striking the post. He stood and looked at the girl, who was in turn looking at Billy-Bob. Billy-Bob could tell by the way the man's body froze that he knew someone had arrived. His hand tightened around the stick and he twisted his head slowly until it bore upon Billy-Bob and the wog. His mouth opened.

The face was one he'd never seen before, yet in it Billy-Bob saw something familiar. Free of dirt and beard trimmed to a tight stirrup of hair following his jawline, he still knew that face, and the faint yellow remnant of a vanishing bruise in the middle of his forehead. The misshapenness of the cloak made sense because they concealed his enormous wings.

"Gordimer!" said Billy-Bob.

Gordimer brandished the stick.

"You!" said Gordimer. His eyes fell to the wog in Billy-Bob's arms. "That!"

"Welcome!" said the translucent image. "My name is B."

Gordimer rapped the post with his stick.

"Go away!" said B.

"You can't be here," said Gordimer. "You have to leave. It's all we have left."

"Where is here?" asked Billy-Bob.

"This is Beta," said B, cheerily. "Go away!"

Billy-Bob looked around. In the distance behind him stood the forest. In the other direction grasses stretched in a wide river beyond the waterfall of the horizon. Apart from that, nothing. Even though finding Beta was no longer a priority, he couldn't help feeling disappointed.

"I'm not looking for Beta. I'm following the wogs. Have you seen them?"

"No," said Gordimer. Billy-Bob saw him wrestle with his curiosity and lose. "Why?"

"To stop them."

Gordimer strode with purpose to Billy-Bob and squinted at him.

"You can't stop them. They can't be stopped. How?"

"Find their treasure chest," Billy-Bob answered.

"What?"

"Don't ask," the wog chimed in. "No idea."

"It's because you're different," Billy-Bob explained to the wog, and Gordimer, though he doubted either understood him. "They're changed, like the post giving the wrong information. They don't realize what they're doing other than they know they're doing what they're told. Maybe I can change them back. Like the post."

"No," said Gordimer. He clutched at his head in frustration. "You're not a hero. They can't be changed."

Not long ago this would have upset him. Now he wanted to believe he could make a difference without being a hero. Ordinary people could do great things too. Maybe the world was unchangeable and wrecked. Maybe not. He could only think of one word to express the possibility of an alternative, and didn't expect it to sway Gordimer, but tried anyway.

"Unless," said Billy-Bob.

Gordimer's head snapped up, the corners of his mouth full of weight, eyes glazed. He gripped the front of Billy-Bob's shirt in both hands, and his mouth opened, but nothing came out. In his eyes Billy-Bob saw what he could not say, a hope restrained that finally broke free in a single bead that rolled down his cheek and dropped away.

"Unless," Gordimer whispered.

"Go to Beta," the post B interrupted. "Meet them there."

"I thought I already found Beta."

"You did," said the wog. "But that doesn't mean you're there."

"They come with regularity as part of their search," said B. "It is high time they came again."

"It's here," said Gordimer, gesturing to the lip.

Billy-Bob moved forward. For several steps he saw nothing but a gentle rise of grass that settled down again before sloping away, only to rise again in the distance. He almost turned back to say he didn't see anything when a silver glimmer at the far edge caught his eye. He took another step and more of the silver shaft revealed itself. He reached the edge of a sharp slope and saw the entire shape of a tall craft, and knew this is what he'd seen exiting the world at the end of the streak of smoke.

The craft lay at the center of an empty, blackened circle at the terminus of a long causeway, from which a network of smaller veins extended through the pit. The clanks of metalworking, gears moving, and other minor clamors that had been somehow muffled only a few steps further away carried up to him. A sparse forest of windmills labored slowly atop the short buildings, themselves made of wood mortared with clay, but unlike the sagging structures of Dirtburg they remained in good condition, straight-backed and tidy. A faint stinging taste of oil and metal rose out of the city.

"This," said the wog, "is Beta."

In spite of so many uniquenesses, he felt certain he'd seen it all before.

"They'll be here soon," said Gordimer. "You need to hurry."

"How do I get down?" asked Billy-Bob.

"Lean forward," said Gordimer.

Billy-Bob leaned forward, gazing down the slope that slanted sharply to the main thoroughfare.

"Careful," warned the wog.

"More," said Gordimer.

"I'm not sure I can," said Billy-Bob.

"You can," said Gordimer.

On the far side of the crater he saw a long, gentle ramp leading from the top edge to the floor. This must be what Gordimer wanted him to see. Gordimer never told him anything, preferring to have him discover it himself instead. He appreciated this. It gave him confidence. Any teacher could provide knowledge. Belief in oneself was a gift only the most skillful of teachers could give.

"I see it," said Billy-Bob.

"Good," said Gordimer.

Billy-Bob straightened, carefully, when he felt a hand on his back give a gentle shove. He wheeled a free arm to help regain his balance, tottering on the precipice, and for an instant he managed to reverse the fall and save himself.

"That was close," he said.

Then he felt two hands, harder, and found himself leaning much too far over the emptiness, staring down at the ground far below. The wog in his arms sighed, then they were falling. It was a long way to go, and Billy-Bob could hear Gordimer calling after him.

"Don't worry, you'll be fine! You're special!"

Gordimer whispered a quiet afterthought he probably meant to keep to himself.

"Unless."

A CHANGE OF TREASURE

At some point the wog must have come free of his grip because Billy-Bob was cartwheeling through the air with his fingers webbed over his eyes. The wall was not as steep below him and he struck the slope of grass hard, but the curve of the embankment reduced much of the blow and started his body on an uncontrollable somersault. The world alternated between grass and light and grass and light and grass and light until it ended resoundingly on grass and he sledded the rest of the way on his chest, picking up clumps of turf in hair, face, and mouth before coming to a stop where the slope flattened into the street. He clutched his fingers into the fibers of grass to remind himself that the ground remained steady beneath him, even though he could still feel it turning.

A sound like a tin can full of bolts clattered to a stop beside him.

"That wasn't so bad," he heard the wog say.

Billy-Bob pushed himself onto his hands and knees and looked down the main avenue separating the two hemispheres of Beta. At the end a silver dart stood against the black vertical face of the crater's far side. The buildings stood removed from the craft, safe from the propellant that scorched the stony crater ground and walls. Up close he could see a few windmills atop the buildings, grinding out slow circles. Here too people stood atop the buildings, a practice Billy-Bob found unusual, because surely there were less elaborate ways to build devices to make oneself feel taller.

A grinding noise came from the nearest building as one person dragged the ladder they'd just climbed onto the roof. He spotted Billy-Bob and hesitated, looking about to see if any other ladders remained lowered. When he saw all had drawn up already, he beckoned to Billy-Bob and tilted his ladder back toward the street.

"Hurry!" he called.

Billy-Bob put one foot forward and pushed himself into a standing position. The world still turned slightly as he recovered from his dizziness, but he managed to remain upright. He held up a hand to the man in thanks.

"I'm okay."

Perplexed, the man lowered the ladder further, though not all the way to the ground.

"They're coming!"

Wogs. That must be what he meant. He needed to meet them.

"Good," said Billy-Bob.

"Who are you?" asked the man, dumbfounded.

"Not anyone," Billy-Bob confessed.

It was the truth. He'd seen his biography. He could not do the things a hero needed to do, but this no longer troubled him. He did know he wanted to protect the girl from the wogs, and anyone else who might fall prey to them, and he knew stopping them was something he could do. Wogs were not inherently evil, but as with all things they could be led astray and serve an evil purpose. One only needed to bring them back. That, Billy-Bob had decided, was what he would do.

The man on the roof shrugged his shoulders, drew the ladder up, and sat down on the ledge to watch, his expression betraying his belief that he expected some form of tragedy to ensue. Others on the rooftop watched as well, their eyes alternating between Billy-Bob and the slope behind him that he'd recently navigated. They would come from that direction, he guessed.

Billy-Bob turned to await the wogs, and gazed up the slope. As he did so a deep chime of familiarity rang in his head and his mouth opened.

Grass wagged at his elbows, waving in a gentle breeze that swept down the sharp ramp leading out of the crater. Where the slope ended the atmosphere began, and plump white clouds plodded across the pasture of the sky. With the sight came a powerful sense of belonging.

"My dream," he murmured.

Movement at the crest of the crater made his heart snap in his chest. Was it the girl? Was this his dream? Was she up there waiting for him to come and take his hand? What would happen when he arrived? Was he dreaming now, and if so much of his memory was nothing but a dream, what would he wake up to?

Then the shape spread its wings and leapt off the ridge, gliding overhead. It was Gordimer.

"They're coming!" he cried.

A new shape appeared, a bump on the lip of the crater that soon widened as more shapes joined the first. Not the girl. Wogs.

Down they came in a violet sheet like a curtain dropping on a stage. Some held their feet and slid, others tumbled end over end, their asymmetrical bodies causing them to bound high in the air and sail past him.

"I'm not going to be able to help you," said the wog.

It edged closer to him, nevertheless. Whether to protect him or to seek protection, Billy-Bob wasn't certain. Perhaps both.

"You won't need to," Billy-Bob responded.

"This time I think you should run."

"Why?"

"You can't handle all of them at once. Get to the roof. Talk to them from there."

The wog spoke faster than its normal, thoughtful pace. It sounded tense and urgent.

Billy-Bob stood.

"All right."

By now the wogs sliding down the hill had reached the floor and ambled toward him. Those that bounced past had regained their footing and began to close off his retreat, leaving a path to just one building. No one stood atop the building and no ladder stretched down from it, but the awning seemed low enough to grab with a well-timed leap. Once atop the roof he should have no troubled defending it from the leaps of wogs. He could simply catch them or knock them away.

Billy-Bob lifted the wog and ran. Behind and around him wogs flowed eagerly into his path like rainwater running into a trench.

Gordimer swooped down and settled on the roof where the citizen had offered to let him up.

"Who is that?" he heard the man ask Gordimer.

"That is Billy-Bob."

"Billy-Bob?" called someone from an adjacent roof. "That's a terrible name. What is he doing?"

"Being a hero," Gordimer called back, "I think."

"A hero?" said the man beside him. "No. He's too short."

"That could be a disadvantage," Gordimer agreed.

"He's going the wrong way," the man added.

Even though Billy-Bob had become accustomed to carrying the wog and to running, he found himself unable to do either well while trying to do both. The path ahead narrowed as a few wogs closed in from the sides, and at the this slower pace he knew he couldn't make it to the only building that remained accessible. He'd have to leave the wog if he wanted to escape the others and face them on more favorable terms.

"I won't make it," said Billy-Bob. "I'm sorry."

"I understand," the wog responded. "Thank you for everything. I will do what I can to slow them."

"That won't be necessary."

"What do you mean?"

With an effort, Billy-Bob spun in a circle, using the wog's centrifugal momentum to hurl it over the wogs closing in from the sides and onto a rooftop where it caught a citizen watching the events full in the chest.

"Oh no!" she cried, assuming the worst. "Why!?"

Freed, Billy-Bob accelerated toward the building ahead. Its awning stood well out of his normal reach, but a barrel stood before the building. The barrel looked sturdy. It had a lid with a rope handle looped into the top. A long leap separated the barrel from the building, but not too far for Billy-Bob. It could not have been coincidence such an item had been placed arbitrarily in the best possible place to aid him. Something else had to be at work, some unseen force that favored him had set the barrel precisely where he needed it to escape.

He reached the barrel and leapt atop it in stride, planting a foot and pushing off in a single, smooth motion. The rooftop stretched out like an open hand. Billy-Bob found himself unable to suppress a smile.

Something tugged at his foot and Billy-Bob looked back to see the rope hand on the barrel's lid caught on the toe of his shoe. This would hamper his jump, and, sure enough, when he looked to the awning again it was not approaching with the same comforting rapidity. His smile faltered. Before he reached the building the arc of his leap turned sharply downward, just before the rooftop. His fingertips brushed the lip of the roof and slid away, and the barrel lid attached to his foot caught on the decorative handrail at the edge of the walkway below.

Billy-Bob wondered, as he spun out of control and braced for a crash against the building, what role fate had played in this episode. Had it placed a mechanism to allow his escape in the road and had he misused it, or had it been the intention of fate to give him false hope and intended for him to fail? More likely, he decided, the presence of the barrel had been nothing more than a fortunate coincidence, and fate had no part at all.

Then he met the building with his shoulder and fell to the ground, feeling the pain of the blow move up and down his body like an echo in a canyon.

He heard sighs from the rooftops in all directions. They had the heavy tone of familiar disappointment.

"You see," someone said. "Too short."

Running away had failed. But running away wasn't the plan. This only sped it up. He rolled onto his back and sat up.

The ground had become an ocean of purple lapping against the buildings. Wogs burst upward like swordfish toward the people on the rooftop who, with grim poise that came from experience, swatted them out of the air with two-handed rackets designed for just such a purpose.

The tide surged toward him eagerly, swarming up over and around the rails, and a tickle of concern touched him. It was possible this would not work. He didn't have a good idea of how wogs functioned, or how to do what he planned. He knew wogs could open a passageway from one mind to another. He hoped doing so was automatic, a reaction, and that they had not taught themselves how to avoid doing so. As the wave began to break across him, Billy-Bob, believing he was doing the right thing, or at least the only thing he knew to do, opened his arms.

Seeing this, the foremost wogs realized they'd fallen into a trap and tried to turn back, but the surge from behind pushed them forward and they swarmed over Billy-Bob.

The sounds of the city faded away under the blanket of wogs. The metallic knocks from wogs being struck by citizens and thumping back to the ground, the shouting of citizens as they called out directions to their fellows to sweep wogs away that managed to leap onto the rooftops, the clamor of wogs tumbling down the crater slope—all mute. He felt their weight on him, felt their bodies churning against him as those below tried to get away as still more piled on top.

Billy-Bob could see little in the darkness created by the heap of bodies apart from a solitary, luminous, translucent wog, its arms folded across its chest. Wogs had rigid faces that limited their ability to make expressions, but their creator had thought to give them eyebrows, and Billy-Bob could see this wog was annoyed.

Since the wog was a projection of its mind, Billy-Bob imagined it could have appeared in any form it chose. Yet these wogs had chosen to appear larger and little else. Wogs must have very little imagination or felt very comfortable with their appearance. Billy-Bob wondered what he looked like to them, and at the same time didn't want to know.

"What do you want?" it asked imperiously.

"I want to help," Billy-Bob answered.

The wog laughed.

"Then stop getting in our way!"

Billy-Bob looked left, then right, searching. Creating a passageway to the mind of another required craft Billy-Bob did not know or understand. Nor did he understand the fission reaction that drove the sun, the cellular reactions in his body that prevented him from holding his breath indefinitely, or the reason that Gordimer's song filled him with hope and longing. That did not mean he could not use these things, nor take advantage of what the wogs had somehow made. In creating a connection from mind to mind, that passageway had to have an opening at the other end.

Then he saw it—a chest covered in patches of purple fur near the floating wog. A latch without a lock held the chest shut. Billy-Bob reached outward and flicked it open.

"What are you doing?" shrieked the wog. "Leave that alone!"

The open chest revealed numerous iridescent spheres no larger than the end of his finger, each melting through one another in a constant churning tumult, yet remaining distinct.

These must be the memories they had accumulated. Some their own, some stolen from others. He had only to find the memories sent them after the girl and perhaps he could change it, or remove the memory altogether. That, he thought with amusement, would be quite the heroic accomplishment.

He extended a hand toward the open chest, not knowing how best to access the memories, deciding he ought to try touching them.

"Stop!" shouted the wog. "You don't know what you're doing. You do not know how to navigate the memories of another, and certainly not the collected memories of all of us. You will destroy yourself and ruin what we have labored to acquire."

It shook with agitation and concern. The other wogs ceased their assault on Beta, watching, but clearly unable to do anything about it. To have one's mind exposed to another was to be at their mercy.

"Will you leave the girl alone?"

The wog puffed up, as if its frustration built up within it like air in a paper bag, then let it all out in a single, agonized statement.

"We can't!"

"I know," said Billy-Bob. "But I can help."

Wogs, like the post beneath the Institute, had been corrupted, their search tainted, their mission corroded. John, in his ceaseless attempts to disrupt the great mechanism of existence had set a single gear turning against the machine. The post had felt the change but could not resist it; the wogs felt the error but tried to accept it; and the world shuddered as the clockwork struggled against itself.

"How? Why?"

"Because," said Billy-Bob, feeling he had the answer but not the ability to articulate it. Then it came to him. "Because it is right to help."

The wog did not argue and Billy-Bob took this to mean it would no longer try to stop him. So he looked back to the chest of shimmering marbles and plunged his hand through the pile. If the wogs had memories of how this began, it made sense that they would be at the bottom. To his surprise, he didn't feel any resistance when his hand passed through the memories. He'd expected them to part grudgingly, as any heaped objects did when someone tried to force their way through them. The wog had been right. He had no idea how to navigate these memories. What now?

All he could do was remove his hand and ask. Except, he realized, his hand would not come free of the box. Billy-Bob looked up at the wog for an explanation, but all it did was return his look with an expression of despair and offer a minor platitude.

"Good luck."

Then everything vanished in a snap of white.

THE LIBRARIAN

From all around Billy-Bob the roar of fire rumbled like a great engine as it consumed the city. Buildings hovered in the smoky night, illuminated by their own destruction. The fire sucked the oxygen from the air in windy gulps, cracking and snapping as it chewed through one building after another. The acrid smell choked him and he could taste cinder in his mouth that would not go away when he swallowed.

People dashed past, oblivious of his presence. An endless stream of them, more than could possibly be contained in the town burning to the ground around him. On and on they went, as though having passed from sight into the haze of smoke and glare from the fire, they curled back around so they could push past him again.

Indeed, after a while he began to recognize faces as they appeared over and over again, the same terrified expressions, taking the same paths, always shouting the same, incoherent cries. Some went slowly, drifting perpendicular to or even against the flow of people, calling out for others and slipping out of sight, only to reappear where they started.

Somehow he'd gotten trapped by a loop in time, moving forward along a möbius strip on which forward progress was not resisted, but he could only cross and recross the same path over and over. But how had he gotten here in the first place? And where was here?

One person did not reset. She stared back at him, looking suspicious and intent, and Billy-Bob recognized the familiar sandy hair pulled tight against her head immediately. Something about her seemed odd to Billy-Bob, and he realized he could not see through her.

"Dee?" he called.

The girl approached as the crowd continued to wash around them. She took slow, careful steps, watching him with wary eyes, and Billy-Bob knew something about her was different.

"My name is Anne. You are not part of this memory. Why are you here?"

A memory. He was inside the wogs' memories. Now the environment and the repetition made more sense. The wogs' minds were digital, recalling things in precise detail, unlike the human mind where the details fuzzed, gaps filled in to make a sensible whole, and sometimes interacted with other memories to create new, less reliable memories. A human mind was easy to manipulate because in many ways it lent itself to deception. People created memories to convince themselves of truths that fit their worldview even though it contradicted the world. He could find genuine truth here, where he would no doubt run into a mish mash of memory and imagination in his own mind.

"I'm Billy-Bob."

"I know who you are. But you should not be here."

"Why not?"

"Only memories belong here."

"I thought you were someone else," said Billy-Bob. "You look like someone else. Exactly like them. She's a helper."

Anne considered this.

"I look like myself, unless myself has changed since last the wogs saw me."

"Where are we?"

Anne watched the people flow past them for a moment, turned toward the noise of a building falling in on itself, before answering the question.

"This is Alpha, at the end. This particular memory is a poignant one for the wogs. It's when their mission changed from pragmatic to impossible. Look."

Anne gestured to the rear of the crowd at the edge of the street where the burning city ended and the night rested upon the world like a heavy foot holding everything in place.

The crowd cleared and a man emerged from the haze, crouched, zig-zagging back and forth through the street, searching. At last he found something and lifted it into the air. Billy-Bob moved closer to see the object, and discovered it was a wog. The fires continued to belch smoke and send glowing ash drifting through the air, but it created enough light for Billy-Bob to see the face of this man. In spite of the soot darkening his face, it was a face he recognized.

He had met him only once, but the man had made enough of an impression upon him that he could remember the name that went with that lean, grim face. Mardin was a slender man in his prime here, and even though his body lacked bulk Billy-Bob could see the power in his frame by the ease with which he lifted the wog. He also saw something else he hadn't seen before. When he spoke, his voice was clipped and rushed and aggravated. Mardin appeared frustrated, angry, and perhaps frightened.

"You have a new mission," said Mardin. "You must find Anne."

Billy-Bob turned to look at the memory Anne, who watched the encounter intently but without expression.

The wog did not respond. Perhaps it was processing the order. Even though it didn't make sense for an object to think about a command, Billy-Bob suspected the wog did not agree with it.

"Do you understand?" Mardin asked. "Acknowledge."

"Acknowledged," the wog intoned.

Mardin set the wog on the ground.

"Find Anne," he repeated. "Find her, then come back to me. Tell the others. These orders come directly from me. Abandon all other tasks."

"Even protecting the boy?"

The tight line of Mardin's mouth sagged.

"Yes."

The two vanished, the crowd reappeared, and the buildings reassembled themselves and began burning anew. The memory had ended and reset itself.

Billy-Bob turned to Anne.

"He was looking for you. He modeled the posts after you. The girl the wogs were looking for. You."

Anne nodded.

"It was me. But I had gone somewhere wogs could not follow. Then the mission changed again."

"Who are you?"

"A memory."

"I know that, but who?"

"As I said, my name is Anne. I am a librarian, I suppose. I am someone they understood as benevolent and protective. I have evolved into their subconscious, the guide who helps them make decisions. Who better to guard their memories?"

Her answer did not satisfy his question. He wanted to know who Anne was, why Mardin wanted to find her, and the part she had played in the past. Why had her image been chosen for the information posts? Why did the wogs consider her a guardian? Perhaps this information was more than a memory could provide. Could a memory be expected to remember the events that shaped them or details of their existence outside of that memory? Billy-Bob shook his head. This line of wondering only distracted him from the new question her answer had created.

"Why do they need to guard their memories?"

"Memories are the soul of a person, the filter through which they see and understand the world. To tinker with those memories could change the fabric of their being. Tweaking a single memory could rearrange their entire purpose. A minor character could believe they are a hero; a major character could lose their way."

Anne strode toward the haze at the edge of town, the brink of the wogs' memory. She stopped before passing into the cloudy periphery and beckoned to Billy-Bob, then continued on. Billy-Bob followed Anne into the haze, which felt cool and moist on his skin, like a mist. Even though a step or two separated them, he lost sight of her immediately. Panicked, he moved faster, and found himself abruptly teetering atop a boulder in a setting he recognized.

Chest-high grasses surrounded the boulder they stood upon and a forest stood in the distance. Beyond that forest Billy-Bob knew the Institute stood, but he could not see it over the treetops. Below them trampled grasses made a small clearing where wogs stood around the edge, unmoving. Perhaps twenty stood, stock still, in varying stages of decay. Billy-Bob wondered if the memory had frozen, but he felt wind in his hair and saw a the grass shifting as something approached. A single wog stepped forward into the center of the clearing and at the same moment a figure broke through the wall of grass into the clearing and pulled up short as she spotted the wog.

The tangled hair and dirty fingernails gave her away immediately. He could tell by the tension in her posture she knew her danger. It was the girl from his dream, the girl he was trying to protect by coming here, the girl with whom he felt a connection that defied his understanding, the girl who he felt he knew and comprehended despite not knowing anything about her. His heart drummed in his chest.

The girl looked behind to see the ring of wogs close behind her. She turned her attention back to the wog in the center of the clearing. Its beak separated to release a rush of static followed by a rush of words.

"You're her," it said.

"Her who?"

"The one we've been hunting."

The girl stood with her legs apart, ready to fight, the muscles in her forearms flexing as she ran her thumbs across her fingertips in anticipation.

"Why?"

"Because you are a hero."

Billy-Bob straightened. The girl, a hero?

The girl scowled.

"No, I'm not."

"Your opinion is invalid. Your denial is a stalling tactic."

"Then I suppose there's no point waiting any longer."

"The sooner you attempt your escape, the sooner this will be at an end."

The girl nodded.

"On your word, then."

"Begin," said the wog.

The girl turned toward the grasses from which she emerged. At the same time, half of the wogs launched themselves into the air, some ahead, some behind, and some directly at her, calculating she might evade some, but in the process of doing so move into the path of others.

To Billy-Bob's surprise, she made little attempt to dodge the incoming wogs, instead using a few deft movements to redirect those that flung themselves directly at her, sending several careening into one another. It was a beautiful and brilliant eyeblink event, but in the end, as the wogs surely knew, there were simply too many. She was not fast enough to deflect all of the wogs, and one struck her in the back, another in the shoulder. She shrieked, lunging forward from the blow from behind and snapping a hand up to cradle her damaged shoulder. However, she was not, by any means, defeated. In this alone, the wogs had miscalculated, and it was a critical mistake.

It appeared the strike from behind would topple her, bending her backwards and pitching her forward, but as she fell she managed to fling a foot in front to catch herself, turning this lunge into a first step toward the grasses. Her next stride was shorter and more controlled, and by the third she had regained her balance completely. One wog remained between her and the wall of grass, not reacting, perhaps trying to calculate how their tactics had failed rather than enacting a secondary plan. Before it could respond, the girl swept a foot into it and kicked it, sending it swooping into the air to land beyond the clearing. Billy-Bob was surprised by the distance it flew. He knew firsthand the heft of a wog, having carried one across the wasteland, and the force required to propel it so far was extraordinary. While impressive, and probably necessary, the blow must have had a cost, and Billy-Bob could see a pronounced limp in her stride as she disappeared.

The wogs did not move immediately to pursue and Billy-Bob wondered if the memory had ended. Then the wog kicked into the grass returned to the clearing and paused, and Billy-Bob realized the wogs were trying to decide what to do next.

Billy-Bob could see the trail of parting grass as the girl moved into the distance, willing her onward. He knew they could not have caught her in this memory or they would not still be searching when he encountered them in Beta, but he could not suppress a sense of anxiety and fear that her handicaps were too great to permit escape. She needed someone to save her, to give her a few extra moments to hide herself, and he watched the line of her path extend, pained by the slowness of her progress.

As he watched, he saw another figure pop into a clearing, head hanging and gasping for air. He thought he recognized it, but before he could examine the features, it slouched to the ground and out of sight. The girl must have heard the sound because her line had stopped, then started again, bearing toward the point where the new person appeared. At the same time, the wogs made a decision on how to proceed and moved single-file into the grass. Both lines looked to converge on the spot where the new person had emerged from the forest.

Billy-Bob stepped off the boulder to follow them.

"No," said Anne. "This way."

She gestured in a direction perpendicular to the path the girl and wogs had taken.

"We have to follow them!"

Anne was stern.

"You don't belong here. I'm taking you to the exit."

"I can't leave," said Billy-Bob. "Not yet."

"You can, and you must, before you disrupt something further."

"Further?"

"You have not disrupted anything yet, but you might. Entrances and exits into memories are created by gaps in logic, disruptions in memory. Human memories are easy to access because they manipulate their own minds to suit a narrative or belief system, particularly those who feel threatened by a reality that does not agree with them, creating inconsistencies that make entry simple. These pathways should not exist within wogs, whose memories are founded upon a repository of fact. Your presence here is an indication that something is awry. This is a disturbing consideration because the owner of a memory has no way of knowing which memory is faulty."

Billy-Bob understood why the wogs were so determined to fulfill their mission and why it troubled them at the same time. Their mission was a single gear turning against their entire machinery. They understood something about their mission was wrong, but they didn't know why and didn't have any other purpose but to complete it, hoping success would relieve the strain.

"One faulty memory can reorganize the entire purpose of a being. That purpose could be extrapolated multifold when the being is many that shares and compiles memories from a multitude of sensory appendages, like wogs."

Anne's expression became grim.

"All the things wogs believe and the purpose they pursue could be corrupted by this error. The purpose itself may well be an error."

"I can help! I'm not here to rearrange their purpose, but to re-rearrange it. To arrange it back to how it had been arranged before it was rearranged. I'm here to... perform maintenance. But I don't know where I am. I'll need help figuring out where I need to go."

Anne hesitated, considering.

"I understand what you are trying to mean. Perhaps you will find the error you seek in the exit, which should not exist because there is no reason for a gap in logic. They are not permitted. The only way a wog could have a gap in logic is..."

She stopped, unable to continue.

"Is if the wogs agreed to it," Billy-Bob finished. "And now that the memory is implanted, they don't know how to overwrite it. It's hardwired."

Anne did not respond, but her frown deepened with disappointment.

"Take me there."

Anne nodded and stepped into the grass. Billy-Bob followed. He pushed aside one stiff stand of grass after another, trying to keep up with Anne, until finally they broke into the familiar fractured terrain of the wasteland. In the distance the spire of the Institute of Alpha wavered in the heat as though standing on the edge of reality, driven into the terrain like a pin meant to keep everything from flying apart at the seams.

Wogs stood all around them in a motionless blanket that stretched out as far as Billy-Bob could throw a stone, all staring past him. Anne turned around and Billy-Bob turned as well. He expected to see the grasses from which they'd emerged, but instead he saw more wasteland beyond the edge of the gathered wogs. Their herd came to a point where a single wog stood and at this apex a man faced the crowd—one Billy-Bob knew well.

"You are John," said the foremost wog to the towering man.

This was the man he remembered from Alpha, the one Mardin identified as an engineer, and who identified himself as someone trying to accelerate the deterioration of the world. He did not appear alarmed by the volume of wogs facing him, nor in any way perplexed by the wog's vague statements.

"I have been called that," John responded.

"We are searching for the girl. Our search has brought us here."

John nodded.

"She is here. But you cannot recover her. She is present, yet absent from the world."

Some of the wogs fidgeted, shifting from one foot to the other as they considered how to continue.

"You must release her."

"She is not my prisoner."

"But you know where she is."

"Yes."

"Where?"

"Beyond the reach of retrieval. All those who go to the place where she resides are lost. Forever."

Billy-Bob looked back at Anne, who listened without expression. If she had any feelings about the discussion, a discussion about the fate of the person she represented, she did not betray them. Nevertheless, he could feel the sense of loss and desperation in the wogs, as though something they needed was very near, yet somehow out of reach. They rocked and hummed and revved their gears, trying to resolve a simple problem that defied them.

"It is our mission to retrieve her."

"Then your mission is in vain. She cannot be retrieved."

The foremost wog did not speak immediately, but made a staticky noise that continued for several seconds. Could wogs feel frustration? How did a machine respond to a mission it could never fulfill?

"We cannot desist in this mission," the wog said at last.

"Ah," said John. He raised a finger to his lips. He did not smile, but Billy-Bob heard the delight in his voice and knew, without question, that within this point in the memory lay the corruption that allowed Billy-Bob to enter their mind and housed the error that had misguided and made them a menace. "Then perhaps you do not understand your mission."

"Our mission is to find the girl."

"Which girl? There are many. A mission is not a mission if that mission cannot be accomplished. It is a folly. Wogs are too precise to commit folly. Is this not true?"

"This is true," the wog agreed.

"Wogs must have a mission that can be completed, rather than one of futility. Wogs are meant to have purpose, and futile missions have no purpose. Is this not true?"

"This is true," the wog agreed again.

"I ask again. Which girl do you seek?"

"The girl," the wog repeated, stopping in mid-sentence. Then the wog made a noise like a stick caught in a fan blade. The scene froze while the noise continued, and Billy-Bob pressed his hands against his ears to dull the hammering noise. The whole world shuddered with it.

Through the noise he heard something else, like someone shouting to him through a wall. Behind him Anne was pointing to a space beside John and he saw her mouth shape the word "there."

Billy-Bob picked his way through the stationary wogs and approached the giant form of John, his mouth bent upward in one corner as though quietly celebrating the success of a secret trick. A line stood beside him, like a bit of world folded over itself. He walked around it and found a door, all but invisible from the side.

Abruptly, the noise stopped, and the wog resumed.

"The girl, Poppy. She is not many."

"No," John agreed. "She is not. Your mission is to seek her. Find her. Bring her to me. Or bring me to her, correct?"

"Affirmative."

The scene froze, tugged to one side, and started again. Billy-Bob reached for the door, then remembered his mission here, unlike so many others, was not to escape. Anne stood amidst the wogs, watching.

"What do I do?" he asked.

"I don't know. Maybe you already did."

Billy-Bob didn't know how to alter a memory, and John had started to weave his manipulative web of words. Not knowing what else to do and uncertain it would have any effect, Billy-Bob threw his shoulder into John's side. Maybe this would disrupt the memory or at least remove John's influence on it.

John's bulk, even in a memory, proved considerable. The initial blow stung Billy-Bob as though he'd run against a tree rooted in the ground, and he wondered if all the objects here were fixed and immovable, resistant to change. Then he saw John's heel separate from the ground and redoubled his efforts, pushing against the dirt that slid from beneath his feet in long stripes. John continued to speak all the while, oblivious to his predicament.

"I ask again. Which girl do you seek?"

Then came the bone-shaking noise of a memory that had snagged. At the same time John tipped forward, momentum took over, and the pressure on Billy-Bob's shoulder went away. John crashed to the ground before the wogs. Abruptly, the noise stopped, and the stillness of the frozen memory shuddered back into motion.

The wog serving as spokesperson looked about as though released from an enchantment. It looked at John, lying face-down on the ground, then Billy-Bob panting beside the still form of the giant.

"You," it said.

"What is your mission?" asked Billy-Bob.

"Find the girl, Poppy."

"Why?"

"Because that is the mission we received."

"No. It isn't. I was there to see the mission you received. You allowed the mission to change."

The wog did not respond immediately.

"We have no memory of another mission. It has always been the mission to find the girl."

"Yes, but the *girl* has changed. Do you remember Anne? She was your mission. You abandoned her."

Anne stood amidst the wogs, her expression stoic. A memory could not be expected to feel sympathy for the plight of the person it represented, but she folded her arms across her chest when he spoke of her, as though protecting herself from the topic, and he could see a finger tapping restlessly upon elbow of a folded arm. It hurt to be forgotten, and if a memory could have a memory, then as well as she obscured her feelings, this conversation surely made her unhappy.

"She was a mission that could never be completed. We found this frustrating."

If the memory of an artificial creature could have feelings, the wogs themselves could feel frustration. The wog he carried across the wasteland had expressed emotions such as empathy and concern, and Mardin seemed both surprised and pleased by the fact it verged upon independent thought after been left so long to its own devices. While loyal to their missions, they had developed rudimentary emotions that allowed them to feel frustration. It would not surprise him to learn they wanted to feel a sense of accomplishment—something their unadulterated mission had not permitted. Like Gordimer, they had grown frustrated with a mission that offered no possibility of success. Wogs were tools, and in their desperation they had allowed themselves to be manipulated in order to restore their usefulness.

Perhaps these emotions could be of use.

"Does your mission make you happy?"

Again, the wogs did not answer immediately. A proper wog would not allow emotion to factor into their opinion of a mission. Based on what he'd seen from the interaction with Mardin, wogs ought not to have had an opinion at all.

"No. It does not."

Billy-Bob smiled.

"Old mission parameters have been altered to permit success. I propose a new mission."

"Our mission cannot be changed until it is completed."

"It won't. Continue efforts to locate the girl: Poppy."

The wog did not object, so Billy-Bob continued.

"Once accomplished, the mission is complete."

"Mission accepted," said the wog.

"Once this mission is complete, you will have a new mission: Protection."

"Protect the girl, Poppy?"

"Yes. From all harm. You are familiar with the protocols of Protection?"

"Yes. This was a former mission, overwritten in favor of Locate and Acquire."

"Do you accept this mission?"

"Corollary mission accepted."

"Excellent. Initiate mission."

The wog faced the other wogs, unspeaking. It must be communicating the updated orders to the others. It turned back to Billy-Bob.

"Mission engaged."

The wogs began to disperse, fanning out across the terrain. Then the scenery shook, and all the wogs had resumed their places. The memory had started again. Except this time John was gone. It his place stood a thin, hunching boy in clothing that appeared slightly too large. He recognized the boy as himself, and felt somewhat saddened by his unimpressive appearance. He wanted to straighten the boy's back and say something to give him confidence, but nothing came to mind. Then he spoke in a voice, resonant and self-assured, and in no way fitting the appearance of the boy.

"Does your mission make you happy?"

He looked at Anne, who stood in the crowd of wogs, wondering if she would remember the old mission, or if her memory had changed as well. He thought about asking her about the old memory, but decided in this case ignorance was best. There was a way to test the effectiveness of the new memory.

"Well?" he asked her.

She looked at Billy-Bob.

"Yes," she said. "They are happy."

Satisfied, Billy-Bob walked to the door and pulled it open. As soon as he set a foot through the door he could feel something pulling him through. There was no turning back now. Even as he sucked through, he had a thought and looked back to Anne. She had not departed, and held up a hand in farewell.

"You know me," he called. "Who am I?"

She walked forward to the door to avoid shouting. He was halfway through and the pull became stronger the further he went.

"That information is restricted," she said.

"Why?"

"I cannot disclose why information is restricted. I can tell you who you are based upon my observations. You have reversed what no one else could. You have relieved the bitterness of beings who believed themselves beyond retribution. It should be clear."

This didn't tell him anything. He knew what he'd done. It was what had to be done. Doing what one must didn't make anyone anything. It didn't tell someone anything about themselves. The pull was irresistible, leaving him only a moment before it would take him entirely, and he could see Anne was holding something back.

"Who am I?" Billy-Bob pleaded.

Anne smiled and closed the door. As she did so, she leaned forward and whispered through the last sliver of an opening.

"You are a hero."

* * *

Billy-Bob found himself seated on the walkway of a building in Beta, surrounded on all sides by wogs. The projection of the wog had vanished and they stood arranged in ranks stretching from Billy-Bob's feet to the embankment he had fallen down. He wondered if he'd imagined the entire experience. Had the new memory stuck?

"What will you do now?" asked Billy-Bob.

A single wog stepped forward.

"Complete our mission," it answered. "Protect the girl. Good luck in your own."

"Thanks. I'm not sure what my mission is."

The other wogs turned and began ascending the wall, leaving the spokeswog behind.

"I'm certain it will present itself," it said, then turned to join the others.

Billy-Bob stood, stepping into the sunlight of the street. Those standing on the rooftops said nothing. How could they know what happened? Their mystification was evident in their silence. A surge of joy and pride filled him, and he didn't know how to spend it. He had reached Beta. What did he do now? Gordimer had told him he needed to defeat Ultimate Evil, that he could not find it, it must find him. He'd rather it didn't and felt confident ultimate evil, whatever it was, wouldn't recognize him. But should he seek it out to prevent others from being subjected to it? How did he help it find him?

As if in answer, a flutter of wings settled behind Billy-Bob and he recognized a bird with a sack of skin hanging from its beak and neck. From the corner of its mouth a golden band shimmered. The beak opened and clapped shut again, and the golden band disappeared back into the pelican's mouth.

Before Billy-Bob could alert the rest of the town to the coming peril Kilgoth slammed to the ground at the end of the street and he knew his next task had found him.

VERSUS

Gordimer watched the tide of wogs recede, draining out of the street and washing back up the wall they had descended only moments ago, like a waterfall in reverse. Whatever had happened, they had achieved something and now moved to a new mission. The leaping of wogs had ceased soon after they caught the boy, and since he was beaten they had lost interest in the citizens of Beta. This, Gordimer tried to tell himself, was a good thing.

The world had been spared another villain. Yet Gordimer did not feel relieved by Billy-Bob's defeat. That small bit of hope, a slim possibility of Unless, kept it from him. Instead, he blew a few tired notes from his half-remembered song, trying to detach himself from his disappointment, and knowing without a new hero his test had started again when it had seemed so near the end.

"It didn't have to go that way," said the man sharing the roof with Gordimer, a clever fellow named Simon with wide and curious eyes that pinched when he thought.

Simon was very good at understanding things, such as how to calculate the trajectory of objects thrown into the air, how rockets worked, and the contents of texts produced long before Gordimer had arrived. Simon had picked up where others had left off, giving those people that remained here the opportunity to begin again elsewhere, escape the inevitable rather than be pulverized by it. He rocked restlessly at the edge of the roof, chewing on the end of his thumb, his face taut and distressed.

"He could have escaped, but he didn't really try. Now look. Why did he do that?"

Simon had a strong urge to understand things, how they worked, and why they behaved the way they did. No doubt, he found Billy-Bob's behavior counterintuitive and deeply troubling.

"This is better," said Gordimer.

"How?" asked Simon.

"If he had succeeded, something else would have followed. And after that another and another, until something against which no one could prevail would find him. In the process, your city would join the rest of the world in ruin."

Simon scowled and pinched his eyes. He did not like the answer, but Gordimer knew he would try to understand it.

An exceptional mind could accept what it did not like if it made sense. That this trait tended to be an exception was one of humanity's great hindrances. Vast amounts of time were wasted on trying to prove things people wanted to believe, even after it was clear they were impractical, impossible, or wrong. The human mind was a beautiful and profound device capable of the most staggering ignorance. The hardest thing to do was to change a mind that had already decided what it wanted to believe.

"You might be right," said Simon. "I suppose we'll have to see."

Gordimer hesitated, his wings half spread.

"My test," Gordimer explained. "I have to find another hero."

"Oh. Don't you want to see what this one does, first?"

The question jolted him.

"What do you mean?"

With great effort, Gordimer's wings folded and he turned toward the street on legs that felt reluctant to hold him. What Simon implied excited and terrified him, and even though he understood, his mind resisted, unwilling to believe because it didn't seem possible, even though everything leading to this point suggested it was. He continued to resist Unless, even as it asserted itself more fully as days passed. Why? Because it was so much easier not to believe. After all he'd seen, he'd come to the understanding that only the impossible could alter the pathway to destruction, and the impossible was, underpinned by the most conspicuous logic, not possible.

He looked into the street. There stood the boy, mussed, but unharmed.

The strength went out of Gordimer's legs and he dropped to his knees. The boy had survived again. Trumpets blared a fanfare in his mind, and his eyes welled with relief and joy. He fought the urge to lunge into the street and congratulate Billy-Bob, ask how he had done it, and search for the way home that had surely opened. At the same time he reminded himself of his own prediction. The wogs were gone. But something else would come to fill the gap they left.

No sooner had the thought formed than a white shape flashed down from the sky and settled in the street, shaking its head and padding around in a small circle as though preparing a place to sit and rest. A pelican.

"That doesn't seem so bad," said Simon. "For a worse monster."

Indeed, Gordimer saw nothing threatening about the bird, but the boy had tensed and his hand crept toward the gun at his hip. The bird opened its beak as if to speak, and for a moment Gordimer thought he saw something sparkle and disappear into its mouth. It did not appear frightened of Billy-Bob, but edged away from him nonetheless, spreading its wings as though preparing to grapple.

Behind Billy-Bob at the opposite end of the street came the boom of something very large falling to the ground. A thin screen of sand rippled out from the point of impact and Gordimer saw Billy-Bob's shoulders fall, as if he'd been expecting it and was nevertheless disappointed by being right. Gordimer looked down the street, expecting part of the crater wall to have fallen in or a much larger pelican. Instead he saw a giant, red creature, nearly twice the boy's height, with black wings that spanned the entire street that shrank as they collapsed against its back. The creature had black eyes, so Gordimer could not tell where it was looking, but it faced the pelican, which waddled back and forth, wings spread, squawking as though shouting its half of an argument.

Between the two of them stood Billy-Bob, flimsy and dismayed, like the hollowed out sticks that were once trees in the wasteland.

What was this new creature? Gordimer had explored deserts and cities the world over and never encountered anything like this. Huge and huffing and angry.

"Oh," said Simon, extending the word for a few seconds. "This *is* worse."

* * *

At the far end of the street, Kilgoth glowered. Only the rumble of his breath and the slow, restless opening and closing of his hands betrayed the fact that he still lived and felt, and was more than a grotesque statue. His black eyes seemed to see nothing while looking at everything, and by observing barely perceptible turns of his head, it was clear he was watching the pelican as it danced behind Billy-Bob.

The pelican tottered back and forth, flapping its wings and making pig-like snorts, trying to see Kilgoth around Billy-Bob, who had placed himself in a precarious position between the two and felt very much like a nail waiting to be struck.

It was apparent the pelican enjoyed tormenting Kilgoth, and so long as Kilgoth stayed, so would the pelican. At the same time, Kilgoth held himself in check, knowing if he approached the pelican it would fly away and the chase would begin again. Instead he stood, and watched, enduring the behavior of the pelican, while his insides smoldered and his hands clenched and unclenched, waiting for a chance to strike.

Neither intended to go anywhere for the time being, which, Billy-Bob decided, was both good and bad. Good, because Kilgoth had reasoned the best decision was to stay still, and if Kilgoth could still reason, perhaps Billy-Bob could reason with him; bad, because Kilgoth meant to retrieve his test by any means, meaning conflict reminiscent of what took place in the forest was inevitable and the city would not survive it.

The obvious first step was to return what had been taken from him.

Billy-Bob faced the pelican, which stopped prancing and clucking when it realized it had gotten the attention of something else. The pelican appeared cautious at first, then began wauking and flapping its wings again, directing its taunts at Billy-Bob, the golden band dangling from its beak.

With the pelican distracted, he felt a faint jolt in the ground followed by another and another. Kilgoth had found his opportunity.

"Drop it," said Billy-Bob.

Immediately, the pelican knew it had something Billy-Bob wanted. The pelican spread its wings and wauked at him defiantly, dashing toward him and ducking away again, just out of reach.

Billy-Bob stood, trying to remain calm as Kilgoth approached. He didn't have the luxury of looking back to check his progress. The pelican dashed in again, and Billy-Bob reached out and set his foot on top of one of the pelican's paddle feet. When the pelican discovered it could not dash away again it flew into an immediate rage.

Unable to escape, the pelican began to caterwaul with great intensity, pounding Billy-Bob with his wings, but Billy-Bob did not withdraw. The pelican pecked and smacked its head against Billy-Bob until, finally, as he knew it must, the pelican opened its mouth to bite him. With a quick grab, Billy-Bob reached into the wet pocket of the pelican's beak and snatched out the wristwatch. He lifted his foot and the pelican stumbled backward. It regained its balance and squawked a few more times in defiance, then spread its wings and flapped away. Even in the face of defeat, the pelican's pride demanded a flourish.

When he turned, Kilgoth had closed half the distance so only the length of a few buildings separated them. His gaze did not follow the bird as it pumped high into the air and headed back to the forest. He stood with knees bent slightly, wings partly open, as though preparing to launch himself forward.

From so near Billy-Bob could read the expressions on his face and in his behavior. He looked like a beast enraged, but Billy-Bob detected a few stains of regret. His breath came in long rasps through a hard scowl like air escaping through the fracture in a boulder, yet his brows rode high and his black eyes opened wide. For all his rage, there remained a sense of despair and fear.

Billy-Bob looked at the wristwatch in his hand. It was an ordinary band connected to a numbered face with arms that clicked and twitched. Jim had given this to Kilgoth, this test. Kilgoth's attachment to the wristwatch was the test. He had failed to release it because it was precious to him and he continued to fail so long as he pursued it. Did everyone undergo such a test? Billy-Bob wondered what cherished object Jim could test him with by taking it away and whether this was a test he, or anyone, could ever pass. Billy-Bob didn't know if returning the test would allow Kilgoth to redeem himself, but it made sense to try.

He held the wristwatch aloft. Kilgoth, who crept closer as Billy-Bob considered the watch, went rigid. Billy-Bob hurled the watch to Kilgoth, who caught it in a giant hand.

"You've got it back," called Billy-Bob. "Now go."

Kilgoth regarded the wristwatch, looking at it with fascination and compassion, but his consternation did not subside.

"Hoo!" called a voice from the rooftop. He saw Gordimer trying to pull a man away from the edge of the roof. "What was that?"

Kilgoth looked up from the watch and balled it inside a fist.

Billy-Bob's shoulders fell. The first resort of the mighty and jealous was never to protect what they had, but destroy what they considered a threat, real or imagined. The mighty and jealous saw threats everywhere, and that made them dangerous.

"Oh no," said Billy-Bob.

Without a word, Kilgoth took two great strides to the building closest to him and swung out an arm, sweeping the front away in a cloud of splinters. The building leaned forward and collapsed. Those standing on it scrambled to an adjoining roof. Kilgoth moved to the next building and crunched through the material, then moved on to the next.

In appearance and behavior, Kilgoth was the embodiment of what he'd expected Ultimate Evil to be. Giant, powerful, unstoppable. The same Kilgoth who had been so kind and willing to help, who had failed his test and been set upon a path of widespread and arbitrary destruction. It stung him to know this was not the real Kilgoth, that the helpful and kind Kilgoth was somewhere unreachable, his thinking self secluded within the shell of this destructive beast. And like the Forest Monster before him, Billy-Bob had to stop Kilgoth because Kilgoth could not stop himself. It had happened just as Gordimer said it would, but not as Billy-Bob hoped.

Billy-Bob drew his gun.

If it had not been Beta it would have been somewhere else. If not Billy-Bob, someone else. Kilgoth had failed his test and could not unfail it. He would be subject to these rages to the end of his existence. Unless someone set him free.

“I guarantee,” said the gun, “that every time you involve me, even if events transpire the way you want, you will regret the result.”

“I understand.”

Kilgoth had pounded his way through the shell of a building and it collapsed around him. Billy-Bob followed with the gun and found Kilgoth standing in the rubble, staring back at Billy-Bob, waiting. He did not move forward to attack or duck down an alley to hide. He did not appear enraged or malevolent. More he seemed devoted to a chore. This is what he had become. He did not like it, but it was what he had to do. And he understood what Billy-Bob had to do now.

Billy-Bob raised the weapon. He felt unusual and unpleasant, motion sick even though he stood still, and wondered if this was heroism.

Kilgoth waited.

“You don’t have to do this,” said the gun. “You know it. I wouldn’t say so otherwise.”

Did heroes kill when the opportunity stood before them, inviting them to do so? Billy-Bob had shot at the Forest Monster, but never expected to hit him. His mind was always focused on escape. This was not what Billy-Bob wanted, but what he had to do, what a hero ought to do.

Billy-Bob realized he did not like being a hero. But perhaps he didn’t quite need to do what he ought.

With the end of a life came the end of a chance for redemption. Redemption is what Kilgoth deserved, and though he might not be able to give it to him, he could give him the opportunity by allowing him to live.

The barrel trained instead on Kilgoth's shoulder.

Billy-Bob squeezed the trigger and watched the hammer clap against the charge. The bullet ejected with a flash and puff of gray smoke, churning toward the monster, covering a short stone's throw in an instant that lasted quite a long time. It would injure Kilgoth, not destroy him. It would prevent him from doing further damage. These are all the things Billy-Bob expected the bullet to do when it reached Kilgoth. Instead, much to his surprise, it bounced.

First it sank into Kilgoth's shoulder, pressing inward without penetrating, then sprang backwards. Billy-Bob had a harder time following the bullet when it came back toward him, but he felt it bite through his left shoulder and continue past him. He felt more surprise than pain, just enough of the latter to prove something unexpected had occurred.

"I tried to warn you," said the gun.

Billy-Bob aimed the gun again, strengthened by disbelief as much as the knowledge that he had to stop Kilgoth and could not think of another way to do so. His left arm dangled limp at his side and he felt something wet on his fingertips, like moisture draining out of a wet shirt. He squeezed the trigger again and again the bullet had no effect on Kilgoth.

This time the bullet rebounded from Kilgoth and struck Billy-Bob in the right shoulder. It didn't hurt much, but the blow pushed him back a step. The strength in his arm departed and the gun dropped from his hand. Without the weapon, Billy-Bob didn't know what to do. Thinking about the problem didn't help because thinking had become suddenly very difficult, which Billy-Bob found frustrating. He dropped to his knees and, once there, couldn't help dropping to his side as well. He could see the gun resting within reach and tried to stretch for it without success. His arms did not respond. His body had become so heavy he could not raise it.

Kilgoth crunched his feet in the wreckage of the building in frustration, the approached Billy-Bob. Billy-Bob expected Kilgoth to crush him out of existence, but instead he whispered in the calm voice Billy-Bob remembered from the forest, albeit touched with despair.

"How do I end this? If not this, how? If not you, who?"

Billy-Bob wanted to tell Kilgoth he could help, he just needed more time to think about it. He wanted to give Kilgoth hope for salvation, even if hope was a silly thing that couldn't be trusted. Hope did serve a function, even if it was false, because the hopeful person who pursued their hopes had a better chance of achieving them than the cynic. This is what he wanted to tell Kilgoth, to give him a faint belief that in that hope lay the salvation he desired. He wanted to tell him not to go, to let him to gather his thoughts so he could offer a better solution. He wanted to tell him not to give up. Instead, all he could muster was a single word.

"Don't."

Even that word was hard, and it took everything. Even his vision had gone and the world lost its color. So he laid his head down in a wet patch of grass and let the tiredness overtake him. Maybe after a rest he could try again.

* * *

Gordimer watched the boy slump to his knees and fall to the side. He saw the dirt around the boy darkening, then his eyes filled and blurred his vision.

He heard someone shrieking the word "No!" in a long and agonized cry, in a voice that sounded familiar but he could not place. Then he felt the ache in his throat and twinge in his knees and ankles as he leapt from the building and landed in the street, and knew it had been his own.

Maybe this was another deception, another trick of circumstance where Billy-Bob had proven successful yet again and Gordimer's skepticism made him blind to it. Maybe the boy was whole. As he approached he could see the whiteness of his face and the discolored grass below him, and the hope that the boy would spring to his feet and surprise him diminished.

Kilgoth faced Gordimer and roared, clutching whatever Billy-Bob had thrown it, and leapt into the air. Gordimer felt unexpectedly fearless, and shooed the monster away as it lifted off the ground as though it were no more than an aggravating insect, determined to get to Billy-Bob.

He skidded to the ground beside the boy, his knees resting in matted grass, not knowing what to do. He had never been anything more than a guide from one place to here, uninvolved and trying to remain detached, focused on home. Even now he heard himself whistling a shaky version of the tune he could only remember in a small part. The boy's shirt was a morass of sticky fluid where the bullets had passed through it. Should he take it off? Should he find a shirt without holes? Gordimer's mind had made itself useless.

"We need to staunch that."

Simon had descended after Gordimer and knelt beside him.

"Where is the physician?"

Simon pointed a finger to the sky, then tore off one of Billy-Bob's sleeves and began to wind it around the boy's shoulder.

"We're all that's left. And that." He pointed to a sleek craft pointing upward out of the bowl that held the city. "That will take the last of us."

"Where?"

"There's a place at the far edge of the planets that still functions, constructed long before I've been around. You too, maybe. We can stay there and keep an eye on things here. If there's any improvement, maybe we'll come back. You should come, too."

If Gordimer went with them he could escape this place, though he couldn't complete his mission. He had to save the boy, otherwise there would be no one left to be a hero and he would be trapped here forever.

"I can't go!" Gordimer cried.

"Why not?"

"I've got to get out of here!"

"You don't even try to make sense."

Simon shook his head and returned to his work, pulling another sleeve free and winding it around the other shoulder. Simon had preserved the expertise of the past in his mind, but he was not a medical practitioner. Gordimer needed more than preserved expertise, he needed something restorative, something that could do for Billy-Bob what the girl had done for the forest.

Gordimer jerked to his feet, astounded by his leap of judgment.

The girl had restored the forest, she could restore this boy. She could be a hero, as he'd always hoped, if he could convince her it meant something to be so. If he could convince her being so was not hopeless. But how to find her? And how to convince her of a belief that had only recently been ground away by the force of Billy-Bob's endurance and conviction?

Her father had been a hero, the last hero, and she had lost him. She'd become bitter, misanthropic, and ventured out by herself for the singular purpose of being alone. Maybe if she had the chance to save a hero, a hero worth saving, she would come back. Even though coming back would expose her to those searching for her. To find her, he realized, he needed to find those whose mission it was to search for her.

Turning in place, Gordimer scanned the town, then strode to intercept an injured wog as it limped toward Billy-Bob. He didn't think wogs had any distinguishing features, apart from varying states of disrepair. Nevertheless, he couldn't shake the feeling that this wog looked familiar.

"You," said Gordimer. "You can help me."

"Helping you is not my mission," the wog replied.

The wog did not have features that permitted expression, but it looked to the spot where Billy-Bob lay and labored around Gordimer with earnest. It cared, Gordimer thought. Or, at the least, the boy played some part in its mission.

"To the contrary. Helping me is very much your mission."

"Why?"

Gordimer hoisted the wog into his arms. The tiny creature was heavier than it looked, and when he spoke his words came out with a gasp.

"Because the other wogs know where to find the girl, so you know where to find her."

"That's quite a leap of judgment," said the wog. "Why do I want to find the girl?"

"Because she can save him."

For a moment the wog did not respond and Gordimer could hear the threshing of gears and cylinders inside its body. Then it raised an arm back toward the slope below the Information Post.

"That's the last place we saw her. We should start there."

VARIATIONS ON A THEME

Billy-Bob lay on the familiar slope leading back to the forest outside Beta, curling and uncurling his fingers in the soft strands of grass, watching fragments of broken clouds scatter across the sky.

A prickle in his shoulders made him reach up and scratch them. This only made them itch more, so he attempted to ignore the sensation instead.

At the edge of memory he recalled confronting Kilgoth, though he could not remember the result. At no point did he remember defeating the goliath, which meant he had, in all likelihood, lost. Possibly he had perished in the effort. Could one still ponder things once they ceased to live? On the other hand, the familiar setting might make this his dream. If this was death, apart from the fiendishly itchy shoulders, it did not seem so bad.

The effect of death on his shoulders reminded him of Gordimer's chronically itchy wings. Had Gordimer finished his mission or had he already departed on the long path back across the wasteland to find a new hero? If Billy-Bob had lived he could have asked the wogs to help Gordimer. Surely a few could be spared from protecting the girl.

The girl.

If this was his dream, she was here, too. Billy-Bob rolled onto his stomach and pushed himself up, clambering up the slope to where she should be waiting.

And there she was, up the hill, staring into the forest, oblivious of all else. Dark hair kicked at her shoulders and the wind sent ripples through the grass at her knees. Sticks and leaves poked through her hair and her hands, dangling at her side, were stained with dirt and dark under the fingernails. She was filthy. Filthy and beautiful, even as a dark silhouette at the top of the hill.

Billy-Bob gazed at her in awe. This girl, fashioned by his own head in all her imperfection, beautiful in ways he could not understand, only feel, had all his life been illusory, imaginary. Something beyond reach, but visible from an incomprehensible distance. Something he'd heard of but never expected to see. Hope, a confounding tickle, unscratchably remote, had toyed and fooled and teased, never expecting to be seen in fullness.

She was real. Not here, but in the world. Somewhere. And now, thanks to his efforts, protected.

Pulling at grass and clawing at the turf, he ascended until he was at her side.

The girl gazed over the green plain between Beta and the forest where a man in white sat at a table. Even at a distance he seemed large, dwarfing the table and crouching uncomfortably in a chair that was much too small. He didn't remember him from any prior dreams, but perhaps he simply hadn't been paying attention.

The girl gestured and a tree pushed up nearby, unfolding like an umbrella beneath a stormcloud and blocking his view of the man in the distance. Her head cocked, admiring the world in silence because that was how beautiful things were best appreciated.

Strange. The dream usually ended here, like a great book, at the most poignant and promising moment, leaving a reader to wonder about events beyond the final pages, as if the people inside kept going on.

What to do? Talk to her? What to say? That he knew her? That he had nonsensical dreams about her? Right now, in fact. There must be something he could do that wouldn't send her fleeing down the hill in horror. This was a dream made by his own mind. What would it mean if his own brain caused her to reject him?

He took her hand, waiting for the gritty fingers to pull away. Instead they tightened around his and a powerful surge of Everything pulsed through him. He'd never felt a sense of Everything before, the notion that a summary of his existence, of his hopes and efforts, could be encapsulated in a single item that, to anyone else, might mean something completely different or have no value at all. The girl. She was Everything. Being a hero had nothing to do with it.

A new thought crashed into his head like a thunderbolt in a cloudless sky. Bold, and startling.

Did he want to be a hero? It occurred to him heroing wasn't important, so long as he could have what everyone, in their most simplistic combination of hopes, desires, aspirations, and necessities, wanted: to love and be loved. Was heroing no more than a means to that end? If he could have this without heroing he would take it. Instantly. Without thought. This was enough by itself.

On the dream went.

Now her face was heavy with disappointment. He felt heat on his cheeks and followed her gaze.

His face opened.

Fire raged in the forest and on the plain before them, blotting the sky with smoke that choked him and scalded his eyes. Everything lush and green had gone, eaten into ash. No living things remained, only the spikes of glowing embers that had been trees. Everything once beautiful was dust in the hot air, irreparably fragmented. Grass had curled and blackened on the buckled land where abrasive sands swirled up into brief vortexes that drilled at the ground before collapsing in exhaustion. Slivers of light punched through the haze in splintering bolts, shocking the terrain with malevolent impunity.

Amongst the lightning strikes he could see people struggling with one another. Here again he heard the familiar roar of sound he thought were cheers as people clashed, not as two opposing armies, but as a single morass of human conflict, with no aim but the destruction of one another. He saw no order, no objective, nothing but a general anguish expressed by a compulsion to eliminate all but themselves.

"I'm not afraid," he murmured. The words sounded peculiar because he should be frightened, yet wasn't. He wondered why.

His hand tightened on the girl's and he turned to face her. At least, though everything was lost, he still had her. He could still escape this place with the girl. But when he saw her, she was frozen, dark hair rigid and powdery gray, eyes locked in terror. He touched her, searching for animation, and a flake peeled away where his fingertip met her face.

He drew back, but it was too late. The girl shortened slowly in the wind, then exploded into dust and scattered in the air.

Billy-Bob screamed and the world around him shook with his despair. Why would his mind dream up something wonderful then destroy it in front of him? What did that mean?

Terrain around him shattered, cracks opened into canyons that ate what remained of forests and cities, draining the last bits of rivers and oceans and sent their steaming remains into the swirling atmosphere. The ground beneath him rose up in a swallowing mouth and closed around his neck, leaving all but his head buried. Wind rose, breaking apart the few blackened trees and turning the world to a blur of dust with Billy-Bob screaming inside it.

Why should it be this way? This was his dream after all. If dead, he could do nothing. If all proved a manifestation of his roving imagination, he ought to have some control over it. So Billy-Bob squinted and shook his head, trying to empty it of everything. He cracked one eye open.

The world remained, not empty, but restored to a state of peace. He remained at the top of the slope with Beta behind him, and ahead the field and forest. The girl no longer stood beside him, leaving him alone in this familiar yet frightening world.

A flicker of motion on the opposite side of the field caught his attention. No. Not alone after all. In an opening in the grass just before the trees the large man in white remained at the table. He wore a broad-brimmed straw hat and waved an arm over his head, beckoning.

This dream was immense. Unpredictable. Horrifying. Wasn't he dead?

Maybe the fellow would know.

THE RELUCTANT HERO

Poppy knelt at the edge of the forest over the sprig of a new tree, a few fingers of branches extending from the slender trunk like an outstretched hand. The trunk had snapped in the middle and the hand sagged to one side, as though too fatigued to hold itself upright.

For a moment she considered using her father's glove to restore the tree, a remnant of the technology rediscovered when it seemed humanity might redeem itself. But the power to use it had to come from somewhere. She didn't have the strength to give any more of herself and to take it from the world around her meant destroying one thing to save another.

She stood the tree upright and wound several long strands of grass around the frayed elbow. It stood stiff and straight inside the bandage despite its injury, stalwart and brave, though it must be hurting. Would it heal itself? She didn't know. But she hoped. Not because she believed hope could shift events in one direction or another, but because without hope the compulsion to try evaporated, leaving only one possibility.

Poppy raised her head until she could see over the top of the grass. No shapes moved against the background of the horizon, though that didn't tell her much. Her hunters stood well below the level of the grass. She cocked her head, listening for the sound of a branch broken underfoot, heavy breathing, or the telltale knocking of a wog's machinery. Nothing.

The silence, however, only made her wary.

Wogs had gotten smarter. They disguised their passage in the ambient noises of the world, walking when the wind blew a rustle through the branches or remaining still and silent until she crossed their path. They'd almost caught her the last time doing just that, forcing her to flee through grasses so knotted she had scarcely succeeded in pushing through them. Now she had to watch for narrow paths trampled in the grasses, footprints in soft dirt, fibers of hair caught in branches. Soon, she realized, they'd figure out how to hide those clues, too.

The broken tree was probably a lure in a trap. She stopped anyway because they knew as well as she did that she could not turn away, even if it meant danger and more running. Even now she expected them to leap out of the grass, pin her in place, and work whatever malevolence they had intended for her after years of fruitless pursuit. Still nothing.

Why the wogs had turned against her, she didn't know. Her list of questions without answers underwent regular turnover, but some remained forever. Wogs had once been friends; her father had once been here; the world had once seemed on a path to recovery. The circumstances had changed for each, and she suspected, somehow, the reasons were related. Where her father's mission had been conspicuous and designed for attention, she carried out that mission alone and in secret.

Everything had changed when her father disappeared. All the buoyancy and belief that the world could recover had evaporated. She stayed away from people, stayed away from the city and fought this battle herself, because she knew the disappearance of her father was, in the end, her fault. Isolation was her self-inflicted punishment. If not for her, he might still be here, might still be guiding humanity to recovery. Maybe if she punished herself long enough he might come back.

Poppy shook her head and squinted away the mist that started to sting her eyes. She had wasted time and watered countless plants with thoughts like this, wondering if she could have made him stay and if her efforts to rekindle life in the world would someday reverse and pick out her careful stitching.

Until it happened, she would mend broken saplings while the forest deleted line by line, like a story unwriting itself, removing all its traces and all the means through which it might have told its tale. That such disasters could spring from an act of kindness and mercy shattered the hopes she had for this world. She had saved a person, a man named Mardin, who later pushed everything her father had saved to the brink of destruction. In the process the world had stopped its recovery, people began to isolate themselves, and her father had never returned from his mission, leaving only shards of a fragmented hope.

No movement came from the grasses other than a few waves from the breezes passing through like the sweep of a hand. She gripped the heavy branch she'd set aside while she tended the sapling and straightened, her back and legs groaning with the effort. A lifetime of running, of fixing, then refixing the work she'd just completed, left her in a permanent state of fatigue.

"There she is!"

The voice came from above and to the side. She hadn't expected an approach from the air and cursed herself for the oversight. How didn't matter to her, she needed only to escape. No one with good intentions ever came looking for her.

With a quick turn of her hips, she swung the branch toward the approaching creature and struck it from the air as it approached. The branch shattered, leaving her defenseless, but the flying creature spun half a cartwheel and fell to the ground in a heap. A small animal let out a whoop of surprise as it flew from her attacker's arms. It rotated through the air just long enough for her to identify it as a wog before dropping out of sight into the grass.

Wogs could not be defeated, only escaped. She backed toward the grass behind her, her legs shrieking in anticipation of what would be another long run. Then a head popped up from the grass followed by a waving arm.

"Wait!" said the head. "It's me, Gordimer!"

Gordimer. Her mind rambled. Gordimer was a name she hadn't heard in some time. Why did he have a wog? Had it corrupted him to its purpose? Could they do that to people now? Even if they hadn't she doubted he'd have anything of interest to say. He never had before. Just the same desperate plea to save the world so he could leave it behind.

"I don't want to be a hero," she muttered, and stepped back into the grass. "I can't save everyone."

"You don't need to save everyone!" Gordimer called, panting as he heaved into the clearing. "You just need to save one."

The wog joined him in the clearing, its body half mashed.

"Please," said the wog.

Poppy stepped forward again. Wary, but curious.

"Wogs don't say please," she said.

"Please," the wog repeated, its voice warbling. "It is my mission to protect him. I need you to help me do so. I will never have another opportunity. I do not wish to be permanently saddled with the memory of failure."

"Failure is a part of existence."

"The threat of failure is equally instructional. And this failure is personal."

She had expected the wog to cast aside the ruse of an injury and lunge forward. Instead it remained still, pleading. It was an unfamiliar and compelling tactic, and she wondered how the wog would take advantage of her, and wondered also if it was already too late to escape.

On the other hand, she understood failure, or rather, understood the frustration of watching success slip slowly from her grip. Her father, the receding forest, the people leaving this world for elsewhere, her disintegrating resolve. More and more she wanted the fight to end, but she could never bring herself to surrender.

"We need to get back to Beta," said Gordimer.

He seemed anxious to leave. He rocked restlessly, creeping in the direction of the city, as if each fingerlength he traveled now might save him precious instants later.

"Can I trust you?"

"Yes, of course!" cried Gordimer.

"How do I know that?"

Gordimer's mouth opened and closed several times without a sound.

"I don't know how," he said at last. He wrung his hands in frustration. "I didn't think about it. You have to believe me. That little bit of hope we all cling to so stupidly, it's here. It's bleeding to death in the street as we speak. But you can save him. You must."

"If I don't?"

"The boy dies," said the wog.

She'd met a boy not long ago. He seemed pleasant, if awkward. And though awkward, he had not been a fool, blathering on meaninglessly just to have something to say. Most people with nothing to say chose to speak anyway, their mouths were trapdoors and every thought that entered their minds fell through the gap, filling the world with noise when they would do it greater service by remaining silent. Few possessed the wisdom to keep their mouth shut.

He had helped her, without thought, and without concern for his own safety. Against her will, she liked him, though to what extent she could not say. Liking someone without knowing them did not make sense, and she prided herself on her sensibility. Her feelings on the matter annoyed her because they did not behave sensibly, but she did not regret them or try to flush them away.

In retrospect, she'd used him as a buffer and may have left him to his destruction. She returned later, looking for him, but he had vanished. This relieved and disappointed her. Glad he'd escaped, saddened he had not lingered. Not surprised. Just part of the pattern. Everyone left.

She wondered if the person Gordimer wanted her to save was that boy. It didn't seem likely, but she couldn't resist hoping, even though hoping always led to disappointment. Against her judgment, she wanted Gordimer to convince her to help, though she didn't want to make the convincing easy. He would have to earn her aid. In earning it, it would prove worthwhile. More than anything she wanted to have something to believe in. But if she were to have something to believe in, something in the world would have to change significantly.

"I'm listening. Convince me."

Gordimer smiled, jittering excitedly.

"I will!" he cried, then raised a finger, as though he'd come to the perfect solution. Then he spoke a single word, as though it carried some great, unspoken meaning. "Unless!"

"Unless," murmured the wog. "Of course."

AN IMPERFECT PLAN

By the time Billy-Bob reached the table the giant man seemed to have forgotten he'd invited anyone. Instead, he sat crunched in his chair working at a piece of wood with a small knife, removing a few splinters at a time that he blew off the table with gentle puffs of air. Only when Billy-Bob rapped gently on the table did the man raise his floppy straw hat, and in that moment Billy-Bob knew him. Even crunched down at the table his size was unmistakable.

"Jim," said Billy-Bob.

Jim nodded.

"Have a seat," he said.

"Yes," invited the rough wooden chair beside the table. "Have me."

Billy-Bob sat and the chair creaked and gave a grunt as it took on his weight. It wobbled and Billy-Bob had to hold onto the table to keep it from falling over.

"So this is how we meet," said Jim, gesturing in a circle with his knife before returning to the task in his hands, flicking out bits of wood with deft turns of his wrist. Jim had the stature of someone profound and important, yet he spoke with coyness and amusement of a lunatic. His eyes squinted and his mouth twisted one way then the other, as though teetering upon the precipice of a smile. He was anxious or excited. Maybe both. "It's nice here, don't you think?"

"Did we need to meet?" asked Billy-Bob. "Did I have to die to meet you?"

If Jim was a being of omnipotence, it made sense to find him lord of an afterlife.

"Of course not. No need for such drama. We would have met no matter what. Nothing would change that. It was simply a matter of opportunity. This is your dream. Don't you recognize it?"

"Then you're a dream, too."

Jim blinked, as though he never thought of this before. If he was part of a dream he may never have considered the possibility he wasn't real.

"Perhaps."

Billy-Bob felt a prickle in his shoulder. He reached up to scratch but his arm stopped short, as though something were resisting. He strained and his hand crept closer to his shoulder until he was able to claw at it with his fingers. Instead of relief, however, his shoulder burned, and he decided he'd try to ignore the urge to scratch because this was worse.

"Why am I here?" asked Billy-Bob.

"You fell asleep."

That made sense. Maybe the strangeness of his dream was an indication that his mind had started losing bits of itself like the wood giving up little chips as Jim worked at it with his knife. Each ablated flake brought him a splinter closer to senility and oblivion. He wondered if death was something he could escape.

"How do I leave?"

Jim shrugged.

"You wake up. Surely you have better questions than this."

If this was his dream, the only familiar element was the setting. He'd seen the world around him, but the table, this conversation, and Jim were all new. The cheering people gave him a sense of belonging and purpose, and the girl provided the enjoyable fantasy of companionship. What purpose did Jim serve?

"Why are *you* here?"

"That's better!" Jim dropped the wood and knife and brought his hands together with a clap of pleasure. "Because you're afraid. Because I am the natural alternative to a lack of information. Because you're looking for a task to complete, another stepping stone on a path toward heroism. Go west, find Beta, save the girl, defeat Ultimate Evil, fourteen acorns." Jim counted his fingers as he went through the list with a tone of familiarity and boredom. "You've heard all that. I'm here to tell you not to let them leave. I'm the push from behind when you would turn back."

Billy-Bob tried to sort out everything Jim had told him, but could not. He tried to focus his attention on just the last bit, about preventing people from leaving. Rather, he assumed Jim meant people. It might mean wogs or trees or all or none. He didn't know who he was supposed to stop from leaving, nor how to show them doing so wasn't necessary, nor why they shouldn't go. His shoulders itched terribly.

"And yet, at the same time," Jim added wistfully, "they're all tied up together. The ridiculous, the impossible, and the mythical. You can't do just one. You've got to do them all."

"Don't let who leave?" asked Billy-Bob.

Jim did not answer. He smiled and waited for Billy-Bob to figure the riddle out himself. He reached beneath the table and picked up a handful of dirt, then stopped himself, as if he realized the time hadn't yet come to do so, and opened his hand to let the dirt sift back to the ground. He sat back in the chair, scratched his nose, flicked at the scraps of wood on the tabletop, picked up the wood and peeled off a thin curl with the carving knife, and did an altogether bad job of appearing patient. He drummed his feet, bit his lips, stared with expectation and impatience. Nevertheless, Billy-Bob could see he was determined to resist the temptation to answer, as though not answering had greater value.

Riddles never made sense without a special insight or a leap of intuition Billy-Bob lacked. Riddles did little more than exploit the ignorance of one person in a conversation. Jim knew, but he wanted Billy-Bob to guess. Naturally, Billy-Bob had no idea, and the harder he thought, the more foolish he felt for not knowing and the more his shoulders itched.

Maybe a rock would know. They always seemed to know when he didn't. So he picked up a small, dirty stone the leg of the chair had pried out when he sat.

"Who can't I let leave?" he asked the stone.

"What?" the stone shouted back. "What? Speak up!"

Billy-Bob rubbed his thumb over the stone, clearing away the dirt caked on its surface and repeated himself.

"Who can't—"

"Why?" the stone interrupted.

"I don't know."

"How am I supposed to solve an equation without any variables? I'm just a hunk of limestone. I'm not *magical.* Limestone doesn't lend itself to magic. This sounds like a riddle. Riddles are obnoxious."

"Are there any magical rocks around here?"

The stone made a noise like two rough blocks groaning as they scraped past one another.

"Don't be escapist. Figure it out for yourself. Too many people waste their time searching for magical rocks instead."

Billy-Bob saw Jim watching him from the other side of the table, gnawing at his lip as though straining to avoid interrupting. Billy-Bob felt suddenly foolish and the last thread preventing Jim from asking his question snapped.

"Does it answer?" Jim blurted.

"I'm not crazy," said Billy-Bob. Though in truth he was uncertain about the claim.

"No, no," said Jim, excitedly. He leaned forward onto the table, as though they'd finally gotten on a topic he'd been waiting to discuss. "Those voices are your own."

"What?"

"What what?" asked the stone. "You didn't know?"

"The rocks and dirt only have the voices and thoughts you give them," said Jim.

"No. They always know more than I do."

"They know only as much as you do. Perhaps you know more than you know."

Billy-Bob eyed the stone.

"Is that true?"

"Of course it's true," the stone responded. "I know only what you tell me. I know your name, your parents, lots of important stuff. I thought you knew. I did."

"Who are my parents?"

"You really should have figured it out yourself by now. I have."

Billy-Bob stared blankly at the stone, then set it on the ground.

He didn't know which astounded him more: that the stone had identified his parents or that all this time he'd been speaking to himself and couldn't remember the things this stone claimed to know. He didn't feel crazy, but most people with cracks saw the thin fissures of fractured sanity in everyone but themselves.

"My thanks," said the stone. "And a thin layer of dirt, if you please."

Using the side of his shoe, Billy-Bob pushed loose dirt over the stone. He knew the stone didn't have a voice or petty concerns, but he did it anyway. The dirt muffled the stone's response, but it sounded appreciative with a touch of finality that ended the discussion.

"It was me," said Billy-Bob.

The realization did not comfort him. He preferred to be crazy than alone in a quiet, lifeless world.

Jim shrugged.

"We look for advice in the inanimate, as if they would have a perspective outside our own, but in truth what they tell us is only a reflection of what we already know and felt uncomfortable thinking about. They can seem brilliant or odd, and we let them tell us what we believed without admitting it to ourselves. Or we can dismiss them, satisfying the need to express an idea without having to respect it."

"But it seemed real," Billy-Bob continued. "And if it seemed real but wasn't, how do I know what is real from what isn't? How do I know I haven't imagined you, too?"

Jim tapped the flat of his knife against his mouth, thoughtfully.

"Ask yourself the same question. Are you real? How do you prove it to someone else? You have an easy bias toward your own existence, but how could I convince you that I am real, or that anything you see or touch or feel is not something you built yourself, one of a million tiny tricks your mind plays upon itself—a little bit of madness to prevent the complete madness that would come from total isolation. It's an idea that terrifies everyone, so they accept what might be an illusion, even if that illusion is a nightmare."

"But other people see you."

"Maybe I'm a shared delusion. Maybe I play by rules, or maybe the rules exist to explain my behavior. Maybe you're having this entire existential conversation with yourself. Maybe all of existence is the happy dream of an unhappy and neglected boy."

How better to explain his survival so far?

"So…"

"So the only existence you can prove with any certainty is your own. It's the only thing you can be sure of. I know I'm real, but there's no way for you to know that without being me. Of course, what more convincing illusion is there than one that believes in itself? That's the best I can do. The rest you have to decide for yourself."

"Then I can imagine whatever I like."

"Assuming you made everything up, yes. But there's always the possibility that you didn't."

"And I'll know I didn't if things don't go as I wish."

"Unless you imagine that, too. Gives it a dash of reality if you program a few frustrations to trample your accomplishments. It would make everything a challenge, worthwhile. That's the conclusion I came to."

Billy-Bob sighed.

"Thinking is hard."

"I don't know why you say that," said Jim. "You're clearly very good at it. Particularly if you made everything up. I mean, this is a pretty elaborate place. I should thank you for making it. For making me."

"Unless you made me."

"That's a possibility, too. But we can't be sure who imagined who first, can we? Then again, there's the tantalizing possibility that we're all real."

Or none. How much of the world did he imagine? Had it been only the voices of rocks, dirt, and other voiceless objects? What about the girl, the writer, Gordimer? Had he imagined the whole of everything just to seem significant?

"I know what you're thinking," said Jim, "and I'd like to point out that thinking about it won't change anything. However, you can change things, if you choose to do so. I'm interested in seeing how it all turns out."

He could not let them leave, Jim had said. All he could change was whether or not someone left. Who? To where? From where? If he had the answer to the most important question, he realized, he would know how to make them stay.

"Why do they want to go?"

"Ah. Simple. Because they wish to escape the slow atrophy of the world rather than face it. People protect themselves by putting distance between themselves and what threatens them."

"Isn't it better to escape?"

"It would seem so," said Jim. "Seeming so is the nature of the easy path. The quick solution. Immediate results, but no lasting fulfillment, and worse, no resolution. You know that. It's why you run away. But separating people loosens their connection with one another. Separated peoples emphasize their differences. And it's the perception of difference that brings disaster. People look for difference. They fear those differences. They are instinctively suspicious and fearful of what they don't know and don't see every day. Isolation provides an illusion of safety, but at the immense cost of innovation and exchange of ideas. When you isolate yourself, you regress, sometimes reducing so far that everyone else becomes inhuman, they become monsters. You can see it in the world around you. Driving themselves apart will invariably bring them together in war. They don't understand they are all one, in spite of the differences they insist upon seeing. In destroying a bit of others, they destroy a bit of themselves, a bit of their own humanity. You cannot let them leave."

Go where? As he formed the question, he knew the answer. The craft he'd seen leaving the atmosphere was an indication they'd already started.

"How do I make them stay?"

"You have to give them a reason to believe."

Sounded like a hero's business.

"I don't know," said Billy-Bob. "I'm too..."

Slow, weak, stupid, crazy. A wall of words rose up before him. He thought of the statue in Dirtburg and his failed attempt to leap onto the roof in Beta. He thought of his repeated failures and compulsion to escape rather than confront his adversaries, and the recent disaster when he decided not to flee.

"Short," he finished. "And dead."

Jim wagged a finger.

"Not dead," he said. "Only dying."

"Is there a difference?"

"A temporary one. You're worrying about the wrong characteristics. One does not need might or beauty or brains. They help. One needs compassion and the bravery to act upon feelings that well up from it. Fate doesn't predestine someone for greatness or infamy. Your fate is stretchy, flexible, malleable stuff. Make it for yourself. That's what a hero does. Even in failure a hero can succeed. Because a hero doesn't always save the day. A hero succeeds when he or she inspires people to save one another, that it's worth the effort to try."

"Then it isn't fate, is it?"

Jim smiled.

"No. I suppose it isn't," he said. "You're smarter than people think."

It sounded like a compliment. Cheery and friendly rather than a sarcastic snap of short words.

"What are you whittling?"

Jim looked at his hands and jerked, as though surprised to find them busy with something. He turned the object over in his hand, oblivious to the attention he'd paid it, trying to figure out what it might be, then leaned forward and blew away a few curls of wood that had gathered in a furrow he'd made. He watched in fascination as his hands drew together again and resumed their project.

"I suppose I'm working toward the same thing all parts of this world are subtly fixated upon—determining what a hero is. A part of me is a part of you, after all."

"I'm not a hero."

Jim held up the product of his efforts. It was shaped like a mashed sphere with a single leg extending from the bottom, not unlike a wooden mushroom. Jim set the globe on the table and leaned to the side. He scooped a handful of dirt then dumped it on the table where it settled in a pile.

"Hey, hey, hey!" the table protested. "Impolite!"

"Before trees were trees, they were this," said Jim, jutting the knife at the dirt. "Before it was dirt, it was a grain. Before that, a molecule, an atom, a simple electrical charge. And before that just a bit of whimsy floating at random through the ether. They all came from somewhere. If there is greatness locked up in something so simple as this." Jim pinched the top of the mound with his fingers and rubbed them together, and a thin waterfall of grains misted back onto the pile. "Think what wonderful things something more complex can create. Plants. People. You, perhaps."

"Hear that?" sneered the dirt. "I'm the building blocks of everything."

"You're a lump of dirty dirt making me dirty too," the table snapped.

"Maybe I'll evolve into a rhinoceros right now and break your legs off!"

"I'd like to see you try!"

"I'm evolving right now!"

John had said people were stuck as they were, that they were hopeless, that they could change nothing on their own, that they were nothing more than puppets incapable of helping themselves.

"Nothing changes," he muttered.

Jim raised an eyebrow.

"You're right. Nothing changes. Unless."

The word rang in Billy-Bob's ears. The message from Kilgoth. But what difference did it make? He was dead. Or dreaming. Who could trust the advice of a dream? Random, fanciful, full of nothing but the things he feared and for which he most hoped. Of course a dream would tell him everything he wanted to believe.

Jim sighed, eyes scrolling wistfully across the grasses as if he expected them to poof away into a bleak, heat-blurred dustland at any moment.

"Nothing is as it is without purpose. The world is horrible for a reason. Were the world not horrible, people could never understand or appreciate its goodness. It has to be this way first," he said, clenching his fists, and Billy-Bob knew he wasn't merely stating a fact, he was trying to convince himself as well. "It has to be this way so people can realize they want to change it."

"The world is horrible because John wants it that way."

"John thinks making the world horrible will help spread his pain thinner, and it will self perpetuate. That is his plan."

"It's working," Billy-Bob remarked.

"Perhaps. But I have a plan too."

"How do you know your plan will work? Why hasn't it worked already."

"Because I was waiting. Because I have faith. In the plan. In people. In you."

Billy-Bob gazed at his hands. Thin, knobbed. If he ever clutched something like love or victory or fame, how long could he hold them? He wanted to help people. Could he? Rather than be loved by everyone, he preferred just one person. Just one girl. That would be enough.

"What if I don't want to be a hero?"

For the first time Jim's wall of enthusiasm shook. His smile did not fade, but Billy-Bob saw his shoulders dip and knew it was not a question he'd expected. A hint of despair, surprise, defeat. It stung him, briefly, then it was gone. Billy-Bob wondered why such a simple question would jolt him.

"It is, of course, a choice only you can make," Jim answered.

"If I win, will they stay?"

"Winning is not the right word. Winning implies a loser."

"Am I a hero?"

Jim shrugged.

"Maybe."

"Then I can win."

"Not exactly," said Jim.

"Then why bother?"

Jim gnawed his lip, brain working furiously in an attempt to explain.

"A hero's purpose is not to win, conquer, or defeat. Not everything needs to be destroyed. Maybe not anything. That's the crux, you see, the lynchpin of being a hero. The other way. The way to win without defeating anyone. A victory from which everyone benefits. It's always there. Always. Tiny, hidden, elusive. It's not the obvious path. Finding it is what makes you a hero. But it's not enough to be a hero. What people want, and what they need, is an example. Humanity loves examples to which they can compare themselves; a goal to which they can aspire. That love has spawned words like simile and metaphor and analogy and parable."

Billy-Bob stared at Jim. He understood the compulsion to resist what seemed wrong. He did not understand how to combat wrongness without suppressing it.

Jim could see his confusion and pulled at his face in frustration, as though he hadn't yet worked out the idea himself. His mouth chewed on the thought, before saying what he needed to and it became apparent to Billy-Bob he'd been trying to think of a good way to describe a bad thing.

"It is the role of a hero to take on the suffering of others," he said, and allowed himself a grin for having arrived at this solution.

If a hero relieved the suffering of others by taking it on, were they doomed to a life of misery? The fate of heroes was to be great and loved for their greatness. The fate Jim suggested was the complete opposite. Were that true, why be a hero at all?

"Who takes on the suffering of heroes?"

Jim's grin faltered and he looked back across the empty plain.

"Well," he murmured. "It's not a perfect plan."

At that moment the ground shook violently, rolling Billy-Bob from his chair. The sky all around was darkening as though night was closing them up in a giant bag. Jim looked about alertly and his face became urgent. He worked at the object in his hand with gritty paper until a thin layer of dust covered the table, then blew across the surface of his project.

"I suppose that's all the time we have. I hope you're ready. Take this." Jim set the whittled ball in his hand. It felt heavier than expected. "You made me make this. It must be important. My gift to you."

The object had become a yellow-brown metal rather than wood, though that didn't seem possible. The table shook its legs and bolted into the forest as the hinges of reality began to tear free and his dream fell apart. Billy-Bob's face stretched hideously on the brassy surface and his ugliness saddened him in the escaping light. The world distorted as it disintegrated, and darkened. Had he exhausted his remaining bits of life on this fantasy?

"Am I dying now?" he asked.

"No," said Jim. "You're waking up. The world wants you back."

The darkness had swallowed everything but Jim, who leaned forward on his chair, staring at Billy-Bob, determined to keep his eyes on him until the very end.

"Why?"

"Everyone gives something great to the world," said Jim. "Remember that."

Jim was visible only as a vague glimmer in the darkness and the itch returned to Billy-Bob's shoulders with renewed intensity. Darkness reminded him of loneliness and loneliness made him think of the parents he didn't know and why they'd left. He knew Jim would not tell Billy-Bob who they were, but that didn't mean he wouldn't tell them what kind of people they had been. That could well give him the insight he needed to identify them.

"What was it my parents gave the world?"

A row of white showed in the dark where Jim smiled, then laughed. An echoing, hearty laugh as light faded. His voice, when it finally came, sounded like a whisper in his ear.

"Silly boy," he answered. "They gave it you."

A HERO RESURRECTED

Idiot boy.

Andrew stood just inside the doorway of the building where he'd arrived, watching the still form of Billy-Bob on the porch, floorboards staining red around his bandaged shoulders, face chalky and cadaverous as the color ran out of him. The rest would probably be gone by this evening, then it would be over. All this way for nothing. Down through the mineshaft of time, over a parched and scavenged world, dragging himself across a treadmill of dust only to depart with an overlong tale of disappointing mediocrity.

Andrew should have felt elated, relieved his journey had come to an end. Instead his jaw ached from clenching and his fingernails bit into the palms of his balled fists.

Why the boy insisted on confronting Kilgoth, even after watching the beast tear the stitching from the buildings, Andrew did not know. Better to let a monster exhaust its fury and move on. After all, Billy-Bob had not driven the monster into a rage, so it wasn't his responsibility. But the boy knew everyone else was too sensible to resist a creature of Kilgoth's stature and demeanor, to prevent it from reducing their community and accomplishments to wreckage. That wisdom led him to act insensibly. What kind of ignoramus accepted the burden of someone else's error?

"It's not your fault," said a familiar voice.

The statement slipped between his ribs to stab him in the heart, because though it may have been intended for consolation, Andrew knew it was a lie. Jim surely knew, too. If anyone could be blamed for Kilgoth's rage, it was Andrew. If blame could be laid upon anyone for Billy-Bob's current condition, heels on the crumbling precipice of extinction, that too would be Andrew.

He wanted to ask how to help, how to take back the punishment intended for him, yet when the question emerged it had transformed between his mind and his mouth, changing shape and meaning under the influence of his fear and humiliation.

"Why are you here?" asked Andrew.

Jim sat with his back to Andrew on a bench before a small, upright piano, knees butted up against the underside, the wooden bench bending into a strained grin in an effort to support him. He curled over and set a giant finger on the keyboard. Two detuned notes sounded and made Andrew's ears squint. Jim regarded his enormous hands with a sigh.

"I'm everywhere," said Jim. "Don't worry. Help is coming. Probably."

"How do you know? How do you know it isn't too late?"

"It's all about finding the right parts," said Jim, "and making sure they're in the right place at the right time."

Jim reached for a sagging chair, its joints worn so it could scarcely stand under its own weight. He pulled a leg free and used the foot to press an individual note on the piano. Pleased, he looked over his shoulder to Andrew.

"If you can do that, they should all come together when they're needed, like notes in a chord."

Andrew looked out the window, down the street to the silver ship then up the other way toward a sharp green slope, empty in both directions. Everyone had hidden, except Billy-Bob, who could not, and a man named Simon, who tended Billy-Bob with the temerity of someone who had reached the limit of their expertise and did not know how to proceed. Every so often the boy would reach up and scratch at the dressings, and Simon would pull against him in futility to prevent him from tearing his wounds.

"Zounds, he's strong," Simon would say, and put all his weight into holding the hand back, only to fail. "How is he still so strong?"

Simon and Gordimer had been the only people brave enough to rush into the street after Kilgoth departed, though only after. Doctrine told Andrew he could not interfere, that a recorder of history should not make themselves part of that history, though he imagined everyone who shook away their conscience had a similarly frail latticework of excuses.

"It's not your fault," Jim repeated.

"Yes it is. Of course it is."

Had he not taunted Kilgoth, drove him to a rage over a matter of semantics, they might have passed into Alpha unscathed.

"No it isn't," Jim insisted. "It's Billy-Bob's fault. He took it from you. That's what a hero does."

"What?"

Little wonder heroes didn't last long in this world. Their entire purpose pointed toward their destruction. No matter how strong the hero, eventually the weight of responsibility taken from others would crush them. They accumulated enemies and burdens such that victory became impossible. Unless.

Unless Andrew took his fault back and redressed it himself.

"Then I want it back!"

Andrew left the building, feeling a sense of urgency and purpose, even though he had no idea what to do once he got outside. Taking those first steps, though, proved energizing. Movement meant little without direction, but movement nevertheless proved more fruitful than remaining static because movement was proactive. He didn't know exactly what to do, but he knew he had to do something. The first step was taking the first step.

At the edge of hearing, Jim's voice reached him.

"That is what a *great* hero does."

Simon looked up at Andrew and regarded him with uncertainty and caution. After a moment of cogitation he apparently decided it didn't matter. He looked back at Billy-Bob with the same urgency Andrew had, knowing he needed to do something but didn't know what.

"Why did Gordimer leave?" asked Andrew.

By Gordimer's account, he had seen this play out many times before and must have seen a few heroes recover. If anyone knew how to save Billy-Bob, it would be Gordimer. Yet, after hovering restlessly over the boy for a short while, Gordimer left in a gust of anxiety.

"To find another hero," Simon answered.

Andrew should have guessed. The winged man said finding heroes would let him go home. If Billy-Bob failed, it made sense to find another. Everyone wanted to leave. The presence of the ship at the end of town was evidence of that.

"Jim?" the boy murmured.

Billy-Bob squinted his closed eyes in a fit of delirium. Andrew looked back through the window of the building he'd just left but the bench and piano where Jim had sat were empty. Where had he gone? Not that it mattered. For some reason, Andrew knew Jim would not help. Jim would feel deep disappointment if the boy expired, but helping was not something he did. He wanted people to help themselves, even at the risk of failure for his plans.

Even though he knew Jim and Gordimer had gone, he couldn't help searching for them, looking for aid, because he didn't know what else to do. Andrew turned in place, scouring the city, but did not find them.

Instead, he saw a shape at the top of the hill where the street led out of town. Even at this distance Andrew could see it lacked the characteristic halo of a straw hat. It waved as though beckoning to someone who had fallen behind, then skipped down the slope, a parachute of wings opened behind it to slow his descent, then dashed across the flat ground and up the street. Gordimer had returned. He waved his free arm urgently toward a shape now picking its way down the hill, took a few more steps into the city, then turned back again as though his follower would give up without constant encouragement.

"I did it! I brought her back!" he called to them, then laughed. "Maybe I'm a hero, too!"

Gordimer trotted up the street, chest thrust forward and beaming with accomplishment. He hesitated every few paces so the slow-moving shape following him could catch up.

A wog rested in his arms, in poor condition. Even though the only difference between wogs seemed to be their various states of decay, Andrew thought he recognized it as the one Billy-Bob had captured. The wog wormed in his arms and Gordimer released it, crashing to the ground with a rattle of loose parts. The wog pulled itself along with its one working side until it stood within reach of Billy-Bob, then turned about, standing like a stump.

Soon the trailing figure came into focus, stumbling wearily behind the winged man. A girl. As she drew nearer Andrew could see her disheveled clothing, wild and witchy hair, and the dirt that covered her body in crusty patches. For a moment Andrew thought the girl could be a Forest Monster and counterpart to the one from Dirtburg. But where the Forest Monster moved at random, the girl moved with determination and purpose, even if her steps shuffled under the weight of fatigue, as though making a final push toward a finish line.

"Who is she?" asked Andrew.

"A hero," Gordimer responded with pleasure. "Of a sort."

Simon looked up, then jerked to his feet when he saw the girl approaching. He regarded her with an open mouth.

She didn't appear any more impressive than Billy-Bob. Less so, perhaps. She scowled as she struggled up the street, resentful for having been brought here. What made her special?

"I didn't think you would come," said Simon. "I didn't think you would help."

The girl snorted.

"Maybe I won't."

"Then why are you here?" asked Andrew.

The girl looked at him before responding, top to bottom and back, and Andrew wondered what degree of disappointment would result from her analysis. Like Simon, she did not recognize him and Andrew could see her determine it made no difference. She shouldered Simon aside and crouched over the boy, examining his injuries while she answered.

"Because Gordimer told me everything I already knew. That the world is doomed. That my forest will be destroyed. That my father is lost forever. That everything I do is in vain. That I will linger alone as the world withers around me. He outlined a path to obliteration and said it could not be changed."

Andrew didn't think Gordimer had made a compelling argument, and she looked up grimly. Gordimer smiled.

"Unless," she added, wistfully.

The wog, quiet until now, grunted disdainfully.

Of course, Unless, thought Andrew. For all the rigidity of the future, imperceptible pinholes existed, like stars in the night sky, and through them slipped the thin beams of Unless. On their own they had no strength, but gathered together they cast enough light to navigate a darkened world.

"Unless what?" Andrew asked.

"Unless is different for everyone. For me, Unless this boy. Which could itself be a failure. Unless… well, Unless."

It seemed everything connected to everything else by thin filaments of Unless, and all the forbidding certainty of destruction withered away in its face.

What was Unless, Andrew wondered. What was it to Andrew? He would never return home. Unless. He would never succeed here. Unless. The boy would perish, even though he deserved triumph. The boy was not a hero by any stretch of the imagination, even though he should be. Humanity often received what it deserved in comeuppance but rarely what it needed to preserve itself. Unless. Unless. Unless. The word swung back and forth in his head like the clapper in a bell.

Could Unless be Hope? Hope, that insipid but powerful thing, resisting the inevitable with its incorruptible and insuperable stupidity. Unless is all that kept Andrew in pursuit of Billy-Bob, hammering through barriers such as fear, enduring the torment of his isolation from Bree, and driving him onward when it would be easier to lay down and expire. Unless motivated a belief that things could be other than they were. Anything could happen in the fullness of time. One needed only the endurance to last long enough to see it.

The girl's expression had softened during the course of her examination of Billy-Bob and she reached out to brush the knotty hair from his face. Billy-Bob's eyes fluttered and centered on her. His head raised for a moment.

"I love you," he blurted.

The girl said nothing in response. Her mouth opened, but no words came out. Billy-Bob watched her response in earnest, then the strength went out of him and his head knocked against the walkway. The rigidity returned to her face and she grabbed his shoulders and shook him. His eyes opened dazedly.

"Prove to me that you mean me no harm," she said sternly. "Not me, the forest, or anything. Prove you are worth saving."

Billy-Bob hesitated, thinking, and Andrew worried this might be his undoing. It didn't appear he had an answer, and his faculties had surely been impaired by the loss of blood. Then he saw the boy's hand crawling into a pocket like a wounded insect seeking the darkness. It disappeared, found something, and withdrew. When he opened his hand an acorn rested in his palm amidst a powdering of desert sand.

"I brought this across the wasteland," said Billy-Bob, "but I didn't bring enough."

The girl's mouth firmed into a thin line. She took the acorn and put it in her pocket, then reached into another pocket and withdrew a glove. She donned the glove carefully, pressing the fabric down into the vee between each finger.

Again, the boy's eyes fluttered and his head knocked hollowly against the walkway. Instead of trying to revive him, the girl stood and addressed the city in a loud voice. She seemed to know this place and Simon certainly knew her. Yet she seemed an outcast, not unwelcome, but unwilling to be here.

"Does anyone care to save him?" she called.

The buildings remained still and silent, as though she had addressed an empty city. Gordimer stood nearby, looking content having already done his part by bringing the girl. Even Simon had climbed back to a rooftop. Andrew knew the other citizens were there, hidden and reluctant. He could see hints of their presence in knuckles curled over roof edges and brief glimpses as faces popped over the peaks to survey the street below, and knew they were frightened. He was frightened, too. But he also knew, as Billy-Bob often demonstrated, the best way to overcome fear was to confront it.

It seemed an eternity passed while the question hung in the air, and an eternity again before Andrew's mind caught up to the decision his muscles had already made.

Andrew stepped forward, knowing full well he would regret it, as he had regretted each time he'd done so before. And yet he did so willingly, embracing the agony that would surely follow. Why, he wondered. What reward did he expect? Gratitude? Some acknowledgement for this bit of bravery? Or, perhaps, the gratification of a satisfied conscience. If it was right, Hobert had said, someone would be doing it. Billy-Bob's epiphany was the recognition that he didn't need to wait until someone else acted in order to act himself. If everyone waited, no one acted. If he knew acting was the right thing to do, he could serve as the catalyst himself.

The girl drew another glove and donned it on the other hand. The glove had blue circles on the palm and fingertips, much like the dull disc on Andrew's chest that had the power to send him home.

"Give me your hand," she said.

"What is that?" asked Andrew.

"The last resort."

If successful, this would only return Billy-Bob to the world through which he bungled and upset. And yet it felt appropriate. It felt as though he were returning balance to a mechanism out of kilter, and this thought surprised him because it assumed Billy-Bob to be of disproportionately great value, though he had scarcely proven himself more than a minor impediment to greater powers.

"Why do you need me?"

The girl looked at him with slouching shoulders. Even through the layer of dirt he could detect the exhaustion in her eyes.

"Because I've given everything to the world around you and I don't have anything left." She looked at the hand furthest from him and her eyes ticked across information he could not see. She looked back to him, a surprised arch in her eyebrow. "And because you're a donor match. For both of us."

Andrew reached a hand toward her and she took it, tightening her grip so his bones ground together.

"Will it hurt?" he asked.

She did not answer, and Andrew knew she was trying to determine if she should answer with the truth or a lie. When her grimace deepened, he knew she had settled on the truth.

"Yes."

In a flurry of small movements, she touched the thumb of her free hand to the ends of her fingers with the fleetness of a spider working its intricate embroidery. When finished, she spread her gloved fingers wide and pressed her palm against one of Billy-Bob's wounded shoulders. Andrew became aware of a low humming coming from the hand. A pale light emanated where she pressed against the boy's shoulder, and Andrew saw the girl's hand in his also grow bright.

The girl looked up at him and said, "Get ready," then looked away, tightening her body as best she could with both arms outstretched.

Andrew set his heels against the ground and gritted his teeth, feeling he was as prepared as he could be. Still, when the time came, he discovered he hadn't been ready at all.

The hum increased to a sharp pitch in his ears. A great yank in his chest felt as though someone had flung him across the street, yet he remained standing, stunned and immobilized, unable to pull his hand away from the girl, unable to tell her to stop, certain this process was destroying him from within, certain Simon and Gordimer, watching from afar, could see his eyeballs melting out of his head. He felt impossibly heavy and locked his knees against the weight, expecting at any moment to punch through the surface and plunge to the center of the planet. The girl was hunched and unmoving, muscles taut, teeth gritted. The dried dirt on her mud-caked forearms fractured like the broken ground he had crossed to reach this place.

It was more than pain. A feeling that thoughts and memories were being stripped from his mind, as if his essence and the things that made him distinct were being forcibly siphoned off. Only the process of unmaking a person and reducing them to a featureless puppet could explain a degree and brand of agony he began to feel would be with him forever. It went on interminably, continuing for what seemed so long Andrew became resigned it would never end.

She released him, abruptly, and Andrew dropped to the ground in a clatter of unresponsive limbs. He took a sharp and prolonged breath that sent needles into his lungs. For a moment all he could think about was the memory of that profound agony and the belief that it was destroying him, certain scars from the experience would never fade, having forgotten the reason he'd agreed to it in the first place.

The pain did leave, though, draining from his arms and legs, and out through his nose in what felt very much like a flow of warm fluid. It left him feeling cleaner and stronger, but thoroughly exhausted. He knew if he tried to stand his legs would not support him. His vision blurred with every ragged thump of his heart. With an effort, he found he could move, and did so, turning his head one way and the other, then lifting himself onto his elbows.

Billy-Bob remained unchanged, unmoving, his eyes staring blankly into the yellow-tinted atmosphere, mouth ajar.

For a moment Simon's head protruded over the edge of the roof.

"You killed him!" he cried. "Just like a monster!"

The girl sighed and wiped a hand under her bloody nose. He could see the shiver in her hands, but she had recovered quickly. Her strength astounded him. Andrew felt something wet on his lip and rubbed his thumb under his nose. It came away smeared with red and he wondered what components of his mind had been sheared away. He felt saddened by their departure, even if he had no means of remembering what he'd lost.

"He's not dead," said the girl. "He'll be all right. He's stronger than you think." She stood, shakily, and looked at Andrew with mud-ringed eyes and an expression of smug satisfaction. Then she turned to Simon and her expression darkened. "You all give up too easily."

Abruptly, Billy-Bob sat up. He pulled blankly at the saturated bandages, which came free with minimal resistance. His shirt remained torn and stained at the shoulders, yet apart from the dried crust clinging to his skin that pulled away with his shirt, he appeared whole again. His wounds had closed.

Billy-Bob itched his shoulders absent-mindedly, looking around in wonder as though waking from a long and disorienting sleep.

"You're alive!" cried Simon.

Billy-Bob looked at him, then looked around, noting the buildings, Gordimer, the ship at the end of the street, the slope of grass at the other.

"I'm back in Beta," he observed.

The girl staggered into the street and sat down hard. Apparently she had not recovered as quickly as Andrew or the girl had thought.

She had saved Billy-Bob. She was a hero. Was this the girl the wogs had sought? Little wonder. Maybe they didn't want to capture her to remove her from the game board, but to save themselves. Maybe the Forest Monster knew of her, too. Perhaps the Forest Monster wasn't so dull as he thought. Perhaps it was looking to be healed.

"Woman?" called a familiar voice.

With an effort born of terror and regret he twisted his head against the screaming resistance of corroded muscles to face the slope.

The figure on the edge of the crater stood beyond the focused sphere of his vision, but he didn't need to see it up close to remember the details. The deep set eyes and body bent into the shape of a fishhook, bare except for a scant remainder of pants held together by a few atoms of dignity and a supporting framework of dirt and grime.

Could he have summoned the Forest Monster simply by remembering it? They had only just recovered from Kilgoth's attack, and according to others the wogs just before Andrew arrived.

"It can't be," said Gordimer. "Can it?"

Andrew detected a familiar tone of despair. No sooner was one threat overcome than another appeared on its heels. The world and its remaining defenders had every reason to feel exhausted and defeated.

"Does it matter?" said Simon. "Threats and Evils abound in this world. They converge here in an effort to destroy us. What option do we have but to escape?"

"Resist!" screamed the girl, pounding a fist against the street.

She struggled to her knees, teeth bared, and pushed herself to her feet. She had a will Andrew had never seen and wondered who might resist her at her full strength. She rose against the power of a world determined to pull everything down, and Andrew felt a sense of joy that people like her existed. How could he remain still when she gave even when she had nothing left? And yet, for all his efforts, he could do nothing but sit and watch as the Forest Monster paced along the precipice as it searched for a path into the city.

"Will you wait until the world runs out before you stand your ground? Will we abandon a wasteland we created, shrinking from the responsibility of fixing it? Once we built spacecraft capable of traveling to other worlds. Look how far we have fallen. Using wooden constructs built into a larger launch complex. Why would we allow ourselves to continue on this downward parabola? Why do we surrender? Where has our will to resist and overcome fled? When did we begin to exist for the sake of existing? Where is our purpose? Our drive? Why am I the only one who bothers to ask these questions?"

"Every bit of resistance ends in failure," Simon muttered. "All the odds have a way of turning themselves against us."

"And what will stop those odds from following wherever you flee? I'm tired. Tired of running. Maybe it's my time to face failure. But I'll face it rather than let it run me down from behind."

At the edge of town the Forest Monster tested the drop carefully with a foot. He overreached, howled when he realized he could not recover his equilibrium, and down he went in a pinwheel of appendages. The fall became less haphazard as the monster approached the bottom, settled into a tight ball that rapidly gained speed and hurtled into the town. The Forest Monster sprang out of the ball and arced a short distance before landing on its feet, not more than ten paces from the girl.

She straightened, ready to engage the creature.

"No!" cried Billy-Bob. "I just found you!"

The boy raised himself to a knee and began to straighten. His legs wobbled beneath him and he collapsed. He tried to push himself up again with his arms, but they would not hold him. Determined, he began to push feebly with his legs against the street and moved a few feet closer before he ran up against the heavy form of the damaged wog.

"Why aren't you protecting her?"

"That's not my mission," the wog responded.

"Then I change your mission! Protect her!"

"She's not in danger."

Andrew felt similarly what he saw in Billy-Bob's face. How could the wog know the Forest Monster wouldn't harm her?

"We cataloged his mind long, long ago," the wog explained. "Barring damage, a mind doesn't change much. I'm a very good judge of what is and is not dangerous. He will not harm her."

A few paces away the Forest Monster gave all impressions of being dangerous. It watched the girl, stepping one way and then the other, never coming closer but not retreating either. It feigned curiosity, but Andrew knew it was simply looking for an opening to strike. Strange that such a dull animal could strategize.

The girl stood with her weight on her back foot, turning ever so slightly to keep the Forest Monster in front of her. In her weakened state, she would not be able to resist him. Perhaps even at her strongest, she might not resist him. The Forest Monster had been defeated once, and then quite by chance when caught unawares. Surely it was more wary now. Indeed, every once in so often it would flick its gaze away from the girl, as though looking for an unexpected shovel and reached up to cover a mark on its forehead where the grime had worn away to reveal a purple welt.

Andrew wished she would run away.

When it struck, the speed startled Andrew. In one moment the Forest Monster stood several paces away from the girl, arms limp at its sides. In an eyeblink it reached her guard, arms outstretched, groping for her head. For all its speed, the girl was somehow faster. She jerked her left hand straight up, catching the Forest Monster under the chin and snapping its head upward. It was a blow that would have felled anyone. The Forest Monster was not anyone.

The Forest Monster absorbed the blow, jerked back, and lunged again. This time the girl changed tactics and gripped the monster by the wrists. As the monster's hands flexed, clutching at her face, she appeared to catch a glimpse of the writing on its hands, but could not hold them steady enough to read them. She looked hard into the wells of its eyes, searching.

"Who are you?"

"Woman," the Forest Monster said in response.

The girl released one of the Forest Monster's hands and coiled to throw a punch. She directed it at the monster's face, but the monster caught the fist in its hand. They stood locked in one another's grip, each holding the other's opposite hand.

The Forest Monster's head turned slowly to look at the gloved hand. It's mouth opened, but it did not utter its standard phrase. Andrew thought he saw something fall from the Forest Monster's face. He squinted. Sure enough, another fell. And soon several fell in rapid succession.

The Forest Monster was crying.

Had the girl struck a painful blow? Had she defeated it? Andrew couldn't tell. The Forest Monster's hand directly before the girl's face opened, perhaps in surrender, perhaps to snatch at her hair if it came in reach. The girl did not appear to look for another opening. Instead, she squinted at the open hand, and Andrew knew she was trying to decipher the writing. She blinked and reread it, then whispered to the Forest Monster through gritted teeth.

"You can't be," she said tightly and squeezed her eyes shut. "Not this."

Very carefully, she released the Forest Monster's wrist. The free hand did not swing at her or drop away. She pulled her other hand free. The Forest Monster remained motionless, both hands raised, as though petrified.

The girl pressed one gloved hand against the Forest Monster, then tapped out a pattern on the other hand and pressed it against her chest. The gloves glowed blue and she shrieked and writhed.

The Forest Monster's deep-set eyes jumped open as though he'd been jabbed in the back by a fork of lightning. His mouth opened, uttered a silent scream, and shut. Andrew felt prickles through his body and saw the hair on his arms stand, the fallout energy filling the air with static. He watched a nail lift itself gradually from the floorboards of the walkway. Then the Forest Monster began to change. His blocky head narrowed, straggly hair shortened, and his back straightened. The eyes, buried deep in his head, surfaced from the bottom of their sockets.

The girl released him and the two fell apart like the halves of a bisected fruit.

"Impossible!" cried Gordimer, and Andrew couldn't tell if he was furious or delighted. His eyes bulged and he strained like a prisoner in his own body. "You were destroyed!"

In place of the horrid, mindless Forest Monster was an exhausted, panting man. Not old, but almost. Tattered clothing hung loose on his body, his bewildered face garbled with overgrown hair. His eyes fixed on the girl and he smiled.

"Poppy," said the man in a raspy voice.

Poppy sat up and stared at the man with a rumpled brow as though staring at something familiar through the distortions of stained glass. When she spoke, Andrew's mouth fell open.

"Daddy," she murmured, voice quavering as beads of dirty fluid dropped from her cheeks. "Where have you been?"

ONCE UPON A PLAN

Even though they had come a fair distance, leaving the ruin of their home far behind, Alexander could still feel the heat at his back from the burning city, as though the memory had branded itself on his skin, crisp and stinging. He ran all night, knowing the further they traveled, the more unfamiliar the people, the safer they would be.

The boy in Alexander's arms was slight and wiry, with legs too short to carry him quickly enough to their destination. Yet he felt heavy. Some part of Alexander's strength had departed, leaving him with a sense of depletion even as he plowed through the night, across the separated plates of the dried up terrain indicative of a world pulling itself apart.

Until now he'd worked to bring people together and protect them only to discover how easy it was to undo his efforts. Only a few days before he had felt invincible, in person and purpose, guiding others from the wilderness to the sprawling city of Alpha, through the savage lands where those whose minds had built fortresses impregnable to reason sought to waylay them. The war against ignorance and fear had gone on so long as Alexander could remember, but only recently had he ever had the sense that they were winning. To have achieved so much only to retreat with this slender thread between his fingers as proof they had done something great struck at the tentpole of his confidence.

The boy in his arms clung to him as Alexander traveled, yet it was Alexander who clung to him.

He couldn't remember the last time he felt despair, and now he could feel it in the reluctance of his legs as they churned onward and the ache in his neck where the boy's arms wrapped and hung from him, gazing into the distance from which they'd come. These pains had always been present, lingering at the edge of his awareness. Until now he had muted them, the soreness of his feet from a million steps on the sharp and uneven world, with the understanding that a little suffering was a small price to pay for the consolidation of humanity and the great things that would come from the united strength of so many interlocked hands. The evidence of prior greatnesses could still be found in the world, broken and gray from neglect and misunderstanding, if one ventured far enough.

"Do you see anyone following?" Alexander asked.

"No," the boy replied.

Alexander had not looked back, afraid of what he might see. Rising smoke or the remnants of those he could not protect as they fled like ants from their immolated hill to be stamped out as they scattered.

Like barbarians, those who destroyed Alexander's home saw it as a prize to be plundered and a threat to their wayward existence, even if that existence was confused and meaningless and hostile. There was comfort in that confusion and hostility, not because it was an easy way to live, but because it was familiar. Fear was familiar, and they dwelt in it perpetually, like amphibians sheltered beneath the slick surface of a rancid pond.

People who didn't understand something tended to fear it, and the first impulse was not to understand what was feared, but to ridicule, strike at, and destroy it. Alexander and Mardin had traveled a small portion of the world in an attempt to introduce awareness, purpose, and understanding, to bring savage folk together with the knowledge that distance caused estrangement. Those they had not yet reached remained scattered and would never pose a threat unless some malevolent force sought to unite them.

Not only did that force exist, Alexander learned, it had a name. Alexander had never met him, but Mardin had. Shrewd and calculating, with gears turning behind gears, knowing a twist of one could affect another far distant in the machinery, and the manipulation of one meant the manipulation of all. Alexander knew of a similar entity, but they were not the same, according to Mardin. Not Jim, Mardin had said, but a more nefarious creature called John.

Alexander opened his hand and read the words inscribed upon it. They were a reminder that some things he did because he must and because no one else could do them. Poppy had written them for him, and most times when he read them he was reminded not of his purpose, but of her.

The boy pressed a finger against Alexander's face and drew it back, looking at the sheen of perspiration before wiping it on his shirt. The boy watched him and Alexander became aware of the chugging breaths he took in and released, punctuated by his footfalls. Alexander saw the boy frown and knew he could see the despair in his face.

"I will not always be a burden."

"You are not a burden," said Alexander.

"Yes I am. You can't continue like this."

"I can," said Alexander. "I must."

"Why?"

"It's what I have to do."

"What about Poppy?" the boy asked. "They'll chase her, too, won't they?"

They would.

"Poppy will be fine on her own. She's a strong girl."

Even as Alexander said it, he believed himself. He worried, as parents did for their children, even when they had proven their perseverance and competence, even when they had taken that perseverance and competence from their parents. She was older than this boy, but not much. Poppy had always been different, and in that difference he saw distinctness in her directness, skepticism, and ability to judge character with alacrity where most people would find disconcerting strangeness. Most people gladly blended into the unoffending beige of humanity. Others stood apart, an oak rising above the shrubberies. Yet those who stood apart also made themselves visible and vulnerable. Their Institute had been designed with that in mind, in defiance, and it had been lost. In spite of her ability and impulse, Alexander hoped desperately that she would hide.

"Sometimes I dream about her," said the boy. "I miss her."

"So do I," said Alexander. "And her mother. They make me strong. They remind me I have something to stay strong for."

"We should go back. You can't fix a thing by running away from it."

Little wonder Jim considered this boy important. So much like his father. So keen on resolution, on confrontation. A special few could hear the cries from gears that had come out of joint, plucking sympathetic notes that compelled them to set the machinery right. In a world of few friends, at the acme of his power some years from now, he would make a formidable ally, a tide-turner. Or, he thought ruefully, a dangerous adversary.

"We run to buy time. To gather strength."

The boy cogitated and they continued on for a distance in silence. He would not agree. He would say running away expended strength in the wrong direction. He knew it because that is what Mardin would say, and in so many ways the boy reflected his father. Like his father he was a thinker, capable of bending all the lights of thought at his disposal upon a problem until a solution stood out like the moon on a background of night.

It was difficult not to agree with the boy's logic—it appealed to Alexander's deep desires, which made it dangerous. The further they traveled, the more the tether connecting Alexander's heart to home tightened, and the more difficult each step became. He wanted to go back, too, to throw himself into a final, decisive battle. But he knew that's what their adversary wanted as well. With tremendous effort wisdom had resisted compulsion, but only just.

Ahead, a town rolled over the horizon and Alexander slowed to a walk. Two low rows of buildings rested atop a threadbare carpet of grass that appeared to be losing its grip on the terrain. A forest stood wearily in the background, brittle and leafless, attached to the city by the frayed cord of a wooden fence that separated one meaningless possession of dead land from another. The wide mouth of a chasm opened before them.

They had come far enough, Alexander decided. They had certainly never come further. He let the boy slip out of his arms.

"Do you know this place?"

"Yes," Alexander answered. He pressed his palms against the base of his spine and leaned backward, then forward, feeling the refreshing ripple of cracks as vertebrae decompressed. "This is Dirtburg."

The gorge separated the plates of land from which they had come and the place they were going by a distance much too far to hurdle, and maybe too far to throw a stone across. A bridge connected the two sides and Alexander was glad to see it still in place. Some of his efforts remained intact and that gave him hope that if enough survived it may recover in time.

They approached the bridge and a familiar image appeared. He wondered how the boy would respond when he saw her, though he probably knew no more about what had happened than Alexander. He might certainly draw conclusions. Why wasn't she here with him, after all?

"Greetings, Alexander," said the woman with her familiarly genial tone. Alexander felt his throat tighten. She looked at the boy and smiled. "Hello, William."

"Best not to use our names," Alexander interrupted raspily, and cleared his throat, "given the circumstances."

The image wavered a moment as it updated its profiles.

"Understood. You have come quite some distance. According to my records your last known identification was two days ago at the Institute, though I am no longer receiving updates from that location."

She relayed this information while staring down at the boy, who stared back at her, scrutinizing the translucent image. The boy might consider her comforting and familiar or an unpleasant and hurtful reminder. Alexander didn't know what to expect, and per the norm the boy behaved unexpectedly.

"What are you called?"

"My designation is D," the image replied.

"Dee," the boy repeated thoughtfully. "We have come a long way."

"Yes," Alexander agreed. "We still have a little way to go yet."

Alexander stepped onto the bridge and beckoned for the boy to follow. Soon the three of them had crossed and for the first time Alexander looked back across the emptiness they had traversed to get here. The uniform terrain made it seem they could have started anywhere and gone on for days without making any progress at all, trapped on the rolling log of a single landscape that simply repeated itself over and over again. But somewhere out there Alexander knew a city burned and a people scattered.

The consequence of that destruction would be the unleashing of Mardin, and even though Alexander's mission as a hero was completely opposed to it, Mardin might be the only person capable of destroying their enemy. If Mardin could not, and despite his greatness it seemed unlikely, they needed a plan for the future, bleak though it may be.

Alexander looked down at the boy, who surveyed the town ahead. This boy was the plan. Anyone who recognized them was a liability, a link back to the enemy and a way John could find them. So Alexander had taken the boy and fled to where no one would know them.

"Citizens approaching," said Dee.

Alexander looked ahead. A dozen people approached them in a wedge. He didn't recognize any from his previous visit.

"Where are the original citizens?" asked Alexander.

"Fled," said Dee. "I recommend exercising caution."

These, then, were agents of John. His influence extended to the very edge of understanding. Was there no escape?

"Ho there! Who might you be?" called the foremost of them, a soft and saggy man like a piece of spoiling fruit. A pipe extended from one corner of his mouth. He stopped well beyond the reach of the Alexander and the boy, and his grim posse stopped warily behind him. Among them towered a very tall man with a gentle, mischievous grin and a wide, straw hat.

"Jim?" asked Alexander.

"Jim," the man with the pipe repeated. "You don't look like a Jim to me, but I s'pose you can keep it. Jims are usually taller. Name of Hobert. From where do you hail, and whither are you bound?"

Alexander's attention returned to Hobert. He could learn Jim's purpose here later. Jim's defining characteristic was inscrutability. Better to sort out this situation first.

If Hobert thought Alexander's name was Jim, so much the better. A carefully crafted lie would obscure their retreat. Still, Alexander disliked deception. It was not a weapon he was accustomed to wielding and strengthened the myths and rumors and falsehoods he'd strove to dispel. Before he could confirm the lie, the boy stepped forward.

"I'm William," he said. "Pleased to meet you."

Alexander tensed. They'd come so far to escape anyone who might know them and the boy had already given away his identity. And why not? He was fearless, or didn't yet have the good sense to fear anything.

"That so?" asked Hobert. He crouched before the boy, jabbing a finger into his chest. Testing. The boy staggered back, more surprised than unbalanced. "We're looking for a girl, though, not a worthless Billy-Bob."

Alexander stiffened.

Did they mean Poppy? If they were looking for Poppy it meant she was in danger, but it also meant they had not found her, and her cleverness would surely allow her to evade almost anyone if she didn't want to be discovered.

Experience allowed Alexander to remain motionless and refrain from betraying any knowledge or feelings for the girl. The boy, however, lacked that training. He scowled deeply.

"Don't know the girl, do ya?" asked Hobert.

Hobert, apparently thinking he had the advantage over the small boy, stabbed a finger into the boy's chest, enjoying his superiority. It was a mistake.

The boy took Hobert by the wrist and guided the hand aside, and Hobert followed after it, stumbling forward, with nothing to catch his fall but the fist the boy swung out to intercept Hobert as he went by. Inertia or the fist by themselves wouldn't have caused much damage, but the combined motion crunched the knuckles against Hobert's nose like the head of a hammer. Hobert dropped into the dirt without a sound of dismay or discomfort, senseless, his nose flattened against his face.

That would certainly get attention they didn't want. And any attentions would surely find their way back to John, and John would find his way to them. Alexander faced Dee.

"Collapse the bridge," he said. "Don't extend it again except by our request."

Dee vanished and Alexander faced the crowd. He heard the clanking of the mechanical bridge as it retracted and drew itself into the side of the chasm. For a moment he thought the people who had accompanied Hobert would withdraw or throw away their allegiance, but their numbers gave them confidence, and they began to fan into an arc, trapping them against the edge of the crack that dropped far, far away, past layers of rock hundreds of millions of years old. To fall from this place was to fall back in time. If only escape were that simple.

They appeared empty handed or simply armed at best, with rocks or boards with nails jutting from one end they had peeled from the skin of the buildings. They probably had no skill in fighting, just meanness, which would make them cruel rather than calculating. He could see it in the snarl of bared teeth they had no other aim than to do harm. That was a hallmark of the wilderness—a purposeless existence bent on malice because violence posted immediate results. It offered rapid gratification that patience and planning, often undone by the malevolence of others anyway, did not. In the wilderness violence was the only thing hasty enough to take root, and a violent realm was an impatient one, a self perpetuating attitude.

Violence came easy to people. Violence was rash and rapid, and its unpredictability made it dangerous. But Alexander was faster.

The first to lose hold of their restraint held a rock as a bludgeon. Alexander saw his weight shift incrementally forward, the rock arm begin to rotate, so Alexander stepped toward him, inside the arc of his slow-winding swing. He saw the man's eyes begin to pull toward the corners, trying to follow Alexander, but by that time he was already hurtling backward, the breath whooshing out of his chest where Alexander had struck him with his shoulder, the stone spinning out of his grasp. He would rise again in a few moments and reclaim the rock. By then this should be over and he would know better.

Alexander turned to the person on his right, grabbing him by the arm, and with a quick turn hurling him toward the woman behind. The two would crack together and tumble to the ground. One or the other might be unconscious. At the least they would be tangled for a short time. Alexander didn't have time to confirm. By now the rest were in motion too. He blew threw them in a single, forceful gust, without wasted motion or loss of momentum, each movement flowing into the next, like a wind that beat down and broke the long grasses in its passing.

The gifts of strength and speed Alexander had always had. Their proper application had come after a time. He could easily have become a tyrant. Most people with uncommon strength, be it of arm, intellect, or resources did. Tyranny was easy and obvious. Perhaps the need for difference prevented the tyrannical in him.

"Uncommon strength begets opportunities to exploit the weakness of others. Few with it can resist the compulsion to extort their fellow beings. But some are special. Some are better than impulse. And the rest of the world is made better, too."

Jim had told him so. That same Jim who stood just outside the fracas, arms crossed, his expression mischievous, watching Alexander systematically disarm and disable the rapidly diminishing semicircle of aggressors. It would not surprise Alexander to learn the enigmatic Jim had joined these people and sought to destroy them, or test them. Jim delighted in tests. Most things with great power, as Alexander suspected Jim had, cared little for the doings of lesser creatures, apart from occasionally engaging with them for their own amusement, proffering hopes and assistance only to snatch them away again at a crucial moment and watch their victims founder in incredulity and despair.

Had Jim played a part in the destruction of Alpha? Perhaps. Nothing indicated his involvement, but Alexander couldn't help wondering. What he knew about people, what he knew about the powerful, made the thought inevitable.

"What does one do if they are strong?" Alexander had asked the boy as they ran through the night.

He hoped to impart some of the knowledge he'd acquired. Doing a thing for the sake of doing it made it a chore, an item on a list to be accomplished. Understanding was a breath of life that brought purpose.

"Advantages lead to exploitation," the boy answered, echoing Jim's observation.

"Absolutely. The overriding impulse strength gives a person is to use it for yourself. Uncommon strength begets opportunities to exploit the weakness of others."

"Tyranny."

"That's it. These tyrants come and go with regularity. They are predictable and expected. Those who have strength use that strength to dominate others. Are there no other uses?"

After a moment's consideration, the boy answered.

"To protect the things one cares about."

"Exactly. And what if we were to expand upon that notion, to protect not just those we care about, but all those who need protection? What if strength was used to defend against those who would exploit the weakness of others? What if we took the strength of tyrants and turned it against them?"

"Then," said the boy, with a tone of morbidity and cynicism in which Alexander heard the echo of the boy's father, "we would be vastly outnumbered."

Only a handful of the assailants remained standing. One appeared to have lost the inclination to attack, cowed by the prospect of being painfully disarmed, no doubt, and fled back toward the town. A second appeared to be making the same calculation, albeit somewhat slower. Alexander knew this person wouldn't pose any more problems. Once thought started, it couldn't be stopped, except through brainwashing or stubbornness, and thought invariably led one away from violence.

The first, however, had already reached his feet, already strode back to the fray. This time he made for the boy. Others had also recovered, raised from defeat rising like corpses with unfinished purpose. When had he become so slow?

The first assailant reached across his body toward the belt sagging on one hip as he approached. A chill ran through Alexander. He couldn't see the weapon there, but he knew what it must be, an archaic tool built with the singular purpose of ending life. Perhaps rusted by disuse or poor care, rendered inoperable, but that was not a chance he could afford to take. Alexander hurried back through the attackers in their various states of recovery, artless and violent, ignoring some and knocking those in his path aside. Speed meant everything. Speed was the only thing that could return him in time. Speed, which he knew as he saw the gun emerge, that would not be enough.

Young though the boy was, and inexperienced, he was not helpless. As his attacker unsheathed the weapon the boy stepped forward. He was no more than half the height of the man bearing down on him, so the boy would not overpower him. Instead, he closed the distance, reached out and intercepted the barrel as it rose, and the gun came free of the man's hand as easily as though he'd meant to hand it over. Rather than grabbing the boy, the man grabbed for the gun, his scepter, his symbol of power, forgetting his initial purpose. That's what power did. Taken away, one grasps to recover it rather than trying to finish the mission for which it was intended.

In a single smooth motion the boy had reversed the gun in his hand, cocked the weapon, and had a finger resting beside the trigger, the gunmouth gaping at his foe, who stared crosseyed into its black maw, hands close around the gun yet not close enough, his face and the weapon separated by no more than the spread of a hand.

"Stop," said the boy.

Alexander stopped. The attackers stopped. Only passing dust that hissed against the cracked terrain as it blew by escaped rigidity. Alexander didn't know what to do. The most minor mishandling, error, or twitch would end a man's life. Even if the man had intended to kill them, Alexander felt remorse at the idea of destroying him because it meant a person lost rather than recovered. It meant they never had a chance to become other than what they were right now. It meant this distorted, wretched form of humanity was all they could ever achieve. It took away more than life, it took away redemption. Alexander despised weapons of this sort because they did not allow for mistakes, were too simple to abuse, and had a habit of falling into the hands of the mistake prone.

"Now what?" asked the man at gunpoint.

"I paint the sky with your face," the boy answered. "Or you leave me alone."

The man dipped as his knees began to give way beneath him, and Alexander could see he wanted to reply, though he feared any movement might be interpreted as a foolish act of aggression that could end his life. Fainting might prove his best option, and he seemed on the verge of taking that route, but he somehow managed to keep his feet and take a cautious step backward. As he retreated he unbuckled the holster and let it fall to the ground as a token of utter surrender.

It wouldn't matter. Defeat at the point of a sword meant nothing. It created a puzzle. How could he regain the advantage? How could he remove this boy that defeated him? Power made those subject to it resentful. To make people leave you be, you had to trust them and make them trust you.

Possessing the gun, a physical representation of mistrust, would never allow that.

The boy swept the gun barrel slowly across the group, pausing to let the path of the bullets touch each individual so they knew the warning was meant for each of them. Slowly, those still able to rise did so, and they retreated back into town, leaving a single, giant man who hadn't joined the fight standing in their midst.

Jim.

"You're not afraid of death," said the boy.

"I don't die," said Jim. "I become obsolete."

Alexander set a hand on the boy's arm. It shook faintly, and lowered. Alexander exhaled.

"A weapon like that is full of anger and thoughtless vengeance," said Alexander. "I think you should put it away."

"Jim is not an enemy?"

"No," said Alexander. He looked at Jim, who smiled back at him. "I don't think so."

* * *

The three of them sat outside the town into which their assailants had sifted like a quick throw of sand into the wind. Only Hobert remained, his mind dazzled, collecting dust as his senses wandered. Alexander massaged and rotated his shoulders before they could stiffen, feeling a soreness in his muscles that took longer than usual to regress.

"What happened here?" he asked.

Jim pulled at his beard and exhaled. He smiled before he spoke, but the expression didn't match the anxiety and distress of his behavior. He didn't seem comfortable or happy. He looked restless, pensive, as though something carefully weighed was in danger of becoming unbalanced, and he could do nothing should the mechanism go out of kilter. Like most dealing with something close to their heart, he didn't want to make a mistake, and was either uncertain how to proceed or uncertain they had made the right choice.

"The residents of this place found themselves forced out by newer, more aggressive marauders. I could not convince them to stay, to resist. Too easy to flee. I imagine they made their way toward the Institute."

"I don't remember anyone coming to the Institute."

"No," said Jim. "I doubt they arrived."

The residents had not been warriors, but artisans. Masons, primarily. Wall builders and erectors of statues. Alexander had told them of the Institute himself, and of its purpose, and his enthusiasm for their success, the encouragement that any who sought it would find shelter, and when they investigated, seeking the protection he promised, they in all likelihood found a trap awaiting them.

Jim pointed to the great figure standing over the town, pointing back westward.

"Before they fled, they started a statue. A thank you, a reminder, an homage to the world they hoped for. The one promised to them, in time. An indicator of the direction one should take in times of need. Does it seem familiar?"

Unfinished, the statue lacked many details. Alexander could pick out major body parts, the head, arms, legs, the outstretched hand, though its feet remained an unfinished, stony slab. Nothing lent itself to identification.

"Don't you recognize it?" asked the boy. "It's you."

Alexander's shoulders fell. Of course the boy was correct. Who else? He had told them where to go to find safety with a similar gesture. Even now he could see his features projected onto the blank template of the statue's face, the pride and self assurance in the posture, chest out, feet wide, shoulders back. He had inspired them to construct a tremendous mouse trap in disguise, promising security with the brazen arrogance of a few recent successes. All turned against him. How many others would follow that gesturing fool to destruction?

"We can't stay here," said Alexander.

"To the contrary," said Jim, "you can't fix a mess by spreading it around. You need to stay here."

The boy stood and clasped the gun belt around his waist. It was an ill fit, almost wrapping twice around him.

"You should get rid of that," said Alexander.

"I'm keeping it," the boy replied. "As a deterrent."

"An implied threat will only make people suspicious and fearful."

"Is that not how you make people leave you be?"

"Of course not. People are conditioned to respond to threats. You want to eliminate a response."

"Oh? And how does one do that?"

"Make them trust you."

"Have we not made enemies of all of these people? How do we earn their trust?"

"Forgiveness."

The boy's face turned stern and skeptical, but Alexander could see his mind working. If an obstacle to peace stood between two people, such as vendetta or vengeance, the best thing to do was remove the obstacle. Forgiveness sounded frail and meek, a form of surrender others would take advantage of, but that was why the strong could afford to offer forgiveness. They could endure its perils. And forgiveness, given time to work, always succeeded. Always.

"It won't be enough," said Jim.

The giant man lifted his hat, turned it, and set it down on his head again before lifting and setting it down once more. He appeared to be looking for the right fit, as though the only way to know what would work best was to explore every permutation. A man who had the patience to explore every possible option in order to find the best result ought to be trusted with advice. He spoke with the decisiveness and gaiety of a scholar who has found an opportunity to dispense the knowledge he's spent a lifetime accumulating in the hope that it might one day prove valuable.

"Not victory, not forgiveness," he continued. "The rumor of what you have done will drift westward. Even if it flakes away under the sun before reaching its destination, wherever you go, there will be more confrontations, more rumors of your endurance, marked by your victories. John will hear of you eventually."

"Then we fight," said the boy. He gripped the handle of the gun.

"Absolutely not. That's more ridiculous than forgiveness."

"Then what?" asked the boy. "Defeat means destruction."

"Avoid confrontation entirely."

"How?"

"Hide. Not in a box or a building, where you might be discovered. Not just from everyone else. From yourself as well. Give nothing away by having nothing they can take."

"We came here to hide," said Alexander. "They know who we are, or will soon, and they'll certainly find a way to cross the chasm and report to John. Yet you think we should stay."

"I do not think you should stay. You must stay. You will stay. There is nowhere further east, and to the north and south a peppering of barbarians like those who stole possession of Dirtburg by force. Your exploits and achievements were great, Alexander, but you live in a large world full of isolated, suffering, and angry people."

"Where do we hide, then?" asked the boy.

Jim pointed to the building closest to them.

"It's the one place they'll never think to look. The one place they cannot enter."

The boy's face scrunched. Alexander found it difficult to believe any building could prevent others from finding them. It looked no different than the others, a tired and tilted edifice made from wooden boards that had warped and withered over time, allowing ribbons of light to slip through the gaps.

"How long?"

"Until you reach your full strength, at least. There must be no rumor, no trace, no thread they can follow. You must be gone, utterly."

"And once I reach my full strength. What then?"

"Use your strength to make others strong. Obviously. One who can do that, who can raise others up to face the tyrants, to wrest their power from them or mute it altogether, those people are surreal, they become larger than life itself, they become figureheads, symbols, rallying points, legendary, immortal. They have their images cast in stone and raised in the street."

"Heroes," said the boy.

"Yes," Jim agreed. "And there is no greater calling for a person with strength on a world in distress."

The boy considered.

"Was my father a tyrant or a hero?"

Jim shrugged.

"To know that, one must know his story."

"Has someone written it?"

"I'm certain someone will, in time."

The boy exhaled sharply. He remained skeptical of this plan. Alexander could not help sharing his uncertainty.

"That building?" the boy asked.

The boy looked at Jim, squinting, his face full of disapproval and doubt.

"Here," said Jim.

Jim raised his hand, one finger extended, over the boy's head. The boy watched it descend toward him. It touched lightly against his forehead and the boy's eyes fluttered, then opened wide, as though Jim had conferred clarity and comprehension upon him. His body stiffened, not in pain, but realization.

"I understand," he said, then his eyes clapped shut and he fell to the ground.

"The one place they'll never think to look," said Jim. "The one place they cannot enter. You must hide within yourself. I can help you do that."

Alexander jumped to his feet and rushed to the boy's side, afraid the betrayal of a mercurial being had manifested at last. A cursory observation showed the boy continued to breathe normally. No damage showed where Jim had touched him. Apart from succumbing to an unprecedented fit of narcolepsy, he appeared unharmed. He looked at Jim, who stood over them, arms folded, satisfied with his work.

"Dee!" Alexander called, and abruptly the image stood beside him. "Is he all right?"

Dee's expression glazed for a moment as she conducted her analysis.

"His breathing, heart rate, and cerebral function all appear normal."

He turned to Jim.

"What did you do to him?"

"I built a wall between his knowledge and his personality. The latter will not be embittered by the former. And it will give him something he might not have otherwise had: humility. But that boundary won't last. He has a strong mind, like his father. It will fight its way free in time."

He looked at the boy's face, relaxed, unfettered by the distress of the great burden on his shoulders that had been hidden from him. The boy had always been happy and pleasant. Alexander pitied him, knowing it would not last, and when the truth came it would arrive on a peal of thunder.

"Will it be time enough?" Alexander asked. "Or too late?"

"Don't you trust me to know? Come. Pick him up. We'll take him there."

Again Jim gestured to the building.

Alexander lifted the boy in his arms and he felt the familiar weight of a hope he'd carried across the wasteland. The floorboards of the building groaned beneath them, as though voicing displeasure in the burden they were meant to endure. He lay the boy down and stepped back. Jim remained outside.

"You want me to leave him?"

"You are too conspicuous to watch over him," said Jim. "You worry about detection by those who can identify him while forgetting that you are one such person. He will be all right."

The boy groaned. One eye opened and he stretched out a finger to touch a nail that had lifted its head above the floorboards as if to survey the world around it.

"Who am I?" he asked, as though responding to a question. "I… don't know. Where am I?"

Alexander felt Jim's hand on his shoulder. It guided him away from the door and down the street.

"You see. Already his mind is trying to break loose, to alert him to a false reality."

"And where do I go, if not here?" asked Alexander.

"You must hide as well. From others. And yourself."

"Who will protect him if I am hiding? Who will protect others?"

Jim nodded, as though he'd identified a problematic component in an otherwise flawless plan.

"Without you, the descent of humanity will be more rapid and the slope the boy must climb so much steeper. But if you are discovered, if anyone can use you to find the boy before he is ready, he'll never have a chance to make that perilous ascent at all."

"It isn't wise to have a single, slim recourse to victory."

"No, it isn't. But this one can grant it in totality."

"Then we can win?"

Jim shrugged.

"Maybe. He will be a wall against the wind. I hope. Perhaps they'll find him anyway. Perhaps he can't do what is necessary when the time comes. Maybe he fails, too. Many have before him."

"Then this could be for nothing."

"Absolutely," Jim agreed. Then he raised a finger, an exception. "Unless."

Alexander had heard Unless before. He didn't like it. Too much a wish or prayer, something that relied upon the whims of fortune. Fortune was random, fickle, and sometimes malicious. Anyone who relied on fortune stood upon a trap door, trusting fortune to hold it shut, never knowing when its strength would fail.

"Maybe, perhaps, unless," said Alexander. "Never any certainty. Why do we do this?"

"We live in a universe of possibility. Only the ignorant are so brazen as to deal in absolutes. We do this to swing the odds in our favor. We do this to have a chance, because without trying there is none."

"You're describing hope."

"Maybe. Perhaps." Jim grinned mischievously, then added, as Alexander knew he would, "Unless."

Alexander clenched his fists. He did not like this plan, but at the same time felt resigned because he had no alternative. He knew Jim was right.

Powerful though Alexander was, he would not be able to protect the boy, nor keep him hidden. The forces arrayed against them would continue to hound and eventually overwhelm them. They had to hide, convincingly, and it made sense that to hide completely they would need to conceal their identities from themselves as well.

"Very well," said Alexander. "I will do what I must."

"You always do. It's what makes you a hero."

Jim raised his hand and extended a finger.

Alexander stepped back.

"Will I forget everything?"

"Not everything," said Jim. "Most things, except the thing you must protect. Focus on it, and it will remain with you."

Jim's hand lowered and Alexander braced himself, squinting his eyes shut as he prepared to absorb a blow. To have his memories quarantined was tantamount to losing himself. Who would he be without the things that made him what he was? What would remain of him? Kindness? Strength? Would everything fashioned by experience and memory be lost, and how would a stripped down version of himself manifest? Would he be a being of pure power, and would that lead him to oppress others? Was a human an innately good creature, a civil being in its most primal form?

He could keep one memory, and that was the memory of the thing he must protect: the boy. So he would. It was an acceptable sacrifice, and Alexander was no stranger to sacrifice. So much he did was a because it must be done. Even so now. Even though it meant forgetting his daughter, Poppy, because this meant securing the hope of a better future for her.

Again his mind turned to worry. Would she be safe? Could she protect herself? And if not, who would protect her? Someone must protect his Poppy, his girl. How he missed her, how he wanted to keep her safe. How in his mind he searched for her, mortified by the knowledge that he did not know where she had gone.

Alexander's eyes popped open, hoping she would be there before him, with him, her girlish smile giving him purpose and her confidence stirring his. What greater gift than a believer's belief, which increased his belief in himself?

She was not there. He stood amidst the squat buildings and swirling dust of Dirtburg, missing his daughter, the bright sun over Jim's shoulder making him squint until his eyes became useless slits, and he felt a horrible, bleak emptiness and longing.

And at that moment of despair he felt Jim's finger touch his forehead.

A HERO REMOVED

With an effort, Billy-Bob lifted himself until he sat with his back against the wall of the building. The writer, Andrew, stood nearby, looking haggard and depleted, and leaned heavily against the same building not far from him.

An unpleasant weight gathered in Billy-Bob's abdomen and he felt regret and embarrassment heating his face. He had failed to recognize the Forest Monster as a great hero in disguise, and rather than save the man from his fate in Dirtburg he'd almost destroyed him. He found his hand resting on the empty holster and recoiled, then scrubbed the hand against the front of his shirt, as if doing so would scrape the guilt away. The gun still lay in the street, partially obscured by grass, where it had fallen from his hand during his confrontation with Kilgoth. He watched it, willing the ground to open up and swallow that representation of his shame. But shame remained, and even if he buried or hid it, he could not hide from it. He would always know it was there, always see through the camouflage. He could never destroy it, he could only keep it secret and make silent atonement for it.

No one here knew of his encounter with the Forest Monster in Dirtburg, except for Andrew, but he did not utter a word of the event. Instead, he struggled weakly with his notebook, which had swollen considerably since Billy-Bob had first seen it, flipping to the back in search of white space to jot some new note.

"That's where you've been all this time," said Poppy.

"It's where I've been," Alexander agreed. "A prisoner in the labyrinth, searching for a way back. Apparently I've been searching for you."

"And the boy?"

Yes, thought Billy-Bob. The boy interested him greatly. Had he become a hero? Had he recovered from the peculiar malady with which Jim had afflicted him? Had he embraced the destiny Alexander expected of him? The expectations for one boy daunted Billy-Bob. Could the world truly be the responsibility of one person to save? It seemed too large a challenge for an individual, too cruel a burden. To be a hero was a daunting task; to be *the* hero sounded impossible and frightening. The expectations for such a hero were galactic in scale, stretched beyond the realm of functionality for any normal person. To be a hero was to do the right thing when the choice presented itself, a choice not always simple to make. *The* hero was a force for right that asserted itself everywhere, a force of nature no one could resist.

It fascinated Billy-Bob to think he and the boy had both been in Dirtburg, walked the same dusty paths and choked on the same sandy air. He didn't remember any other boys in the city, so he must have departed long before Billy-Bob arrived. Too bad. The description made him seem someone Billy-Bob would have liked to know, even if Billy-Bob would have proven little use to a person of such caliber.

Alexander shrugged and hung his head.

"Lost," said Alexander. "I don't know. I suffered a single moment of distraction and in that moment he slipped away. He could be anywhere. Or nowhere. If you don't know, he has not asserted himself. I have failed. Not just myself. Everyone."

"No you didn't," said Gordimer, bounding into the street. "I found him. Mardin's son."

Poppy's brows raised.

"You have?"

Alexander approached Gordimer shakily and his voice came out in a soft breath.

"Where?"

Gordimer pointed toward the building where Billy-Bob sat. He shared the thrill of Alexander's excitement. To be so close to a hero of legendary renown made his heart knock hard in his chest. He wondered what a hero looked like and if he would recognize him from Dirtburg. He wondered what characteristics made up a hero and the image they cast, and whether he would see him in action performing the deeds Billy-Bob had attempted and met with resounding failure. He longed to see heroics performed with grace and ease, with the fluidity economy of motion of a painting completed in a single, elegant brushstroke. The building began to slip from behind him, but he didn't have the energy to resist, so he fell to the side with a halfhearted and reluctant thump, coming to rest on the wooden planks of the walkway and threads of grass growing up between them.

Poppy and Alexander canted their heads sideways until they were parallel with Billy-Bob. He felt very much in the way of what they meant to see.

"I'm sorry," he said, sheepishly.

Alexander approached and knelt before Billy-Bob, then reached out and propped him upright. He looked at the bloodstained shoulders of Billy-Bob's shirt and up to his face.

"Of all people, you have the least reason to be sorry," he said. "You have had a long and difficult journey."

The journey had been long, Billy-Bob thought, across the torched desert, around the snapping jaws of villains intent on their destruction, and through a forest occupied by a messenger gone mad to reach this place. Alexander's words carried the weight of a trek greater in scope than the one Billy-Bob remembered making. He felt strongly and with some consternation they were not thinking of the same thing. Alexander smiled, and the expression struck him as distantly familiar.

Behind Alexander the girl looked on with an expression of wry satisfaction and Gordimer jittered from one foot to another with restless excitement. The three of them spent an inordinate amount of time on him before moving on, and for that Billy-Bob was grateful. It soon became apparent they had no intention of moving on, that they knew their destination and had arrived. With that attention came a prickling suspicion. That all the minor coincidences between Alexander's story and Billy-Bob's had not been coincidences at all, that the gaps in his memory were caused by blockades rather than absences, and, as Jim had suggested, the voices of the world had been his own mind screaming through closed doors what he had already known.

"Oh," said Billy-Bob quietly, his voice shuddering under the weight of a realization at which the others had already arrived. "It's me."

Alexander's face struggled with itself, unable to decide between a frown and a smile. He blinked his eyes and took several deep breaths as the two expressions waged a war for possession of him, struggling to hold in what desperately wanted out. In the end he said nothing, pulling Billy-Bob against him for a few moments instead.

Billy-Bob's legs lay upon the walkway like dead trunks. They tingled, so he could still sense them, but they had become much too heavy to raise, and a woeful unpreparedness weighed him to the ground. The urge to stand and flee was great, but his limbs did not respond.

Alexander released Billy-Bob and stood. He looked the red stains on his shirt. Billy-Bob had revived, but a faint throb of pain lingered deep in his shoulders.

"He'll be all right," said Poppy. "He just needs time."

Gordimer stood before him as well, smiling. The smile began to fracture at one corner, however, then underwent a slow collapse like the crumbling of an unsupported cliff. He began to bend at the knees, as if a great weight was building on his shoulders and his hands snapped up to clutch at his head. His face pitched upward and he shrieked in agony.

Poppy looked to Alexander, who had also seen the slow transition of Gordimer, but rather than ask the winged man what caused him such pain he had turned and scanned the town. He seemed to know the reason already and meant to find it amongst the rooftops and rubble.

"Time!" a voice boomed.

The words thundered down from somewhere above and shivered the buildings as it rumbled through the city. A shape dropped into the street, raising a short cloud of dust and grass that quickly settled, and Billy-Bob felt boards rattle under him. He could not see the figure through those surrounding him, but he slipped sideways again and struck the wooden walkway, allowing him to view the speaker through their legs.

"Time you have not," the voice added.

Even from far away, unhunched and fully visible rather than shrouded in the shadows of a hut beneath the Institute, Billy-Bob recognized him by his height and breadth. In the light he lost none of his intensity or muted malevolence. Broad-shouldered and grim, with the faintest of smiles. Billy-Bob could not forget the voice that made his spine turn icy.

"John," Billy-Bob rasped.

John set his hands on his knees and bent to look at Billy-Bob.

"Hello again, well-kept secret."

"You aren't welcome here," said Alexander.

John straightened.

"A fascinating story, Alexander, particularly useful for the knowledge one gains from learning history. True history. So *that* is how Jim did it. That's where you've been. Standing right out in the open, yet invisible. Such a clever ploy. All undone. All undone. Too bad."

"Not undone," said Alexander. "Not yet."

"An anachronism, yes. I spoke out of turn about an inevitability," John replied, dismissing the statement as a mere technicality. "Had you plans of resisting me?"

"I don't need to," Alexander replied. He stood aside and gestured to Billy-Bob. "He can do it himself."

Billy-Bob fluttered his fingers anxiously. He could do little else in his current state. How Alexander expected him to fend off this monster he had no idea. His heart rattled the bars of his ribcage, and the activity provided fuel for his body that allowed his fingers to twitter faster. Even at full strength, he had no idea how to confront the behemoth. He'd surprised himself before, often through escape, but what he needed to succeed in this situation went well beyond the capacity of mere surprise.

John laughed.

"Unless!" he countered.

The word rattled Alexander. Billy-Bob saw a shiver run through him that he caught and clenched when it reached his hands. Anyone with any sense knew Unless was fickle and unpredictable. Unless hinted at the splinter of a possibility that, should all the haphazard odds somehow fall in one's favor, something miraculous and impossible could occur. Unless was a sword held carefully by the blade. A single slip and all the delicate designs would fall apart in clatter of severed fingers. John had merely taken hold of the handle on the other end. Unless was, after all, highly improbable, uncertain, and unlikely.

Where once Unless offered hope, Alexander now found himself at the point of its limited mercy.

"Unless," Alexander repeated. The confidence of a moment ago had fled. "Indeed."

John shifted his gaze onto Gordimer and smiled. Gordimer had spoken about meeting a creature so detestable it made his mind shriek in agony. It served as an alarm when John was near. Until now Billy-Bob had never seen the alarm triggered and doubted whether a beast existed that could provoke such a reaction. Gordimer huddled on the ground, eyes squinting.

"No no no!" cried Gordimer. He shoved himself across the ground, scudding turtle-like toward the building where Billy-Bob lay, hands gripping his ears. "Not this one! Not this time!"

"Ah, Gordimer," said John. He spoke softly, with faux compassion that made Gordimer shriek all the louder for its wickedness and falseness. "I'd like to thank you for locating him, and the others for whom I've been searching. I can only imagine how shattering this must be. I did warn you long ago about the consequences of locating heroes. Still, you should be glad to learn that I am here to help you complete that cycle. I'm going to make your boy a hero. I will help you go home."

Gordimer's pinched eyes opened long enough to find Billy-Bob. In his eyes Billy-Bob saw an apology and knew Gordimer had abandoned him, not by choice, but because he had no alternative and it was better to save something than lose everything. He continued backing away until he met the wall and could go no further, then huddled his arms about his knees. His wings extended and he gave Billy-Bob one last piteous, hopeless frown before folding them over his head and crouching inside them like a creature retreating back into the safety of its shell.

As Gordimer hid himself, Billy-Bob saw a small shape skitter past him, like a whittled down tumbleweed propelled by a powerful gust. It stopped abruptly at Poppy's feet, who took a cautionary step away. The creature stood as high as her knee and faced John with its giant eyes on a background of purple tuft. It knelt slowly and took a pebble in one hand, then returned to its upright position and stood motionless.

Soon another wog appeared from between the buildings across the wide street and placed itself beside the first. A third quickly followed and before the latest had reached Poppy, ten more had appeared, then ten more after that. As the number of wogs grew they arranged themselves before the girl until they stood in ranks three deep, then hoisted themselves atop one another, creating a wall of silver and dirty, worn-through purple.

John regarded the wall with amusement.

"You have located the girl, have you?" he asked.

"Indeed," said a wog from center of the wall. "We are fulfilling our mission."

"Of course. What else could you be expected to do?"

"To protect her."

John squinted.

"Protect her? From whom?"

"From you and anyone else who might do her harm."

The tightness in John's jaw told Billy-Bob this was not what he expected to hear. Had Billy-Bob not felt so terrified, he might have smiled at the unlacing of a plan John must have believed beyond alteration. For a moment John looked at Billy-Bob, perhaps entertaining the idea that someone had changed what he had distorted. He recovered quickly, dismissing the revelation with a wave of his hand.

"Irrelevant," said John. "I'm not here for her, nor for Alexander. I'm here for him. With his discovery all other searches become unimportant. What say you to that?"

The pillar of wogs slouched to the ground and the girl emerged again, scowling. She started to step forward but found herself restrained by Alexander. He shook his head at her, indicating she ought not interfere.

The wogs followed John's outstretched arm to settle on Billy-Bob. They looked back and forth between John and Billy-Bob, but made no outward motion. It was not their mission to protect him, after all.

"I thought not," John continued. "Your task may have changed, but you have selected the wrong mission for this particular situation."

"I have not."

One wog separated from the group, misaligned gears grinding within the creature as it moved, until it interrupted the connection between Billy-Bob and John's pointing hand. It did not pant or cough, but the effort left it in what could only be described as a state of exhaustion. Billy-Bob recognized the wog that had traversed the wasteland alongside him, standing on the brink of ruin as the result of its determined companionship.

Of these many wogs, this one seemed the most aware of itself outside of its mission. It had selected its own mission, after all, rather than relying on the direction of someone else. This wog had made a choice, and that made it distinct amongst wogs and humans.

"You stand against me?" asked John.

"It is my mission," the wog replied in a clipped metallic voice.

"Only one programmed to resist would attempt this foolishness. Every sensible being steps aside." John pointed to Alexander. "Even a hero."

"It's not programming," the wog retorted. "It's what I have to do. It is what I have chosen to do. Someone must. Or none will."

"So then," said John. "Do what you must."

The wog sprang at John. John's eyebrows raised, perhaps as surprised by the attack itself as the idea that anyone would attempt it. Yet for all the wounded wog's speed and strength, John clapped his hands together faster still and caught it with ease.

"What has your failure accomplished?" asked John.

"Failure does not make the decision unjust."

"I see," said John. His face twitched with a flicker of understanding. "Perhaps it is you who is the hero of this story."

John raised his elbows and his arms pressed inwards. The wog did not struggle or make any attempt to free or defend itself, as though it had come to its purpose and embraced it. For a moment the ovular form shivered as the sturdy frame resisted compression, then the pressure became too great and the wog's body flattened between John's hands, sending out a jet of white sparks. John opened his hands and let the flattened disk of metal fall. It struck heavily and stuck in the ground, sending off faint tendrils of black smoke.

"This is what happens," said John, dusting his hands together, "when you do what you think is right."

The world shook and Billy-Bob realized he was in motion. The sideways world righted itself and John, though he stood motionless in the street, rushed closer and clearer, his expression one of moderate surprise. He moved forward as he did in dreams, under his own power yet as an observer, with strength he thought had left him, uncertain where it had come from or where it would take him.

He tried to think, but his mind was a blur of static, of broken thoughts that touched and fell apart again, all puzzle parts searching in vain for their matching piece. Occasionally he caught a glimpse of a familiar memory, of a wog providing him with a useful piece of advice or stringent objection, and it saddened him to think these events had relegated themselves forever to nostalgia.

He could see in the reduced motion of the world around him that he must moving very faster. Poppy's eyes tracked slowly across the space where he had been rather than where he was. The world blurred, perhaps from the pace of his passing, though even objects that came nearer did not come into better focus, and he could feel a stream of moisture trailing back across his face and a sourness in his stomach. Not sickness. Despair. And something else. Something angrier.

A silver and brown shape lying against the green of the street caught his attention and he scooped it up without thinking, then raised his arm and brought it to bear on John in a smooth, swift motion.

He moved his other arm across his face and the wet sheen that made the world glare and go out of focus cleared. He looked down the shaft of his arm and saw the gun in his hand, and beyond that stood John. Billy-Bob's throat ached and in the distance he heard a muted shrieking. At the end of his arm, Billy-Bob watched the gun hammer snap forward, pull back like a battering ram at a castle gate, and crash forward again and again against empty chambers.

Billy-Bob found himself suddenly out of breath. The gun fell from his hand and thumped against the street, and he folded at the waist, propping himself up with his hands at his knees. Sweat beaded on his forehead and stung his eyes, and water bubbled out of his mouth when he breathed as it ran down his face in a relentless torrent.

When he looked up again he saw John watching him, patiently. At his feet lay the crushed disc of what had been a wog.

"Why?" asked Billy-Bob, raggedly.

For a sliver of a moment, John appeared remorseful. He acknowledged what he had wrought, and even though this was what he must do, he regretted the necessity. It came and went almost undetected.

"Unlike my counter engineer, I am willing to interfere at the expense of elegance. Most times I am satisfied to allow plans to play out as I have crafted them, while in others I am compelled to see them through myself to add a level of certainty and… satisfaction. I want the futility of resistance to be abundantly clear." John gestured to the crushed metal. "At times it is necessary to provide… metaphors."

A rock lay by Billy-Bob's feet, rounded and small enough to fit in his hand, as if provided by providence. He'd thwarted the Forest Monster with a rock, and he'd heard the writer speak to the effectiveness as weapons wogs had made them. Appropriate, he thought. Justice. Billy-Bob knelt and took the rock in hand.

"Hey," said the rock. "What would you like to know? Hey. Hey. Are you listening? Hey."

He had no questions for this rock, only a mission. The rock continued trying to get his attention, repeating Hey even as Billy-Bob wound the rock behind his head and hurled it at John, whistling on its path and leaving a long and ululating Hey as it hurtled toward John's center.

The rock met John in the chest, but it did not knock him backwards, bounce aside, or shatter. Instead the rock passed into John and went silent. It did not exit the other side and John appeared unaffected by the addition of the rock to his body. He could hear the breath rush out of Alexander and Billy-Bob guessed they thought the same thing. He might not have expected success, but he probably had not expected John to be invincible.

"You cannot harm me," John explained. "I am the event horizon of things that are. Those things that pass through me become nothing, removed from history. It is why, I suspect, you have none. Because I will make you a proposal, and afterward you will accept oblivion."

"Why?"

"Because I cannot be defeated, but I can be stopped. You can stop me, if you agree to surrender."

"Why surrender?"

John pointed to the lip of the crater that led into Beta. A stream of animals circled the brink and made their way around, but so many had come that a waterfall began to pour down the slope and into the city.

"My forest!" cried Poppy.

She reached out to touch passing wildlife as it pushed by, birds and bears and bees, shoving on in a torrent that pooled in the city and dissipated amongst the buildings.

"They are coming," said John. "In numbers more numerous than when Alpha was overcome. They would gladly throw themselves at you as a means to extinguish their despair. Even should you somehow survive, all the hard work you have accomplished here will be destroyed. The remnants of your civilization will be lost, and I will pull them up wherever they set down roots."

John looked hard at Billy-Bob.

"You can save them from me. You can be a hero. All you need to do is surrender. Give up. Join me. Is that not the essence of being a hero? To sacrifice oneself for the good of all?"

"Surrender and be obliterated?"

"Obliterated? No. You would simply become obsolete. It's not quite the same thing."

"Why are you doing this?" asked Billy-Bob. "Why work so hard to undo everything?"

John's expression darkened.

"Because I must. I've explained this."

"If I agree, how can I know you will let them be?"

"You don't, I suppose. But you don't have any alternative."

Billy-Bob considered the offer.

He had failed in his attempt to avenge the wog, as he'd failed so many times before. He'd failed to safely thwart the Forest Monster, failed to prevent Kilgoth's fall, and failed to recover him when he reappeared. All the faith placed in him by Alexander, or Jim, and Gordimer, had been misplaced. He hadn't prevented destruction anywhere and it followed him everywhere. This time, however, he might save everyone simply by giving up.

It was a surprisingly easy choice to make.

"What do I do?" asked Billy-Bob.

"Move forward." John opened his arms. "Come to me."

Billy-Bob did so. Wildlife crossed between them in an anxious rush as Billy-Bob approached John's outstretched arms, all searching for somewhere to hide and unable to find a secure location in the now cramped city, running into one another and hooting in alarm and dismay.

He saw Andrew begin to take a step into the street, an unexpected movement from the reluctant writer. The step hung in mid stride, then he fell backwards, disappearing through the opening of the building behind him like a fish plucked from the ocean.

Nearby, the carapace of wings Gordimer had created unfolded enough to allow him to see through a gap near the top.

"I'm sorry," said Gordimer.

Billy-Bob nodded. Gordimer would understand. Launching himself into a contest with John would only delay the inevitable and likely cause unnecessary destruction in the process. He didn't like this option, but knew it was the best one.

"Go home," said Billy-Bob.

Gordimer covered himself again.

He wondered what Alexander thought, if this resolution surprised him or if he had expected it. Billy-Bob did not turn back, fearful of the despair he'd see in Alexander's face, an indication that his plan had gone horribly awry. Better to imagine this was how it was supposed to be, since it could not be any other way.

Billy-Bob approached John's giant torso and the grinning face above it, uncertain what to expect other than a collision. He shut his eyes as the monster filled his entire field of view and continued on, waiting for contact that never came, wondering if John had played one final trick by moving out of the way.

He opened his eyes, expecting to see John behind him, laughing. Instead he stood near a forest, a group of people gathered ahead of him. He looked behind to find John and ask where he'd arrived and found a door without a knob standing in a frame without a wall, as though he'd been invited into a new world and discovered he'd been locked inside.

A TEST COMPLETED

When the wog's crushed husk struck the street, white sparks snapping as its circuitry tried to send signals across broken synapses, Andrew felt nothing. Not because the meaningless destruction did not upset him and not because he disliked the wog. The wog had proven clever and kind and wise; the sort of creature a person wanted as a friend. So many emotions, despair and rage and sadness, all trying to squeeze through an aperture large enough to accommodate only one, lodged themselves in the turnstile. If he felt anything, he felt sore on the inside from the collisions of so many large emotions banging against the exit in an attempt to express themselves at the same time.

The world no longer seemed real, as if he had been separated from reality by a thick glass wall through which everything became unfocused and distorted. He saw John's mouth moving, feeling rather than hearing him utter something poignant and relevant, a sardonic eulogy for the eradicated wog. His words sounded blurry and indistinct. All noises had dulled, until a single, piercing shriek returned Andrew to clarity.

Billy-Bob was on his feet, something Andrew had not thought possible, and from him came an otherworldly scream that articulated everything the logjam of Andrew's feelings could not. Moments before, the boy appeared inert, doomed, too weak to hold himself upright as John waded effortlessly through a low pool of milquetoast guardians offering weak resistance, confident in their inane decision to allow the immobilized boy to fend for himself.

Not long ago that decision had seemed absurd. Now Andrew wasn't so sure. Had the wog known this would happen? Had this been its final resort in protecting Billy-Bob, kindling a rage-fueled strength to save himself? No sooner had the wog's smoking body struck the grass than Billy-Bob was in motion.

The boy had already crossed into the street in a blur before Andrew registered the wail of agony and rage as a sting in his ears. John stood his ground with profound aplomb. It would not surprise Andrew to learn John had not reacted because he didn't have time to do so. Billy-Bob made directly for the gun lying in the street, sweeping it up and targeting the giant, then hammering out a series of empty shots with such rapidity they sounded like the short snap of a drumroll. John hid his astonishment brilliantly, but Andrew saw him lean then correct himself, preventing a cautious step backward.

Agitated, the boy flung the gun to the ground, the barrel planting itself in the turf like a bulbous, brown weed. Now he took up a rock.

For all of his confidence and bluster, John feared something in Billy-Bob. It was a subtle fear, buried under the self assurance of long planning, but Andrew saw it. He didn't know what to fear, only that the boy surprised him, and the unexpected shivered his confidence like a sledgehammer blow against the sensitive root of a mountain.

The rock came at John with a velocity no one could hope to dodge, so John remained motionless. He had little alternative. With no small thrill Andrew saw the two objects draw nearer until they touched. And John remained unaffected. The rock did not bounce away nor cause a deep indentation, nor even make a sound to mark its arrival. It simply vanished.

Again Andrew felt a curtain of confusion draw between himself and the world, muffling anything John had to say. Andrew had no interest in his rationalizations. Could nothing stop John? Could nothing affect him? How could an entity of such incomprehensible power ever be defeated? Andrew disliked resorting to fairness as an excuse or defense, it reflected a failing in oneself to comprehend or adjust accordingly to the circumstances, but this inexplicable invulnerability was undeniably unfair. How could one hope to contend against a being that was physically unassailable?

That, perhaps, was the flaw in the approach. Perhaps physical assault was not the appropriate response to an antagonist. What then?

John continued to speak at length. Andrew did not process John's words, but he felt them plink against his face like grains of sand caught up in the wind. An unceasing annoyance that had never deterred him as he crossed the wasteland, though a distraction that peppered and eroded his ability to concentrate on anything else.

He watched Billy-Bob and saw the effect the words had on him. He saw the rage from moments ago give way to disdain and then, at last, he could see the boy give up. If Billy-Bob spoke, no sound reached Andrew. It didn't need to. Andrew read his body.

Shoulders slack and brow furrowed, his downcast eyes in deep cogitation as he considered what John had told him. Andrew understood why he might surrender. John was an indefatigable adversary. But Andrew wished he hadn't. He wanted Billy-Bob to push on, to persist, to find a way even he could not see.

The boy had surrendered, but Andrew did not. Andrew had come too far to see it end this way. Billy-Bob had come too far not to take another step. All he needed was a push.

Yet no one moved forward to deliver it. Someone must, or nothing would happen. The wog had said as much prior to its annihilation. Would Andrew suffer the same fate if he interfered? Perhaps. Perhaps the push would prove too little. Perhaps the boy could not be pushed. Perhaps John would withstand the boy even after his impetus had been restored. Perhaps everything anyone did to resist John was futile and the world would grind itself down to a splinter.

Unless.

Andrew righted himself and took a step toward the street. As he leaned forward a hand caught his shoulder and pulled him back through the opening of the building. A most inopportune time for the appearance of another Forest Monster, Andrew thought, wondering what unfortunate person had been converted in order to hide them from John and what misguided mission they had adopted to occupy themselves.

The hand spun him around and Andrew found himself looking into the bearded, smirking face of Jim.

"I'd rather you didn't become involved," said Jim.

"Now that I realize what I need to do, you won't let me!"

Andrew gripped Jim's hand and tried to fling it away. He may as well have tried disconnecting one of his own appendages. The hand did not move.

Jim laughed.

"You don't know what you're supposed to do or you wouldn't be rushing into the street."

Jim's hand abruptly released him and Andrew toppled backward. He rolled over and looked up in time to see Billy-Bob pass into John, just as the rock had before him, and vanish. Andrew pounded a fist on the floor, rattling the wooden floorboard.

"I could have stopped him!"

"Maybe," said Jim. "Unless. I have something better planned."

"What could possibly happen now? How can losing your hero be a step toward winning?"

Jim lifted Andrew to his feet and guided Andrew away from the doorway. A moment later Gordimer entered, glum and distant. Andrew knew he had come here not because he had an errand but because he didn't know where to go, and his listless gait had taken him through the first doorway that seemed to lead away from the catastrophe he'd just witnessed.

"Gordimer," said Jim.

Gordimer recognized the voice and raised his head. Andrew, seeing his questions wouldn't be answered until Jim finished his conversation with Gordimer, made his way to the piano bench and sat. He rubbed his fingertips across the cracked, yellow keys, trying to think of a tune that would occupy his mind.

"Congratulations," Jim continued. "You've met your quota. You are welcome to return home."

"Home?" Gordimer echoed hollowly. "Where?"

"Through that door," said Jim.

Andrew threw a brief look over his shoulder to find a door against the wall to his right. The door would lead to an alleyway between buildings. Andrew couldn't help watching, anticipating Gordimer's disappointment when the promise proved a ruse, as did the hope that the boy could withstand something superhuman. Gordimer appeared decidedly unenthused, approaching the door because he had nothing better to do with his time, perhaps expecting the same as Andrew.

Gordimer pulled on the handle and the door opened, letting sunlight pour through so everything beyond became a shining morass. Andrew couldn't see beyond the door, but an alleyway still seemed most likely.

"Hmm," said Gordimer. Apparently it was not what he expected, and not a complete disappointment. Then he seemed to spot something that interested him and he dashed through the door, uttering a single word before he left. "Oh!"

The door swung closed behind him. Gordimer had escaped at last. Something Andrew had no expectation of doing any longer. His goal had become simply to resist.

He turned back to the piano keys and picked out the notes he'd heard Gordimer whistle to himself over and over again. The melancholy tune had embedded itself in Andrew, instilling a sense of need, but for what he didn't know. He pressed a single key, letting the detuned note touch each corner of the room before moving to the next. He played it through once, then again. He meant to play it a third time because it somehow made him feel better to know an escape existed and someone had gotten away, when a door swung open on the other side of the room.

Andrew watched in astonishment, a finger hovering over the next note, as Gordimer stepped through. Gordimer's eyes were glassy and his face ran with joyful tears. The door swung shut and the crack of the wood against the frame made Andrew blink. When he recovered the door was absent.

"The song!" Gordimer cried. "It's the song! I'm home!"

"Home?" asked Andrew. "No you're not. You're back where you started, just on the other side of the room."

"Right! Where I started! I started here!"

The light of epiphany lit in his eyes and he took a sharp breath.

"That can mean only one thing," he said in a hushed, excited voice.

Gordimer rushed toward the door and Andrew called to him as loud as he dared without raising the attention of the giant man outside.

"What?"

The winged man stopped at the doorway leading out of the building and looked back, gripping the frame like a dream he feared might vanish in the light of day if he didn't cling to it tightly.

"The boy wins."

Gordimer hurried out the door and into the street. Andrew didn't have a chance to remind him Billy-Bob was already gone.

Andrew gave Jim, who had seated himself on the bench beside Andrew, a puzzled look.

"I don't understand," said Andrew. "I thought you sent him home. Is this a joke?"

"I did," said Jim. He pressed his finger down on a sour note. "He is home. This is home. It's all a matter of perspective. Most of what you see of the world is shaped by *how* you see it. One person sees the world as a place destroyed by avarice and neglect, another sees it as a place full of potential. One sees it as broken, the other views it as just out of tune. Both see the same world, they just see it differently, and that shapes how they approach it."

"Bullsh…," Andrew started.

Something in Jim's smile and gaze made him stop. Jim was looking past Andrew. At what he couldn't guess, but it made a shiver drop down the back of his shirt. Behind him he heard a door creak on its hinges in the place where Gordimer had appeared and there was no door.

"Just as his perspective changed, so can change that of a boy who is told repeatedly that he can be a hero," said Jim. "It doesn't make him one, but it puts his mind to work, it makes him more likely. He needed only this chance, this crucial moment, to push him over the edge."

"But the boy is gone," said Andrew hoarsely.

Jim's smile stretched tighter and his eyes sparkled with scarcely restrained joy, as though something for which he'd long hoped had finally come to pass.

"Is he?"

The door creaked again and clapped shut. Andrew twisted away from Jim and saw Billy-Bob standing in the room with them, looking around as though trying to remember this place. He spotted Andrew and Jim, and smiled softly, looking plaintive and calm, as if they were markers that allowed him to determine when and where he was. Something about the boy appeared different. Billy-Bob remained the same lithe, coiled spring he always appeared to be, but now his actions had a certainty and decisiveness they had lacked. The boy looked upon them with temporary fondness, as though he knew he had more important things to do yet wanted to take a moment to indulge himself by giving his attention to those he had not seen in some time. He gave them both a sharp, decisive nod, and strode out the door.

Andrew jerked to his feet, banging his legs against the keyboard in his rush and sat back down again. He remained seated an instant, paralyzed by his astonishment and unable to make his legs work, then slid off the bench and started to follow. Again the hand from behind caught him and turned him about.

Jim shook his head, then gestured to Andrew's chest. Andrew looked down and saw his shirt emanating a dim blue pulse. He grabbed the hem of his shirt and shook, raising a cloud of dust that revealed the blue disc Mardin gave him glowing brightly.

"This part of your test is over," said Jim.

Before Andrew could comprehend what this meant or explain his desire to stay and learn how events would unfold, Jim poked a finger into the button.

"Now serve your purpose."

The world went white, Andrew felt a sudden sense of acceleration, and abruptly he was standing at the edge of a platform ringed by grass. He realized abruptly his mission was over and, from relief or exhaustion, his legs wobbled and folded underneath him, his eyes fluttered shut, and the world went dark.

INVENTION FINDS NECESSITY

The process was painless, much to Billy-Bob's relief. Not unlike passing through a sheet of water. He clenched his eyes and took a breath before moving, then there was a faint wash of cold, and he was through. And the world had changed.

Like all places, this one had a particular odor. Dirtburg had a dry, old smell as the dust of another layer of dead ground peeled away in the wind outside; the forest near the Institute smelled of bacteria rotting down lifeless material to reconstitute into food for new plants; the rolling fields beyond the forest had flowery aroma from pollens exchanged by corresponding plants in long-distance relationships; Beta had an oily metal odor of machinery.

This place smelled wet. Not like a large body of water, but something able to retain moisture, verdant, more akin to Poppy's forest between Beta and the Institute.

To his surprise, he found the Institute standing on his left, radiant atop its platform, with grasses and trees extending to its base and beyond. The forest had grown through and beyond it, and past the Institute the beginnings of a city. Several of the buildings appeared familiar. As he stared at it a thin wisp of smoke began to rise from the center, and he knew this was the city that burned in the wogs' memory.

Closer, a group of people crouched around a man laying face down on the ground.

Determined to discover the nature of this place, he took a step toward them and his foot caught on a stone. Without thinking, he picked it up and turned it over in his hand. Rocks came in a shape and texture of incalculable variation, yet the weight and look of this one appeared familiar. Where had he seen it before?

As he approached the group he could hear the murmur of their voices more clearly.

"A rock. From out of nowhere," said one. He knocked his knuckles against his forehead and clicked his tongue. "Right in the cabbage. Who does a thing like that?"

Billy-Bob looked at the rock in his hand.

"Already in trouble," it said, and Billy-Bob knew it was the rock he'd thrown that disappeared into John. "I expect next time you'll just ask me a question."

He dropped the rock.

The thump as it hit the ground drew the attention of those gathered around the fallen man. These people were as variegated as the rocks populating the universe, men and women and children, clothed in pants, skirts, robes, overalls, tight-necked shirts, some barechested, others clothed in naught but layers of paint in places, tattooed in others. A fascinating menagerie that gave no indication of where they had come from, except everywhere, a term of ghastly and unhelpful imprecision.

A woman in a blouse with white puffed sleeves and a long, black skirt approached him. He could see in her face deep curiosity, as though he was less a person and more a problem to be solved.

"Bonjour. There is nothing to fear. My name is Marie. Who are you?"

"My name is…," Billy-Bob started.

"William," someone interrupted. The voice was familiar, but he couldn't quite place it. "I'd know that face anywhere. Any time."

The woman closest to the fallen man's head rolled him over. He was barefoot, robed, and filthy, with long, dirty fingernails and a fluffy gray beard. If he had wings, he might have been Gordimer. He sat up, eyes squinting, cradling the back of his head, and waved the others away.

"Είμαι καλά, ευχαριστώ," he said, then stood.

The woman stood and strode toward him, touching Marie on the elbow, who nodded and backed away with a hint of reluctance at leaving a mystery unsolved.

The approaching woman had a confident and wide smile, and her sandy hair hung at her shoulders. Of course the voice sounded familiar. He'd spoken to her several times. She was the most helpful person he knew, if it was correct to refer to her as a person.

"Hello," said Billy-Bob. "Where am I?"

"This," said the woman, extending her arms to gesture at the world surrounding them, "or rather, these, are John's memories. Quite the trove of information."

All these people, these places, specters of what had once existed. It made him curious and sad. With access to John's experiences he could see how the world appeared before the erosion had come so near completion.

"How did I get here?"

The girl pointed to a space behind him. In that space stood a door, in the same spot where Billy-Bob knew he had arrived.

Billy-Bob approached the door and the girl followed, amused. Standing by itself, without a wall or building, the door did not connect an inside to an outside. It hung on rusty hinges clinging to a pale wooden jamb suffering from dry rot, ready to disintegrate and let the door fall from the frame. The door did not have a knob, only a small hole midway up the door where a knob belonged. He poked a finger in the hole and felt nothing, and when he tried to look through the darkness was impenetrable. He pushed on the door, and it flexed, but did not move. He kicked the door, and he heard a bolt rattle in the catch, yet despite its flimsy appearance he felt the rigidity of something that could not be broken without significant effort.

"Leaving so soon?" the girl asked.

"Can I?"

The girl shrugged.

"You would be the first."

He knew he had traded his freedom for the safety of those in Beta, though he did not trust John to honor the bargain. On the other hand, should he escape, that might negate their arrangement. Leaving might bring destruction upon Beta and he had no idea how to stop John if he managed to get out.

"Trapped," he muttered.

"Perhaps. We've tried beating it, knocking it down, prying it open. Nothing works. Here we remain, outside of existence. There is no getting back. I think that's the message here." Her head rocked back and forth, thoughtfully. "Unless."

"Then there is a way out."

"No idea. Not for lack of trying, though."

Billy-Bob looked at the woman, disappointed. With such vast reservoirs of information at her disposal, he'd anticipated a better answer. At the least, he'd expected a hint, a direction of some kind.

"You seem surprised," the woman said. "Is that not the answer you expected?"

"I expected you to know."

"Surely if we knew the way out we would not still be here."

"You always know everything."

"That's flattering, but untrue."

Something seemed amiss. The girl struck him as less academic than he remembered, less rigid. He looked around her and behind himself, searching.

"I don't see your post," he said.

She shook her head, puzzled.

"My post?"

"Yes. I fixed one already. Maybe it's hidden. Maybe you don't need one here."

Her eyes widened.

"Oh! My goodness!" She laughed. "You think I'm a Waypoint Interface!"

"A what?"

"A hologram. Not real. I warned Mardin it would confuse people if he used a representation of a genuine person rather than an amalgam. He argued with compelling and smug blarney. He believed people would trust me. Not convincing but touching. He did it anyway."

"What?" Billy-Bob repeated.

She reached a finger toward him and poked it against his forehead. It surprised him when his head reeled back from the contact. Billy-Bob blinked at her.

"Real!" she said.

The image from the posts had come from a real person, according to Gordimer. One who was lost. When Gordimer said the girl was lost, Billy-Bob assumed she had died or been destroyed. Perhaps that is what he believed. Perhaps they all believed this. Everyone, that is, except Mardin.

"You are the one the wogs are looking for, aren't you? John sent some after Poppy, but that was a distortion of their original mission. It's you they sought. And they could never find you, so they became frustrated."

The woman blinked, and Billy-Bob knew he'd found a piece of information she'd never had.

"Mardin," she breathed.

"Yes. Why is he looking for you?"

"Because he did what his heart told him rather than listen to his head."

"Is that wrong?"

"No. But there should be a discourse between them, and the head is usually more sensible."

Despite the fact that this girl was limited by her humanity, she was bright and wise.

"Who are you? How long have you been here?"

She looked hard at his face, as though she could count the years of her absence in them.

"Not long. Not as long as some. And yet, longer than I would have liked. There's so much I've missed. My name is Anne."

She canted her head and looked at him, her expression skeptical.

"You have no memory of me?"

His only memories of this person consisted of encounters with the devices that borrowed her image. She seemed significant and urgent, surprised and disappointed by an absence in his recollection, and this saddened him, but he could think of no answer to comfort her.

"You have always been very helpful," he said. "I don't know what else I should remember."

"You know Mardin," said Anne. "That's half of your equation."

Billy-Bob stared at her helplessly, not understanding. According to Alexander, Jim had erected partitions in his memory, and some rooms must remained inaccessible. Any hints that ought to have made their relationship plain provided no illumination.

"If that is meaningful, I don't remember why. Alexander said Jim…," he tried to explain.

"Alexander and Jim," she interrupted. She shrugged. "That explains much. It will come to you. Let's focus on the task at hand."

"Okay," Billy-Bob agreed, even if he didn't understand what that task might be.

"Follow me," said Anne.

She set off across the landscape, eastward into the emptiness he'd spent days trying to cross. It took a moment to convince his legs to follow. They remembered the ceaseless, repetitive tramping and blanched at doing it again. He leaned forward, forcing them to extend and prevent him from falling, and his momentum carried them reluctantly onward.

"Do you know what this place is?" she asked.

"It's John's mind. You told me that."

"Yes," she said.

She stopped in an empty space in the ground that held no apparent significance, then extended her arm, feeling about as though searching for a wall in the darkness. Her hand flattened against a surface he could not see and drifted lower until it gripped something as though giving it a handshake. She twisted her wrist and the outline of a doorway became clear as it opened.

"It's also where he keeps those he considers dangerous to his test," she continued, then stepped through, beckoning him to follow.

On the other side of the doorway a circle of buildings surrounded a large, black stone, darker even than the night beneath the cloudy sky. A chain extended from the stone and at the other end sat a boy, sleeping. Anne continued on without stopping until they reached one of the buildings where no lights burned on the porch. She pushed open the door and Billy-Bob followed her through.

They found themselves not within the interior of a building, but treading through a grassy street. Anne crossed and Billy-Bob followed behind. She made her way toward a doorway, the lone portion of a crushed wooden structure to remain standing. Billy-Bob abruptly knew where he was. Beta. He stopped.

Just a few paces away stood John, the wog in its outstretched hands. People gathered at the edge of the street and on the ledge of rooftops, but none engaged, none rushed forward to prevent the catastrophe he recalled, restrained by a persistent belief that they were incapable of helping themselves, that salvation must come from elsewhere, and interference brought not vindication, only destruction. Nor could they interfere now—this memory had set itself in time. Unless.

Billy-Bob rushed to John's side and gripped a forearm. He strained, heaving with all the might available to him, yet he could not pry it away from the wog. He could not alter this memory. He released John with a gasp and regarded the wog helplessly. He'd proven just as impotent as those who refused to help.

"I'm sorry," said Billy-Bob.

"It's all right," the wog said quietly, almost too quietly to hear. "I understand."

Before he could respond, John spoke in a whisper.

"Can you make it?"

He saw John's eyes flick past the wog, past the city, and up the slope. At the peak stood a filament, scarcely perceptible against the background of pale sky. The Information Post.

"Yes," said the wog. "Do what you must."

"I always do."

The wog's eyes flickered a moment, then the white dots of its electronic eyes went dark. John raised his elbows and crushed the empty shell of the wog, then dropped it at his feet.

"Come on!" called Anne.

Billy-Bob stumbled toward her. John had allowed the wog to escape somehow. Wogs had received updates and provided information to the posts. Did the wog have the ability to transfer its entire consciousness? The notion brought him comfort, but the idea that John had permitted it confused him. Was he not diabolical? A remorseless creature seeking destruction as a salve for the torments of his existence?

"Through here," said Anne.

She held a canted door open that led into the wreckage of a collapsed structure. Billy-Bob stepped through and Anne pulled the door shut behind them.

"Where are you taking me?"

Anne continued moving, heading along a bare pathway toward a towering building. Far above a word circled the structure. It passed overhead twice before Billy-Bob could determine what it said: WELCOME.

She spoke, but did not answer his question.

"All of the places and many of the people here are memories, but not all. Some were wrenched from reality and brought here. John considers this a prison. But a prison does not allow you to explore its inner workings, to show you the process of its construction, to provide the details of its use. This is a vessel of discovery. When we learn and we understand how something works, we can effectively disrupt the machinery."

John had said the same in his secluded library beneath the defunct Institute. Understanding granted powers of disruption. It was why he was reading. Learning strengths and weaknesses to blunt one and exploit the other. He wondered if those present had an influence on him, or whether his thoughts influenced those here. Had John assimilated the idea from Anne, or did she absorb it from him? Perhaps his strategy of absorbing people had a disadvantage so he selected only a few crucial characters to remove.

Billy-Bob understood the advantage understanding gave, but it struck him as an incomplete solution. You could attempt to crush a problem, but rather than destroy it, it shattered into thousands of shards that might grow of their own accord into still more numerous troubles later. Could one repair a world by breaking one of its components?

Regardless, one enormous obstacle stood in the way of this plan and made the entire notion of plotting irrelevant.

"Does it teach us how to escape?"

This dampened her enthusiasm.

"No."

"Then what is the point of the learning?"

"For when."

When they escaped. However that happened.

"How did everyone get here?"

"The same as you. He offered us a choice: remove yourself and save those you care about or see them destroyed. It's a simple choice to make. No one ever refuses. The sort of people who would refuse him are the sort he wants in the world. They serve his purpose."

"Then we're trapped."

"Yes."

"Why is he doing this?"

"Why? Isn't it obvious?"

"No."

"Then that is where I am taking you."

* * *

They stood on a white plain, blank as an empty page. The air had no odor, no motion, and all around them he could not pick out any objects. Something supported them because Billy-Bob could walk across it, but he could not see what he stood upon.

"There," said Anne.

Before them stood two figures, both clad in white. One taller and lankier, the other nearly as large but stockier. He did not recognize them immediately because nothing existed here with which to compare them, though he identified them by voice when they spoke. One looked everywhere, searching for something upon which to anchor himself. The taller one stared at the one searching the emptiness, then reached out and set a finger on the stockier figure's chin and gently guided his face until their gazes connected.

"What is your name?" asked the taller one with Jim's voice.

"My name? I don't know. What is your name?" The stocky one hesitated, perplexed. "How do I know how to speak?"

"One of the mysteries of existence and purpose, I suppose. My name is Jim. You are intelligent and perceptive. Do you know why?"

The stocky one looked thoughtful.

"Because I must be."

"Yes. Because your test will be the most challenging of all."

"Did you make me?"

"I did not."

"Who did?"

"Those who made me."

A brief silence passed.

"You should have a name, I think. A way to identify yourself."

"Can I be Jim, too?"

"I'm afraid not."

"Then can I be John?"

"Of course."

John turned in place, observing the unpopulated emptiness.

"I like this place."

Jim's smile faded.

"So do I."

His survey complete, John faced Jim again.

"What is my test?"

"To undo all other tests."

John frowned.

"Why?"

"Because without resistance, all other tests are without meaning."

"What is your test?"

"To make myself unnecessary."

John considered.

"I do not like this test."

Jim set a hand on John's shoulder.

"I know. Which is why you are so important."

Jim and John exchanged expressions of reluctance and resignation, then the scene fluttered and began again.

Anne coughed and Billy-Bob's concentration broke.

"Now do you understand why John behaves as he does?" she asked.

"This is his test," Billy-Bob breathed.

"A test no compassionate entity can ever fulfill. And yet he strives. He is the most loyal, most true, and most frustrated. He does this because he believes in the tests and knows his is the only test meant to fail. Of all beings, he should be the most pitied, the least envied."

No wonder his frustration and anger. John had attempted to convey this to him when they first met, but Billy-Bob had interpreted it as the ravings of a madman bent on ruining the world for some inscrutable and hostile purpose. Some people delighted in the misery of others, filling a psychological void with the unhappiness they created that most satisfied with love. Much to his surprise, John was not that sort of villain.

Further, if John absorbed those who resisted him and those people influenced his thoughts, adding those people to himself would only make his test harder because he would believe in it less. Their presence would create a dissonance in his thoughts. He wondered if John's mind would spring back to its original shape after they escaped, removing that permanent influence, or if it would remain permanently distorted. Only a creature of colossal will could struggle onward with such a weight upon his mind.

"Jim gave him this test?"

Anne nodded.

"He is the giver of tests."

"Is he evil? What kind of monster would do that?"

"He is whatever we make him. Give me your hand."

Billy-Bob extended his hand. She took it and pinched the skin on the back of his hand. Billy-Bob jerked his hand away.

"Why?" he asked.

"Do you prefer pain or pleasure?"

"That's a silly question."

"And how would you have known without experiencing both? Our appreciations are discernible only through contrast. Without experience we cannot say that we prefer pleasure or pain. We require pain to appreciate pleasure, or at the very least the absence of pain. So it goes with all of our sufferings. It is up to us to overcome them."

Billy-Bob did not have a follow-up question, nor did Anne continue. She let him think in silence, which he did for long enough only to notice the silence. Neither Jim nor John spoke either.

The two beings stared at them, perplexed. Then John started toward them, his visage folding into a stern scowl.

"Who are you? What are you doing here?"

Billy-Bob took a step backward while Anne watched the approaching man in awe. Beside Jim, with an empty template for a world in the background, he appeared by all accounts normal in size. His immensity became apparent as he neared and his anger felt like a harsh sun on Billy-Bob's face.

"Get out!" shouted John.

A wall rose up before them, smooth and silver, doorless, too high to leap and too sheer to climb, without a seam or rivet to serve as a point to grip. Anne touched the wall, fascinated.

"I've never seen that happen before. He's thrown us out of a memory."

This did not surprise Billy-Bob. He had encountered memories inside wogs that he'd been able to influence. It made sense that a creature so sophisticated as John could become aware of someone else watching his memories and perhaps trying to manipulate them.

He wondered, if he could alter the memories of wogs, could he also alter John's memories? And if so, with which memories could he most effectively tamper? Perhaps to remove the memory of the people trapped here would allow them to escape.

"Now what?"

"I'm not sure. Observe. Jim has a plan, so it will all work out."

Jim had mentioned a plan, though he hadn't seemed confident in its success. Then again, that encounter occurred in a dream and might prove unreliable.

"If Jim thinks I'm the one to save everyone, why doesn't he wish us out of here?"

"Jim does not ply the miraculous. He is a tinkerer, an arranger, moving seemingly unrelated parts around a cluttered roomful of jittering gizmos and creating a sequence of favorable events, like a machine built to bump and clatter haphazardly and without purpose until all the turning gears catch at the same time, and the purpose of his innocuous hints and gifts become plain to everyone."

"Hints and gifts," Billy-Bob murmured, enthralled by the poetry of her monologue. Then the epiphany struck him like a fist, ringing his ears.

Jim had sculpted something for him in his dream. A gift, Jim had called it, without explaining what it was. He had imagined that experience in a dream world not unlike this one. Could he imagine it here, too? How much of reality traveled with him to this place and how much imagination could he take from one realm to another, or did they all interweave, permitting journeys between them all as seamlessly as walking through a doorway from one room to the next?

Billy-Bob slid a hand into his loose pocket and felt acorns, grit, a scrap of leaf, and beneath them, a heavy, rounded object. He drew it out and held it in his open palm.

"What is that?" asked Anne.

It was disbelief that asked the question, because she knew what it must be and knew what it meant. But even though she believed she must have felt awe that all those promises and hopes could finally manifest in the palm of someone she had not seen in years and wished to be the salvation she expected. He knew she felt this way because he recognized the same feeling of hesitation and restrained joy in himself.

It was a doorknob. But not just a doorknob.

"The way out," Billy-Bob answered.

* * *

Billy-Bob picked the knob off the ground and clicked it into place against the door again. The next captive approached, a small, bald, dark-skinned man wearing a long towel looped around the narrow rails of his limbs and wireframe glasses pressed into the jut of his nose. He smiled at Billy-Bob, a childish and wild thing apart from the gray mustache and missing teeth, then Anne, and opened the door to a small town where others in similar garb moved about, carrying water to patches of gardens in a dusty land. They smiled and greeted him in passing, and he returned the greetings warmly, as though he had never been away.

The door swung closed behind and the knob once again fell to the ground.

The long line of prisoners dwindled until only Billy-Bob and Anne remained. All returned to what Billy-Bob guessed was a point relatively near their time and space of departure. Each time the door the scene had changed, drastically in many cases, some returning to worlds cluttered with people and the noise of motorized vehicles, while others arrived upon roads made of dirt and traversed by horse-drawn carts.

He picked up the knob again and set it against the door, then turned to Anne.

"Where will you go?" he asked.

Anne moved forward and flung the door open.

A burnt out town, still smoldering and stinking of hot ash revealed itself in glimpses as small breezes pushed aside low clouds of gray smoke. Billy-Bob recognized this place because he'd seen it in the wogs' memory at the time of its burning. Had Anne been there, too?

Billy-Bob felt himself drawn to the place. He wanted to know more, to learn where that place existed and what she had been doing there. He took a step forward, and another, then the door closed in front of him. Billy-Bob started.

"Not where I was," said Anne, "but where I am needed. To find someone who has been looking for me for some time."

Everyone was searching for something, it seemed. Gordimer for heroes, Alexander for his daughter, the wogs for Anne, Billy-Bob for a myriad of waypoints on the route to heroism. It was a prolific and familiar story. What did it mean when one finally found what they sought? Without the search, at the end of the journey, where did purpose go?

Lost in his thoughts, he didn't notice Anne approach until her arms had enveloped him, pinning his own against his sides. She did not cling to him with a sense of yearning, but more akin to a parent reluctant to leave a child to fend for themselves.

"You're not just another victim, another pawn taken off the board to shift the advantage to John," she said. "You're here for a reason. You're going back for a greater reason. You're the one who will save us. You are a hero."

"How do you know that?"

Anne released him and rubbed a forearm across her face, removing dust or something else that had accumulated and obscured her vision.

"Because you were meant to. Because you can. You don't know me, so it seems possible you don't know yourself so well as I do. Don't imagine I encourage you because… because I know you so well, or because I have outrageous ambitions. I do it because you are brilliant, because your life has been structured to prepare you for this confrontation, and because you are *meant* to win. I believe in you because it cannot end any other way."

She tightened her grip on the door handle, then looked at Billy-Bob.

"Are you coming?"

The prospect of facing John again remained daunting, though he had a much better idea of how to approach the creature and a vague idea of what he might do. Nevertheless, despite the assurances of the destiny placed upon him, he was reluctant to return to do what so many expected of him: defeat John. What troubled him was whether or not he should. The recollection of his confrontation with the Forest Monster rattled him. The Forest Monster had been a hero in disguise, misled by his memories and desires, one who had carried him to safety in the hope that Billy-Bob could accomplish what he could not. And Billy-Bob, in a spate of shortsighted proactivity, had nearly killed him.

John was not so different. Not a villain bent on ruin, but a creature fulfilling a task. Defeating John did not seem the correct thing to do, though clearly necessary. More than he wanted to win, he didn't want to be wrong, and he certainly wanted to avoid winning for the wrong reason.

"I can't go."

"Why?"

"I have to stay. To know more. To understand."

Anne did not respond, so Billy-Bob tried to explain better.

"So when I do something, I know it's the right something. Not just for everyone else, but for John, too. Even though he means to destroy everyone. Maybe the effort to understand is misplaced. Maybe he is a monster. Maybe it's a waste of time."

"Unless," Anne finished.

And any sliver of Unless deserved exploration.

A tear ran down her face, followed by another and another. From someone so joyful and certain they struck him as strange and abrupt, and he knew he had wounded her incredibly. The dual streams of disappointment joined at her chin and fell to the ground.

"I think I know what my test is. It isn't to save the girl or prevent people from leaving. It isn't fourteen acorns or defeating Ultimate Evil. It's something else."

Anne did not respond.

"I'm sorry," said Billy-Bob. "I know everyone hoped for better."

"Better?" she asked incredulously, then laughed. "This is why Jim chose you. Why he didn't give the means of escape to anyone else. Because you see John, a creature whose sole purpose is to undo all the tenuous connections formed throughout the world, as someone to save rather than overcome. If I had doubts about how events would transpire before, nothing remains of them now."

Anne twisted the doorknob again and pushed.

The door opened into shadow that stretched for a distance before ending in an arc of sunlight, as though a great edifice stood over them. In the shade Billy-Bob could see other structures, dirt hills like huts, with doors set in them, and he knew they must be underneath the platform of the Institute.

A figure approached cautiously in the sunlight, clothed in black crusted with dirt as though it had been buried in the ground with him. One hand gripped the front of the figure's hat, holding it in place as though the sunlight might try to tear it free. It leaned forward, peering into the darkness.

Anne stepped through the doorway and into the shadow. Somehow the figure must have seen her because it straightened up in surprise.

The figure spoke with a voice Billy-Bob almost recognized, though it cracked and sounded hesitant and unsure.

"Have I found what cannot be found?"

"It's me," Anne responded. "And I found our boy."

The man fell to his knees and his hat blew away in a gust that seized its opportunity when he released the brim. The sun shone on his face and Billy-Bob knew him.

"Did you?" Mardin laughed. "So did I!"

Anne turned back to the door and swung it shut. Before the door closed he saw her smile one more time and heard her whisper.

"Save them," she said. "All of them."

The doorknob fell to the ground. Billy-Bob picked it up and placed it in a pocket, and gazed at the vast world around him.

"I suppose I should begin at the beginning," he said.

"The beginning," observed a familiar rock, the rock he'd thrown at John, which still lay in the spot near the door where he'd dropped it, "is a sensible place to begin."

A TEST UNVEILED

Billy-Bob faced a wooden door he had passed many times in his travels here. He found it everywhere, offering itself to him, tempting him, begging him to leave.

How much time had passed since he had come here, Billy-Bob did not know. He felt fuller, not older, and his hair and nails had not lengthened during his stay, making the passage of time indeterminable. The only difference between then and now was then he did not understand, and it made him apprehensive. Now that apprehension was gone and the best way he could think to describe the term of existence he'd spent here was Enough.

He set the doorknob against the wooden door and turned it, hearing the bolt slip out of the strike plate and feeling the door lose its grip on the frame. He leaned forward and the door opened into a room filled with chairs, tables, a piano, and Jim.

Jim looked at him, beaming, unspeaking. Beside him sat the writer, unchanged from the last time he'd seen him, weathered and raw, sunburnt by an environment to which he was unaccustomed. Billy-Bob removed the knob and dropped it into his pocket and the door clapped shut behind him.

The writer turned when he heard the door and Billy-Bob smiled, but he didn't have time for pleasantries, so he nodded and strode forward, out the front of the building.

The street teemed with creatures, elbowing one another in an attempt to get where they were going. Ahead of him Poppy stood in the center of the street where Billy-Bob had confronted John, moments or ages ago. Beside her stood Jim, which gave Billy-Bob pause. He turned and looked back into the building where Andrew gawked, and Jim towered over him. The giant man waved him along so Billy-Bob turned back to the street. Poppy had started to flee, upstream against the flow of animals coming down the slope, pushing away from whatever had driven them here.

He approached Jim, who awaited him, arms folded, an expression of satisfaction on his face. Behind him on the other side of the street Alexander sat, watching him, perhaps wondering if his decision to flee Alpha and take Billy-Bob with him so many years ago had been correct. Billy-Bob wanted to reassure him, but he couldn't. Not yet.

"Hello," said Jim. "Do you know what you must do?"

Almost nothing, Billy-Bob realized. Because he knew so clearly what he needed to do, leaving him free from the anxiety of doubt. This is how the certain viewed the world, as a tornado of events through which they could see a path of calm, which they followed to their destiny.

"Yes," said Billy-Bob.

"Very well. There he is."

Billy-Bob turned and found John, a few paces removed from where he'd left him. He appeared less sure of himself than he remembered, less confident in his plan. He seemed diminished somewhat, as though the great exodus that took place had left him without the strength and cunning of those he had taken in.

"You can't be here," John stated.

"Here I am anyway."

"Why?"

"It's my test," Billy-Bob explained.

"What is?"

"You."

John chewed on the inside of his cheek, considering his meaning. He walked to the edge of the street and the building Kilgoth had eviscerated in his rage, and reached into the rubble. He drew out a long beam of steel he wielded with one hand. Billy-Bob could see the weight in the beam as it swung sluggishly through the air.

"Your father was a fighter," said John. "He could not defeat me. You are not your father."

The beam dipped and bowed in John's hand, like a great baton conducting a ponderous and sludgy symphony through a slow passage. Then he raised it high to strike a staccato orchestral chord and brought the beam whistling down upon Billy-Bob.

Billy-Bob could only raise his hands in a futile attempt to protect himself. He managed to catch the end of the beam, though an observer would hardly call that a victory any more than a fly could celebrate intercepting a blow from the snap of horse's tail. Billy-Bob felt his body begin to crumple beneath the blow.

The shock of the impact rippled through his body and his knees buckled. The ground cracked beneath him and his body began to compress like a soup can under a heavy heel. He managed to move to one side and the beam slipped past to crash against his shoulder instead of stamping his head through his clavicle. This triumph too might be overrated.

Even as this played out Billy-Bob could see citizens pausing to watch over milling animals, their expressions a menagerie of awe, sadness, resignation, and general despair. What enthusiasm they might have felt upon realizing he had somehow returned flagged quickly as they saw John crush him under a beam no ten of them could hoist with their joint strength.

But the beam did not crush the boy. He had bent and his feet had driven themselves into the ground like tentposts. The beam, however, had stopped beside his head. Not just stopped. It began to rise, slowly. And, impossibly, the boy's legs straightened. Billy-Bob tried but failed to restrain a faint grin when John's mouth opened in disbelief. Then the boy gave the beam a quick twist and it spun out of John's grip and thudded against the ground with a heavy clang that scattered all the animals from the street.

"I am not my father," Billy-Bob agreed. "We are the same, but different."

"You cannot destroy me, for all that you may remove!" cried John. "The thing that drives me will always remain—my test."

"I don't want to destroy you. I don't want to destroy anything or defeat anyone."

He could sense the puzzlement in the citizens and John as well.

"What?"

"I offer you the same that you offered me." Billy-Bob extended his hand. "You gave me, and those before me, a choice. You have a choice, too, but it must be your decision."

John smiled briefly, with relief or skepticism or amusement, but that smile faded quickly.

"No," said John. "Never. That would mean failing my test."

"You're wrong. You don't have to fail. I can *change* your test."

To this John took a step backward.

"No."

"You don't have to suffer any longer by making others suffer. It pains you. You've done it long enough to know that causing misery in others does nothing to assuage your own. I can end that pain."

"No. My test is all that I am, all I have ever been, and you would take it from me."

"Certainly not. I would never take it from you. You must give it freely. You must do so willingly, otherwise your mind will resist, it will try to break free and correct the disparity between memory and reality."

"Then why don't I just change the test myself?"

Billy-Bob smiled and bobbed his head.

"Preposterous," said John, "I can't do that. That would eliminate the purpose of having a test. No one can change their test."

Billy-Bob raised a finger to interject.

"Don't say it," said John. "Don't you dare."

The word that signified a slender thread of possibility so strong it prevented the world from flying to pieces. Billy-Bob said it anyway.

"Unless."

Billy-Bob took a step toward John. It didn't matter if he passed into John, he knew the way back. John took a step back, fearful allowing Billy-Bob back in would give him access to his memories.

"Stay away!" John cried.

John hurled objects in his reach as he retreated, barrels and loose timber, stones he ripped from beneath the ground. All these Billy-Bob slipped away from or batted aside with a few deft movements, and continued moving forward. This little bit of his test might come to an end today, if John allowed him. John had never known anything but his test, and not unlike a normal human being, he feared what he did not know. Billy-Bob guessed he worried about becoming unfamiliar to himself, or perhaps it was difficult to throw away the work of millennia, no matter how nefarious.

At last John realized Billy-Bob would not stop and he could not stop him, so he turned on his heel and fled, but there was nowhere to go in that direction. He ran up the street toward the wall at the back end of the city where a ship stood, and fidgeted frantically while Billy-Bob continued to approach. John was trapped.

To Billy-Bob's surprise, John entered the ship. In a few moments white smoke jetted from the base of the ship, then flame, and the craft rose into the air, steadily gaining speed until it pierced the sky far overhead and disappeared into the night beyond.

"What are we going to do now?"

Simon stood nearby, looking up into the sky where the craft had departed.

"They take so long to make," he said ruefully, then looked to Billy-Bob, as though he might have an answer for the question. As if he could tell them what they needed to hear to continue on when it seemed there was nowhere else to go.

And he did have an answer, but it could wait. Something more important needed his attention. Billy-Bob turned toward the slope on the other side of the city where smoke rose above the forest beyond and a shape crouched on the edge of the crater.

It occurred to him that if that ship had been the last, he had accomplished a mission. He did not let them leave, they couldn't leave, and now they had to confront the ruin of the world around them.

At the moment that wasn't important. The rope that held him to a particular destiny had a considerable amount of slack, and he could choose his own quests, or none at all, so long as he didn't try to wander beyond its reach. He had chosen a new task, much like the wog before him. It waited at the top of the slope.

A FAMILIAR REALITY

Poppy knelt in the trodden-down grass where Billy-Bob last stood while animals yelled and brayed and charged up and down the street around her, with no sense of direction or purpose other than to flee madly in search of something they could not articulate. Shelter, relief, nourishment, a place away from the sun. Confusion drove creatures to madness and recklessness they resolved through meaningless action.

All things John wanted.

John stood not far away, pleased with himself, watching the animals carom hither and thither, crashing through buildings and barrels and any fixed object subject to destruction, making a general wreckage of the town while citizens scrambled to escape them. So the world reduced itself. John smiled when their eyes met.

"This is just the froth pushed ahead by the true tumult."

The smug elation hurt her and he knew it. Even so, his smile faltered and became a frown.

Amid the motley tapestry of clashing animal noises, she detected a faint sound, scarcely noticeable. Footsteps scraped to a stop beside her and she looked up at the towering figure in white. Jim.

Jim, a being of great insight who had all the knowledge necessary to save people but expected them to save themselves. Yet everything they strove to achieve was invariably swept away by the relentless waves of the very folk she and the others hoped to rescue from their ignorance and fear. The process had become so predictable that no one confronted these dilemmas any longer, they simply looked for ways to escape them. She wondered for some time if she ought to do the same.

"Does this seem familiar?" he asked.

Jim had a habit of not looking at whomever he was speaking. Even now his gaze cast randomly over the town, watching the inhabitants scramble in futility and noise with a smirk on his face, as if he knew this would happen or wanted it.

Of course it was familiar. She recognized the city and its inhabitants. Destruction too was a common thing. The presence of animals made it strange, but this too was oddly familiar.

On a porch on the opposite side of the street sat Simon, a wog and three penguins, their heads swiveling and recoiling quietly as they watched animals parade by.

She saw her father, hands propped on his backside, striding about the town as it filled with wildlife, surveying the wreckage and petting animals that came near enough, as though all this discord somehow fit within the contrivances of an elaborate and succeeding plan.

"Marvelous," he would say, kick over a stray plank of wood, observe as a frog flopped away in search of darkness, and repeat himself. "Marvelous."

Something about the unfolding scene clicked and she froze, horrified. This was familiar.

"Oh no," she murmured, eyes glazing in the moment of realization. "My dream."

Then she was moving, crossing the city and pushing through the locked gear of jammed bison, climbing the hill as tortoises made their slow way down, her shadow fluttering along the rumpled grasses as it tried to keep up. She knew what she would find as the peak neared, having seen it times beyond counting, then snapping awake in shivering, miserable terror. A world of scalded, broken rock, torn by conflict. It was the inevitable disaster. Her vision blurred and her eyes filled as she neared the top of the slope.

As a dream she could awaken, shuddering, and slowly the terror and anxiety would ebb. There would be no such comfort in reality.

Worse, no one could save it. Her father had returned but could not be expected to stand against John. They needed heroes. Not because people were helpless and silly, but because they were hesitant and frightened, and needed someone to show them their hopes were not impossible, to see a reassuring hand on their hopes and tell them It Can Happen.

The boy might have been a hero to assuage the hopelessness, to show them everything awful could be made beautiful, and even those who seemed weak and foolish had purpose. But no sooner had he been found, and restored, he had been lost again. This time forever. Undoubtedly, this was the crux of John's plan, to break the keel of humanity and send any hope of success straight to the darkened bowels of the world.

She clambered to the peak and stood, her eyes pinched shut as a hot spray of dust hissed across her face. She smelled ash in the air, heard the distant crack of fire and the inebriated cries of the arsons working their destructive mischief, and knew her forest was burning. A world she'd hoped to restore trampled and plucked of its beauty by mindless ruiners.

A warm dot of wetness trickled down her face and she crouched, hugging her knees, clenching her teeth so they would not chatter.

She had always felt alone, preserving the world thanklessly, even preferred loneliness to the blundering stupidity of those who didn't wonder or marvel at anything, hating one thing then the next when the old hatreds wore themselves out. But never did she feel so alone as when she'd been dreaming, waking to find herself clutching a stone or a handful of grass. Anything to suggest there was someone who understood her despair, to comfort, a hand in her own.

One person did understand. She knew it when she touched him. Because when she revived him a bit of his mind touched a bit of hers. He understood striving and desperation and isolation. She did not know why, but she felt them there.

Poppy opened her eyes as the first of the destroyers emerged from the forest, wild-eyed, swinging at anything that came near enough to strike. Crazed and terrible people instilling everything around them with their madness. They had come from the Institute, the most agonizing of ironies, sending all the occupants of the forest before them into confused flight. As she watched him another emerged, then others.

She knew what she had to do. She had to confront them, even though she did not have the energy to be successful. She knew if she did not, they would go on as they were, unsatiated, ruining the world and one another, just as surely as a small fire never eats to its fill, but grows to consume all it touches. Just as John planned. She knew also that to resist now meant her own destruction. Maybe it was enough to stop them here, maybe not. She'd never dreamt that far. The fear in her made her more exhausted still, but it would not stop her.

Too tired to take another step, Poppy let herself fall forward. Perhaps her sense of self-preservation would prompt a jolt of energy allowing her to throw out a leg to prevent falling into the grass. What might provide the strength for the next step she did not know, but this first step would propel her forward, carried on by the irresistible momentum of fate.

But there was no footfall, no stumble forward, no final, gallant charge. She hung leaning, then felt herself draw back. Something was reversing fate. And now she stood at the top of the crater and felt a hand clenching her own.

Poppy turned and looked at Billy-Bob, who stared at the considerable horde gathering before them. Nothing had changed since she'd first seen him in the knotted weeds. Wide-eyed and breathing through an open mouth gave him an expression of astonishment. Deceptively simple. But something was changed. Nothing suggested new daring or power or supernatural that made him otherworldly or capable of great deeds. Nothing had been added.

But now there was no fear.

"What..." Her throat was dry. A mixture of happiness and anxiety came upon her. An unfamiliar sensation that left her feeling light-headed and confused. She swallowed. "What do we do now?"

He continued staring toward the burning forest, as though seeing beyond the anvil of a punished planet. Beyond the silly, scrabbling people as they galloped forward. Over the horizon and out into space past the frayed ends of the universe, accepting it without shock or hurry or excitement. It was as if he saw things of greater consequence than mere humanity, and gentle roads stretched out before him like the reaching fingers of an open hand. There were greater problems to be met, and the thought saddened her, because it meant he'd been lost to the existential and would abandon them to ruin while he ascended to a higher plane of existence where their feeble pleas could not reach him.

His eyes ticked across the horizon. Probably he wasn't even listening. Then his gaze fell, and she could see him counting the members of the approaching horde, measuring his response, and ascribing to each of them a carefully detailed obliteration. She started when he answered.

"Simple," said Billy-Bob.

He turned to face her and his mouth quirked and grinned as though the answer could not have been otherwise. He pointed to the slavering, mad people, stripped of their senses as they bore down on them, cracking the air with the screams of the ideologically deranged.

"We save them."

SO LET IT BE WRITTEN

At first, Andrew didn't know where he was. Clouds scrolled lazily along overhead like grotesque sheep, stretched across a blue pasture of sky as they migrated toward a more verdant patch of atmosphere. Grass brushed the backs of his ears and he sat up. Ahead of his legs were his feet, right where they ought to be, and beyond them stood a shimmering, glassy structure. Andrew blinked.

The Institute. He'd come home.

Not far from him two figures wavered on the edge of reality. He squinted, an expression that had become second nature in the glare of the yellow past, but rather than resolving into a broken tree or vanishing when the prismatic effect of the sandy air twisted light into shapes he longed to behold, these sharpened when he paid attention to them. With a few more blinks to steady his vision, the two figures became clear and he could see they were moving away from him.

One he recognized by a characteristic glower identifiable even at a distance: Mardin. The figure beside Mardin he had no difficulty recognizing. He had seen it walking past more times than he could recall, straight-backed and confident, a gait indicating she had no need for anything but herself and her ambitions to feel complete. Even though he had succeeded in returning, he felt a familiar sense of loss. Even this close, she always seemed to be moving away from him. But what had he ever done to deserve her attention?

The two stopped, and the extra moments they remained in view made Andrew smile. Mardin leaned toward her to speak, and the girl's head snapped back in the direction from which they came. She saw Andrew and he stiffened, unsure how to respond in this rare moment of recognition. She looked away.

Mardin and Bree looked at one another, unspeaking. Mardin's eyes might have flickered toward Andrew, and the curl at the edge of his mouth might have been a smile, but he hid them well, and turned to continue on his way.

Bree hesitated, then walked stiffly toward Andrew, as though trying not to run. Andrew felt a flutter in his chest, as if a foolish bird had gotten itself trapped in the cavity and sought frantically for a way out. When she arrived Andrew realized he'd wasted his time watching her rather than trying to figure out what he should have said. Now his mouth hung open, unspeaking.

"You're back," she said in a gush. "I didn't know if you would be back."

Bree leaned forward tentatively and brushed his forehead with her fingertips, and he felt flakes of burnt skin crumble away.

Considering why he left, Andrew couldn't help a hint of suspicion that ground a heel into his happiness. As much as he longed for them to seem sensible, this expression of compassion and affection didn't make sense.

"You sent me away."

She sat beside him, nodding.

"Mardin told me you could be great."

"Mardin? Great at what?"

"If you wanted. You just needed a push. Figuratively." She hesitated, questioning her assumption. "And literally, as it turned out. I'm sorry about that. He told me it was important that *you* go. He said you would understand what needed to be done, but you had to understand on your own. Because we all have to decide things for ourselves rather than be guided by others. That's not real. It's not living. It's not honest. And it sets us up for failure when that latticework is pulled away."

"A push," Andrew repeated.

How like Mardin, who seemed to believe the best taught are self taught. It wasn't enough to tell someone they could do something. He forced you to do it. Better, Mardin thought, to allow them to discover their abilities, to hurl them into the churning seas and let them struggle to the surface. The risk and terror of drowning was a secondary concern to him.

"I'm glad you're back," said Bree.

Andrew nodded, unsure how to respond. Was she more concerned for him or his mission? Several long moments passed in which his uncertainty gave way to awkwardness, forcing her to speak again to fill the silence.

"Where is it?" she asked.

"Where is what?"

"The reason you were sent."

Andrew removed the notebook from a pocket. Tattered and abused, the scribbles and images he'd drawn showed through the cover in places, and a few leaves of paper had come free of the binding. He'd used it as much to protect himself from the sun and swirling dust as to write, and the faded book had a large crease through the center where he'd rolled it up to swat at insects and branches in his face. The notebook had swollen, having absorbed dirt from the air and moisture from the wide leaves and wood he'd added to supplement the book when he ran out of pages.

What started as a loathsome mission had become steadily more important and Billy-Bob fascinating anomaly. He often acted against the self-preservatory impulse. His mind, in the guise of simplicity, had proven strong and complex enough to overcome instinct. It was human nature to be selfish in the vast majority of circumstances. In that respect the boy had shown himself to be, in a fashion, superhuman. More surprising was that Andrew had begun to question his own impulses, and found himself braver than before. Those challenges once evaded Andrew now confronted and discovered they had lost their menace, and he knew Billy-Bob had made Andrew's mind stronger as well.

He handed the book to Bree, who accepted it with gentleness as though receiving a new child. The book crackled when she opened it, and hissed as sand poured from between the pages. She dragged a hand across the page affectionately, touching the few words amidst large black swaths of scribbled out text.

"What do we do with it?" asked Andrew.

"We give it to Mardin," said Bree. "He is the librarian. But he doesn't keep them. Where they go, I don't know."

Andrew's bones turned to ice. Billy-Bob had mentioned a giant man who kept a dank library beneath the abandoned Institute, hoarding the stories of everyone who was and had been and perhaps might be. That same giant man had confronted Billy-Bob in Beta, and had a preternatural understanding of how things should happen. Could Mardin be giving the books to him? Could that same person have been the one to develop the obelisk that permitted time travel, all so he could safely send writers to record histories, and then send them to himself in the past to prepare himself to derail any successes in the future? It seemed a convoluted conspiracy, but the parts fit.

"Do you think...," Andrew began. He had difficulty getting the words out and had to begin again. "Do you think Mardin would betray us? Would he give histories to someone who could use them against us?"

Bree frowned. Not because she disagreed, but because, perhaps, he had confirmed a suspicion she had as well.

"I don't know what he means most of the time. He speaks in contradictions. We can't change what happens in the past, but we can change how the past happens. That's what he tells me."

On the surface, the statement was a contradiction. Andrew's eyes widened. He understood. Mardin was not a traitor. Instead, in his way, he was trying to guide them, subtly, as had Jim, all while lulling the giant John into believing they were aiding him. In a lightning bolt strike, his epiphany touched him, and all the blurred images on the horizon to which Mardin and Jim had hinted suddenly became sharp and clear.

"I know what I can do! I know why I was sent!"

Andrew grabbed the book from Bree and the pages fanned into a brief peacock tail as Andrew flipped to the back. Then he grasped the last few and wrenched them free.

Bree stiffened.

"What are you doing?" she rasped, her voice clenched to avoid attention.

"I'm doing what no one else can. I'm doing what I was meant to do. The reason it's me. I'm going to save him."

"You? What?"

Andrew slid his writing stylus from his pocket and met Bree's eyes with certainty and purpose, then brought the stylus to paper like the sure blade of a guillotine.

"I'm going to kill him."

Her mouth opened in horror. The reaction made him laugh. His mirth mortified her at first, then he saw the lights of understanding flicker to life.

"Change his triumph to destruction," said Bree, distantly. "He will find victory in defeat and death."

"Yes! Yes! Mardin told me readers trust me, that my honesty is considered sacrosanct. I can write *anything I want*. We can't alter the past, but we can alter *the record* of the past. It's what historians have always done."

"But it's a lie."

"The best lie. To protect the truth and prevent that lie from becoming the reality. By the time he realizes the history is false it will be too late."

Andrew became aware of a tapping noise, even and slow, and knew it had gone on for some time. He had focused so intently upon the book and Bree that he had only noticed it now. It sounded familiar yet he could not place it. Not from Bree. She sat motionless beside him, pale and wide eyed. Andrew followed her gaze, suddenly alarmed that someone had discovered their plan.

Mardin stood before them, one foot tapping, his arms folded. He did not glower, as Andrew expected of a person who overheard the engineering of a conspiracy. Instead, he appeared amused by having taken them unawares and delighted in their mortification.

"Have you finished, then?" he asked.

Andrew raised the notepad toward Mardin. Mardin scowled and stepped back.

"No," he said. "Have you finished? I cannot accept a work that has not received the appropriate embellishments and abridgements. Do you understand?"

Appropriate abridgements. Did Mardin instruct him to remove portions of the story?

Cautiously, Andrew extended the hand that had remained behind his back. The hand containing those pages he had removed in an effort to hide the boy's destiny and resistance, and what the state of the world implied had become a triumph.

Mardin regarded the pages in one hand and the notebook in the other. He took the notebook from Andrew, but did not reach for the other pages.

"I am pleased that you understand the gravity of your assignment," he said sternly. "Nothing of importance can be excluded and I trust the chaff you have removed will receive an appropriate disposal. I trust this comprises the complete and accurate account of your travails. To offer anything less would amount to a terrific deception."

"Yes," Andrew replied. "Everything that needs to be there is there."

Still scowling, Mardin attached a blue tag to the book, identical to the one he'd placed on Andrew at the outset of his journey. He pressed his thumb against the gelatinous blob, causing it to glow blue. It pulsed with steadily greater intensity until a snap in the air and an odor of ozone and Mardin's hands were empty again.

"You have performed a trivial task with admirable aplomb," said Mardin. "Your efforts contribute to a greater good. Any dismissal of this product is proof of its success."

Andrew slowly returned the missing pages behind his back. Even though Mardin gave no indication that he wanted them, no hint in the puzzle of his words that he would acknowledge them, Andrew felt a shiver because he knew he was involved in the trickery of a creature that made it his mission to annihilate humanity. Whether fear or excitement, it didn't matter, the mere practice made him realize all the world, which had seemed so clear and straightforward, was shrouded in a haze of competing deceptions.

His task complete, Mardin turned away.

"Have I done well?" Andrew called after him.

Mardin raised his arms and gestured to the world around him as he continued on.

"What additional evidence do you need?"

It cloyed at him to know this place, a place of reason and truth, protected itself through deception. It was a poor foundation. Something he needed to resolve or their triumphs meant nothing more than a shift from one false foothold to another. That meant the boy's story, the true tale of events, must be told.

"Will you still write the story? The real story?" asked Bree.

"I have to," said Andrew. "Maybe just for myself. Maybe just in my head. But it will be there."

Bree closed her eyes. She did not speak for a moment, and when the words came they emerged with a strange, mystical cadence, clinging by the fingertips to comprehensibility.

Why silent are the bells that rung
In glory yet with bitten tongues
All are mute as far as flung
Such deeds resplend remain unsung

The words reverberated, unlike those silent bells, as though they matched a frequency in his body and his chest resonated with them.

"It's from a book I read as a girl," she explained. "An adventure full of inarticulate big ideas, as though the writer had an inkling of something that troubled him, but didn't have the mind to wrap his head around and resolve it. Not that all problems require resolution. Sometimes it's helpful just to recognize them, to think about them. Maybe the ideas are tossed out there in the hope that someone else can fix them. It's been so long since I read it, I don't recall the rest, but it seemed appropriate."

She looked at him and blushed. To see her in this moment of vulnerability made him eager to set her at ease.

"It's perfect," said Andrew. "I think I know where I can use it."

"You have an idea for your book, then? Do you know what you'll call it?"

"I think, *The Least Envied*."

Bree squinted.

"That's not a very good name," she said.

Andrew's eyebrows pulled together and he opened his mouth to issue a stern retort, but she was already speaking again.

"I suppose the name isn't important," she continued. Her face scrunched, as if the contraction allowed her to focus all her thought on a single point. "It's a decoy, isn't it? To hide it. To keep it safe."

Of course it was. But he didn't need to tell her. She knew.

Andrew loved this girl. She had uncovered his plan effortlessly, as though he had left a doorway open in his mind and she needed only to walk through. Her brilliance and beauty gave him a smile that hurt, too big for his face, and made him rash. Without thinking, he lurched toward her, kissing her even as he realized his daring had been a miscalculation, and in that moment he knew he'd destroyed all the bridges he'd built to her by trying to cross too soon.

What he'd done was wrong and unwelcome, and he felt embarrassed and ashamed. Andrew felt her body stiffen, recoil slightly, but she did not push away or bite. To Andrew's astonishment, she reached arms around to pull him tighter, and everything wrong with the world blew away like the smoky remnants of a satisfied djinn dismissed after granting a final wish.

ABOUT THE AUTHOR

This author has held several positions in recent years, including Content Writer, Grant Writer, Obituary Clerk, and Staff Writer, and is under the false impression that these experiences have added to his character since they have not contributed much to his finances. He was awarded a BFA in Creative Writing and Journalism and a BA in Technical Communication by Bowling Green State University because they are giving and eager to make friends. He has a few scattered publications with The Circle magazine, Wild Violet, Toasted Cheese, and Lovable Losers Literary Revue, and resides in the drab, northeastern region of Ohio because it makes everything else seem fascinating, exotic, and beautiful.

Made in the USA
Coppell, TX
27 February 2021